Book 8
of the
Cornish Chronicles

Somewhere Out There

Ann E Brockbank

Copyright © Somewhere Out There.

by Ann E Brockbank

First published in Great Britain as a paperback in 2024

Copyright © 2024 Ann E Brockbank

The moral right of Ann E Brockbank to be identified as the author of this work has been asserted in accordance with the Copyright, Designs and Patents Act 1988

All rights reserved. No part of this publication may be reproduced, stored in a retrieval system or transmitted in any form or by any means, (electronic, mechanical, photocopying, recording or otherwise) without the prior written permission of the publisher. Any person who does any unauthorised act in relation to the publication may be liable to criminal prosecution and civil claims for damages.

Somewhere Out There, is a work of fiction. All incidents and dialogue, and all characters with the exception of some well-known historical and public figures, are products of the authors imagination and are not to be construed as real. Where real-life historical or public figures appear, the situations, incidents, and dialogues concerning those persons are entirely fictional and are not intended to depict actual events or to change the entirely fictional nature of the work. In all other respects, any resemblance to persons living or dead, events or locales is entirely coincidental.

Front cover by © R W Floyd, from an original oil painting

All rights reserved.

ISBN: 9798325642043

Somewhere Out There

For Lynne,

for the joy you bring to every occasion.

By Ann E Brockbank

Cornish Chronicles

1. A Gift from the Sea – Set between 1901 - 1902
2. Waiting for the Harvest Moon - Set between 1907-1908
3. My Song of the Sea - Set between 1911 -1912
4. The Path We Take – Set in 1912
5. The Glittering Sea - Set between 1912 – 1919
6. Our Days in the Sun – Set in 1919
7. The Hand that Wrote this Letter - Set between 1922-1923
8. Somewhere Out There - Set in the 1880s & 1923

Historical Novels

Mr de Sousa's Legacy – Set between 1938 – 1960

Contemporary Novels

The Blue Bay Café
On a Distant Shore

Somewhere Out There

ACKNOWLEDGMENTS

My huge and heartfelt thanks go to you, Angie, for your editorial help, support, and historical guidance. You have no idea how much I appreciate your generous time, friendship, and expertise. Also, to Hazel, who helps me polish this manuscript ready to send out to the world.

To my partner, Rob, for every single wonderful thing you do, especially the beautiful artwork you do for my book covers – they always add a special quality to my novels. Thank you also for listening to me droning on about the story before, during, and after I've written it. It can't be easy living with someone who spends so much time in another world.

To the amazing staff at Poldhu Café Cornwall and to Ginny at The Bookshop in Helston, thank you for selling my novels and your continued support.

To Lynne, for the joy you bring to every occasion. This book is dedicated to you.

To my darling late husband, Peter, you are forever in my heart.

My heartfelt gratitude goes to Sarah and Martin Caton and their lovely family for allowing me to use their beautiful home, Bochym Manor, as a setting for my 'Cornish Chronicles' novels. My partner and I were lucky enough to live at Bochym Manor for a few wonderful days in the summer of 2023. That stay inspired this novel.

And last, but certainly not least, my grateful thanks go to all you lovely people who buy and read my books. I so appreciate your continual support. You are all wonderful, and I'm enormously privileged that you believe in me and chose my books to read. Special thanks, as always, go to Kim, my friend, who continually champions my books on social media so that they reach a larger audience.

ABOUT THE AUTHOR

Ann E Brockbank was born in Yorkshire but has lived in Cornwall for many years. Somewhere Out There is Ann's eleventh novel and the eighth in the Cornish Chronicles series. Ann lives with her artist partner on the beautiful banks of the Helford River in Cornwall, an integral setting for all of her novels. Ann is currently writing her next novel. Ann loves to chat with her readers, so please visit her Facebook author page and follow her on Twitter and Instagram.

Facebook: @AnnEBrockbank.Author
Twitter: @AnnEBrockbank1
Instagram: annebrockbank

Somewhere Out There

1
Thursday 15th June 1922

It was late – eleven o'clock. The sun had set over an hour ago, but the waning gibbous moon gave enough light for Henry Penhallow to make his way home from the Wheel Inn, Cury. He staggered, inebriated, and wore a supercilious grin - he'd had a good night on the proceeds of market day.

Halting at the entrance of a field, he grabbed the farm gate for stability while he relieved himself. With a sigh of satisfaction, he buttoned himself up and set off again on his way. It was a good mile walk home to Wild Cliff Farm, which stood at the very pinnacle of Poldhu Hill. He was keen to get to his bed and the woman who kept it warm. He sneered as he always did at the thought of his wife – she gave little more than cold comfort. He'd been married to Maia for over three years and still had to beat her into submission to conform to his marital rites. Thank the Lord for the barmaid, Edith, Edna, or whatever her name was. She appreciated his tall, good looks and had been more than willing tonight to please him out in the backyard of the inn, thus whetting his appetite for more when he got home. The wench had probably given him more than he bargained for, though, by the irritating itch he felt in his trousers.

As he approached the steps to Cury Church, he snorted, then belched loudly and laughed – that was a good old-fashioned beer burp to be proud of. Suddenly, he slipped. His feet went from under him, and he hit his face on the rocky earth. Howling in pain, he pushed himself up with the flat palms of his hands. Tasting blood as it trickled down his nostrils and the back of his throat, he spat furiously, cursing loudly. Using the church step wall to help drag himself up, he rested one hand against the wall as he tried to steady himself, cupping the other to his bleeding nose as he scanned the white, glistening ground beneath him.

'What the hell! Snow. In June!' he muttered, and then a movement above made him look up at the figure looming over him. 'You!' he roared. In the next instance, an almighty blow to his head floored him, and the discomfort of his broken nose worried him no more.

*

Maia Penhallow was roused from her bed at Wild Cliff Farm just after dawn by someone furiously knocking on her door. Lifting the sash window, she leaned out to find a police officer at her front door. Her heart leapt into her throat. 'What is it?' she called down to him.

P.C. Thomas cleared his throat. 'Begging your pardon for disturbing you so early, Mrs Penhallow. Could you let me in? It's about your husband.'

Maia paused and nodded. 'One moment.'

Closing the window, she glanced at the wicker linen basket and the leg of a pair of dirty trousers poking from it and quickly tucked it under the lid. Dressing quickly in a rough cotton dress with a woollen cardigan to ward off the early morning chill, she pulled her fiery red hair into a ponytail and then glanced in the mirror. Her face sported a swollen black eye and split lip sustained the day before. She could do nothing to hide them, and why should she?

P.C. Thomas removed his helmet, nodded gravely, and stepped over the threshold into the stark, drab kitchen.

'Mrs Penhallow, Maia,' his tone gentle, having noted her battered face. 'I'm afraid I bring bad news about Henry.'

Maia stood very still, despite the effervescence in her tummy.

'I'm sorry, but we understand he was attacked with a heavy implement and robbed - they cut his money pouch from his body.'

Maia felt her eyelids twitch. 'His body!'

'Yes, I'm afraid Henry is dead.'

Maia grabbed the back of one of the kitchen chairs to steady herself.

P.C. Thomas rushed to her aid and helped her sit. 'I am so sorry - this must come as a terrible shock.'

'Where is Henry now?'

'He has been taken to the undertakers at Cury Cross Lanes. Forgive me for asking, Maia, but were you not concerned that he did not come home last night?'

Lowering her eyes, Maia answered, 'Henry doesn't always come home when he's been out drinking after market.'

'I see.' The constable tutted — his disapproval of Henry's behaviour was evident. 'I'm so sorry,' he added. 'Maia, forgive me for asking, but your face...?'

'I had an argument with the pigsty door yesterday,' she answered flatly.

He put his hand gently on her shoulder. 'You must take more care of yourself.'

Maia suppressed a sardonic laugh but was grateful for his sympathy. 'I will from now on.'

'Can I get you a cup of tea or something?'

Maia shook her head. 'No. Thank you.'

'I am on my way to inform Jago now about his brother. Do you want him to come to you?'

'No!' She answered sharply, then added softly, 'Thank you, but no.'

'Can I get anyone else to come to you?'

Maia felt a great emptiness inside. *There was no one else.* 'Thank you. I'd rather be alone for the time being.'

P.C. Thomas nodded. 'As you wish.'

'Tell me, officer, have they found a weapon?'

'Police officers from Helston have been brought in to search the area. Whatever it was, it was heavy - possibly a lump hammer, something like that!'

Maia nodded.

He picked up his helmet to leave. 'I'll see myself out. I have no doubt the Helston police will come and see you later.'

'Me!' Maia's eyes widened. 'Why?'

Just routine questioning to establish a motive – things like that.'

When P.C. Thomas left, Maia closed all the curtains in the house to show respect - and hopefully to keep people away. After stripping the bed - a scene of many violent episodes, she remade it with fresh, clean linen, boiled buckets of water on the range, and washed everything she could lay her hands on – even though it wasn't Monday.

The familiar hammering on the door inevitably came, but Maia ignored her brother-in-law Jago's attempt to gain entry. Later, she stepped out into the yard to peg her washing on the line. The warm, sunny June day filled her heart with joy. The fields surrounding Wild Cliff Farm looked greener than they had ever looked before. The birds twittered more loudly between the burgeoning leaves on the orchard trees, and Maia threw her head back, laughed, and shouted to the blue sky. 'He's gone! I'm free at last!'

*

Out of the corner of her eye, Maia caught sight of a figure walking towards her when she was feeding the pigs. Her blood ran cold for a second, thinking Henry had returned from the dead, but it was Jago, her brother-in-law. Taking a deep breath, she placed her pigswill bucket on the ground and watched him saunter to her in his self-assured way. He was as tall and darkly good-looking as his brother had been, though not as pudgy faced as Henry had become due to the amount of drink he regularly consumed.

'A tragic day, Maia,' Jago said grimly.

Maia remained silent.

'The police have conducted an extensive search of the area but cannot find the weapon used to kill him.'

'I know,' she said darkly. 'The police were here earlier and told me as such.'

Jago's eyes travelled the length of her body, faltering as they settled on her bruised and battered face. Even on this day, the day his brother had died, Jago could not disguise the fact that he coveted her. 'I have arranged with the undertaker for Henry to be brought back to the farm until the funeral, which I have booked for Monday.'

A curl of disgust and anger erupted within her. 'Well, Jago, I suggest you rearrange it because Henry is not coming back here!'

Affronted by her vehemence, he countered, 'This is Henry's farm! He should reside here!'

'It's *my* farm!' she corrected. 'Bought for me by my aunt.'

'That's as maybe, Maia, but as Henry was your husband that makes it *his* property too, and as his brother, I shall be taking over the running of the business.'

'Business! You have your own business to run. I am quite capable of running my own business, thank you.' She folded her arms.

Jago laughed gently and shook his head. 'Maia, you know you cannot run it by yourself - this farm has made nothing in the three years you have been running it.'

'That's because Henry drank all the profits!'

Jago's mouth twitched, knowing that was true enough. 'I am a good businessman – you only have to look at the success of my motorcar showroom. So, I shall deal with the finances. I will also arrange for someone to come and help you with the livestock.'

'No, Jago. You will not!'

'For God's sake, Maia, someone needs to look after you now.'

'I need no looking after by another bloody *Penhallow!*' Maia dropped her voice to a low hiss.

'I know things have been difficult for you in the past, but Henry is dead. I don't think we need to bring up his shortcomings as a husband. Don't tar me with the same brush - I would look after you much better.'

'I need no looking after,' she reiterated.

'Well, I beg to differ. Look at the state of your face. Henry said you were clumsy – forever falling and hurting yourself.'

'Did he!' She gritted her teeth, feeling the fury building again. 'Well, I think you will find I won't be *falling and hurting* myself from now on!' She locked eyes with Jago in a steely gaze.

'You are understandably upset. We will speak more about this after the funeral. The undertaker will bring Henry home to the farm tomorrow.'

Thumping her fists into her hips, she said savagely, 'Then he will find my door well and truly locked! I never want to see Henry or his mortal remains in my house again!' She picked up her bucket and stormed back to the house.

He followed her to the back door, scattering the hens as they picked and scratched in the yard. 'This is highly irregular, Maia,' he said, trying to keep his annoyance at bay.

'Good day to you, Jago,' she said firmly, closing the door on him before pulling the bolt across.

2
14th June 1923 - 1 year later.

It was the day before the first anniversary of Henry Penhallow's demise, and not a trace of him ever being there remained in the cosy interior of Wild Cliff Farm. The fireside chairs, no longer hard and uncomfortable to sit on, had been adorned with brightly coloured cushions and throws, and soft, warm rugs lay underfoot. A black kitten, Prudence, so named because of her good judgement of anyone entering the farmhouse, purred contentedly on her cushion in the window seat. Prudence had been gifted to Maia by her good neighbour, the dairyman David Trevorrow, to keep her company - and company she was, for Prudence followed Maia everywhere she went. Rows of books now adorned the shelves, and a gramophone filled the house with music to while away the contented hours Maia spent cooking, reading, or shaping her pots out of clay, which, as a new venture, was already reaping good rewards. Before Maia was married, she had practiced the art of ceramics to much acclaim, but Henry had put paid to all that she loved to do. It was good fortune that Lady Sarah Dunstan, the Countess de Bochym, remembered the quality of Maia's work from before and had encouraged Maia to start up again after Henry died, offering the use of the Bochym kiln. As soon as Maia accumulated enough money, she invested in a potter's wheel. Once she started to produce her beautiful bespoke pottery, Lady Sarah invited Maia to join the prestigious Bochym Arts and Crafts Association. Maia worked from home, converting her back parlour into a studio. Her fellow artisans in the association worked at the manor and liked to socialise, and though Maia often joined in with them, she needed peace to create her beautiful pots. Life was as near-perfect as possible.

Henry's killer had never been found, nor had the weapon that had put a favourable end to Maia's marriage.

Maia knew there were rumblings and rumours hereabouts surrounding his death. People wondered if perhaps Maia secretly knew something about it but was not telling. It was common knowledge that she'd had a deeply unhappy marriage and that Henry had spent all their money in the Wheel Inn and on the barmaids, who offered more than a glass of ale. Maia was aware that she had probably fuelled those rumours by not openly grieving Henry's passing. She also stubbornly refused to wear mourning clothes and instead wore bright Edwardian silk and satin colonial clothes, which were passed down to her when her aunt and guardian, Lady Martha Jefferson, who had spent many years in Mombasa, Africa, passed away.

Henry's brother, Jago, had not avoided suspicion either, because he had never hidden the fact that he coveted Henry's wife. It was understandable why he wanted to step into his brother's shoes, regarding Maia. With her long, fiery red hair, she was beautiful, if not a little wild and eccentric in her dress. What puzzled everyone, including Maia, was Jago's mission to take control of Wild Cliff Farm. Jago was a wealthy businessman dealing in motorcars – he certainly did not need another business.

It had been a struggle for Maia to keep Jago at bay – indeed, he had tried to move into the farmhouse the day after the funeral, continuing to argue that, as it had been his late brother's farm, he should, by law, take over the running of it. In desperation, Maia eventually sought advice from Lord Dunstan, who had arranged for his lawyer to check the deeds in order to settle the argument. Thankfully, the ownership was in no doubt. Lady Martha Jefferson, who had bought the farm for her ward, Maia, had put Maia's maiden name on the title deeds – the document was watertight. This had not quelled Jago's quest to make himself indispensable to her, as he tried to wheedle his way into the farm and her bed. He regularly turned up at her door like a bad penny - normally quite soon after she had suffered a spate of vandalism at her farm. This had been happening regularly over the last year when the fences had been kicked down, her yielding vegetable patch desecrated, and her livestock released from their pens. These unsettling episodes were the only fly in the ointment in Maia's new life.

*

After a fine start to the day, a storm blew up late that afternoon. Maia had ridden her horse, Shadow, to Poldhu beach that morning – something she had done most mornings since the death of Henry - and had noticed the swell building as the blow of the wind turned south-westerly. It was very different weather to last June, Maia recalled, when the temperature had soared into the nineties for several days, hardly dropping during the night. Not so this year - after a warm, sunny spring, the weather had been quite changeable – almost chilly on certain days.

Maia knew she had to prepare against the storm and secure her livestock in their pens before it blew in. She glanced with dismay at her burgeoning rose garden, just about to burst into flower, and prayed the blooms would survive. Shadow had been stabled for safety, and the house window shutters were secured. Standing high upon Poldhu Hill, facing Poldhu Cove, the farm was not named Wild Cliff for nothing. The building always bore the brunt of the strong westerly winds, which rattled the rafters on the roof in extreme weather.

Once all was secure, Maia stood in the yard and glanced down at the ocean swell, hoping her friend, Ellie Blackthorn's tearoom, would withstand the high tide pushing relentlessly up the beach. Her gaze turned to Jago's house, aptly named Penn als Cottage - Cliff Top Cottage - as it was situated precariously atop the cliff between the mighty Poldhu Hotel and the Poldhu Tea Room. Over the years, the land surrounding the cottage had suffered from coastal erosion. Maia had noted earlier that the sandstone cliffs, eroded by the nesting sand martins, were crumbling onto Poldhu beach. Would Penn als Cottage withstand this coming storm? Might it take Jago Penhallow with it if it fell down the cliff? An uncharitable thought, she knew, but he was the only thorn in her side in her new life.

After supper and happy that the farmhouse was secure, Maia donned a long leather apron, selected a slab of clay, and began the arduous process of wedging the slab by kneading it on her tabletop. This was to remove the air bubbles and align the clay particles to achieve an even consistency. As always, she began to sing softly to herself as she worked, old Cornish folk songs her late mother had sung to her. As she worked, Maia pushed a lock of hair from her hot face with the back of her hand. When happy with the slab, she slammed the clay onto the centre of the wheel head, kicked the flywheel, wet her hands, and…... bang! The noise stopped her hands from moulding the clay, her foot ceased, and the wheel stopped. Her mouth dried as she turned this way and that, listening and wondering what on earth could have banged. All doors and windows were secure! Swallowing to moisten her mouth, she stepped away from her wheel, the words of her song still in her head as she wiped her hands on a rag. After re-checking that the windows were secure, the doors bolted, and nothing had fallen, she wondered if the house spirits were angry. This was an ancient farmhouse - many people must have died here. It was inevitable that she shared this space with them - perhaps something had upset them. Her thoughts turned to Shadow in the stable – she had better check on her. Lighting the storm lamp, she undid the bolt to the back door, and as she opened the door, Prudence jumped down from her cushion to follow her to the door, rubbing languidly against her leg.

Maia crouched to stroke her - if danger were afoot, Prudence would alert her, but instead, she just purred.

Shadow was twitchy, but not unduly frightened, as Maia lifted the lamp in the stable to check on her. All seemed well as she snuffled gently into Maia's hand for some nuts. She watched with interest as Prudence moved with stealth towards the second stall, her ears pricking at some noise. Again, there was no sign of alarm from the cat, so Maia moved the lamp higher to illuminate the rest of the stable. Her nostrils picked up on a strange smell, it was earthy, with a tang of old sweat. Someone was here, hiding! Lowering the lamp, she turned to leave, Prudence happily following her.

'Please, don't steal my horse!' she said as she closed the stable door behind her.

*

After holding his breath for what seemed like an age, Josh finally exhaled long and low, wondering if the woman with the lamp would bring the constable. He listened intently, but all he heard was her back door closing and the bolt engaging. Josh knew who she was, having seen her twice on the beach with her skirts tucked in her belt, revealing long, pale legs as she walked barefoot in the surf beachcombing. He had watched her mount her chestnut mare to ride up Poldhu Hill, her long, red, curly hair flowing freely in the breeze. Jago had no intention of stealing the horse or harming her. All he needed was a dry place for the night to shelter from this storm.

*

The presence of someone in her stable was unsettling to Maia's concentration, so when the pot she was trying to throw collapsed, she gave up for the evening. After washing the clay from her hands, she brushed her long hair a hundred times like her mama had shown her as a child, and then took herself to bed. With Prudence curled at her feet, Maia clutched the covers to her chin as the storm raged outside, and her thoughts turned to the stranger in the stable. Maia had an idea who he was, having seen a stranger huddled on the black rocks at Poldhu fishing with a line earlier that day. Before leaving the beach, she had spoken to her friend Ellie at the tearoom about him. Ellie said he'd been about for a couple of days, clearly sleeping rough. She had taken him a mug of tea and a couple of scones, which he gratefully accepted. She added that he was very polite but looked tired and weary. She also mentioned that the stranger reminded her of someone, but she could not quite place who.

Maia wondered who he was and if she had been a fool to leave him in the stable, but if he had meant any harm - he would have rushed at her when he had the chance. She would assess the situation in the morning and hoped once again that he would not steal her horse.

*

The storm had passed by the morning, which was beneficial, as Maia needed to transport her pots to be bisque fired at the kiln at Bochym Manor. It was still breezy - small white clouds scudded across the pale blue sky, and down in the cove, rollers crashed onto the beach in a frenzy of white foam. The barometer had moved that morning – better weather was on its way. Maia glanced at Jago's house, still standing, and felt a pang of disappointment. She knew he watched her from his window – she had seen the glint of a telescope on several occasions when the sun hit it.

Her thoughts turned back to the stranger in the stable, wondering if he was still there. After washing and dressing in her work clothes, she fed and watered her livestock and ate a slice of bread to break her fast. The remains of the loaf were left on the table next to the jam and cheese. Fetching the tin bathtub from the hook on the washhouse wall to the kitchen, Maia put two large pails of water in the range to warm. When all was ready, she dressed more presentably to visit the manor, just in case she met with any of the more senior members of the Dunstan family. She buttoned up her jacket, pinned on her hat, and walked across the yard to her cart. She secured her box of pots onto the front seat before making for the stables and Shadow. Hearing a scuffle at the back of the stall, Maia surmised that her presence had woken whoever was sleeping there. She waited a moment, but whoever was there stayed silent. After harnessing Shadow, she led her out into the yard and attached her to the cart before returning to the stable.

Maia cleared her throat. 'May I ask you if you are the man who has been living on Poldhu beach these last two days?'

There was silence for a few seconds, then a male voice answered shakily, 'I am.'

'I see. I am going out, but I should be back just before midday. I have left you water warming in the range for a bath, food on the kitchen table, and tea brewing in the pot. Please keep the back door locked until I return. Do not let anyone in. Do you understand?'

'I understand,' Josh said, in disbelief. 'Thank you, kindly.'

*

Josh stepped out of the stable, blinking and scratching in the bright sunlight. He had bites on his face and neck from the mites in the straw he had slept in, and sniffed himself – he did smell awful!

The back door needed a shove to open, but once inside, the kitchen held a welcome sight, and his eyes watered at the kindness bestowed on him. The black cat on the cushion in the window seat watched him cautiously. After a minute, it purred and settled back into slumber.

Slowly peeling off the clothes he had worn for the last couple of weeks, he stepped into a gloriously warm bath while eating a slice of bread slathered in strawberry jam. Having scrubbed himself with carbolic soap, he submerged to rinse himself clean. As he luxuriated, he glanced around the kitchen for a towel, noting that it was next to a pile of neatly folded clothes on the chair. My goodness, this lady was heaven-sent! Unwilling to move from this luxury, Josh flopped his arms over the side of the bath and relaxed into a blissful state of euphoria. For the first time in fifteen days, he felt settled.

When his skin turned wrinkly, he reluctantly got out of the bath. He quickly dressed in the clothes waiting for him, realising they had belonged to a man much taller and with a larger chest than he, but they were good quality, clean, and hardly worn. He had just finished rolling up the shirt sleeves when a car pulled up, and a wrap of knuckles came to the back door. Josh sank back into the shadows behind the curtains and held his breath.

'Maia!' A gruff voice shouted as he hammered again. 'Are you in there?'

The man tried the door. Silence ensued momentarily until the man called through the closed window. Hearing footsteps walk away, Josh peeped around the curtain, noting that the visitor was about the same age as him: broad-shouldered, dark-haired, handsome, and well-dressed. The caller must know the lady of the house, and a thought ran through his mind that the clothes she had left out for him might have belonged to this man!

Peeping tentatively around the curtain, Josh watched as the man checked the stable, shrinking back when the man retraced his steps to the car. Josh knew little about cars but knew quality when he saw it, and that it was a magnificent machine. Perhaps he was the lady's sweetheart.

Nevertheless, Josh heaved a sigh of relief that the man had gone because he had no idea how to explain who he was or his arrival in the community to anyone. Even so, Josh knew he'd have to explain who he was to the lady of this house - she would want to know why he was living rough and sleeping in her stable. Would he tell her the truth?

With the coast clear, Josh stood at the window, admiring the magnificent vista before him. Poldhu Cove stretched out in front of him in all its spectacular beauty as his eyes travelled up to the vast Poldhu Hotel on the top of the cliff. The sea was rough today, whipped up by the storm. He could see the waves crashing against the black rocks where he had been fishing. The bread and jam the kind lady had left him had come as a welcome change from eating raw fish. Perhaps if he asked her, she might know where he could find work because he desperately needed money and a roof over his head before the end of summer. He hoped and prayed that he could find a safe harbour here for a while.

*

Bochym Manor was bathed in watery sunshine as Maia steered her pony and cart down the long, dusty drive towards the Arts and Crafts workshops at the back of the manor. The peacocks were strutting around the manor grounds, emitting loud cries, which made Shadow quiver.

'It's all right, girl,' Maia said gently, but when one of the peacocks approached and opened its feathers with a loud shuttering sound, Maia struggled to keep her horse steady. She quickly turned off the main track towards the workshops, hoping these exotic birds would stay at the front of the house.

En route to Bochym, Maia had questioned her rash decision to allow the man in her stable free access to her house, but the fact he did not steal Shadow almost justified her decision - she hoped she was right. It was clear that the man needed some help, and if he turned out to be a decent sort of chap, he might be able to help her on the farm. With ideas to increase the farm's livestock, she would need an extra pair of hands to help. Perhaps with a farmhand about the place, the vandalism may cease. None of her neighbours were suffering from this persecution. Jago was forever knocking on her door, trying to make himself indispensable - which he wasn't – and calling regularly to see if she needed anything fixed, which she never did! She needed to somehow stop him from dropping in so often because he had started to hint that, as it had been a year since she was widowed, she should think about marrying again and that if the persecution continued, it might not be safe for her to be at the farm alone anymore. Dismounting from the cart, she stroked and kissed Shadow's nose. No amount of persecution would ever make her yield to Jago. She disliked him almost as much as Henry - he was just as manipulating, and Maia feared that one day he would not take no for an answer.

3

Josh was dozing in the chair when he heard the clatter of hooves come into the yard and rushed to hide again. Whoever it was, took their time, and as he waited in the shadows, the cat watched him with curious eyes. A key in the lock told him that whoever it was, this was their home, and Josh should not be skulking in the corner of the room. He stepped out to greet whoever was coming back in, feeling his shoulders tense with apprehension. His body relaxed when he saw the lady of the house enter. She looked startled when she noticed him, as though forgetting she had left him there.

'Oh! You made me jump – I thought the spirit world was upset again.'

'Spirits!' Josh frowned. 'Do you mean ghosts?'

She nodded and put her wooden crate down on the table. 'Sometimes they are restless, though not so much this last year,' she said calmly. After placing a heavy earthenware pot into the range, she turned to Josh, smiled, and asked, 'Are you all right?'

'Yes, thank you.' Josh put his hand to his heart. 'I stayed to thank you for your kindness to me last evening and this morning. I appreciate what you did for me, the bath, the food, and the clothes you laid out. I take it they belong to your husband?'

Maia smiled. 'They did, but my husband does not need them – he died a year ago.'

'Oh! I am sorry.'

'Don't be,' she waved a hand. 'I'm not. He was a hateful man.'

'I see.'

'If the clothes fit, they are yours if you need them – I threw most of them away but kept some back to wear whilst working on the farm – though they are too big for me, and..,' she glanced at him, 'slightly too big for you too by the look of it.'

He laughed. 'A little, but thank you - I do need them.'

'There you go then.' She smiled, tied an apron around her waist, and began to busy herself again at the range.

'You had a visitor earlier.'

Maia turned her head sharply.

'A man knocked and shouted your name – that's if... your name is Maia?'

Maia nodded and frowned. 'He didn't see you, did he?'

'No, I kept out of sight until he drove off in his car.'

'It was probably my brother-in-law,' she said sourly.

'Do you not like him?'

Maia busied herself at the kitchen table. 'Not particularly. I don't want him here, but he believes he has some claim on me and my farm, but he hasn't.'

Josh glanced at his saviour with admiration - she was truly lovely. She stood about five feet six, with a nice trim body and beautiful long red wavy hair to her waist – he couldn't blame the brother-in-law for his interest in her.

'You are very trusting,' Josh said presently. 'Giving me access to your home and then leaving me here.'

She looked up and smiled warmly. 'Well, I decided that because you didn't steal my horse, you wouldn't rifle through my house. Besides, Prudence trusts you.' She nodded to the purring cat.

Josh smiled. 'Well, I thank *you both* for trusting me.'

She nodded, pulled down a brown ceramic pot from the shelf, and tipped a pile of flour into it. Making a hole in the centre, she poured in a beaten egg, milk and cheese and gently began to mix the dough together to make four scones.

Josh edged to the back door. 'I'll take my leave of you now - I can see you are busy. Thank you again for your kindness.'

Maia stopped mixing. 'Do you have somewhere to go?'

'Well, no, but...'

'You'll stay for dinner then.' It was a statement rather than an invitation.

'Gosh! Thank you.'

'It's just a stew with scone cobblers on top. I cooked it yesterday. It's just warming through now and will be ready when these scones bake on top of it.'

When Josh began to smell the rich beef aroma, his stomach rumbled, despite the bread and jam he had eaten.

She placed two glasses of water on the table and cutlery and then sat down. 'I don't have any ale, I'm afraid.'

'No matter. It's a while since I drank any – stream water has been my preferred tipple this last month.' He gave a crooked smile.

Maia put her hands on her hips. 'Are you a fugitive?'

He bit down on his lip and nodded. 'In a fashion, yes.' She tipped her head questioningly. 'It's a long story,' he added.

'Maybe you can tell me after dinner?' She raised an eyebrow.

He nodded resignedly.

'So, you appear to know my first name.' She wiped her floury hands down her apron and reached out to shake his. 'I'm Maia Penhallow.'

He shook her hand. 'I am pleased to meet you.'

'And you are?' Maia waited for him to offer his name, then prompted, 'I trusted you - you must do the same.'

He took a deep breath. 'My name is Gideon Walsh, but I hate the name. Ma wanted to call me Joshua – Josh, after Grandpa, but Pa wouldn't hear of it. She always called me Josh in private - bless her.' He smiled at the thought of her.

'And is Josh your preferred name?'

'Yes.'

'Josh it is then,' she said, fetching the rich-smelling warming stew out of the oven to place the scones atop. She grinned when Josh's stomach growled again. 'Goodness, I hope you can wait another twenty minutes for the scones to bake?'

Josh laughed. 'I've waited a long while for a decent meal, so yes.'

'Now I am intrigued.'

When the meal was ready, Maia put two plates on the table, ladled out the stew, and sat down to eat with him. They ate in silence, but not out of unease. When they finished, Josh patted his stomach with a sigh. 'That was the best meal I have ever had!'

'Gosh, my husband used to push his meals away! He thought I was a terrible cook, but nothing pleased him – least of all me.'

Clearing the plates, she began to wash up, and to her astonishment, Josh picked up a tea cloth to help. When they had finished, Maia put the kettle on and invited him to sit. 'So, Josh. I think you have a story to tell me.'

'I do. If you were to ask the captain of my ship what my story was, he would say that I jumped ship,' he said indignantly.

Maia placed two cups on the table. 'By the connotation in that statement, I take it that wasn't what happened.'

He shook his head. 'Well, I certainly left the ship, but it wasn't something I wanted to do.'

Maia poured him a cup of tea and gestured for him to continue.

'My father enlisted me in the Navy in 1919 for four years – he didn't ask me - he just did it and forged my name on the papers. He was always an unpleasant man, but when he came home from war, angry and resentful, he called me a wastrel and a coward because I had not volunteered to fight. It did not matter to him that I had not been old enough - my eighteenth birthday was not until Christmas 1918. Not pacified, he insisted that I enrol in the Navy to make a man of me. I refused, but he forged my name and signed me up anyway. It has been four years of hell. Our captain was brutal; punishment was harsh for the slightest misdemeanour. On my father's orders, the captain was told not to spare the cane and to make a man of me. He took my father at his word and was brutal.'

A crease appeared on Maia's forehead as she prompted him to continue.

'I only had another month to serve – a fortnight on board before we docked at Portsmouth and a further fortnight land-based.' Josh dropped his head and shook it. 'We had left Liverpool and were on course to sail into Portsmouth when Captain Wright summoned me.' Josh paused and closed his eyes, forcing himself to think back to that fateful day.

*

I had been in high spirits for the first time in four years – my time on that damn ship was coming to a close. Just a few more days, and my nightmare would be over. My back was still smarting from a beating I had taken only the day before for doing nothing more than accidentally bumping into another shipmate in front of the captain. It had been a lonely time for me aboard – no one had dared befriend me, for if they did, they risked receiving a flogging by association.

I couldn't help but feel apprehensive when I was called from my bed in the early hours to the captain's quarters. I'd been summoned many times for tiny misdemeanours, most of which the other shipmates would have got away with. When I entered the captain's quarters and stood to attention, Captain Wright was smiling.

'I see you have a month left of your initial service in the Navy,' Captain Wright said flatly. 'No doubt you thought it beneficial that we would be docking in Portsmouth soon.'

'Yes, sir,' I answered cautiously.

Captain Wright snorted as he pushed a document over to me: 'This is your next four-year contract.'

I could not believe my ears. 'What?'

'Your father does not want you home. I cannot blame him. So, we have arranged for you to serve another four years on this ship – under my command,' he said, a cruel smile curling on his lips.

'I'm not signing that!'

'Too late, boy, your father signed and postdated it when we docked in Portsmouth two years ago.'

'But? You can't do that!'

'It is done. So, I have the pleasure of your company for another four years. I shall enjoy trying to flog some sense and obedience into you, as the last four years seem not to have made you into the man your father needs you to be.'

I shook my head. 'I will not do it. I will seek advice when we get to Portsmouth. This,' I stabbed the document with my finger, 'is not my signature, therefore not a binding contract.'

Captain Wright steepled his fingers and smiled. 'Do I take it that you refuse to honour your contract with the Navy?'

'Correct.'

'Flintman,' the captain called one of my colleagues in. 'Bring Able Seaman Savage to me - I have a job for you both.'

When both men came and stood to attention, my heart was hammering inside my chest, and I braced myself – would I be beaten again for insubordination?

'Walsh is about to desert the ship.'

I glanced between the men, puzzled.

'Grab him.' The two burly sailors each grabbed an arm. 'Right, throw him overboard.'

Flintman hesitated and glanced in alarm at his shipmate, Savage, who looked equally stunned.

'Overboard, Captain?' Flintman questioned.

'Yes. Walsh is deserting the ship.' The captain turned to address me. '*If*, and that is a big *if* you survive, know this. There will be no hiding place for you. You will be found out, court-martialled and imprisoned for your desertion.'

'But, Captain,' Flintman questioned, relaxing his hold on Josh.

Somewhere Out There

The captain narrowed his eyes. 'One more word from you, Flintman, and you too will go overboard.'

Outside on the deck, it was still dark. The ominous sea below looked black and terrifying, and I began to quake. 'Oh, God. Don't do this,' I pleaded with them.

'I'm sorry, mate. We can't go against orders,' Flintman replied. 'If it's any consolation, I can smell land - follow the north star if possible. Here, take this.' Flintman pushed an old lifejacket into my arms. 'God help you, mate. If you manage to survive, I implore you – don't tell a bloody soul who you are.'

I barely had time to wrap my arms around the life jacket before being picked up and flung into the icy waters of the Atlantic. The shock of the impact made me gulp and swallow water, and I'd lost hold of the lifejacket. Panic ensued in the swirl and swell of the waves. Seawater stung my eyes, muffled bubbles impaired my hearing, and I couldn't breathe for shock. Blind, deaf, and disorientated in the darkness, my body shuddered in horror. The rolling swell of the waves tumbled me over and over. *"Relax, Josh."* My grandpa's voice came into my head, reminding me of the wise words he said to me after we found ourselves caught in a rip tide. *"Turn on your back and relax."* Terrified, I tried desperately to settle my breathing, but with each wave that washed over me, I truly believed that I was going to drown! *"You won't drown,"* his grandpa's voice said. *"Turn on your back, put your head back, and float."* I did so, but I was coughing and choking as the waves relentlessly engulfed me. *Relax, relax, relax.* This time, it was my own voice in my head, and then panic ensued when I felt something bump against me. *Oh Christ, now I'm going to be eaten by something.* I flayed about in the water to frighten whatever was nudging me, until I realised it was the lifejacket! Grasping it, I noted a split in the sky – dawn was breaking! Would I, could I, live to see the day? Frightened tears blurred my vision. Soon, I would lose my bearings on the north star. Feeling my body chill, I knew I would not last long in the wild Atlantic. I also knew I must get out of my uniform, as it was dragging me down. The lifejacket Flintman pushed onto me was from a pile of old, damaged, discarded stock. With the ensuing light of dawn, I held it aloft to inspect it, only to find the strings had broken. I slipped it over my head, but with no strings to secure it to my body, I just had to hope for the best. Thankfully, the kapok within it had not been compromised and was still sound, therefore able to keep me afloat to a certain degree.

It took an enormous effort to keep the lifejacket from drifting off while I unlaced my shoes to kick them off. I tried to remove my trousers, but I sank underwater as I kicked them down my legs. My lifejacket started to float away. I panicked, swam to grab it, and it took several seconds to calm my breathing when I caught it. Holding the lifejacket with one hand, I tried to pull my tunic over my head. This proved to be an impossible task, being one-handed. Deciding to use the lifejacket as a float, I shoved it under my belly, unbalancing myself several times before I was able to roll the tunic over my shoulders and finally over my head. By now, I was utterly exhausted. I slipped off the lifejacket and began to sink. Was all this effort worth it? How much longer could I survive? Would it be better to let myself continue to sink? It would be so easy to disappear into the depths. My body was numb, with cold and tiredness prevailing. Let this hell end, I prayed. Suddenly, the thought of drowning – water filling my lungs was too terrifying to think about. *No. No. No. I will not die here!* Gathering strength from deep within me, I powered back to the surface and had to swim quite a distance to catch hold of the lifejacket! I put it over my head and held it tighter this time, but I was shivering relentlessly. The sky had lightened slightly, and I squinted into the far distance. If I was not mistaken, the horizon looked lumpy. Oh, Christ, was that land? I dearly hoped so. A sudden movement in the water told me I was not alone, as a large black shape swam alongside me. A seal! Did they bite? I crossed my arms over the lifejacket, trying to find some comfort and safety from it, as the seal circled me a few times before heading off, much to my relief. When the adrenalin waned, I began to feel incredibly tired again but forced myself to keep my eyes open. A few moments later, I had the strange sensation of something huge behind me and felt my legs lift as a massive body of water picked me up and projected me forward. Caught within a terrifying water tunnel, the great wall of water behind me suddenly collapsed. Down I went into the mighty swirling surf, tumbling over until I had lost all coordination. I couldn't find the surface – this time, I *was* going to drown! The lifejacket had gone - I had nothing to help me cling to life. Suddenly finding fresh air, blinded by salty seawater, I coughed and gasped, pulling great gulps of air into my lungs until the next wave hit me. Once again, I felt myself projected forward at a speed that took my breath away. When the water broke, I braced myself, tumbling over until I felt the seabed beneath me. Panic ensued as the wave pushed me down, but then the force of the water tumbled me further forward until I could breathe air again. Before I could gather my senses, the next body of water pushed me up and spat me onto the jagged rocks beneath a massive cliff face. Grasping hold of a rock to stop the waves from sucking me back into its deathly, watery mouth, I mustered all my strength to scramble to higher ground where the waves could no longer reach me. Blood was pouring from various cuts, and it took a few moments to gather my senses. I howled with anguish at what I had just gone through. Although I was relieved to have survived, I couldn't stop the wracking sobs shaking the very core of my body. I felt utterly empty, spent of all other emotions.

Eventually, I calmed, and I lifted my stinging eyes to look around. To the side of the rocky outcrop was a small fishing cove where a boat rested above the waterline. I started to stumble over the sharp, slippery rocks, conscious of the pain and blood dribbling down my face from what felt like a large gash on my head. I swilled the blood away from my face with rock pool water in the hope the salt would help to heal and seal it. Approaching the boat on the beach, I felt strangely relieved to find the rowlocks missing. I had no urgent desire to go near the sea again for a while. Glancing around, I noticed the path up the cliff and surmised there to be a village or house nearby. My first mission was to find out where I had been washed up, albeit without alerting anyone to my arrival. I was, after all, shoeless and clad only in my underclothes. With that thought, I touched the pocket in my underclothes for my good luck charm - a four-leaf clover set in copal resin that my grandma had given me. Amazingly, it was still there. Good luck, eh? A bit of a double-edged sword, I remember thinking. Where was the luck when I was thrown overboard, eh? Still, I *had* survived, so there may have been something in it after all.

Climbing the rocky coastal steps, I kept my head down as I approached the summit. There was a house perched on the hillside, so I skirted the coast path, ducking from one gorse bush to another. At the gate to the house, I could see washing on the line, and fortunately, no one was about. Opening the gate, I cringed when it creaked but sprinted across the grass and pulled a pair of trousers, two pairs of socks, and a jumper from the line and was back out of the gate without anyone seeing me. I peeled my sodden underclothes off and dressed quickly, feeling the instant warmth of the clothes, especially the jumper and socks. The trousers were huge around my waist, and at half-mast, the owner was a completely different shape from me, but beggars could not be choosers. The socks gave some padding to my feet, so I moved swiftly along the winding path until a small hamlet came into view, dominated by a square church tower. The church clock said five thirty – hopefully, I could get through this village without being seen. I passed the granite church steps, glancing at the sign: St Senara's Church, Zennor. Where on earth was Zennor? I'd never heard of it! My first thought was that I had washed up on one of the islands that made up the Isles of Scilly, as our ship had been en route to Portsmouth. I hoped that it wasn't the Isles of Scilly. I remembered from the maps I'd seen that the islands on that archipelago were tiny, so I would have been caught very soon and sent to the mainland for punishment. I didn't think anyone would believe my story of being thrown from a ship.

Continuing along the path, I passed a public house called the Tinners Arms, and it dawned on me that I must be on the mainland in Cornwall. As far as I knew, history had taught me that there were no tin mines on the Isles of Scilly.

Having left the village without being seen, I came to a crossroads and a granite road sign. Land's End was to my right, St Ives to my left, and Penzance straight on. As a sailor, I knew of Land's End and its dangerous stretch of water. The Lizard, which was further along the coast, was similarly difficult to navigate. So, I was at the bottom of the country - far enough away from Portsmouth and any risk of being caught. Grandma's family had come from Cornwall, and she had told me that she had once lived and worked in a manor house on the Lizard near the hamlet of Mullion. It seemed like a good enough place to head. Perhaps I would find work there, change my name, and settle down. I glanced at my feet, clad only in socks. Would I make it? It would be a long walk, but I remembered Grandma telling me how beautiful this part of Cornwall was – so walk I must. So, with determination in my step, I set off in search of Mullion.

4

With his story retold, Josh felt thoroughly exhausted. Taking a large intake of breath, he looked at Maia, noting she had paled significantly.

'Goodness me, Josh, how dreadful for you.' Reaching out to gently touch his hand, she was quite unaware of the warm sensation she inadvertently sent shooting up his arm.

'So, tell me, have you worked while en route here? I see you managed to acquire footwear.' She glanced down at his worn boots.

He shook his head dejectedly. 'No one would employ me. I was in a terrible state - battered, bruised, bleeding, and dressed in stolen clothes. I looked like a beggar.' He twisted his mouth to the side. 'I am a beggar. As for the boots,' he tried to wiggle his squashed, sore toes. 'I stole them from outside a farmyard door. They are a size too small and killing me, but I couldn't have walked without them.'

Maia cupped her face with her hands in sympathy. 'You poor thing. What size are your feet?'

'I'm a size ten.'

'Henry was size eleven. If you are not averse to wearing a dead man's boots, you can wear his until we can get you some that fit.'

'Beggars can't be choosers. Thank you again for your kindness.'

Maia folded her hands on her lap and asked him, 'How long did it take you to walk from Zennor?'

'Just under two weeks. I was ill and laid low for a few days near Lamorna. I ate some berries, which didn't agree with me. I felt quite weak and drained afterwards from the sickness. It was an effort to carry on walking.'

'So, without money, what have you lived on then?'

'Very little. Raw fish,' he grimaced, 'carrots and potatoes from a field, wild strawberries - things like that. I dare not touch the mushrooms – I'm not knowledgeable enough about which are poisonous. The most I had to eat was when the kind lady at the tearoom down on Poldhu came over and gave me a bag of scones and a mug of tea. I thought all my Christmases had come at once.'

Maia smiled. 'That is Ellie, my friend - she told me what she had done.'

'I am incredibly grateful to your friend and to you, Maia, for inviting me in and feeding me so well.'

'Well then. Now that you have made it here, are you planning on settling nearby? I take it you feel safe here?'

'I would like to settle here, but as for being safe, I don't know,' he said nervously.

'I take it you were enlisted in the Navy under your real name?'

'Yes.'

'Perhaps a surname change is essential as well.'

'I have been thinking the same. I thought perhaps Josh Harding had a nice ring to it.'

'It does. It suits you.' She tipped her head, studying his handsome features, particularly his striking blue eyes. 'You know you remind me of someone, but I can't think who it is. Ellie Blackthorn at the tearoom said the same. Perhaps you look like one of these new silent film stars we see in the paper. Has anyone else mentioned that you look like someone famous?'

'No.' He laughed. 'And I have never seen a silent film, so I would not know if I resembled a film star.'

'Did you have that beard in the Navy?'

'No, I was always clean-shaven.' He rubbed his chin. 'It feels hot in this weather - I would like it gone!'

'Well, I still have my husband's cutthroat razor. You could use it if you want, though it may be beneficial to keep the beard – it might hide your real identity. Perhaps just a trim might be cooler for you.'

'Thank you, I will trim it.'

'So,' she smiled warmly, 'you need work?'

He nodded. 'Do you know of any?' He asked hopefully.

'Well, I need a farmhand - can you farm?'

Josh felt tears prick behind his eyes as a great sense of relief washed over him. He nodded enthusiastically. 'I can turn my hand to many things. Grandpa was a gardener on a large estate. As a little boy, I tilled the soil and planted vegetables with him. I spent a lot of time with my grandparents. They were always who I ran to when Pa had been too handy with the belt.'

'Your father sounds dreadful.'

'He was. He was a bully,' he said darkly.

'Is your grandpa still alive?'

'Alas,' he sighed, 'I don't know. When we last docked at Portsmouth two years ago, he was ill with consumption. I've had no word since. Letters were few and far between on the high seas.'

'Well, Josh, I own this farm. My husband left me penniless, and it's been a struggle for the last twelve months, but things are on the turn. I can offer you some work if you wish. I cannot pay you much, but it may help until you find something better.'

'I would be eternally grateful to you, Maia, if I could work here.'

'That's settled then. I'll let you have some money now, in case you need to buy any essentials, and then I'll pay you a wage every Friday when I've been to the bank. If anyone asks about you, I will say that you moved down from Exeter looking for work, and I just happened upon you in Helston.'

'Oh, Maia.' He placed his hand on his heart. 'I don't know what to say except thank you again.

Maia glanced at the clock, as though she needed to be elsewhere, then smiled at him. 'Welcome to Wild Cliff Farm, Josh. Let me show you around.'

Shod now in Henry's gumboots, which were more comfortable than the stolen shoes, Josh stood with Maia at the rear of the farm in the afternoon sun, surveying her land as it stretched out before them.

'As you see, it's only a small holding but large enough to manage. The building you see, two fields away, is David Trevorrow's dairy farm at Polhormon. David has been a great help to me since Henry died. I thank the Lord for good neighbours.'

Maia then took him to meet her pigs and goats. 'Bertha the sow has twelve piglets, and Bruce, the father, lives there,' she pointed to the next pen. 'He likes to wallow in the mud underneath his favourite bush.'

Turning to the goat pens, she said, 'The goats had kids in late March, and I had to separate the does from the bucks last month to avoid any accidents. The buck kids can become sexually active within weeks of being born!' she added with a raised eyebrow. 'They'll go to slaughter at the end of summer. It breaks my heart, but needs must. I milk the goats twice a day in this shed. Their milk makes the most delicious creamy cheese. I sell it every fortnight to the nearby manor.'

They walked further along the field, past where the hens were clucking and scratching the earth in their pen.

'I hope you like eggs,' she laughed.

'I do indeed.'

She smiled as she threw a handful of seeds at them. 'Good, because they are prolific layers, all of them!'

'Happy hens then!'

Her eyes glistened with joy. 'Yes.'

They came to a thicket of trees where the light filtered through the branches, sending shafts of golden sunlight to the ground. High above them, birds twittered and flittered about.

'What a lovely, peaceful place,' Josh breathed. Each and every wonderful thing at this farm seemed to break over him like a wave. He turned to see Maia watching him as he embraced the moment. 'Everything is lovely here - after years of being at sea and the last two weeks of anxiety, this is just bliss.'

She placed her hand on his sleeve, and again, he felt a deep warmth at her touch.

'I'm glad you're finding some peace here. I inherited this orchard. I harvest quinces, figs, pears and apples, which I preserve and make pies and jellies with. There's a cherry tree, but unfortunately, the blackbirds take them before harvest. Over there, I have a small rose garden for pleasure and a large market garden where I produce the food I eat. Any excess, I sell from a stall on the roadside.'

They started to walk back across the field until they came to a shepherd's hut. 'If you need accommodation - and as you slept in my stable last night, I believe you do, you are very welcome to this.' She opened the door, and a strong, musty smell attacked her nostrils. Wrinkling her nose, she said, 'It smells damp because it has been closed up for a long while. It will need scrubbing and clearing of spiders, but it is yours to live in if it suits.'

Josh stepped inside and looked at the elevated space at one end, where the bed was. It had a stove next to the door and enough space to the right where he could have a chair and a table one day. He turned and smiled at her. 'Accommodation, as well as a job! I can hardly believe my luck.'

'I think the luck runs both ways. I need help, and so do you.' Her eyes twinkled gently. 'You'll need to drag that old straw mattress out and put it on the compost heap. I have a spare horsehair mattress and an easy chair in the loft you can have, and I'll sort some linen out for you.'

'Maia, I cannot tell you how grateful I am to you. I do believe you have saved my li…' His sentence was cut short, and they both turned when they heard a man shouting Maia's name.

'Oh dear.' Maia sighed heavily, watching Jago stride over to them. 'My brother-in-law has returned,' she explained as she began to walk to meet him.

'Who is this then?' Jago Penhollow demanded - his stance almost threatening.

'This is Josh Harding - my new farmhand,' Maia answered calmly.

'A new farmhand! Why was I not consulted, and why is he wearing my brother's clothes?' Jago lurched at Josh aggressively.

'Jago.' Maia grabbed him by the arm. 'Josh mislaid his suitcase on the train. I have lent him some of Henry's clothes for now.'

'I ask again, why was I not consulted about hiring a farmhand?' He snarled at Maia. 'I know plenty of men who need work — men *I* can vouch for. Who the hell are you anyway?' He leered at Josh. 'I've never seen you around here before!'

'Jago, Please come up to the house,' Maia said firmly. 'We can discuss it there.' She turned to Josh and said, 'I shall be back shortly.'

Josh nodded reluctantly, but he was full of unease, hoping that he hadn't caused Maia trouble by being here.

*

Maia opened the kitchen door and gestured for Jago to go inside. Prudence woke from sleeping contentedly on the chair, hissed, and arched her back at the sight of Jago.

Jago glared at the spitting animal with mutual hatred. 'Bloody cat.' He lifted his arm to take a swipe at her.

'Leave her be,' Maia snapped.

He dropped his arm, threw the tool roll he was carrying onto her clean table, and sat down, expecting a cup of tea. 'So, who is he then – this farmhand?' he demanded. 'He's not from around here.'

Maia picked his tool roll up from her clean table and put it on the spare chair, unaware that his lump hammer had rolled out of the pouch to settle at the edge of the cushion.

'You're right, he isn't. I met him in Helston today,' she lied. 'He was looking for work, and I need someone to help.'

'I bloody well help you. Don't I?' Jago snapped. 'In fact, I'm here to mend the lower fence. I believe someone broke it again,' he added.

'Do you?' she asked curiously. 'How do you know that? I haven't mentioned it to anyone.'

He paused before answering. 'I saw it earlier when you were out picking up random men from Helston,' he said with a snarl. 'So, I thought I would come back and mend it.'

'There is no need.'

He thumped his fist on the table. 'I will not see my brother's farm go to rack and ruin!'

'*My farm*!' Maia reminded him stiffly. 'And the farm is not, as you say, going to rack and ruin.' She folded her arms instead of putting the kettle on to boil. She hoped Jago would take the hint that he couldn't stay long.

'Henry was my brother. It is right that I should feel responsible for his wife and his farm.' He stood up and started to pace the kitchen, making Prudence hiss at him again.

Maia was tired of defending her right to the farm. 'No, Jago, I have told you before. This is my farm, bought for me, and it is my sweat and toil in this ground. The court has ruled in my favour. I will not tell you again.'

He growled in annoyance and continued to pace.

Maia watched him apprehensively. Jago was not as tall as Henry - though he proclaimed he was six feet two, he was a good three inches shorter, but his angry presence in her kitchen seemed overbearing. He was a well-dressed, well-groomed, and self-assured man. He was more handsome than his brother had been. His dark brown eyes added to his good looks, but would turn almost black when annoyed – a trait they were showing now.

Jago paused his pacing, put his palms flat on the table, and narrowed his eyes at her.

'Henry would want me here. *I* want to be here!' He began to pace again. 'I would not treat you the same. I would be a good husband to you.'

'No. Jago. I have no wish to marry again.'

'God damn it, woman. I love you!'

'I'm sorry, Jago, but I do not feel the same. I enjoy my independence, and I intend to work my land on my own!'

'With the help of Josh bloody Harding,' he sneered.

'Yes, with the help of Josh Harding,' she replied firmly.

'Where is he from anyway?' he growled.

'Exeter, that's all I know.'

He snorted. 'Is there no work in Exeter? How do you know you can trust him if you don't know the first thing about him?'

'I trust him. Now I must ask you to go. I have a lot of work to do.'

Jago shook his head. 'You weren't so keen to brush me off before. You were happy for me to help!'

Maia took a deep breath, thinking of all the jobs he had claimed to do, jobs that she had had to put right as soon as he left.

'I'm grateful for all you did for me, and I hope I can still call on you should I need to, but I need to make my own decisions about *my* farm. Now, I have a pottery commission to complete before the end of the month for Bochym Manor, so I need to get on.'

'Commission,' he muttered, unimpressed, as he pulled the kitchen curtain to one side and looked across the field to the shepherd's hut. 'I shall be keeping an eye on that one,' he snarled.

'You will do no such thing. Josh is my responsibility.'

'Just so you know, Maia, I am not giving up on you that easy.' Jago's eyes flashed as he retrieved his tool roll, tucked it under his arm, and stormed out of the kitchen.

His statement made her shudder, and her anxiety was mixed with an overwhelming sense of relief at his departure. She watched to make sure Jago had got into his car and not, as she thought, set off down the field to threaten Josh. Turning from the window, she stooped to stroke Prudence, who was purring contently now that the threat had passed.

'Good girl.' She felt the vibration from the cat calm her nerves, and then something caught her eye on the chair. On closer inspection, she found the lump hammer that had rolled out of Jago's tool roll, with his initials burned into the handle. The tool felt weighty in her hand, and she remembered P.C. Thomas telling her that Henry was most probably killed with a heavy implement – like a lump hammer. She quickly dismissed all thoughts of Henry from her head and climbed up to the attic, where she kept an old leather chest. Lifting the lid, which creaked with age, she placed the lump hammer inside it and closed the lid on it. Dusting down her skirt, Maia collected a bucket of water, a scrubbing brush, a broom, and a duster and walked back to Josh.

'Could I leave you to clean the hut and settle in? I have such a lot to do today. I'll be back in a few hours, and we can feed the livestock together.'

'Of course.'

He must have seen the disquiet in her eyes because he smiled and asked searchingly, 'Is everything all right, Maia? I've not caused trouble for you, have I?'

Despite her inner turmoil, she shook her head and answered, 'Not at all, Josh - everything is fine.'

5

Jago drove angrily down Poldhu Hill, stopping at the junction for the coast road. He watched the waves rolling in for a few minutes, until his fury abated. Damn that woman for her rejection of him. He was a rich, self-made man – far better with money than his brother Henry. Yes, he had made his money profiteering - selling goods on the black market - during the latter part of the war. Since then, when the bottom dropped out of the need for black market goods, he had made enough money to start a successful and legitimate motorcar business in Helston. He moved his hands around the leather steering wheel of his Alvis 12/50. He loved to drive around the town in this motorcar, knowing he was the envy of many men and had the eye of most single women - and a few married ones, he suspected. With his good looks, smooth talk, and charm, he could, if he wanted, have his pick of women, but there was only one woman he wanted: his brother's widow, Maia. He just had to find a way of getting the silly woman to accept him, which, going by her refusal of him a moment ago, might take some time! Over the last twelve months, he had caused one or two problems for her. Things like setting her livestock free in the middle of the night, breaking a few fences, and stealing produce from her garden. Just things that he could come and put right for her. Incidents that would make her frightened about living here alone. Now, with the new farmhand, Jago would have to cease his nocturnal activities until he could get rid of Harding.

He watched, with interest, the hive of activity by the beach cottage next to the Poldhu Tea Room. Several people were walking back and forth with boxes and furniture. The occupiers must be on the move. Glancing up at his home, Penn als Cottage, perched on the cliff top, precariously some believed for the last fifty years, but it was still standing. Over the past year, though, some of the land to the front of the property had slowly slipped down the cliff, and Jago had started to question its stability. Hopefully, it would not go over until he had secured his place at Wild Cliff Farm. He needed that farm - not only to get Maia to warm his bed and for somewhere to live if the house did go over, but there was another more important reason he needed to gain control of that farm and land. He had had it on good authority from a friend who worked at Tehidy Minerals Limited in Camborne that something rather beneficial was to happen soon in Mullion. Tehidy Minerals had granted permission to The Mullion United Mines Cornwall Limited and The Somerset Oxide and Ochre Company Limited to work serpentine rock and metallic minerals around Mullion. Jago had acquired a secret draft document that gave the companies - *"Full and free liberty to dig, work and search for decomposed serpentine rock or green or other coloured earth under and throughout the fields or enclosures of land in the parish of Mullion".* Wild Cliff Farm land bordered one of the earmarked sites. As soon as the farm was his, he would plough through the farmyard, stables, and orchards and charge a fortune for the mining companies to gain access from the main road to the site. As the companies had been given twenty-one years to do the work, Jago would make a great deal of money.

With his anger abating, Jago started his car, and as he drove past the entrance to the beach, his eye caught sight of a pretty young girl carrying a box to a waiting wagon. Noting that the girl had smiled at him encouragingly, his ego urged him to slow his car to a halt and back up to where she was still standing.

'Hello there, my pretty one,' he said, mentally imagining what she would look like naked in his bed. He might want to marry Maia but could put any scruples aside to have some fun with this girl. 'Do you like my car?'

Sophie Blackthorn, or Fee, as everyone called her now, gave a shy smile. 'It is rather lovely,' she answered.

'Perhaps I could take you out for a spin in her. Would you like that?'

He watched her eyes glitter with excitement.

'Sophie!'

He saw the girl's shoulders droop and her face colour with embarrassment upon hearing her ma's voice.

Jago glanced at Ellie Blackthorn, standing on the dunes with her hands on her hips in warning, and raised his eyebrows in amusement. 'Perhaps another time, *Sophie.*'

'Yes, please.' Fee nodded enthusiastically. 'Oh, and everyone calls me Fee,' she whispered.

'Well then, Fee, until the next time.' He winked.

*

With Maia's newly thrown pots in the drying room, she glanced at the clock when it struck four - it was time to go in search of Josh to show him how to feed the livestock. Maia found the door of his shepherd's hut open, so she knocked and called his name, but when she looked inside, the hut was empty. He'd done a fine job scrubbing away the years of grime. The windows were open to air the place with the breeze, dissipating the musty smell.

She turned when Josh emerged from the back of the pigsty with a rubber hose. He raised his hand to wave as he began to fill the water trough.

'I see you have beaten me to it,' Maia said, leaning over to scratch Bertha, her sow's head.

'The water was low in this trough, so I thought I would fill it.'

'Yes, it was low yesterday as well. Unless my pigs are inordinately thirsty, I think it may have sprung a leak.'

'I shall keep a check on it then.'

'The hut looks good. I've sorted some bedding out for you, and as I said, I have a spare mattress in the attic. First, we'll feed the livestock, and then I will show you how to milk the goats.'

'Actually, I already know how to milk them. They had goats at the estate where Grandpa worked - the dairyman used to let me help milk them.'

Maia's relief was palpable. 'Splendid.'

Once the livestock had been fed, watered, and milked, Maia took Josh into the attic, where she had found him a mattress, a chair, a rug, and a pile of linen.

'Can I leave you to move all this into your hut? I need to feed Shadow before supper. I hope you will join me for supper. It's just soup and bread this evening.'

'If you are sure, that would be lovely. Thank you.'

Maia smiled brightly. 'It'll be nice to have the company. Supper will be at six.'

*

Josh made three trips from the attic to his hut with the items Maia had left for him, each time glancing at the large leather chest when he passed it. On his last trip, curiosity got the better of him. He lifted the lid and found it contained only a lump hammer with the initials J.P. on it! He puzzled over it, then quickly closed the lid – he should not pry, especially as Maia had been so good to him.

Josh had just finished making his bed when he saw Maia walk to her garden and gather a posy of roses before returning to the house. Out of her work clothes, she looked more lovely with the wind in her hair and her long bohemian dress flowing behind her. If he had a pencil and paper, he would have drawn her – something he had not felt like doing for a long time. The sight of her made him tingle - something else he was not used to. He had not met with many girls before he joined the Navy - other than the girls he had gone to school with. He had avoided women on shore leave when the ship had docked, having heard of the horrific diseases some of the sailors had caught from them. Now, he had only known Maia for a few hours, but there seemed to be an easiness between them, and she gave him a feeling of well-being. He hoped that they would become firm friends.

Without a watch, he could only go by the angle of the late afternoon sun to give him the time, so he set off to the farmhouse, hoping he was not late for supper. Maia beckoned him into the kitchen, the delicious aroma of chicken, herb, and vegetable soup teasing his nostrils. A loaf sat on the table set for two, and the posy of flowers now stood in a vase. Maia smiled at him when she took the cauldron off the range and ladled a generous portion into each bowl.

There was a record on the gramophone in the other room, filtering music through to help take away any unease there might have been as they sat together to eat, which there wasn't.

'Goodness, I have never been so well fed,' Josh said, mopping the remains of his soup with a crust of bread. I can't understand why your husband didn't like your cooking. I have never tasted anything so good before.'

'Ah, well, Henry didn't like anything I did. As for the cooking, I cook with herbs and, if I'm lucky, I get spices from the East, which I buy from a travelling salesman in Helston. Henry hated the heat they gave to the food. He said I was trying to poison him!' she grinned.

'Well, I think your meals are wonderful.' He involuntarily scratched his beard as he spoke.

Ellie regarded him for a moment. 'You know, the scissors and a mirror are in the washhouse near the privy. Why not trim your beard while I make us some tea?'

*

At Poldhu, it had been a busy afternoon for the Blackthorns. Guy Blackthorn, his daughter Agnes, Jake Treen, and Ryan Penrose had all finished early from thatching that day. As the day was dry and sunny, they were all helping to move Ryan and his wife Betsy out of the beach cottage near the tearoom - a house they had occupied since before the Great War. They were moving to a larger home in Mullion to accommodate their ever-expanding family. The move meant that Agnes, the

Blackthorn's eldest daughter, and her new husband, Jake, could move to the beachside cottage. Agnes and Jake had married at Easter that year and had been living with Ellie and Guy Blackthorn since – not the best arrangement for a newly married couple.

The move had gone well, and Ellie was making supper that night for her depleted family. She was feeling troubled, having seen the interaction between her youngest daughter, Fee, and Jago Penhallow earlier. Though Fee had received a stern warning from her not to have anything to do with Jago, Fee was almost sixteen now - she could not shield her from the opposite sex forever. All Ellie could do was warn Fee about unscrupulous men, and Jago Penhallow was definitely in that category. As she dished out the supper, Ellie decided to keep the incident from Guy for now, hoping that Fee would be sensible enough to heed her warning.

*

When Josh returned from clipping his beard, he smiled at her and lifted his chin to show off his trimmed features. Maia felt her stomach somersault. Groomed now, Josh no longer resembled a wild man – he was extremely handsome.

'My goodness, what a difference,' she said with her hand on her heart, willing it to quieten. With his dark blond hair and startling blue eyes, Maia was struck again at how familiar he looked. Handing him a mug of tea, she said, 'I thought we could sit and talk for a while. Perhaps tell me more about your grandma – you said she worked at a manor near here.'

Josh picked up the mug and nodded. 'My grandma, Kitty, was a kitchen maid at a manor until 1882, before being dismissed for some misdemeanour.'

'Goodness me, I wonder what she did?'

'Alas, she would never disclose to anyone what it was, but despite being dismissed, she always spoke affectionately about her time in this part of Cornwall. Her family came from Gweek, but when her parents died of consumption, she was sent first to the workhouse and then to work at the manor. She was there for two years and worked her way up from scullery maid to kitchen maid, assisting a lovely cook called Sissy Blair.'

'Sissy Blair! I wonder if that is Mrs Persephone Blair?'

'Oh!' Josh glanced at Maia questioningly. 'Do you know her?'

'If it's the same person, I do know her, and if so, your grandma must have worked at Bochym Manor – I know the place well.'

'Yes, that is the name – I couldn't remember it, but yes, Bochym Manor. My grandma said Sissy looked after her from the moment she arrived. She mothered her and shielded her from some of the other senior staff, who, by all accounts, sounded quite horrible.'

'Mmm.' Maia nodded and frowned. 'I have heard hair-raising stories about some of the horrible staff there in the past. My friend Ellie lived there as a child and told me stories of shocking goings on before the new Earl and Countess took over when the old Earl died.'

Josh nodded. 'Grandma Kitty would only speak about Cornwall and the manor when Grandpa was out – she said he did not like her to hark back to the past. She told me that despite the horrible staff, she made three lovely friends there, and her few precious days off brought her some of her happiest memories. Grandma mentioned the glorious gardens at the manor and how kind the gardeners were. She spoke passionately about the beautiful fields, woods, and hedgerows surrounding the estate and, of course, the lovely coast in this part of Cornwall. So, when I found myself washed up in Cornwall, my heart brought me here, to where Grandma was once happy.'

Maia smiled and watched Prudence jump up and settle on Josh's lap as he spoke.

'Mrs Blair is still there, you know!'

'Really?' This piqued his interest. 'Do you think Mrs Blair would meet me?'

'Why would you want to meet her?' Maia asked cautiously.

'To thank her. Grandma told me that after her dismissal, Mrs Blair did everything she could to help her. She gave her an address for somewhere she could stay and two pounds, which was a lot of money then. She also risked her position by writing Grandma a reference because the nasty housekeeper refused to provide her with one. Grandma said that without Mrs Blair's help, she did not know what would have happened to her.'

Maia tapped her lip with her finger in thought. 'Wouldn't meeting her put your identity in jeopardy?'

Josh pondered this for a while before shaking his head. 'I've changed my name, and Grandma's maiden name was Morton, so no, I shouldn't think it would be a problem, and I would dearly like to thank her on behalf of Grandma. For some reason, Grandpa never wanted Grandma to contact Sissy Blair, and that always made her sad.'

Maia mulled over his request. 'I'm to visit Bochym Manor in the morning. Mrs Blair buys the goat cheese from me. I could mention you and find out if she would see you.'

His eyes sparkled. 'That would be very kind of you.'

Maia smiled at this handsome man before her – the more she looked at Josh, the more familiar he looked. 'You know, you do remind me of someone – it'll come to me soon, I'm sure.' She smiled and got up. 'Let me find you a spare kettle and a lamp for the hut. You will find kindling in the shed near the stables to light the stove. I have put some tea, butter, jam, milk, cheese, and the rest of that loaf in a bag so you can make your breakfast. You're welcome to eat your main meals with me in the kitchen.'

Josh smiled gratefully. 'If you're sure it's not an imposition. I would appreciate that.'

'Cooking for you is not an imposition. I said earlier, I'm glad of the company.'

A vehicle pulled up outside, and Maia glanced anxiously around the curtain.

'Oh, at last. It's Clem with the ice wagon – he's very late!' Maia glanced at the clock. 'I was beginning to worry that my cheese would go off in the cold store if he were any later. Josh, could I ask you to make yourself scarce for a few minutes? If Clem finds you in my kitchen, it will be around this village like wildfire that I am entertaining a young man in my home.'

Josh smiled. 'Of course. Where shall I go?'

'If you go through that door, you'll find my studio – I'll be as quick as possible.'

*

In the studio, Josh stood open-mouthed at the beautifully sculpted pots on the racks, each individually decorated with images of driftwood, seaweed, or shells. Glancing around the room, he noted a floor-length clay-splattered apron hung on the door peg, and the potter's wheel, next to a stool, lay clean and waiting for the next project. Muslin curtains were hung at the windows, possibly to hide these beautiful objects from prying eyes. Without a doubt, these lovely pots would bring a fair price.

'Sorry about that.' Maia breezed into the studio five minutes later. 'Clem was late because he had lost a wheel from his ice wagon again.'

'Again!'

She nodded. 'Strangely enough, the self-same incident happened a year ago today, to be exact - the day Henry died! Clem's wagon had hit a rock on the verge, knocking the wheel clean off, so that he shed his load outside Cury Church. He lost all of his ice that day. It looked like winter in June, though it had all melted by the next day, as we were in the middle of a heatwave. He hit the same rock again today.'

'Goodness. So was the ice lost again today?'

'No. Since the last incident, Clem has installed metal sides on his wagon to contain the ice and keep it cool, so only the top layer has melted while waiting for the wheelwright to assist him. He was not a happy chap this evening, though. Anyway, enough about Clem.' She gestured her hand at the room. 'What do you think of my studio?'

'These pots are amazing, Maia. You're so talented.'

'Thank you. I was taught ceramics in Helston before I married, but Henry stopped me from doing it. When he died, I set myself up again and was so lucky to be able to join the Bochym Arts and Crafts Association. I'm lucky that my work is popular and sells well. It keeps the wolves from the door.'

'Would you allow me to watch you throw a pot one day?' he asked, hopefully.

She smiled sweetly and tapped her lip thoughtfully. 'I don't usually like an audience, but for you, I will make an exception. I'll demonstrate tomorrow evening when we both have more time.

6

Fee Blackthorn rose early for work that morning. She felt a spring in her step after being singled out yesterday by the very handsome Jago Penhallow. Standing before her bedroom mirror, she felt happy with her reflection, despite the black waitress uniform she had to wear. Without a doubt, her inherited good looks had been a factor in attracting interest from Jago. The thought of him gave her a warm feeling because she, and most of the girls she had been to school with, shared a mutual infatuation with Jago. Yes, she knew he had a reputation – her ma had made that quite plain yesterday while berating her for speaking to him. Fee preferred to give Jago the benefit of the doubt just in case it was all hearsay. Anyway, what if he drove about in his fancy car, knowing the ladies were looking at him? Hand on heart, Fee had never seen him walking out with anyone. She smiled to herself. After her encounter with him yesterday, it looked as though *she* would be the lucky one to walk out with him! Yes, she would heed Ma's warning, but she was a grown-up now – almost sixteen— so it was time for her ma to let her gauge her own feelings about his real character. Then, hopefully, she might bring her parents around to accept him.

*

While Josh harnessed Shadow to the cart, Maia first packed the creamy goat cheese in ice to take to the cook at Bochym, then returned with the box of pots carefully packed with straw for a safe journey back to the kiln.

'Do you think you could start digging over the patch of land for my chitted potatoes while I am gone, Josh?'

'Your wish is my command.' He smiled warmly, and Maia felt her heart do a little somersault.

*

At Bochym, Maia greeted her fellow Arts and Crafts members before inspecting the last batch of pots she had fired.

'All present and correct,' a voice behind her said.

Maia turned and smiled at Lord Peter Dunstan, the Earl de Bochym.

'Yes, my lord,' Maia said, suddenly struck by Peter's lovely, piercing blue eyes. It then occurred to her - this was who Josh reminded her of. They shared no resemblance in stature - Lord Dunstan was taller than Josh, and Josh was slimmer in build, though they both had blond hair. At last, she had solved that little puzzle.

'It's always a bonus when they come out of the kiln in one piece.'

'Well, they really are works of art, even before you glaze them.'

'Thank you, my lord.' She loaded the kiln up again with more pots before collecting the cheese from the cart.

'Are these for Mrs Blair?' Peter asked.

'They are.'

'Excellent! I love your goat cheese. I'll carry them for you.'

Concerned that she would not get to speak with Mrs Blair alone, she answered, 'Thank you, my lord, but there is no need. I am sure you have much more important things to do.'

'No matter. I am going that way to meet with my steward, Pearson.'

As they walked through the kitchen courtyard, Denny Trevail, Theo and Lowenna's ten-year-old son stepped out of their cottage. Denny whipped off his hat, nodded a greeting to Maia, and bowed to Peter.

'May I accompany you and Mr Pearson today, my lord?'

'You can, indeed, young chap. Go and find Pearson. Tell him I will be along shortly.'

Watching Denny skip away, Maia smiled. 'That's kind of you.'

Peter sighed and shook his head. 'His poor parents have been so grief-stricken since losing their daughter,

Loveday, last month, that the least we could do is take Denny off their hands for a few hours. The poor lad feels the loss of his sister deeply. I have had him accompany me on my rounds with Pearson on Saturdays, and Hubbard, the gardener, lets him help in the garden on Sundays. The boy seems to have an aptitude for estate management and gardening, even though he is only ten. He'll be after Lord William's job of taking over the estate,' he mused.

'How is Lord William?' Maia asked. 'I haven't seen him since Lady Emma's wedding to Ben. Is he due home soon?'

'Yes. He graduates from Oxford this month.'

'Will he be participating in the London season this year? I suspect he will be looking for a wife soon.'

'No. Not this year. He wants to buckle down to learn about the estate. Perhaps he will do the season when our youngest, Lady Anna, comes of age next year. Perhaps we can kill two birds with one stone and find marriage partners for them both – though, this time, I shall not interfere!' He arched his eyebrow.

Maia smiled, knowing about the disastrous engagement arranged for Lady Emma last year, only to find out her suitor was a deeply unsavoury character.

'Well, thankfully, Lady Emma found the love of her life with Ben.'

'Indeed, she did.' Peter blanched and added, 'I berate myself regularly that I tried to push her towards a wealthy husband. As a father, I only wanted the best for her.'

'Never mind - she is happy now, and Ben Pearson is the best of men.'

'I could not agree more, Maia. Tell me, is it not a year since you lost your husband?'

Maia nodded.

'Are you managing to keep the farm running by yourself?'

'Actually, I have just taken on a farmhand. He isn't a local man, but he seems to be a hard worker.'

'That's good to hear. On that note, I shall drop these off and be on my way. Pearson will be chomping at the bit to get started on our rounds.'

As Peter walked into the kitchen with the box, he bid everyone a good morning.

Persephone Blair – Sissy to only a few close friends – and Mrs Blair or Cook to all who worked with her, smoothed her apron tidy, curtseyed as best her arthritic knee would let her, while all the other maids present dipped a low curtsy and trilled back, 'Good morning, my lord.'

'I shall leave you now, Maia. Good day to you.'

Maia smiled. 'Good day, and thank you, my lord.'

Sissy inspected the cheeses with a satisfied nod before passing them to her kitchen assistant, Vicky, to put into cold storage.

'Thank you, Maia. I was just about to have a cup of tea and a slice of cake. Can I tempt you?'

Maia nodded gratefully. 'Thank you, yes. I wanted to speak to you about something, or rather someone.'

Intrigued, Sissy answered, 'Then we will take our tray outside.'

*

As they settled around the old table in the kitchen courtyard, Lowenna Trevail stepped out of her cottage. Lowenna acknowledged their greeting, gave them a sad smile, and made her way to the manor. With her sunken eyes and grief-lined face, Maia thought the poor woman had aged in the weeks since her seven-year-old daughter Loveday had died of leukaemia.

'Poor Lowenna and Theo,' Maia said with heartfelt sympathy. 'How on earth do you move on from losing a child? Loveday was the loveliest little girl - so full of life and vibrancy. It was such a cruel thing to happen.'

'Yes.' Sissy sighed heavily. 'I don't believe I have ever seen a more heartbreaking sight than watching her little coffin lowered into the ground. That little girl touched everyone's heart.'

Maia agreed. 'And to lose her so soon after the happy affair of Lady Emma and Ben's wedding!'

'Yes. What a day that was! First, a family wedding celebration. Later that day, our butler, Joe Treen, and his wife, Juliet, welcomed their firstborn, Edward, after ten years of marriage. Then, the deep sadness of the news that Loveday died - still dressed in her bridesmaid's dress. And all this happened in the space of twenty-four hours!' Sissy lowered her voice.

'Have Lowenna and Theo returned to their duties in the household?'

'Theo returned as Lord Peter's valet within days of losing Loveday – I think he needed something to focus on. Lowenna returned last week to her duties as Lady Sarah's maid, though she is still understandably fragile. Mrs Johnson, the housekeeper, has to take over sometimes when it all gets too much for her. Oh dear, all this talk of grief.' Sissy reached out and placed her hand over Maia's. 'But of course, you know all about grief, being widowed yourself this time last year.'

Maia shook her head. 'My experience was very different. Henry was a cruel husband to me. I don't mind admitting to anyone that I do not miss him.'

Sissy's brow creased. 'Well, I hope you find someone nice next time. You're too young to be a widow. So, what was it you wanted to speak with me about?'

As Sissy sat and listened to Maia, she looked as though she had had the wind taken out of her sails.

'Lordy me, Kitty Morton!' she said, flabbergasted. 'Goodness, but I often wondered what happened to her! And you say Kitty's grandson is here?'

'Yes, Josh Harding. He's my new farmhand.'

'Is he the son of Kitty's firstborn?' Sissy asked cautiously.

'Josh said he has no siblings. So, I would say yes.'

Sissy folded her arms. 'Why is he here? What does he want?'

Noting that Mrs Blair seemed troubled by something, Maia answered, 'He told me Kitty had fond memories of you and a couple of other people here, despite being dismissed for some misdemeanour.'

Sissy pursed her lips. 'Does he know what that misdemeanour was?'

Maia shook her head. 'Kitty would never speak of it. I take it, you know what it was?'

'I do. But it is not for me to say. Tell me, is Kitty still alive?'

'Josh thinks so, but he hasn't been home or in contact with his family for a while. Josh doesn't get along with his father – he sounds like a cruel individual,' she added.

Sissy nodded as though she understood.

'The last time Josh was home was two years ago, and Kitty's husband, Josh's grandpa, was seriously ill and not expected to live for long.'

Sissy wrung her hands in her lap. 'And Josh wants to come and see me?'

'Yes, he wants to thank you on behalf of Kitty – Kitty says you saved her life.'

'Fiddlesticks, I did what anyone would do for someone in distress.'

'Josh said his grandma says your kindness went far beyond that.'

Sissy lowered her eyes but did not dismiss this comment. She took a sip of tea. 'You say Kitty might be widowed?'

'Yes.'

'Oh, I do hope her husband was someone kind, for she was the sweetest girl.'

Maia smiled. 'Josh says his grandpa was a wonderful man.'

'Yes, I suspect he must have been.' Sissy nodded.

Maia tipped her head curiously, but Mrs Blair did not elaborate.

'Tell him, yes, I will speak to him, but it can't be until Tuesday week. We have visitors at the manor next week, so all days off have been cancelled – not that I do much on my days off nowadays,' she mused. 'You can bring him to my cottage at two o'clock then.'

*

Sissy returned to her kitchen. It was a place she had inhabited for the last forty-five years, first as a scullery maid, then as a kitchen maid, and finally as a cook. Sissy had been twenty-one when she'd taken over the role of cook - very young to have taken over such a prestigious role in a household such as Bochym. Some had muttered that she did not have enough experience, but she had proved them all wrong.

Sissy leaned against her kitchen work table, lost in thought of Kitty Morton. She had never forgotten her or lost the guilt of not preventing what had happened to her. Bochym Manor was not a happy place back then. Some people who worked there were dreadfully unpleasant - cruel to the point of criminality. A far cry from the happy place it was now. Things improved slightly when the old Earl died in 1892, and Peter became the 5th Earl de Bochym. Then, in 1901, when Lord Peter married the lovely Lady Sarah, the new Countess dismissed all the unpleasant senior members of staff who had served under the old Earl. Since then, harmony had prevailed among the staff at Bochym.

Sissy pondered the planned meeting with Josh Harding, wondering how much she should tell Kitty's grandson. Would he ask about Kitty's dismissal? She hoped not. If Kitty had kept the secret all these years, then it was not her place to tell!'

'Mrs Blair. Mrs Blair.'

The voice of Joe Treen, the butler, brought Sissy from her reverie.

'Goodness, but you were miles away then,' Joe smiled. 'Are you quite well?'

'I am well. Thank you, Mr Treen. I was just lost in thought for a moment.'

'Her ladyship would like to see you in her parlour to discuss the garden party in August.'

'Thank you, Mr Treen.' Sissy reached for her kitchen diary. 'At least this year, we will not have Lady Emma's debutante ball the week after – that was a rather challenging time last year!'

'Indeed, it was!' Joe Treen agreed.

*

Later that day, when evening dinner finished, Sissy picked up her basket and made her way back to her little cottage located behind the manor.

As Sissy rounded the Steward's cottage, the magnificent peacocks were noisily vocal in rounding up the peahens from the undergrowth where they had been grazing and preening most of the day. Sissy smiled as the peahens flew up to land on the ridge of the manor roof, trumpeting as they roosted, safely away from a wily fox searching for a tasty treat. Once all the peahens were safe, the more dominant peacock spread his magnificent wings and took himself off to the top of the clock tower to roost for the night. Peace prevailed!

Once inside her little cottage, Sissy slipped on her slippers, put the kettle on for cocoa, and sat down to revisit her thoughts of Kitty. As she dozed in her chair, her mind took her back to 1880 - the first time Sissy laid eyes on that poor little fourteen-year-old orphan, Kitty Morton.

7
Kitty August 1880

As the cart trundled down the long, dusty track towards Bochym Manor, Kitty Morton's jaw dropped – never had she seen a finer house! The apprehension she was feeling flipped to excitement at the thought of working here but soon flipped back again when Kitty was pushed through the tradesman's entrance to be met by a sour-looking woman with her arms folded.

'Kitty Morton, for you, Mrs Bligh,' the cart driver said.

Mrs Bligh, the housekeeper, was clad from head to foot in a black bustle dress, her greying hair pulled back into a severe bun. She narrowed her eyes at Kitty. 'Is that it?' she barked at the driver.

'That's who they sent, so don't blame me,' he snapped back. 'You're certainly getting through a lot of girls - this is the sixth girl I've brought from the workhouse this year,' he added sarcastically.

'And every one of them was lazy, with loose morals.'

'Loose morals! None of them were more than fourteen years old!' he countered.

'It's the older ones that get into trouble. The younger ones have to take their place, but it happens to them all eventually. Disgusting little urchins, they are.' She leered at Kitty. 'She'll have to do for now,' she said, slamming the door on the driver. Grabbing Kitty by the neck of her coat, she yanked her down the corridor and into a small, tidy room.

Kitty stood trembling, fearing she would wet herself if this woman barked at her again.

'Are you clean?'

'Yes,' Kitty's voice trembled. 'Matron paraffined my hair last week, and I had a bath on Sunday.'

Mrs Bligh grabbed her ear and inspected behind it, clearly irritated to find them clean. She turned to open a cupboard and extracted a rough, serge green dress. She held it up against her and then pushed it into her chest for her to grab.

'What belongings have you brought?'

'A vest, two more pairs of bloomers, black woollen stockings, and the clothes I have on now.'

Mrs Bligh nodded. 'You will address me as Mrs Bligh. I am the housekeeper here, and I will stand for no cheek. I expect you to work hard and keep yourself clean. If you don't, you will be returned, in shame, to the workhouse. As the scullery maid, you will get two hours off every fourth Sunday, but only *if* it's convenient for the household.' She pushed Kitty out of the door, grabbed her again by the neck of her coat, and marched her into the kitchen.

'This is Mrs Crabb, the cook, and that is Blair, the kitchen maid. Your duties as a scullery maid will be explained to you by Blair.'

With a shove, Mrs Bligh pushed Kitty towards the kitchen maid, who managed to catch her before she stumbled.

'Blair, you have ten minutes to show Morton her duties, so get on with it. Put her in the cupboard room in the attic.' With that, Mrs Bligh turned on her heel and marched quickly away.

Kitty watched as the kitchen maid turned pleadingly to Cook. 'I need more than ten minutes, Mrs Crabb.'

'Of course, Sissy. Pay no heed to Mrs Bligh. I don't need you for half an hour – that should give you time to explain the job properly to the girl.'

'Thank you, Mrs Crabb,' Sissy said, and then turned to Kitty. 'Come, I'll show you your room first. Though room is a stretch on the word, cupboard just about sums it up.'

Kitty smiled gratefully at her. Sissy was a well-built, plain-looking woman with mousy hair pulled into a tight bun, but she had the most endearing smile. Kitty was glad of her kindness towards her. She followed her up the narrow stairs to the servant's quarters, listening intently to what Sissy was saying, fearing she would not catch everything said.

Kitty's room was the tiniest room she had ever seen. The only window was a six-by-eight slit in the wall.

'Mrs Bligh doesn't like you to open the window – she says it causes a draught in her room, though Lord knows how that's possible – her room is way down the corridor. She likes the occupant to be stifled and as uncomfortable as possible. I suspect you've already surmised that Mrs Bligh is a nasty, unpleasant person, so I implore you to keep out of her way as much as possible.' Sissy smiled amiably at Kitty. 'I occupied this room until yesterday and always opened the window!' She winked. 'I just stuffed the rag rug under the door so she couldn't feel the draught. I suggest you do the same. Now, put your case down and come with me. I'm called Sissy – it's short for Persephone.' She pulled a face. 'I know. It's a ridiculous name for a kitchen maid. I think my mother had delusions of grandeur. What's your name?'

'Katherine, but everyone calls me Kitty,' she answered, hardly able to hide the tremble in her voice.

'Well, Kitty, I cannot lie - you have the worst job in this house! I've done it myself for the last two years until Ethel, the last kitchen maid, got herself in the family way and was dismissed. Now then, the Dunstan family are away from home until tomorrow, but I've cleaned the fires in their rooms and built them with kindling. They'll need a match put to them in the morning. You will rise at four thirty and feed the fire for the boiler so that we have hot water. And then you must light the range so Mrs Crabb can start the breakfast. After that, you must light the fires in the French drawing room, where they have breakfast, the Jacobean drawing room, the Earl's study, Nanny's room, and the nursery.'

Sissy led Kitty downstairs and took a sharp turn down a dark passage to the laundry. 'This is Joyce, the laundry maid. She washes everyone's clothes.'

Kitty smiled at the red-faced, harassed-looking girl, who scowled back.

With a hand to her back, Sissy led her away and whispered, 'If I were you, I'd wash your own drawers. Otherwise, you might not get your own back. The next job is the bedchambers. When the family are at home, all fires burn throughout the day, from September to June. You must enter the bedrooms quietly and not wake the occupants. Feed the fires so they are blazing when they rise.' Sissy opened the door to the Earl's bedchamber first – a dark, foreboding room with oak panelling and dark red drapes at the windows. The Countess de Bochym's room was next – a large, bright, opulent room with drapes adorned with Asiatic pheasants, a matching pitcher and jug, and a beautiful Turkish rug. 'Don't walk on the rug, and keep to the edges of the room, but keep your footsteps quiet. I used to walk in my stocking feet, so I didn't make a noise.'

Kitty nodded - she would do the same.

When they arrived at the nursery, Nanny was in residence with a young boy.

'Hello, Nanny,' Sissy said. 'This is Kitty, our new scullery maid – I'm just showing her around. Kitty, this is master Peter Dunstan – His Lord and Her Ladyship's son.'

'Oh, hello, Master Dunstan.' Kitty bobbed a curtsy, but the child was busy reading.

Nanny shook her head. 'You must not address the child or any family member unless they address you first.'

'Oh! Sorry, I didn't know.'

'Well, now you do. Miss Black, the young master's governess, has just popped out. Best make yourself scarce before she returns – you know what she is like, Sissy.'

Sissy nodded.

'Good luck, Kitty. You'll need it,' Nanny called out as they left.

Kitty felt a tremor in her body as she followed Sissy back down the servant's stairs.

Somewhere Out There

'Now, your next job is to empty all the chamber pots from the servant's quarters – horrible job – stinks it does, but it is your job to empty them. I've already collected them but have not dealt with them yet. So, I'll introduce you to the delights of the scullery in a moment, but first, I need to show you how to get the water up to the bedchambers so His Lord and Her Ladyship can perform their toilet.'

In the boiler room, Sissy showed Kitty where the buckets and large copper jugs were kept and led her to the boiler. The mistress is with child – due in the next couple of months, so she bathes every day to ease her burden. Two buckets of hot water and a jug, all covered with cloths, must be deposited outside her bedchamber, ready for her lady's maid to fill her bath. The Earl requires two jugs of water left outside his room. One of the jugs must contain scalding water, so his valet, Lanfear, can shave His Lordship. The other jug must have warm water for His Lordship to wash with. The Earl only bathes occasionally, but his valet will send for buckets of water should His Lordship want a bath. We keep the boiler going all day, just in case. Once you have deposited the water, you have this delight.' Sissy opened the scullery door and ushered her in.

Kitty wrinkled her nose – it really did stink. 'Keep the scullery door shut so the smell does not escape into the kitchen. If Cook smells it, she goes mad.' Sissy opened the back door to a vast yard where Joyce was hanging out the washing. 'Now, you empty the pots down the privy here – she pointed to the small brick hut. The privy bucket has holes in the bottom to let the pee through to the soak away. Anything hard goes into the barrel for the nightsoil man. I wrap a scarf around my face when I lift the lid. The flies are awful. Once you have emptied the chamber pots, they need scrubbing clean. The servants use the outside privy during the day, so don't put their chamber pots in their rooms until after supper, as they will use them, and they are just for the nighttime. You must check the bucket in the privy every hour to empty the hard stuff out. Mr Lanfear, the Earl's valet, and Miss Howarth, Her Ladyship's maid, will bring the family chamber pots down to you. They are the fancy ones without handles, so they fit inside the commodes in their rooms. Do not break them!' she warned, and she put a comforting hand on Kitty's arm. 'After you've done all that, it will be time for breakfast,' she smiled. 'After breakfast, you will be scrubbing again. First, the chamber pots, in this sink only – the other we use to wash the crockery and such. Once you've cleaned the chamber pots, set them over there on the shelf. Use this to scour the chamber pots. For the pots and pans Cook uses at dinner time, you must use this to clean them.' She waved another scouring pad at her and wrinkled her nose. 'Don't get them mixed up.' She laughed. 'You'll wash all the dishes and cutlery after each meal and put them back where they live – I'll show you where, though you will not be allowed near the crystal or silver - the maids and footmen deal with those. At the end of the day, when Cook has gone to bed, you have to empty the privy bucket one last time, and then the kitchen floor. I'm afraid your working day will be from four thirty until eleven.'

Kitty's eyes watered at the thought of her life from now on.

'How will I get up? I fear I shall sleep too late to do everything,' Kitty cried.

'The nightsoil man will wake you. He arrives at four fifteen every morning to exchange the barrel. The nightsoil man shoots a pea through a shooter at your bedroom window until your face appears.' She pointed up to the tiny window in the cupboard room.

Kitty grimaced, remembering the stinking barrel. 'What does he do with it when he takes it away?'

'He sells it to the farmers to put on the crops, of course. It's fertiliser.'

'Ugh!'

Somewhere Out There

'Listen, Kitty. It's a lot to take in, but I'll get up with you in the morning and do the fires with you so you know what to do. I take it you have lit a fire before?'

'Yes. The workhouse instructed us on how to do all domestic work, but I used to do it at home when Ma and Pa were alive.' Kitty felt her eyes water at the thought of her dead parents.

Sissy, seeing her distress, put her arm around her to comfort her.

'Stay strong, Kitty. I will be in the kitchen all day with Mrs Crabb. If you get stuck on anything or forget what to do next, ask me. Now, off you go and put on the dress Mrs Bligh gave you – I'm afraid it is a bit scratchy – but the material is green and hides the muck.'

Kitty smiled gratefully at Sissy and made her way back up the stairs to her tiny room to find that someone had opened her case and rifled through her clothes. In a panic, Kitty searched the pocket of the case for the one precious thing she owned – the only thing she had to remind her of her parents, who had died of consumption within months of each other – a silver locket that held a sepia photo of them both. Her fingers searched frantically, but the locket had gone.

*

Back in the kitchen, Sissy returned to her work, chopping the vegetables for dinner.

'Has she settled in?' Mrs Crabb asked.

'As well as she can, poor little beggar. She's a pretty little thing, with her chestnut brown hair and blue eyes! I don't think I have ever seen eyelashes that long before!'

'I suspect those eyes will be dulled by hard work soon,' Mrs Crabb sighed as she returned to her stove.

*

Kitty was distraught at the theft of her precious locket, but she knew she must buckle down to her work. If she were dismissed from the manor and sent back to the workhouse, she would be assigned the very worst jobs there. Then she thought of the smelly job she had to tackle here and wondered which would be worse. She pulled on her work dress, which was rough and itchy, and felt thoroughly wretched. Making her way down the stairs, she glanced into the corridor to the laundry and caught sight of Joyce, the laundry maid, with her locket in her hand.

Kitty flew down the corridor and leapt at Joyce. 'Hey, that's mine!' she said, trying to grab it off her.

'It's mine now.' Joyce sneered, holding the locket at arm's length.

Kitty saw red and flew at her again, scratching and kicking until Joyce dropped the locket. Kitty fell to her knees to crawl and retrieve the locket that had shot across the laundry floor. Kitty's hand had just curled over it when she felt herself being lifted to her feet by the scruff of her dress.

'What is going on here?' Mrs Bligh demanded.

'She attacked me,' Joyce whined.

'Did she now!' Mrs Bligh shook Kitty. 'What have you to say for yourself, child?'

Kitty could barely speak due to Mrs Bligh almost strangling her with the neck of her dress, but speak up, she must. 'Joyce stole my locket out of my suitcase.'

'I did not – it was in the pile of laundry sent down to me. So, finders keepers.'

'I did not give you any laundry,' Kitty countered. 'You went into my room and stole it from my suitcase!'

'Enough!' Mrs Bligh yelled. 'Morton, when I asked you earlier what you had brought you did not mention a locket, so, you will go without meals today for fighting and telling lies. I will not tolerate either. Now give me that locket and get on with your work – both of you.' Mrs Bligh turned on her heel, only to be stopped by Mrs Crabb and Sissy.

'Excuse me, but that locket does belong to young Kitty. She showed it to us earlier, so give it back to her,' Cook said, folding her arms, determined not to let Mrs Bligh pass until she had handed it over.

Kitty looked at Cook with astonishment - she had shown it to no one, but Sissy winked at her in the background.

With a large harrumph, Mrs Bligh slapped the locket into Kitty's hand before storming back to the housekeeper's room.

Kitty curled her hand over her precious locket and heard Joyce snarl, 'I'll get you for that.'

Fortunately, Cook heard her. 'Enough of that, Joyce Johnson. We all know that you're light-fingered. If I find out you have done anything else to Kitty, I will deal with you once and for all.'

Joyce blanched as Cook stormed off, leaving Sissy to beckon Kitty into the kitchen.

'Are you all right?'

Kitty nodded, rubbing her head where Joyce had pulled her hair.

'Have you got your locket safe?'

Kitty nodded again and retrieved it from her pocket.

'Good, now tidy your hair, and then start emptying and scrubbing the chamber pots.' She led her to the door of the scullery, but Kitty stopped and turned to address her.

'Thank you, Sissy. Thank you, Cook,' she said, bracing herself to enter the smelly scullery.

'Here's a tea cloth to tie around your face,' Sissy said. 'I suggest you open the back door to get some air in.'

Kitty's eyes watered again at both Cook's and Sissy's kindness.

*

During Kitty's first day at Bochym, Sissy popped in and out of the scullery to check on her progress, sometimes helping when she looked like she was lagging behind. Kitty was dreadfully hungry at the thought of no meals that day, but thankfully, Cook took pity on her rumbling tummy and brought her a dish of stew.

'Nobody working in my kitchen goes without food - no matter what Mrs Bligh says!' she said, placing her finger to her lips for Kitty to keep quiet.

Kitty spent the rest of her day feeding the fires for the boiler and kitchen and scrubbing and cleaning more pots after the servants had had their supper.

'I am sorry to say there will be a lot more to wash up tomorrow when the family arrives home,' Sissy warned when she brought Kitty a bowl of soup and a chunk of bread for her supper. 'Mrs Crabb says you must go to bed once you have eaten this and scrubbed the kitchen floor. I'll see you in the morning to help you with the fires. Oh, and here, I have brought you a ribbon to thread through your locket. Now that Joyce knows about it, it is probably better that you wear it because I suspect she will try to steal it again.'

Kitty's hand closed protectively over the locket in her pocket. 'Why does she not get punished for thieving?'

'She's Mrs Bligh's niece!' Sissy said flatly.

8

After Maia returned from Bochym with the news that Mrs Blair was happy to see him, she found Josh had finished digging over the potato patch, weeded between the sprouting rows of peas and beans, and secured the twiggy frames for them to grow up in! After their midday meal, Josh began to harvest the beetroots while Maia boiled, pickled, and bottled them. Later, they spent a couple of hours happily working together in Maia's garden, tidying up after the storm.

After a very productive day working the land, Maia invited Josh to sit with her outside the back door of the farm to enjoy a glass of her elderflower wine before supper. They sat together, windswept and tinged pink with the sun, enjoying the fantastic view across the sea as far as Newlyn, Mousehole, and beyond. While soft music from the gramophone filtered through in the late afternoon air, Maia felt truly content for the first time in a long time.

*

After supper that evening, Maia, as promised, led Josh back into her studio.

'Are you sure you want to do this now, Maia? You've been working all day!'

'Of course. Making pots isn't work – it's pure pleasure,' she said, putting on the floor-length, clay-splattered apron with a split up the middle. 'This split is so I can sit astride the wheel,' she demonstrated. 'I know it isn't very ladylike, but needs must.'

Josh's eyes crinkled. *If she wore a sack, she would still look like a lady.*

Maia got up, cut a slab of clay from a large piece she had in a damp sack, and placed it on her tabletop. 'Before I put the clay on the wheel, I need to prepare it by kneading it on a work surface - like kneading dough. Kneading removes the air bubbles from the clay to give it an even consistency. Once done, it will be much easier to work with.' She kneaded it for a few minutes, patted the clay into a ball, moved to sit by the wheel, and slapped it firmly onto the wheel head.

'Is that where the name throwing a pot comes from?' Josh asked.

'No, the word derives from the old English word 'thrawan', which means to twist or turn, which is what a potter does with the clay once it's centred.' Maia ran a finger along the edge of the clay and wheel head. 'Doing this creates a seal between the clay and the wheel head,' she explained. 'Once roughly positioned in the middle of the wheel head, I can start to centre the clay properly and shape it smoothly and evenly.' She set the wheel in motion and wet her hands in the water bowl beside her before placing them firmly on the clay. 'By applying force to the clay, I can cone it up and down to make it more central. When I am happy with the centring, I open the clay by creating a dip or hole in the middle using my thumbs and fingers.' A strand of her beautiful red hair fell forward, and she tried to push it back with the back of her hand. 'Silly me, I normally tie it back when I am working. There is a ribbon over there on the shelf, Josh. Could you tie it back for me, please? My hands are a bit of a mess now.'

Josh nodded eagerly. Her hair had fascinated him since he had first set eyes on her – it reminded him of a pre-Raphaelite painting. With the ribbon in hand, he slotted it under the mass of fiery curls. It felt heavy but soft on his hands and fragrant like roses. If he wasn't mistaken, he heard Maia sigh as he tied the ribbon into a bow.

'All done,' he said, stepping back to where he could observe her.

'Thank you, Josh, you have a very delicate touch.' She gave him a look that made his heart flip.

With a little more water on her hands, she set the wheel in motion again. 'Now I push down until the clay at the base of the hole is about a third of an inch thick, then it is ready for me to start pulling up the sides. I do that by pinching the clay at the base on the inside and outside of the pot, then I move my hands up the side of the pot to form the walls, and voila, I have a basic pot.' A shorter lock of hair fell over one of her eyes. She laughed and blew it out of the way. 'I should cut my hair – it would be much easier.'

'Please don't cut it,' Josh said ardently. 'You have the most beautiful hair I have ever seen. You could rival Elizabeth Siddle, Rossetti's wife and muse, for her hair and beauty.'

'Thank you, Josh! That is the nicest thing anyone has ever said to me. I've been taunted relentlessly for my red locks. My school days were a constant challenge, and since I was widowed, I've been frowned on by the older members of the community for not wearing it up. I would not conform to mourning Henry, you see,' she gave a wry smile. 'I do not conform to most things.'

'Bravo!' Josh answered.

Maia tipped her head. 'Goodness, Josh. I think I like you more and more every moment I spend with you.'

Realising the connotations of her unguarded statement, she quickly looked away awkwardly, but her words gave Josh a warm glow.

'Right. Now it is your turn.' She got off the stool and began to take off her apron.

'Oh no!' he protested. 'I will make a terrible mess of it.'

'No, you won't. Here, put this on and have a go.'

He reluctantly donned the apron while Maia cleaned off the wheel and prepared another piece of clay for Josh to use.

'There you go.' She handed him a ball of clay. 'Slam it down on the wheel.'

He did so, though it was way off the mark.

'Pick it up and do it again, but keep your eye on the centre.'

His aim was better that time.

'Now set the wheel going.' She bent over him to lead his foot to the peddle, and he caught the fragrance of her hair again. It took a great deal of effort to concentrate on the task at hand rather than the proximity of Maia.

'Dip your hands in the water and begin the centring.'

He laughed heartily as the slippery clay wobbled in his hands, but Maia stood behind him and slipped her hands over his so they could steady the clay together. Her touch sent shivers of pleasure up his arms. He felt disappointed when she moved them away to let him begin to cone the clay. 'Now keep it damp and insert your fingers and thumb like I did. That's good,' she praised. 'Now begin to build those walls.' Again, she put her hands over his, so they slowly moved in unison up the pot. Josh had to pull on all his willpower to stop the rising passion building inside him, and then suddenly, the pot collapsed, splattering wet clay everywhere. Maia jumped back with a squeal to avoid the worst of it, but Josh was covered. They broke into joyful laughter as they wiped the muddy mess off themselves, then amidst their mirth came a sudden, hard hammering on the front door, which silenced them.

Maia's face clouded, as though she knew that knock.

'Shall I make myself scarce, Maia?'

She nodded anxiously. 'If you would. Go up to the attic.'

*

Maia took her time to go to the door, despite the hammering becoming louder. When she opened it, Jago, his face hot and furious, stepped into her kitchen without invitation.

'Where is he?'

'I beg your pardon.'

'Where is Harding? I know he is here – I heard you laughing.'

'*I* was laughing. I splattered myself with wet clay – see.' She opened her arms to show him the state of her dress.

He narrowed his eyes, as though he did not believe her. 'I bet he had his supper here with you tonight.'

'Josh cooks his own food,' she countered with a lie.

'A likely story,' he sneered. 'You were seen sitting outside with him, and don't deny it, The Old Inn is buzzing with talk about you!'

'How shallow folk's lives are to be bothered by what I am doing.'

'So, you don't deny it?'

'Certainly not. We've been working all day and stopped for a drink for a few minutes.'

Jago bared his teeth. 'It isn't proper - a lone woman here with a male farmhand.'

'Who lives separately from me,' she reminded him.

Snorting derisively, he threw his hat on the window seat next to Prudence, who arched her back and spat at him.

Maia watched, hands on hips, as Jago began to pull out the kitchen chairs. 'May I ask what you are doing?'

'God damn it, woman! I've lost my lump hammer now. I keep losing tools whenever I come here to do a job.'

Maia's face tightened. 'If you remember, you didn't do a job when last you were here.'

'Damn it!' He pushed the chairs noisily back. 'I never found the penknife I was cutting the twine with when I was helping Henry secure the pig fences just before his death – sharp as a razor it was. Both tools have my initials on them - have you not seen either of them?'

'No, Jago, and I would appreciate you not hammering on my door and barging into my kitchen late in the evening as though you owned it.'

'I should bloody own it!' he muttered. 'Anyway, I'll need somewhere to live soon when I lose my house to the sea.'

Maia clicked her tongue in irritation. 'That house has been teetering near the edge of that cliff since your father built it, so folks say.'

'Well, I reckon it's going soon - it creaks and groans like Billy-O now.'

'Then I suggest you find somewhere else to live!' Maia said firmly. 'You're not without money by the look of the fancy car you drive around in.'

'All my money is ploughed into the business. Henry always told me I would have a home here should my house slip down the cliff. It's what he wanted.'

'Henry is not here, and it was not his house to say that. We've been over this, Jago. The farm is mine. I have papers to prove it, and you will definitely *not* be moving in if your house goes over the cliff!'

'So, you would leave me homeless?'

'Yes. Because I do not want you here, Jago, you must look elsewhere, and that is the last I shall say on the subject. Now, please leave. I don't appreciate you being here at this time of night!'

His eyes narrowed. 'Why, are you afraid I will catch you doing something you shouldn't?'

Maia folded her arms. 'What I do here is of no concern of yours. Now please leave my house – you're trying my patience.'

He paused as though to say something else but must have thought better of it because he turned around to pick up his hat, and Prudence hissed at him again.

'Bloody animal!' he said, swiping the cat with his hat before storming out the door.

*

Hearing the raised voices in the kitchen and furniture moving about, Josh was concerned for Maia and struggled with his dilemma. He feared for Maia's safety but did not want to compromise her unless absolutely necessary. While in the attic, hardly daring to breathe, Josh could hear Jago asking Maia if she had found his initialled lump hammer. He frowned and glanced at the leather chest he had sneakily looked into yesterday, knowing that the lump hammer was in there. Why did Maia deny knowledge of it? He shook his head - it was none of his business.

When he heard the back door slam shut, he waited a few moments before returning to the kitchen to find Maia visibly upset. He moved quickly towards her, desperate to take her into his arms to comfort her, but dared not. Instead, he asked, 'Are you all right?'

She nodded. 'I take it you heard all that?'

'I did. I fear I'm making things awkward for you.'

Maia shook her head. 'No, Josh, it is Jago making things awkward.'

'Perhaps we shouldn't eat together?'

'No, Josh. I decide what I do in my own house. Besides, I enjoy your company. Jago does not own me, even if he thinks he does!'

'You said yesterday that your husband was a hateful man – does Jago share his personality?'

Maia pursed her lips. 'Jago may try to hide it, but he's cut from the same cloth, and I have no intention of letting another Penhallow brother into my life – one was quite enough!'

Josh frowned. 'May I ask - if it is not too personal a question? Why did you marry Henry? Did you love him once?'

'Goodness, no, I never loved him!' She lowered her eyes. 'I got pregnant by him.' She turned away from Josh and shuddered with disgust. 'He was my brother's friend – they were the same age.'

'Oh! You have a brother!' Josh's eyes widened.

Maia folded her hands on her lap. 'I *had* a brother. Alec died in the war.'

He cupped her hand for comfort, and she did not pull away. 'Maia, I'm so sorry.'

'So am I. We were very close. Henry was the only fly in the ointment in my relationship with Alec. I never warmed to him - he made me feel uncomfortable. I was devastated when Alec was sent away to war in 1916. Henry, of course, went with him. When we received a telegram to say that Alec died in the trenches in June 1917, I believe my heart broke that day.'

A lone tear trickled down her cheek, and Josh squeezed her hand. Her eyes thanked him for the comfort.

'The few men who did come home just before Christmas 1918 were quiet and withdrawn - as though they'd had the stuffing knocked out of them! But when Henry returned, he seemed to be the same strong-willed, self-assured man he'd always been – a bit like Jago is now. I resented Henry for living while my darling brother died, but Henry kept seeking me out. He'd appear when I was out walking, wanting to share memories of Alec with me.' The latter words came out through gritted teeth. 'Despite myself, his constant talk about Alec kept my brother's memory alive. Then Henry started saying things like, "Alec always thought you and I would make a good match, you know - Alec was keen for us to get to know each other better - and I think it would have made Alec really happy if his beloved sister and best friend could find a future together."

Maia glanced at Josh and shook her head. 'I knew he was lying - Alec would never have wanted Henry for me – he knew how I felt about him. I avoided Henry after that, but then...' Maia's mouth twisted to the side, and Josh wondered if she was about to cry again, but she appeared to shake off whatever demon thoughts had entered her head.

'It was New Year's Eve. I'd gone down to Poldhu Cove. There was a bonfire, music, and dancing to see the new year in, though the thought of a new year without Alec was breaking my heart. I thought Henry would be at The Old Inn, but he was there on the beach! He tried to kiss me, but I pushed him off and ran away, and he followed.' Maia paused and hugged her arms as though chilled.

'Shall I fetch you a blanket,' Josh said. Maia shook her head.

'He caught me up in the dunes, pinned me down, and well...' her lip curled with disdain. 'He was a strong, powerful man - I couldn't fight him off. He said, "Let's give Alec what he wanted," and then he violated me. I screamed, but he muffled my cries with his hand. I was so angry. I was terrified afterwards to venture out, but when I found out I was pregnant, I had to tell my aunt. She insisted that we must marry at once to minimise my shame.'

'Your aunt?'

'Yes. Aunt Martha - Lady Martha Jefferson. Alec and I were her wards. Our parents died when we were very young, and we were brought here to Mullion to live in her fine house over by Polurrian. Though my aunt was disappointed in me, she understood how unhappy I was at the prospect of marrying Henry. To minimise my despair, she bought Wild Cliff Farm as a going concern for me, to give us the best start in life. My aunt died in May 1919, so thankfully, she never saw Henry squander our money - or how he began to treat me – but that's another story,' she said grimly.

'And your baby?' Josh asked gently.

'I miscarried on my wedding night - damn it!' She said crossly. 'If it had happened just one day before, I would not have had to marry him!'

'I'm sorry for the loss of your baby, Maia.'

'Don't be.' She shook her head. 'In truth, I did not want his baby, nor any more with him. I did everything to stop another baby from coming, especially as he showed his true colours with his fist shortly after my aunt died.'

Josh gasped. *With his fist!* He felt enraged that anyone could harm Maia. 'And now that Henry has gone, Jago thinks he has some claim on the farm?' he asked.

'Yes, and on me!' she said indignantly. 'It didn't take long for Jago to declare himself to me after Henry died -

he truly believed that he would take over where Henry had left off. I was having none of it, but I was worried that he might have some claim on the farm, so I sought advice from Lord Dunstan, the Earl de Bochym, and he instructed his lawyer to make my ownership of the farm watertight.'

'The Earl sounds like a decent sort.'

'He is. He has been very helpful.'

'But yet, Jago still tries!'

'Jago is a charmer. He truly believes his charm and money can buy him everything.'

'If he has money, why does he want this farm?'

'Your guess is as good as mine. Anyway, enough about him. We mustn't let him spoil the lovely night we've had.'

'I agree. It has been lovely. Thank you for everything this evening, and I'm sorry I soiled your dress.'

She laughed. 'Think nothing of it - it will wash out. I don't possess a single dress that I've not splattered with wet clay at some time or another. It's an occupational hazard, but making my pots is worth it. The money I make being part of the Bochym Arts and Crafts Association keeps this farm afloat.'

'Is Bochym a nice place to work now, I wonder?'

Maia nodded. 'Everyone seems happy with their work there. Of course, being in service is a demanding job, but I suspect it must have been a lot harder in your grandma's time.'

'Indeed. From stories my grandma told me, it sounded quite unpleasant at times. I'm glad she had a friend in Mrs Blair.'

9
Kitty 1880

Kitty's second day at Bochym was indeed more challenging, but with Sissy's help, she was sure she could manage. Thankfully, Kitty was allowed to eat her meals at the kitchen table with Cook and Sissy, which was much more pleasant than eating them in the smelly scullery!

Lord Randolph and Lady Lucinda Dunstan, the 4th Earl and Countess de Bochym, arrived home at three that afternoon, and from that moment on, the servants never stopped. Kitty was astounded by the amount of dishes coming through for her to wash following tea and then again after the family's evening meal. They just kept coming until, finally, the family retired at around ten. It took another hour for Kitty to finish washing up, so it was half past eleven before she had finished scrubbing the kitchen floor and could finally fall into bed, exhausted.

True to form, each day Kitty was woken from her short slumber by peas shot at her window from the nightsoil man's pea shooter. She scrambled out of bed, knocking her knee on the metal bedstead, and put her face to the window to show the man she was up. After a quick wash, she got dressed to start the day. Once she had lit the kitchen fires, she filled the coal scuttle and set off at a diligent trot along the corridors to tend all the other fires. She had to remember to keep her eyes on the ground if, by chance, she should come across a family member. Under no circumstances was she to make eye contact with them - instead, she had to melt into the shadows. Mrs Bligh had drummed it into her that she was the lowest of the low, and the family would never want to see or hear her.

At the Earl's bedroom, Kitty tentatively opened the door as quietly as possible. The room was hot and stuffy, filled with the most unpleasant odour of expelled wind, which, although the occupant seemed to be asleep, he continued to pass noisily! Trying her best to hold her breath, Kitty built the coals on the fire and swept the hearth, but as she got off her knees, a piece of coal rolled off and clattered into the hearth. With an audible gasp, Kitty tried to catch the hot coal to quieten the noise, burning her fingers in the process. A moment later, a book came hurtling towards Kitty, hitting her just above the eye and causing a split in her eyebrow, which made her squeal in pain.

'Shut up and get out of my room, you noisy little bitch,' the Earl yelled, and Kitty grabbed her coal scuttle and ran to the door just as another book came hurtling over, narrowly missing her but hitting the door as she closed it.

The blow to her head had knocked Kitty sick, making her sway alarmingly. Cupping her face in her hands, she felt the blood ooze between her fingers as she slowly slid down the corridor wall to sit with a thump on the floor.

'Oh, lordy me, Kitty! What has happened?' Sissy whispered, on coming across Kitty as she was en route to start her kitchen duties.

Kitty lifted her tear-stained, bloody face and cried, 'I accidentally woke His Lordship. He hit me with a book.'

'Cantankerous bugger,' Sissy muttered under her breath as she dabbed the wound with her handkerchief. 'I think it's stopped bleeding now. Can you carry on?'

Kitty nodded shakily.

'Come on then.' Sissy helped her to her feet. 'Hurry along now and finish what you're doing. I'll have a headache draft waiting for you downstairs. Try to be quiet, all right?'

Kitty nodded, making her head begin to swim again.

'What is going on here?' Mrs Bligh hissed as she stormed down the corridor.

'Nothing. Everything is fine, Mrs Bligh,' Sissy said calmly.

'You, child, why are you bleeding?'

'She banged her head, Mrs Bligh,' Sissy answered for her.

'Clumsy oaf. Get on with your work. I'm keeping a close eye on you, Morton.'

Sissy glanced at Kitty and nodded for her to go.

'Now, you,' Mrs Bligh jabbed Sissy in the chest, 'get downstairs into the kitchen.'

When Sissy did not move immediately, Mrs Bligh snarled, 'Now, I said!'

'Mrs Bligh, what is happening?' Mr Carrington, the butler, hissed at her as he marched towards her. 'Why are there raised voices outside His Lordship's bedroom?'

Mrs Bligh bristled. 'I'm just dealing with incompetent staff.'

'Please do it quietly then,' he chided.

As Sissy set off down the stairs to the kitchen, it took all of her resolve not to smile at the rebuke that Mrs Bligh had received from Mr Carrington.

*

By the time Kitty had dealt with all the fires, the other servants had risen and left their rooms. Thus began the awful job of gathering the chamber pots, making sure not to spill the contents as she negotiated the stairs with them. Her head hurt terribly, but true to her word, Sissy had a headache draft waiting for her and tended to the cut on her head.

The pain had eased to a dull ache by the time breakfast was over. Kitty had just finished scalding the scullery sink when she saw an older man and a young boy arrive in the back courtyard. She watched as they emptied a couple of chamber pots themselves, and for one awful moment, Kitty thought she had left someone out when she had done the collection. Kitty watched the boy grimace as he emptied his pot, and as he turned away from it, his eyes met hers.

The older man, dressed in an old tweed jacket, dusty plus-fours, and heavy work boots, whipped off his mismatched flat cap and smiled at Kitty. 'Now then, who have we here?'

'Kitty Morton, sir.'

'Oh! Where is Sissy today?'

'Sissy is working in the kitchen now. I'm the new scullery maid.'

'Ah, another newcomer. Freddy here is new too! Aren't you, lad?' He patted the boy on his flat cap.

Kitty smiled at the young boy. 'Hello, Freddy.'

The boy smiled back. 'Hello, Kitty,' he said shyly.

The older man introduced himself. 'I'm Mr John Bolitho, the head gardener, and here is my apprentice, Freddy Hubbard.'

'How lovely it must be to work in the garden instead of this smelly place,' Kitty said wistfully, quickly looking around to ensure no one had heard her.

Mr Bolitho smiled. 'Aye, I don't envy you. Tell me, young lady, what has happened to you? You look like you have bashed your head. Are you all right?'

Kitty's fingers touched the bloody lump that had formed - she winced and answered guardedly, 'I was careless, that's all.'

'Well, you take better care of yourself.' He replaced his hat. 'Give my regards to Sissy. I'm glad she is moving up in the world. You will too, young Kitty - you mark my words. Come along, lad.' He put his arm around Freddy's shoulders, making him break his gaze on Kitty. 'We have flowers to tend to. Cheerio, Kitty. We'll see you at the same time tomorrow.'

As they walked away, Freddy turned and waved. Kitty smiled and waved back. His lovely smile and those big brown eyes looked at her with such kindness, and suddenly, life felt a little better. She would look forward to Mr Bolitho and Freddy's visit every day.

*

By the end of that first week at Bochym Manor, Kitty felt exhausted. The demands on her workload seemed to grow with every day that passed, especially as guests started to arrive on Thursday afternoon for a weekend party. With four more bedroom fires to see to, Kitty's arms ached with carrying coal and numerous buckets of hot water up to the rooms for the guests to bathe in. Some guests were even requesting baths twice a day! From what Kitty saw, these guests, in particular the ladies, did nothing all day except walk the gardens and drink tea. Why on earth they would need to bathe before the evening meal was a mystery to her – none of them could have even broken sweat. Sadly, for Kitty, Sissy couldn't help her with her increased workload – she was also run off her feet in the kitchen, organising the meals with Mrs Crabb for four extra guests.

It turned out to be the male guests Kitty disliked the most – they thought nothing about being sprawled atop the bed in their birthday suits when she tiptoed in to rebuild the fires in the early morning. She had been shocked beyond belief the first time her innocent fourteen-year-old eyes had witnessed it.

'Keep your eyes to the floor, Kitty - that is the best advice I can give you,' Sissy said sympathetically after coming across Kitty, white-mouthed with shock at seeing a naked man for the first time.

Kitty's working days were a lot longer that weekend. The dinner went on late into the evening because the gentlemen remained in the dining room to drink brandy and smoke cigars. It was well past eleven before the footmen cleared the dining table so Kitty could wash up. Kitty was not the only member of staff inconvenienced - the footmen and maids had to be on hand until the guests finally decided to retire. One particular night, to add insult to injury, one of the ladies requested another bath at a quarter to midnight!

'What, now!' Kitty asked in astonishment when Jill, one of the chambermaids, requested hot water from her.

'Apparently, the lady needs a hot bath to relax her - otherwise, she won't sleep!' Jill remarked sarcastically. 'She should try doing a full day's work – she would flipping well sleep then,' she added grumpily.

Kitty took her arms out of the sink, wiped them down, and began filling the buckets, only to be told when she had delivered them to the lady's bedchamber that they were no longer needed - the lady in question was snoring loudly!

The work was relentless for four solid days over that weekend, and Kitty crawled into bed well after midnight most nights, totally and utterly exhausted.

The only bright part of her working day was seeing Freddy and Mr Bolitho, albeit very briefly.

They always had a cheery hello for her, and one morning they gave her a bunch of cherries from the garden.

'Eat the evidence quick, young Kitty.' Mr Bolitho winked.

'These are lovely. Thank you, Mr Bolitho,' she said, savouring the warm, sweet juiciness as they burst deliciously on her tongue.

'Thank our Freddy here. It was his idea to treat you.'

Kitty felt her young heart warm at his thoughtfulness. 'Thank you, Freddy. That's so kind of you.'

Freddy, a boy of few words, nodded and smiled shyly back at her.

The only fly in the ointment during Freddy and Mr Bolitho's visits was Joyce, the laundry maid, who had cottoned on to their little meetings. More often than not, she would stand by the laundry door, arms folded, ready to eavesdrop on their conversations. Kitty knew it would only be a matter of time before Joyce informed Mrs Bligh, who would without doubt stop them from happening.

It was a Monday morning in mid-September when Freddy sustained a deep cut on his hand with his pruning knife. The medical box was on a shelf in the scullery, so it fell on Kitty to administer first aid should anyone need it. Kitty invited him into the scullery and began cleaning Freddy's wound before she dressed it. With his soil-encrusted hand in hers, and despite the blood and the awful smell of urine in the scullery, they shared a tender moment. As she bathed his wound, his large brown eyes gazed at her, and Kitty felt the first stirring tingle of affection for him. For a few moments, they seemed to be lost inside each other - until Kitty heard the rasp of Mrs Bligh's voice.

'Morton. Get on with your work,' she snapped.

Mr Bolitho, who had noted the spark of something between the two young people and had turned his back to give them some privacy, spun around, hearing the forcefulness of Mrs Bligh's command.

Mr Bolitho glanced first at Joyce, who was grinning smugly, then at Mrs Bligh, looming over Kitty and Freddy from the scullery door. Puffing his chest out with indignation, he marched over to her. 'Kitty is assisting us if you don't mind.'

Mrs Bligh turned and glared at him, nostrils flaring. 'Well, I do mind. Morton works for me, not you! I am sick of her slacking and wasting time. I suggest *you* return to the garden and take your grubby little assistant with you.'

Angered now, Mr Bolitho lurched at Mrs Bligh, forcing her to step away from his fearsome stance.

'You,' he said, pointing his finger at her, 'can keep your suggestions to yourself. You have no authority to tell me what I should be doing, but you might want to speak to nosey parker, Joyce, here. She is the one who is slacking and wasting time, nebbing on others rather than doing her work!'

Joyce blanched at being singled out.

'As for us being here, Kitty is tending to a cut on Freddy's hand, at Her Ladyship's request, and who is, at this very moment, waiting in the garden for us to plan next season's borders. Perhaps I should tell Her Ladyship that you would not allow Kitty to tend to the lad's injury. I do not think she will be pleased to know that you are undermining *her* authority, especially after she specifically sent Freddy to Kitty for treatment.'

Mrs Blith's mouth pinched white. Knowing Mr Bolitho had a good relationship with Her Ladyship, she backed down, turned, and grabbed Joyce by the sleeve.

'Get on with your work, Joyce,' she ordered as she pushed her into the laundry, slamming the door behind her.

10

At Wild Cliff Farm, Maia was up with the lark, despite it having taken her ages to fall asleep the previous night. Apart from the unexpected and unwanted visit by Jago, the lovely day she had spent in the company of Josh had delighted and enthralled her. Their evening, especially, had played on her mind well into the early hours, reliving the moment he had touched her hair.

She washed and dressed, and then opened the curtains. Thankfully, the day was bright and sunny for her to take her usual morning ride down to Poldhu Cove and later her Sunday walk to Church Cove. Wearing her late aunt's silk housecoat to cover her modesty, she watched Josh from her bedroom window. He must also have been up and about early, busying himself as always and seeing to her livestock. She would join him after her ride, but for now, she wanted to observe him from a distance. A smile curled on her lips - he had made her laugh last night, something she had not done for a long time.

*

Whereas Maia had had very little sleep, Josh had slept soundly, though the evening had played on his mind too as he dropped into slumber. He had dreamt about Maia. It was nothing specific - he was just aware that she was in his dream, making his life better and safer—something he had not experienced for a while. The cockerel had woken him, as it did every morning, and Josh had risen with a happy heart. He started to fill the leaky pig's trough, again in vain. They had tried unsuccessfully to mend the crack with tar and sacking yesterday, so Maia had decided to purchase a new one from Helston later that week. While winding the hose around his arm to put it away, a movement at the first-floor window caught his eye. He smiled to himself that Maia may be observing him - the thought gave him a good feeling. He wondered if she was as interested in him as he was in her and if there was a future for them. Her life had been quite violent and traumatic with her late husband, by the sound of it – perhaps she may not trust another man – he hoped he was wrong.

*

After an hour of working together in the vegetable patch, Maia announced she was going out and that he should take some time off.

'I'm going for a walk and to have tea with my friend at the Poldhu Tea Room. I've left you a loaf, cheese, and ham to make a sandwich. I'll cook us a proper dinner tonight.'

'Thank you. I hope you have a nice time.'

'You too,' she said gently, 'whatever you decide to do.'

'I thought perhaps I'd walk into Mullion to look around.'

'Good idea. Enjoy your walk.'

He waved her off, with a pang of sadness that they would not spend the day together working.

*

Maia took a circular walk from Wild Cliff Farm to Poldhu via the path that cut through Mullion golf links that led down to Church Cove, Gunwalloe. She was no churchgoer, but on occasions, as long as there was no service at St Winwaloe's Church, Maia would enter the building, if only to cool down after her brisk walk. It was a fine old church – centuries old, and dug into the sandy cliffs. Maia enjoyed the splendid isolation this tiny church gave her. She had a lot to think about this week and a great deal to be thankful for. Josh turning up in her stable had altered her world. This gave her time to concentrate on her pottery, knowing her livestock and crops were in good hands. She had no intention of leaving everything for Josh to do - she had enjoyed working with him over the last couple of days. Without a doubt, he was good company. He appreciated the meals she made and always helped her clear up afterwards. Although Maia knew it had been a risk, sitting with Josh last evening was lovely as they enjoyed a drink overlooking the cove. Of course, it was natural that people would talk, but then they always did talk about her. Since Henry had died, Maia had changed the way she looked. Gone were the dowdy clothes of a work-worn, beaten wife, and in place, Maia had opened the chest of beautiful clothes inherited from her late aunt, which, unbeknownst to Henry, had been secretly delivered to the farm attic after her aunt died. The chest had been full of diaries, books, and fabulous embroidered silk and cotton dresses that her aunt had worn whilst living in Africa as a young bride. Wearing these clothes, Maia was perceived as bohemian, especially because her red hair was allowed to blow loose in the wind. As a widow, it was more appropriate to keep her fiery locks tamed and her clothes demure, but Maia wore her widowhood like a badge of honour. She had hated Henry and had relished every single moment since his demise.

Having cooled down, Maia left the church, blinking furiously and shading her eyes as she stepped out into the bright sunlight of the peaceful churchyard. The tide was out, the breeze was minimal, and the sky was so blue it coloured the sea turquoise. After skirting the water's edge - her favourite pastime - she took the coast path to Poldhu to admire the sea views from up high on Poldhu Head. To her right was St Michael's Mount - to her left, Enys Pruen - the small island nestled in Mullion Cove, or Porth Mellin, as it was known locally. Poldhu Cove and the tearoom looked busy - it always was on a Sunday, but Maia had reserved a table on the veranda as usual. Ellie Blackthorn was a special friend to her. Maia had met her beachcombing one day and felt an instant affinity with her, as she too enjoyed scouring the cove when she had time. Ellie liked collecting sea glass, which she placed in jars on the tables for customers to help themselves to. It was a little bit of the seaside to take home!

Maia sat down on the soft, grassy cliff. It would be another half an hour before her table would be ready, so she turned her face to the sun and took a deep breath of Cornish air. On sunny days such as this, there was nowhere she would rather be.

She glanced down to the beach where families had congregated, picnics set out, and parasols opened to shield from the hot sun. Children played in the stream that ran down Poldhu Valley into the sea, their squeals of delight filtering up on the summer breeze. The swimming huts were being put to good use, trundling backwards and forwards to the water, allowing the more modest of bathers to swim. Her gaze settled on Penn als Cottage, Jago's house. With all her heart, she wished she could eliminate all the Penhallows from her life.

Maia felt like a new beginning was dawning for her and wondered if Josh would be part of the next chapter in her book. With that thought, Maia moistened her lips – tea was the order of the day. She set off to take her place at a table in her favourite tearoom.

*

Ellie greeted her friend warmly, noting a brightness in her eyes that she had not seen before.

'Good morning to you, Maia. I hear on the grapevine you have a new farmhand.'

'I do.' Maia smiled knowingly. 'News travels fast, I see.'

'So, who is he?'

'It's the man you kindly offered tea and scones to the other day. The man who was sleeping rough in the cove. His name is Josh Harding. He's been struggling to find work for a while, so I took a chance on him.'

'How is that working out?' Ellie said with a pencil and pad, poised to take the order.

'It's working out very well,' Maia said, suppressing a smile. Ellie's eyes twinkled mischievously and Maia tipped her head. 'Ellie Blackthorn, what does that look mean?'

Ellie broke into a broad smile. 'I've seen him. Under all that dirt, he was rather easy on the eye.'

'Shocking!' Maia folded her arms. 'You're a married woman – you shouldn't be looking at other men.'

'There is no harm in looking!'

They laughed together. 'I admit. Josh is easy on the eye, but...'

'But what?' Despite the tearoom being busy, Ellie sat down with her.

'Well, having someone like Josh working and living at Wild Cliff Farm, the jungle drums are already going - people are talking. I mean, even you have just insinuated something improper.'

'Oh, Maia.' Ellie reached out to her. 'I'm only joking - I don't mean to offend.'

'I know - no offence taken.'

'I'm only teasing because you seemed brighter in yourself today. I think you like this Josh!'

Maia coloured up. 'I do. Even though I have only known him for a few days. He likes me too, I know he does, but...'

'No buts, Maia. It would be good for you to have someone in your life again. So, if you two share an affinity, let it happen.'

Maia sighed. 'Jago is already annoyed,' she said indignantly.

Ellie huffed. 'Take no heed of Jago.'

'He's angry that I employed an outsider, and he has made it quite clear that it is wrong for Josh to be at the farm alone with me. It's jealousy, I know, but you know what he's like. He was always jealous of Henry. Jago honestly thought he was going to step into Henry's shoes - and his bed, after he died!' She grimaced.

A clatter from a tray of crockery dropped behind them made both women turn to find Ellie's red-faced daughter, Fee, clearing up the mess.

'Is everything all right, Fee?'

'Yes, Ma,' Fee answered.

Ellie turned back to Maia. 'She's got her head in the clouds at the moment. I think boys have piqued her interest all of a sudden.'

'Goodness! Has anyone been brave enough to come forward to court her and face Guy's scrutiny?'

'No one yet, and it will be a brave man that does, but speaking of Jago Penhallow, I caught him speaking to Fee the other day.'

'Oh dear!'

'Exactly!' Ellie sighed. 'She may be nearly sixteen, but she is still our baby girl. We did hope to keep her that way for a while longer, but as you can see, she has developed fast. She's certainly not a child anymore - she has bloomed into a lovely-looking young woman.'

'I wouldn't worry about Jago. He just likes to show off to the women hereabouts.'

'I hope you're right, Maia. She has just settled into the new role as assistant manager here – I don't want her to fall into bad company.'

'You're lucky to have her join the team. She's a real asset here.'

Ellie smiled and nodded. 'She is, and very popular with the customers. It will all be hers when I retire, though I hope that is some way off.' She winked. 'Agnes lives only to thatch, and Zack, well, now that he is in London, I don't think we will see much of him. His music career is going from strength to strength – we are so proud of him. It only seems right to hand the business over to Fee when the time comes.'

'Talking of Agnes. How did the move go the other day? Have Betsy and Ryan settled into their new home in Mullion, and Agnes likewise in the beach house?'

'Yes, everything went well. It's good that Agnes and Jake have their own place now. It wasn't ideal for us all living together – especially for them in the throes of a new marriage, if you know what I mean?' she said with an arched eyebrow. 'Now I must go back to work.' She got up. 'But let me give you some advice, Maia. Take no heed of Jago and let yourself fall in love with Josh. I'll expect you to bring him down to the tearoom with you next week.'

*

Fee had dropped the tea tray she was carrying after hearing Jago's name mentioned in vain. It was as though her thoughts had been infiltrated, for her head was full of thoughts of Jago. After clearing up the mess she had made, Fee stood in the tearoom doorway, listening scornfully to Ma and Maia speak about Jago in a derogatory fashion. Fee surmised that Maia must be completely delusional if she thought, for one moment, that Jago would be interested in her – after all, she was old – she must be at least twenty-three! Why on earth would Jago want another man's widow, especially when he had his pick of any young girl – *preferably this young girl?* She mused. Yes, Maia was still beautiful and a landowner, but Jago was a wealthy man in his own right, so why would he want her farm? No, it was clear that Maia was wrong in her assumption that Jago was interested in her like that. He was probably only trying to take care of her and do the best for his dead brother's wife. Fee set off with her tray of broken crockery to empty into the kitchen bin. One day, when Fee was walking out on the arm of Jago, Maia would see how mistaken she had been about him.

*

It had been a long, hot walk to Mullion. With money in his pocket that Maia had advanced him, Josh was ready to quench his thirst with a small glass of beer, but as he walked into The Old Inn, he felt all eyes directed towards him. He nodded a greeting to a few of the men there, and though some acknowledged him, Josh still felt uneasy. If not for his thirst, Josh perhaps would have just turned around and left, but courage took over, and he ordered his glass of beer. Sitting at a small table near the window, he inhaled the hoppy smell of his drink and could not recall when he had last savoured a beer, and this tasted like nectar. Most of the men in the room had returned to speaking in hushed tones, though occasionally they would look in Josh's direction, quickly lowering their eyes when Josh glanced back at them. As he began to relax, he glanced through the window to see a familiar car pull up. His heart sank, knowing the next man through the door would be Jago Penhallow.

No sooner had Jago walked in than his eyes locked on Josh.

'I didn't realise we served *up country folk* in here,' Jago growled at the landlord and then turned his gaze on Josh. 'So, you can sling your hook. This inn is for Cornish people only,' he snarled.

'No, it isn't!' The landlord slammed his fist angrily onto the bar. 'He's doing nothing wrong, and I say who comes in here, and I don't restrict it to the Cornish, and you know I don't!'

'Well, *I* don't want him in here, and I'm a local!' Jago snarled.

Josh, deciding it was best to leave, left his beer half-drunk and got up from where he was sitting.

'You don't have to leave,' the landlord said, seeing Josh make a move.

'It's all right. I don't want any trouble,' Josh said, moving away from the conflict.

'What do you want then, eh?' Jago leered at him, blocking his way.

Josh remained silent.

'I'll tell you what you want,' he jabbed Josh in the chest, 'to get into my brother's widow's bed. That's what!'

'That is a dreadful slur on your sister-in-law,' Josh countered.

'It's true though, isn't it? You want my brother's wife and his farm.'

Josh could feel the tension in the room and knew he should leave, but felt compelled to respond. 'As far as I know, the farm belongs to Mrs Penhallow, not your dead brother, but that is beside the point. All I want is to work.'

'Maia can't pay you much, so you must be doing it for the love of her.'

Choosing not to answer that, Josh said, 'Please let me pass.'

Jago stepped forward threateningly, but fortunately, another man stepped up to stop him.

'Leave him be, Jago. He's done nothing to you.'

Jago turned and glared at Farmer David Trevorrow. Everyone knew David had been a prize boxer in his time, and he was not one to argue with, so Jago was forced to step down.

'He's queering my pitch,' Jago said with a twist to his mouth.

'He is not, and you know it. Maia was widowed a year ago, and if she'd had any interest in you, she would have told you before now. So, sit down and let the man drink in peace, and I'm warning you now to leave them both alone!'

'This is none of your business, David Trevorrow,' Jago grumbled as he sat down.

'I'm making it my business from now on. You'll do well to remember that!' David loomed over him in warning before returning to his own seat.

Josh gave a thankful nod to David but decided it would be best to leave, so he finished his beer.

As he got up, Jago sneered at him. 'Yes, bugger off, and don't bother coming back here. We don't like you *up country* sort.'

Outside, Josh took a deep breath - he must not let this escalate. His presence here was untenable enough; he knew he must not attract any trouble. His growing attachment to Maia would inevitably cause ructions if it ever came to light.

'Take no heed of that hot head. He's just a jumped-up nobody,' David Trevorrow said, following Josh out of the inn. 'David Trevorrow at your service.' He held a hand out to Josh.

'Josh Harding,' he answered, shaking it. 'It's Maia I feel for. My presence on her farm seems to be annoying Jago.'

'You tell Maia, if Jago becomes a nuisance, she's to let me know, and I will sort him out once and for all. I've been Maia's neighbour for the last four years; she does not need any more trouble or upset. For what it's worth, I'm glad you're working with Maia. I've worried about her - not only because the farm is a lot for her to manage, but because she was alone up there.'

'Maia is lucky she has good people looking out for her,' Josh smiled. 'She has spoken of you and thinks very highly of you. Thank you for what you did in there.'

'My pleasure. Some people need taking down a peg or two. If you come this way, I'll show you a shortcut to Wild Cliff Farm, as long as you don't mind walking through fields and climbing a stile.'

Josh followed him and was glad he had. He found David an amiable chap whom he could now class as a friend. David showed him around his dairy and introduced him to a couple more people who worked in the nearby saddlery. Everyone, except Jago, had welcomed him warmly, and soon the altercation in the inn moved to the back of his mind. It made him believe that perhaps he could settle here safely.

11
Kitty 1880-1881

At a quarter past three on Monday morning, the 4th of October 1880, the residents of Bochym Manor were sent into a frenzy. The doctor was called for, as the mistress had gone into labour and things were proving difficult. Her Ladyship's screams resonated throughout the manor and reached as far down as the scullery. From that moment on, Kitty was not allowed to go to bed but had to constantly deliver hot water to Her Ladyship's chamber in case the baby decided to arrive. The longer the labour, the more Kitty was summoned to take away the cooling water and replace it with another bowl of hot water.

On every trip to the bedchamber, Kitty heard the mistress screaming angry words about the Earl. On one occasion, she screamed, 'That man will never touch me again. I am never, I tell you, never, going through this again.'

'I am sure Your Ladyship does not mean that,' the doctor brushed away her comment. 'You will forget the pain.'

'I will not!' she yelled furiously. She picked up a book and threw it at the doctor, narrowly missing him but hitting Kitty on the hand so that she dropped the bowl of hot water, scalding her arms, and soaking her dress and the Turkish rug.

Mrs Bligh, who was in attendance, stared in horror at the pool of water on the rug. She grabbed Kitty by the scruff of her dress and boxed her ears.

'Good God, child!' she hissed. 'What on earth are you thinking? This expensive rug has been ruined by your incompetence. It will come out of your wage!'

Distraught, Kitty picked up the bowl and looked at the doctor to speak up and say that it wasn't her fault, but no help was forthcoming.

'What are you standing there for, you stupid girl?' Mrs Bligh barked. 'Fetch more water and something to soak up this wet mess.' Again, Kitty felt the sting of a slap to her ear, making it ring and burn alarmingly as she ran back downstairs.

Twenty-five hours later, at a quarter past four the following morning, the mistress gave birth to a daughter, Lady Carole Lucinda Dunstan. The household heaved a sigh of relief. Not only because of the safe delivery, but because everyone had a headache from Her Ladyship's constant screaming.

By the time Kitty had finished delivering water to the mistress's bedroom, it was time to tend all the fires; her working day had begun again, and sleep would have to wait for another eleven hours.

*

A few days into the New Year, 1881, brought the most dreadful weather England had ever seen. From the 12th of January, according to the newspaper reports that Mr Carrington, the butler, began to read out each day after breakfast, Ireland had seen an enormous amount of snow. With Sligo's temperature reaching a record low of -19.1 °C, everyone in the manor shivered at the thought. On the 14th of January, there was a marked drop in temperature in Cornwall, and the family ordered that all fires must burn continually, which made an awful lot more work for Kitty. No matter how much coal and wood she threw on the fires, Kitty was bombarded with complaints that she was not doing enough to keep the chill from the rooms.

On the 15th of January, the newspapers were full of terrible reports of the dreadful weather.

'I wonder if we will get snow here?' One of the footmen asked Mr Carrington at dinner time.

'Don't be silly, boy,' he answered irritably. 'We don't get that sort of weather down here!'

Mr Carrington ate his words because the snowfall started on the 17th of January in the southwest of

England, and at the same time, an easterly gale blew in, with snow drifting in the wind as a consequence. This continued in some places for a good forty-eight hours.

On the morning of the 18th of January, a dismayed Kitty found a wall of snow when she opened the back scullery door. She had over twenty chamber pots needing emptying before she could wash them, and with no route to the privy, people would need these pots! Kitty had buckets they could use, but they were for the transportation of hot water to the bedrooms, and the maids would be ringing down for them soon. At a loss for what to do, she feared Mrs Bligh's wrath, and then she heard voices through the wall of snow, and digging began in earnest. It took almost half an hour until the bright red faces of Mr Bolitho and Freddy appeared through the hole they had made in the snow.

'Stay there, young Kitty, but pass the pots out to us, and we'll empty them. We'll make a path to the privy for everyone later.'

'Never had Kitty been so grateful. The soles of her boots had holes in them. Her feet would have been soaked and frozen if she had had to walk several times across the snowy track over to the privy.

'How on earth did you get through to even start to dig?' Kitty asked in astonishment.

'The drifting is only against the east side of the house, so you got the worst of it. The laundry is blocked in, but we thought we'd clear you first – that nasty little madam can wait until after dinner before we dig her door out.' Mr Bolitho smiled mischievously.

According to the newspapers after the event, it was reported as one of the worst blizzards in history that England had seen. Trains were stuck on lines for days, and Plymouth had been without water for a week. Though the weather turned milder following the big freeze, the manor never seemed to warm up again that winter, keeping Kitty busy until the spring, tending and feeding the many fires.

*

It was the 15th of April 1881 - Good Friday - Kitty's 15th Birthday, when her circumstances changed for the better. It started with Cook and Mrs Bligh bickering over the housekeeper's lack of cooperation to give Cook the essential access to the larder she needed.

Mrs Bligh had placed two wooden boxes of food on the kitchen table. One containing a pheasant, potatoes, and everything needed to make a Good Friday meal for His Lord and Her Ladyship – the leftovers would also serve the valet, butler, and Mrs Bligh. In the other box were mouldering carrots, cabbage, salted fish, and worm-eaten apples!

Mrs Crabb looked at the boxes and then at Mrs Bligh, who stood with her arms folded, waiting for the inevitable argument to start.

'What the hell is this?' Mrs Crabb demanded, pointing to the mouldering box.

'That's for you to make the servants meals. That's all you're getting!'

Mrs Crabb stabbed her fists into her hips and regarded her reproachfully. 'Why, pray tell?'

'Because we have spent too much on coal this winter, Her Ladyship has asked me to cut the household budget where I can. So, from now on, you will tell me what you want from the larder, and if we can spare it, I shall give you it.'

For a moment, Mrs Crabb thought the housekeeper was jesting but dismissed the idea - Mrs Bligh was too nasty for humour. 'I need that key to the larder,' Mrs Crab demanded as she held her hand out. 'This box is not fit for consumption. I am the cook! I need to choose the ingredients myself.'

'No, I have decided to keep a tight rein on the food. I know you are feeding the servants too well. You waste too much food. I've seen you tip the carrot tops and potato peelings in the pig bin. All the good food will be for the family and senior staff, and what is left is for the lowest servants. You will use every scrap of food from now on,' she said in a deep, authoritative voice.

'This is utterly ridiculous,' Cook argued indignantly. 'You cannot make an army march on an empty stomach, and carrot top and potato peelings will not sustain the servants.'

Mrs Blith gave Cook an icy look. 'Overeating makes them lazy.'

'And overeating appears to make you nastier,' Mrs Crabb countered. 'You and your cronies make sure you have plentiful meals, and the junior servants should get the same as you. We are all servants here!'

Mrs Bligh sniffed haughtily. '*We* are senior members of this household; we are entitled.'

'And the junior members of staff are entitled to a decent meal. I cannot and will not feed them scraps and mouldy vegetables!' Cook yelled, waving her chopping knife in the air.

Kitty had crept to the door of the scullery to witness the ongoing argument and exchanged amused glances with Sissy.

'I'm warning you, Mrs Bligh, you give me that key to the larder or...'

'Or what?' Mrs Bligh smirked.

Mrs Crabb's face darkened with rage. 'Or this...' she yelled as she threw the kitchen knife at Mrs Bligh, narrowly missing her ear by a hair breath.

Kitty and Sissy took a large intake of breath as Mrs Bligh turned and gawped in astonishment at how precariously close the knife was to her face. 'I'll...I'll have you dismissed for this,' she spluttered before storming out of the kitchen to report the attack to Mr Carrington.

Mrs Crabb dusted her hands together as a job well done and began undoing her apron.

'Good luck, Sissy. I'm off,' she said, throwing the apron into the box of mouldering vegetables.

Sissy's eyes widened with disbelief. 'But, but... where are you going, Mrs Crabb?'

'To my sisters in Eastbourne to live. I've had enough of dealing with that miserable yard of piss water. It's time for me to retire.'

Mrs Crabb was about to leave when Mrs Bligh came rushing in with Mr Carrington, pointing to the knife as she did.

'Mrs Crabb. I need to speak to you most urgently,' Mr Carrington ordered.

Mrs Crabb turned and smiled. 'If it's about dinner tonight, I suggest you speak to Sissy, your new cook, because I quit. Toodle-oo,' she said, slamming the door after her.

Mrs Bligh and Mr Carrington stood momentarily speechless at Cook's departure, and then Mr Carrington glanced at Sissy, swallowed hard, and pulled his jacket straight.

'Well, erm, Blair, you had better get on with dinner then. You have a Good Friday dinner to prepare, and it appears you are the cook now,' he ordered.

Sissy glanced at the pots cooking on the range, stunned at the turn of events.

'Come on, Blair, get a move on,' Mrs Bligh chided insolently.

From the scullery door, Kitty watched Sissy take a deep, measured breath and turn on the housekeeper.

'It is *Mrs* Blair to you now. If I am to be Cook, I expect you to address me respectfully.'

Mrs Bligh's nostrils flared. 'Nothing is sorted yet about your position.'

'Well, you'd better sort it quickly because I am not cooking until my status as Cook in this house is confirmed!'

Realising that she had to comply, Mrs Bligh started to twitch angrily. 'Oh, very well, *Mrs Blair.*'

'Thank you,' Sissy said, walking to the door jamb to retrieve the kitchen knife, making Mrs Bligh flinch as she pulled it out. 'And I suggest you had better advertise for a new scullery maid because I need Kitty now as my assistant.'

Mrs Bligh narrowed her eyes. 'I shall have to give that some thought – that girl is incompetent.'

'Well, let me help you with that decision.' Sissy took everything off the stove and folded her arms. 'No, Kitty, no meals today.'

Mrs Bligh's eyes began to blaze with fury, but having no option, she turned towards the footmen. 'You. Send word to the workhouse. I need a girl immediately for the position of scullery maid.'

Sissy turned and beamed at Kitty, and then set about making dinners for the household.

When the coast was clear of Mrs Bligh, Kitty crept out of the scullery and into the kitchen. 'I can't help you today, Sissy,' Kitty cried. 'I have all my jobs to do!'

'I know. Don't worry. Most of the preparation is done; I'll manage without you today. But from tomorrow, you will be my right-hand man, so to speak.' She broke into a broad smile.

*

When Kitty relayed the event to Freddy and Mr Bolitho, Mr Bolitho was incandescent.

'That is outrageous. We have plenty of fresh vegetables to go around. I'll go and tell Sissy that I'll leave a box of good vegetables for her every morning in the log store – without Mrs Bligh's knowledge!' He then tipped his head and smiled at Kitty's good fortune. 'Well done, Kitty; we knew you'd move up in the world.'

'Thank you, but it makes me sad that I won't see you and Freddy at the scullery door anymore,' she sighed.

Mr Bolitho laughed heartily. 'We visit the kitchen every morning with fresh produce and flowers for the house, so don't worry, Kitty, we will see you then.'

*

When the servants came in for their midday meal, having heard about the row and that they were to eat potato scrapings for dinner, there were miserable faces all around. They had no idea how good a cook Sissy was, but when she set the meal down, they found to their surprise that Sissy had produced a far more wholesome meal than Mrs Crabb had ever made. All made possible by Mr Bolitho's secret box of vegetables.

Mrs Bligh fully expected Sissy to fail spectacularly in producing a meal fit for the family and had been preparing an advertisement for the local paper for a cook. But when compliments to Cook arrived in the kitchen from Her Ladyship after luncheon and seeing the satisfied faces of the servants, the advertisement was angrily screwed up and put in the bin.

*

The next day, the new scullery maid arrived - a frightened little thing called June. Kitty did as Sissy had done for her, treated her with kindness, warned her about Joyce in the laundry, and helped her as much as she could. Then, moving to a slightly larger bedroom than the box room, Kitty donned a grey dress and white apron before settling into her role as assistant cook, working alongside Sissy - or Mrs Blair, as she had to call her now.

*

In June, Kitty had been in her new job for two months and loved it. Sissy taught her all she knew about cooking, and Kitty was quick to learn, gaining chopping and knife skills far beyond her years.

Every day, Mr Bolitho and Freddy would visit the kitchen with produce for the family and a secret box of vegetables in the log store. It was on one such visit that Freddy passed Kitty a secret letter.

Shocked, Kitty glanced around to see if anyone was about before ferreting the letter into her apron pocket. She glanced up at Freddy, who smiled at her. A warm tingle ran through her body, wondering what the letter might say. She was sure Freddy knew she liked him; she had never hidden the fact. She prayed that his letter confirmed he reciprocated her feelings. It would be later that evening before Kitty got to read the letter, and when she did, her heart was all of a flutter.

Dearest, Kitty.

I respect you greatly, but I would like to ask if you would consider meeting me secretly when you next have a day off. All I want is for us to spend a little time together and get to know each other better. I love our little exchanges when we meet, but I would like to see and speak to you when others are not around.

I am aware that what I ask could get us both into trouble, and it is perhaps not proper for us to be alone together, but Kitty, how am I ever going to know you better unless we take a little chance?

If you agree to our meeting, let me know by return letter in the morning. Mr Bolitho will give me time off when I ask him because he is the kindest of men to work for.

I hope and pray that you will meet me.

Freddy.

Kitty held the letter to her heart. She did not care about the rights and wrongs of meeting Freddy. Of course, Kitty would meet him. She could not wait, but wait, she must. As assistant cook, her days were governed by whether the family were at home or not, but they were due to go to London in a fortnight for a week, and that is what she wrote in her letter back to him.

12

It had been a whole week since Jago had spoken to Fee, and she was desperate to see him again. Each morning, she got up, brushed her rich chestnut-coloured hair so it shone, pinched her cheeks to give them colour, and tried to look her best despite her black waitress dress, hoping this would be the day she saw him. Jago had awoken her interest in the opposite sex, and now that those feelings had surfaced, it was difficult to suppress them. Jago dominated her thoughts throughout the day, to the point where her work was becoming lax. It was rare for Ma to scold her, but she had felt the sharp edge of her tongue that week for not paying attention. On two occasions, Fee had been serving customers when her attention was diverted by seeing the back of Jago's car disappear up Poldhu Hill; consequently, she had got their orders wrong! She was forever glancing up at his house, Penn als Cottage, and it puzzled her how they could live in such proximity and not cross paths for a whole week. Was he avoiding her because Ma had caught them talking? Had he just been humouring her and not meant what he said to her? Perhaps he had decided that she was too young for him. Stop it! She rebuked herself. She must stop these negative thoughts, or her tender heart will break before ever being loved.

*

It was Friday. Maia was getting ready to go to the market in Helston when she glanced at the field adjoining her land with David Trevorrow's dairy farm. The local dairymaids who had been milking there that morning had now finished and were walking towards the fence where Josh was working - no doubt to flirt with him!

Josh had settled very nicely into the work and life on the farm. He had made a couple of new friends since taking a walk last Sunday, namely David Trevorrow, whom Josh had told Maia he had met at The Old Inn at Mullion.

They had walked home together, and David had shown him around his dairy and introduced him to the saddler, Ben Pearson, who had a workshop near the dairy.

Maia watched as the milkmaids stood at the fence. Although still quite early, the day was hot, and Josh had been shirtless while working but had pulled on his shirt after seeing the milkmaids approach him. Maia sighed. He was a fine-looking man – still too skinny, but though he had only been here a few days, he looked much better than when he had arrived. His skin had a healthy glow from working outside, and his gaunt, hollow cheeks had gone now with some good, wholesome food inside him.

Maia felt a tingle in her body and checked herself. Desire was an unusual emotion, and she had never experienced it before. There had never been anything like that with Henry –before and most certainly not after her marriage. Her body involuntarily shuddered at the thought of sharing Henry's bed. He had shown not an ounce of love or tenderness towards her; he had just used brute force when he wanted her. He was cruel, not only to her but to her livestock. They had suffered from his ill treatment, and she had lost a few animals in the weeks after Henry's death, but with love and care, her goats and pigs were happy now. The land now offered her good rewards and supplied her with ample fresh fruit and vegetables. Wrapping her arms around herself, she felt blessed at how her life had changed these last twelve months - and more so now that Josh had come into her life.

Observing Josh from her window as he passed the time of day with the young milkmaids, Maia could hear their giggles as he spoke to them. It was unusual for a new man to come and live in the vicinity. Maia suspected the milkmaids were hoping Josh was husband material. Maia felt a curl of jealousy - another unusual emotion - but then Josh had woven himself into her life - and, if she was truthful, her heart.

*

It was a day of hot, brilliant sunshine, cooled by a gentle breeze. After Maia had pegged the washing out, she harnessed Shadow to the cart and walked across to the pigsty to see if Josh was ready to go to Helston. He would accompany her today to help her with the new pig trough they would purchase from the ironmongers. It was also payday for Josh, and he needed to buy some essential clothes and boots. Henry's cast-offs, although suitable for working in, were far too big for him, despite Maia trying to fatten him up.

Josh was re-filling the old trough for the second time that morning and at first had not seen her approach. When he looked up and saw her, his eyes lit up, and he smiled broadly, making Maia catch her breath at his reaction.

Josh tapped the side of the trough. 'The weather is hot today; I hope enough water stays in until we get home with the new one.'

'It's such a waste.' She sighed. 'The rest of the trough is sound. Never mind; nothing lasts forever. If you're ready, we'll leave in ten minutes.'

He nodded. 'I just need a quick swill, and I'll be with you.'

*

Josh watched her walk away. That slight sway to her hips and the sight of her hair blowing in the breeze stirred up such feelings of desire that it was getting more difficult to suppress them. He glanced back at the trough to take his mind off the subject. There was no need to waste this old one; he had an idea of what to do with it and hoped it would delight Maia.

*

Helston was bustling when they arrived, and Maia greeted several people as they made their way to the back of the Blue Anchor Inn to settle Shadow and secure the cart. Their first port of call was the bank, so Maia could pay Josh his first wage. Then, standing outside Thomas'

Tailors and Outfitters, she said to Josh, 'I'll leave you here. I should think you will be able to get all you need at this shop. I need to do some shopping elsewhere.' Maia suddenly shuddered as a strange, creeping sensation at the back of her neck sent her thoughts hurtling back to her life with Henry. She gasped audibly and reached out to steady herself on Josh's arm.

'Are you all right, Maia?'

'I don't know,' she whispered. 'I have the strangest feeling that someone is watching me.'

Josh looked beyond her shoulder. 'Your perception is correct,' he said gravely. 'Look.'

Maia turned to find Jago had slowed his car almost to a halt on the street and had locked angry eyes on them. She turned back to Josh. 'Just stay with me a moment, would you?'

'Of course.'

Jago glared at Josh for a moment longer and then sped off down the street.

'He's gone now,' he said.

Maia lifted her trembling hand to her heart. 'I'm sorry, I ... just felt such malevolence directed at me.'

Josh reached for her hand to calm her tremors. 'If you are frightened of Jago, you must speak with David Trevorrow. I told you he has offered his service to you should you need it.'

'I don't like to bother people with my troubles. Jago annoys me more than anything. I don't know why I feel so anxious.'

'As I said before, I think my presence with you is clearly angering him.'

'Well, I welcome your presence. Jago will have to get used to you being with me.'

Josh was heartened at the term *being with me* and said, 'Just remember, David will help if you need it, and so will I.'

A smile relaxed her taut features. 'Thank you,' she said with heartfelt gratitude. 'I think we can get on with our shopping now. I'll meet you outside the ironmongers in three-quarters of an hour.'

*

Storming into his car showroom, Jago slammed the door behind him and paced angrily around the cars he had on display.

Sidney, his assistant, looked up from his desk and rolled his eyes, knowing he was about to witness another one of Jago's unpredictable moods. Sidney waited until Jago had stopped pacing. When Jago folded his arms and rested against the bonnet of a 3-litre Bentley, Sidney ventured out of the office to see what the problem was this time.

Jago scowled at him, having been pulled from his reverie, and barked, 'What?'

'I said, What is the matter? You've been like a dog with a sore head all week, and now you look like someone has chewed your ear off.'

Jago hissed through his teeth. 'Maia's the matter!' he grizzled.

Sidney nodded knowingly. 'So, the fair lady has still not fallen for your charms, then?'

'No!' Jago stood away from the car and began to pace the room again. 'And she is unlikely to now that the bloody new farmhand has settled himself into her life. I've just seen them together on Coinagehall Street, as bold as brass they were!'

'You do know that you are approaching this all wrong.'

'Oh, yes!' Jago turned on Sidney. 'And what the hell would *you* know about it?'

'I've been married for eight years, and very happily, I might add. Jane, my wife, was a hard woman to crack, though. She only had eyes for the butcher when I met her; he had money, a business, and good looks, but I didn't give up. A few bunches of flowers, kind words of flattery, and dinner at The Angel Hotel, and she was putty in my hands.'

Jago folded his arms again. 'So, you think Maia needs wining and dining then?'

'Yes. Good God, man, all women like those sorts of things. As for the farmhand, from what you've told me, he doesn't have a penny to his name – if, as you say, he is still wearing your Henry's old clothes. He has no prospects. You, my friend, have everything a woman would want. Just cease boasting about what you have and showing off, and start to court her properly. Tell her how beautiful she is, make her feel special, shower her with gifts, and take her to dinner. If you really like Maia, let her know that you do.' He tipped his head questionably. 'You *do* really like her, don't you?'

'Of course.'

'It's not just her land you want, is it?'

Something struck a cord and made him defensive. 'Why do you say that?'

Sydney leant against one of the cars. 'Because I know you, Jago, there has always got to be something in it for you. You always have an agenda, though Lord knows why you want that farm.'

Jago shot him a sharp look. 'Have you no work to do?'

Sidney turned to walk away from the discussion but stopped and said, 'Just do the decent thing by Maia, Jago.'

Jago bared his teeth; Sidney could always see right through him.

*

Maia met Josh an hour later, only to find him holding several parcels and happily wearing a new shirt, trousers, and a pair of boots that actually fitted him. They had taken tea in Mrs Bumble's Tea Shop on Coinagehall Street and then returned home to don old clothes for the job of wrestling the new trough down the field to the pig pen. Afterwards, they worked together outside. First, they thinned out the burgeoning fruit on the trees in the orchard to allow the rest of the crop to breathe. Then they sowed some autumn vegetables. Maia enjoyed working alongside Josh in friendly companionship. She felt safe having him about the place. Since his arrival, she had not experienced any more damage to her property or felt frightened about living on the farm alone.

After an early supper that evening and before her bath, she had thrown a few more pots and left them to dry before it was time to relax. Maia sat in her cool bath, trying to dislodge the clay under her fingernails. A few more minutes would see them clean, then a dot of lanolin to soften her hands after her bath would stop her from snagging her stockings – an occupational hazard of working with clay. Closing her eyes to relax back into the water, she reflected on the lovely day she had had with Josh, marred only by Jago seeing them together in Helston. She was at a loss at how to deal with Jago now. He was starting to show the same traits as Henry, and that frightened and repulsed her.

Maia always bathed in the kitchen, so she could tip the water straight into the drain under the sink afterwards. With the door firmly bolted, she had thrown the window open to allow the evening birdsong she loved to filter through. Summer evenings always felt sublime. Interspersed with the birdsong was the now-familiar sound of splashing water outside. Quickly drying herself, she slipped her luxurious silk robe around her nakedness, enjoying the soft, sensual feel of the material on her skin, and moved to the open window. The fragrance of honeysuckle wafted in on the warm evening breeze, but it was not entirely the ambience Maia was enjoying. She knew she should not watch, but the sound of splashing water outside inevitably meant that Josh had stripped down to wash from a bowl placed on the trunk of a cut tree outside his hut. Her breath caught in her throat - the sight of him roused feelings of desire again - feelings which had been building since they sat together on the cart on their trip to Helston. She remembered how their thighs touched occasionally - both aware of the connection but neither moving away to put any distance between them. Now her fingers longed to reach out to Josh, to touch his wet skin and feel the muscles on his arms. As he tipped the water over his head, his body glowed in the soft amber light of the setting sun. Her lips parted. 'Josh,' she whispered. 'You are truly lovely.'

*

Josh shook his wet hair, relishing the cool rivulets of water trickling down his warm body. Reaching for his towel, he rubbed his face vigorously and looked towards the setting sun. He'd had such a lovely day working with Maia, but then he enjoyed every day with her now. Wrapping the towel around his waist, he climbed the steps to his hut, glancing up at the farm as he did, and smiled when he saw a figure at the window. He felt no embarrassment that Maia had probably seen him naked. The thought made his heart quicken. A frisson of delight ran through his body; she might really be interested in him!

*

Maia saw Josh halt at the door to his hut and look directly at her. Her breath caught - she should move - but her mind was still processing his taut, toned body glistening in the evening sun. Neither broke their stance for a few seconds until Josh raised his hand and waved. In response, she lifted hers, confirming that she *was* looking at him.

Stepping back from the window, she pulled her robe tighter over her own naked body and held her hand to her heart. Would Josh take this as a sign that she wanted him? Her mouth dried with anticipation - the jug of cold lemonade in the larder beckoned. While quenching her thirst, she spotted Josh, dressed in a new, clean shirt, open at the throat, walking with conviction towards the house. Her heart was hammering in her chest, and she opened the door before he knocked, to feel the full force of his appreciative gaze.

'Hello, Maia.'

'Josh!' she answered, almost inaudibly.

'There is a rare sunset this evening, and the air is so warm, I wondered... would you like to take a walk on the cliff to watch it set?'

'Yes.' She smiled gently. 'Let me get dressed.'

They took the main road to the golf links; what happened earlier remained unspoken. Occasionally, their hands accidentally brushed together, causing a reaction that made them both turn and smile at each other. Settling on the grassy cliff overlooking St Winwilloe Church, Gunwalloe, they had the most spectacular view of the fiery sunset.

It was Maia who finally broke their silence.

'I saw David Trevorrow's milkmaids working in the field this morning; you seem to be quite a hit with them.'

Josh laughed softly and picked at a blade of grass.

'It is quite exciting for them to have a new young man enter their sphere. They will all be looking for a husband, you know!' She grimaced at the slight catch in her voice as she spoke.

'I have no doubt they are, but it will not be me.'

'Because of your secret identity?' she inquired cautiously.

'No, Maia!' He turned and looked deep into her eyes. 'It's not for that reason.'

Maia's heart gave a slight somersault at the unspoken reason.

He cleared his throat. 'What about you, Maia. May I ask, would *you* consider marrying again?'

She circled her legs with her arms. 'If you had asked me that a few weeks ago...' She shook her head and shuddered. 'Henry was such a brute in all aspects of our marriage.'

'I'm so sorry for you, Maia. Abuse isn't nice, is it?'

'No.' She sighed and gently placed her hand on his. 'We have both been abused. I never thought I would trust any man near me again, but...'

Josh smiled. 'Not all men are like Henry.' He tenderly cupped his hand over hers.

Maia glanced at their joined hands and smiled. 'I never thought I would allow anyone to touch me again. You're the first man I have ever felt truly comfortable with; you have restored my trust in men.'

Josh squeezed her hand. 'Thank you, Maia. Your trust in me fills my heart with joy.'

They remained hand in hand as they watched the sun disappear and the sky turn fiery red. This development of trust may be the early days of their relationship, but tonight, they had both taken a small but significant step towards each other.

Maia sighed. 'There is nothing like a sunset over the sea.'

'I have never experienced a more beautiful sight,' Josh answered, not looking at the sky, instead resting his eyes on Maia.

She turned to see him looking at her and realised his meaning.

They sat together in happy companionship until the air turned chilly, and Maia shivered.

'Time to go back while we can still see our way,' she said, gently pulling her hand from his.

Maia had made a bold decision by the time they said their goodnights at the door to Wild Cliff Farm.

'I walk down to Church Cove and then over to Poldhu Cove for tea and scones most Sundays; would you like to accompany me this week?'

His eyes sparkled as he smiled. 'I would love that. Thank you. As long as me being with you won't cause more trouble for you?'

Her eyes twinkled. 'It won't! It is time I started to live again,' she said.

'Well, I'm more than happy to accompany you in your new life.'

'Goodnight, Josh,' she laughed softly. 'And thank you for everything today.'

Josh bowed chivalrously. 'Always at your service, ma'am.'

*

At the kitchen window, Maia watched Josh walk down the field to the shepherd's hut in the fading light of the day. She smiled when he turned and waved – he always seemed to know when she was watching him.

13
Kitty 1881

It was a week before Kitty was due to meet with Freddy in secret, and she could hardly contain her excitement. She had an idea that Sissy knew of her secret but had not yet mentioned anything to her about it. Sissy just kept smiling knowingly at her.

The Earl and Countess were having a luncheon at Bonython Manor that day. Although Mrs Bligh still ran the house like a military operation, this was an opportunity for the staff to take time off that they had in lieu, and Sissy and Kitty had their fair share.

'Kitty, get your coat. We're going into Helston shopping,' Sissy said after the midday meal that day. 'I've informed Mrs Bligh that we are going.' Sissy put her kitchen diary away and picked up the shopping list she had made of all the things that needed ordering. The family was hosting a dinner party for ten in three days' time.

Kitty quickly pulled on her coat. She did not need asking twice. 'Which shops are we visiting, Sissy?' she asked excitedly.

'The butchers and perhaps some other places,' Sissy smiled. 'Hurry, we must catch the wagon at Cury Cross Lanes in twenty minutes.'

Kitty loved these outings with Sissy. She enjoyed the tantalising glimpse of the sea from the road. Kitty had never been to the seaside and longed to go one day. She had in her handbag her purse; with a small amount of money, she had earned before Mrs Bligh docked her wages for ruining Her Ladyship's Turkish rug. Kitty had decided to buy herself a new blouse for her outing with Freddy next week. Smoothing her grey serge skirt with her hand, she sighed, her skirt would have to do; she couldn't afford a new skirt as well. She didn't notice Sissy watching her with a knowing smile.

In Helston, after doing business with the butchers, they went into the bookstore and spent a pleasant hour browsing, each choosing a novel to read. Sissy always insisted on buying Kitty a book whenever they ventured into Helston, and today Kitty chose the book Far from the Madding Crowd by Thomas Hardy, and Sissy bought Henry James's Daisy Millar.

'Now, just one more shop to visit, and then I think it is time to go to Bumbles Tea Shop. I do so love being waited on for a change.' Sissy grinned.

At Mrs Drake's haberdashery, Sissy ushered Kitty through the door, and as they stepped down into one of their favourite shops, Kitty's face brightened. Bolts of material lined the back wall. Rolls of ribbons and drawers of lace and buttons ran along the left wall, but to the right side was a wooden railing with ready-to-wear clothes in various colours and patterns. The sign above read: *ANY GARMENT CAN BE ALTERED TO FIT*. It was to this rail that Sissy steered Kitty.

'Have a look,' she nodded.

Kitty moved the garments until she came to the blouses and picked one with a ribbon threaded through the high collar.

'This is lovely,' she said. 'I think it will fit as well.'

'What about this?' Sissy pulled out a dress, which, if she had not been as rotund as she was, she would have liked for herself! The dress was cream linen, sprigged with embroidered daisies. It was high-necked, with a wide band at the waist, a generous skirt, and leg of mutton sleeves.

'Oh! It's lovely, Sissy; are you buying it for yourself?'

'I don't think I will squeeze my ample hips into this, I'm afraid,' she laughed.

'We might be able to alter it!' Mrs Drake offered, though she didn't sound too confident that the seams would let out enough.

'Thank you for the offer, but I think this would look perfect on Kitty here.'

'Oh, no!' Kitty frowned. 'I mean, yes, it would be perfect, but I can't afford it, Sissy. I need to buy this blouse.'

'There is no harm in trying them both on, just to see what they look like,' Sissy insisted.

Behind the curtain, Kitty slipped on the blouse to find it fitted perfectly, and then she looked longingly at the dress. She knew if she put it on, it would be an awful wrench to take it off and not be able to own it.

'Have you got the dress on yet?' Sissy called through.

'Sissy, there is no point – I simply cannot afford it.'

'Put it on and come out and show me. I want to see what it looks like on someone.'

'Oh, I see. Righty oh.'

A couple of minutes later, Kitty emerged from behind the curtain. Sissy smiled; she looked lovely in it. 'Thank you, Kitty. I might get Mrs Drake to make me something similar.'

Kitty took one more look in the mirror and sighed. It really was lovely. Mrs Bligh had docked her wages for a whole year from last October, so she had another four months to go before she got paid again. If the dress were still here, she could buy it then. Kitty put the dress back on the rack, giving it one last loving stroke.

'Now, Kitty, buy your blouse and run along to the tea shop to secure us a table, preferably near the window. I have some business with Mrs Drake.'

*

Kitty was sitting at the table in the window of Bumbles Tea Shop, trying to keep her mind from thinking about the dress she so coveted, when Sissy came in.

'Goodness, but it's warm today,' Sissy said, slipping her coat off but keeping her hat on as Kitty had done.

Once they had ordered tea, Sissy reached down to her basket and produced a parcel to hand to Kitty.

Kitty glanced at Sissy. 'What is this?'

'Open it!'

She untied the string, unwrapped the paper, and her mouth formed an O. There lay the dress she had just tried on. 'But…' she said, giving Sissy a puzzled look.

'It's a present for you, Kitty. You can wear it when you meet Freddy on Saturday.'

Kitty coloured up. 'When I meet Freddy!' she replied in amazement.

'Do you think I haven't noticed how Freddy looks at you, Kitty, and seen the notes you pass between each other?' She winked. 'I take it you are planning on meeting him since you asked me when the family is away from home next?'

Kitty's blush heightened. 'I am meeting him, yes. So, thank you for this.'

'It's my pleasure to treat you, Kitty; you deserve it. Though why I am encouraging you to go and meet Freddy, I do not know. Lord knows I don't want to lose you from the kitchen if you fall in love and get married, but if I must, I would rather lose you to Freddy than anyone else.'

Kitty's eyes watered at her kindness. 'We are just going for a walk – nothing more.'

Sissy reached over and patted her hand. 'I'm not judging you. I know you're a sensible girl. Freddy is a fine boy; I know he will look after you. Once he sees you in that dress, he will be absolutely smitten with you – if he isn't already. Have you decided where you're going?'

'I don't know, Sissy,' Kitty said excitedly. 'Freddy just said he wanted to take me somewhere on the wagon; he said he'd pay.'

'Did he now? Well, on Saturday, I suggest you tell Freddy to go through the farmyard track to Chypons Road, and you go up the drive. Arrive at the wagon stop separately, and *do not* sit together.'

'We won't.' Kitty held the parcel containing the dress to her chest. 'Sissy, would you keep the dress in your cottage for me until I go out with Freddy?'

'Yes, of course, but why?'

'Joyce in the laundry will know I've been to Helston today, and I have no doubt she'll rifle through the drawers in my room to see if I bought anything new. If she finds the dress, she will steal it. I bought some wool stockings last time we went shopping, and they went missing.'

'Damn that girl! I wondered why your stockings had holes in them. I trust you bought some new ones today?'

Kitty shook her head.

'Why not?'

'I couldn't afford the blouse, and the stockings.'

'What on earth do you do with your wage?'

Kitty lowered her voice. 'I'm not supposed to tell anyone, but I haven't had a wage since I spilled a bowl of water on the Turkish rug in Her Ladyship's bedroom the night Lady Carole was born. Mrs Bligh said I had ruined an expensive rug and that she would have to dock my wage for at least a year. I was not to tell a soul, or I'd be dismissed.'

Sissy's nostrils flared, and she was hardly able to contain her anger. 'Right, well, we shall see about that!'

'Oh, Sissy. Don't say anything; I'll get dismissed.'

'No, you won't.'

'As for your stockings, I shall go and purchase them before we catch the wagon back. You can pay me back tomorrow when you get paid, because I will make sure you get paid! As for Joyce and your stockings, I can guarantee she will not pinch them again. I think it's high time we taught that light-fingered little bitch a lesson.'

*

Kitty left her lovely new dress with Sissy, as planned, but carried her stockings and a small paper bag that Sissy had given her through the kitchen, past the laundry, and up the stairs, knowing that Joyce missed nothing. In her bedroom, she changed her stockings and put the old ones in the paper bag in the drawer and carefully laid the rest of her folded linen on top, tentatively closing it before going downstairs to the kitchen.

As soon as Sissy and Kitty had prepared everything for the evening meals, and with His Lord and Her Ladyship still out at Bonython Manor, Sissy took off her apron and marched up to Her Ladyship's bedroom to inspect the Turkish rug. Finding it in pristine condition, she marched back to the housekeeper's room, found it empty, and grabbed the most recent ledgers for the household budget. There she found the entries stating that Kitty's wages were marked as paid since last October – Sissy was ready for battle.

'What pray are you doing in this room?' Mrs Bligh demanded when she found Sissy waiting for her in the housekeeper's room.

Sissy waved the ledgers at Mrs Bligh. 'These make very interesting reading!'

Mrs Bligh gritted her teeth. 'You have no right to look at those ledgers.'

'Oh, I think I do! Especially as I've found out that you are not paying my kitchen assistant a wage!'

'That girl ruined an expensive rug!'

'She did not, and you know it! According to these ledgers, you have been drawing Kitty's wage but not giving it to her.'

Mrs Bligh's mouth tightened.

'So, Mrs Bligh, you will backdate every penny of Kitty's wages she is due from last October, or I shall go to Her Ladyship and tell her about your fraudulent dealings.'

Mrs Bligh stretched her neck and said categorically, 'Her Ladyship would not listen to you.'

'Oh, I think she would. My position as cook here is more tenable than yours. She will trust me in this matter. I have a rather good relationship with Her Ladyship. You never know - Her Ladyship might find other discrepancies in this ledger – perhaps being light-fingered runs in the family.'

Mrs Bligh swallowed hard.

'I expect Kitty to be recompensed in full tomorrow and make sure she's paid an assistant cook's wage for the last three months!'

Mrs Bligh folded her arms. 'I don't have the money to hand.'

Sissy stared at her darkly. 'Oh, I am sure you have it ferreted away somewhere.' She cradled the ledgers to her chest. 'I shall keep these somewhere safe until Kitty has the money owed - tomorrow.'

*

Shortly after the servant's teatime, Joyce excused herself from the table. Sissy and Kitty were clearing the dishes away from the table and exchanged a glance as they heard her footsteps running up the back stairs to the servant's quarters. Two minutes later, her howls of pain filtered back down into the kitchen, making everyone who was left sitting around the kitchen table look up in alarm. Joyce's footsteps thundered back down the stairs, and she burst screaming into Mrs Bligh's housekeeping room, blood dripping from her fingers in her wake.

Sissy grinned at Kitty. 'I think the little nipper caught a rat.'

The rest of the staff listened on as Mrs Bligh administered a sharp slap to Joyce's face to silence her screams. How has this happened?' She demanded.

'How indeed, eh, Kitty?' Sissy mused with an arched eyebrow.

Kitty suppressed a smile but could not help wondering how much blood had spilled when Joyce's light fingers found the mousetrap hidden in her clean linen drawer. No matter. It would be worth the extra work of washing them all again.

*

The next day, John Bolitho and Sissy watched the growing excitement between the two young people as they planned their outing. They watched little notes being exchanged, unhidden now from them but out of sight of horrible Mrs

Bligh. If Mrs Bligh had found out, she would have undoubtedly found a way to nip their burgeoning friendship in the bud!

'Loves young dream, eh?' Sissy grinned at John.

John smiled. 'I remember it well.'

'It's never happened to me, but I know it when I see it,' Sissy sighed.

'Your time will come, Sissy.'

Sissy tipped her head. 'John! We all know that I'm built like the side of a house and was way down the queue when God gave out good looks. It's not going to happen!' Sissy mused.

'Nonsense! You're a fine-looking woman and an excellent cook – what more could a man want?'

'That's kind of you to say, John, but I think I'm destined to be a *Mrs* in cooks terms only, and I'm fine with that! Cooking is my life and what I love to do. We shall leave the romance to the young ones.'

'Young ones! You're only twenty-one yourself, Sissy!' John said, shaking his head.

They both watched Freddy and Kitty whisper sweet nothings to each other.

'I've warned Kitty about boarding and sitting with Freddy on that wagon on Saturday; otherwise, folks will talk.'

'I've warned him too, but he's a sensible lad. I know we can trust him to do the right thing.'

*

Freddy and Kitty had their heads together but knew Mr Bolitho and Sissy were talking about them.

'They're on to us!' Freddy joked.

Kitty smiled. 'They're just looking out for us – that's all.'

'I know. I can speak to Mr Bolitho better than I can speak to my pa.'

'Same with Sissy. She's like a mother to me. I don't know what I would do without her working here.' *She thought of the wages she had received, which Sissy had forced Mrs Bligh to pay her that morning, and smiled.*

'Well, I hope Sissy knows that I will look after you, and I will not do anything I shouldn't.' His eyes were gentle, and so was his tone.

'Sissy knows, Freddy, and I know too,' she said, gazing into his lovely dawn grey eyes.

'I wish Saturday would come soon.' Freddy sighed.

Kitty's face broke into an excited smile. 'I know - I simply can't wait.'

Everyone in the kitchen turned as June, the scullery maid, rushed in with coal to feed the boiler in the kitchen, whistling happily, albeit tunelessly, through her missing front tooth.

'Morning,' June said cheerily to everyone, grinning a gappy smile. Gone was the timid, frightened thirteen-year-old who had arrived from the workhouse to replace Kitty at Easter.

'Morning, June,' John said. 'Cheery as ever, I see?'

'Ayes. I love my job,' she said, shovelling the coal into the boiler.

Sissy glanced at Kitty, who grimaced - neither had ever come across anyone who liked being a scullery maid before.

'I trust you are in rude health this morning,' John added.

'Ayes, I am. Unlike Joyce,' she cackled. 'She's still like a bear with a sore head this morning. It'll match her sore fingers – proper squashed they are,' she laughed heartily again. 'Silly mare – how do you get your fingers trapped in a mousetrap? Eh? I've asked her how, but she'll not say how she did it.'

'Yes. It's a mystery.' Sissy said, shooting Kitty a wry smile.

June cupped her hand to her mouth and whispered, 'She's having to do all the washing with her left hand only because nobody will help her,' she said, elongating the word nobody. 'Serves her right – nasty little bugger that she is. I've just watched her try to peg a newly washed sheet on the washing line, and the wind took it out of her hand, dumped it in the muck, and she had to wash it again!' she chortled. 'I nearly wet myself laughing. Right. I can't stop - lots of chamber pots to empty – my favourite job!' she said, rubbing her hands vigorously. 'Cheerio!'

Everyone shook their heads and laughed.

'She's a case, that one!' Sissy said to John. 'June takes no notice of Mrs Bligh, you know. Any beratements are like water off a duck's back – it riles Mrs Bligh.' Sissy's eyes twinkled mischievously.

'Right, young Freddy. It's time for us to go too,' John said. 'If we don't get the winter vegetables in the ground these next few days, you might have to work on Saturday.' He winked at Sissy.

Freddy's face dropped as he shot a devastated look in Kitty's direction.

John laughed heartily and put a fatherly arm around Freddy. 'Pick your face off the floor, you daft thing. I'm jesting.'

14

After finishing their chores on Sunday, Josh and Maia set off on their round trip to Poldhu, following the footsteps they had taken on Friday evening along the golf link track to Church Cove. There was no accidental brushing of fingers this time. The intimacy of the other night was curtailed for now; Josh wanted to wait until Maia made the first move, especially after what she had been through with Henry.

The bells were tinkling melodically from the bell tower of Winwilloe Church, calling the parishioners to the service, but Maia led him past the church to look at Dollar Cove.

'Are you a churchgoer, Josh?'

'No. Are you?'

She shook her head. 'I appreciate the architecture. I'll take you inside one day to look around.'

Josh smiled, happy that there was going to be a next time.

They walked down over the pebble beach as she explained the name given to the cove. 'It's named after the wreck of a cargo vessel, thought to have been Spanish, that ran aground in the cove in the 1770s near the base of those cliffs they call Jangye-Ryn. The vessel was laden with silver dollars, and according to reports, some have occasionally turned up on the beach, hence the given name, Dollar Cove. I think we all live in the hope of finding a silver dollar at low tide. I look often, but I've never found one.' She smiled.

As they walked back towards Church Cove, Josh pointed out a flower-laden grave in the churchyard. 'It looks like someone was much loved.'

'Yes, and still is. That's the grave of the author, James Blackwell. He lived just over the Halzephron Cliff there. His widow, Jenna, although she has remarried now, has fresh flowers placed on his grave every week.'

'I know of the author, but I've never read anything by him.'

'Do you read much then?' Maia asked.

'I used to, but my time in the navy put paid to that. I was always kept too busy to read.'

'I have some books at the farm you could borrow. All James's books are there if you want to read them.'

'Thank you. I will. I was browsing your books the other day, itching to pick one out.'

'Well, be my guest.' Maia smiled to herself. There was nothing better than finding someone with a shared interest in books.

*

After a rather pleasant walk over the cliffs to Poldhu, Maia and Josh settled at one of the tables on the veranda of the tearoom.

'I truly believe this is the best tearoom with the most spectacular view. I have to reserve my table out here as it is so popular. But then, you're no stranger to the cove, are you? I remember seeing you on the rocks over there. The day you decided my stable was a better place to sleep.'

Josh laughed. 'Yes, and your very kind friend brought me a mug of tea and scones. I feel ashamed to meet her again today, especially after the poor state I was in then. I was clearly dressed as a beggar, but she was very kind to me.'

'Ellie is a wonderful friend. She would help anyone if they looked in need.'

'Does she know I work with you now?'

'Yes.'

'Well, I hope she sees an improvement in my appearance and circumstances now.'

Maia smiled when Ellie came out to take their order.

'Ah, the stranger from the shore. Welcome, Mr...?' Ellie frowned, forgetting his name.

'Josh, my name is Josh Harding.

'Welcome back, Josh.'

'May I thank you again for your kindness to me the other week?'

Ellie dismissed it with a wave of her hand. 'It was nothing. I was glad to help. I hope you're settling in at Wild Cliff Farm.'

'I have never felt more settled,' he said, smiling softly at Maia.

Ellie threw an amused glance at Maia, who blushed slightly.

Maia cleared her throat. 'It's time that Josh sampled your famous cream teas, Ellie. So, tea for two if you please.'

'Coming up.'

Presented with the cream tea, Josh licked his lips in anticipation of the lovely fluffy scones, the pot of strawberry jam, and copious amounts of clotted cream. 'This looks wonderful; in fact,' he said, looking deep into her eyes, 'being here with you is wonderful.'

There it was again – that tingle running through her body whenever he turned those beautiful blue eyes on her. 'It's nice to have some company. I try to come every Sunday, so I hope you will join me again.'

'I shall look forward to it,' he said, slicing a scone and reaching for the cream.

'Jam first!' She reached out and put her hand on his.

'Pardon?'

'Jam first in Cornwall.'

'Why?'

'We don't have Devon ways down here,' she joked.

Josh laughed and went back to dip his spoon in the cream.

'I mean it, Josh - if you put cream on first, Ellie will never serve you again. Look! She's watching you.'

They both turned to see Ellie standing at the tearoom doorway with her arms folded.

Josh pulled his mouth into a tight line, put his cream spoon down, and moved to the jam, and Ellie winked at Maia.

'Why would it matter?' he whispered as he took his first delicious mouthful.

'It just matters! If you're to be an honorary Cornishman, you must mend your ways.' She giggled.

Maia's attention was caught by Jago driving up Poldhu Hill. It did not escape her notice that Ellie's daughter, Fee, had stopped serving, clutched the empty tea tray to her chest, and was keenly observing Jago drive up the hill with a dreamy look in her eyes.

Maia felt her breath catch, anxious that Fee should give men like Jago the widest berth possible. As soon as the car was out of sight, she watched Fee return to work, having first shot an embarrassed glance at Maia when she realised Maia had been watching her.

'Is everything all right?' Josh asked. 'You look pensive.'

'I'm not sure. I've just seen Ellie's daughter watching Jago drive up the hill. I do hope she hasn't fallen for his charms.'

Josh arched an eyebrow. 'Jago has charms?'

'With the ladies, yes. I think that's why I annoy him – his charms don't work on me, and he is not used to being rejected.'

'He sounds like an absolute rake to me,' Josh said, popping a piece of scone into his mouth.

'Rake is the perfect word for him.' Maia fell silent but wondered if she should voice her concerns to Ellie.

*

Fee walked back into the tearoom with the now-loaded tray, knowing that Maia had caught her watching Jago. Putting the tray down harder than she should, the tea cups rattled noisily, making Ellie glance questioningly in her direction.

'Sorry, Ma, I almost dropped the tray,' she fibbed.

Running her hands down her apron, she took a deep breath to tamp down her annoyance. Whatever that look meant that Maia had given her, she was ignoring it. Maia had no right to object to anyone else being interested in Jago, especially as she had been quite vocal to her ma about not wanting his attention.

*

Shortly after being served their cream tea, Maia smiled as David and Alice Trevorrow, from the dairy, arrived with their youngest son, Jimmy. They greeted each other warmly and sat at their reserved table.

'I see you two are enjoying the delights of Ellie's fine cuisine,' David said.

'Absolutely,' Maia answered. 'One cannot live in Poldhu without visiting this fine establishment. So, I've brought Josh down today.'

Ellie, poised with her order pad, smiled and relished the praise.

'We are here to celebrate Jimmy's 15th birthday,' David said. 'Look at him, though! He's fifteen, going on twenty. I have never seen a lad shoot up and out as much as our Jimmy here. It's like he went to bed one night as a young lad and came down the stairs the next morning as a full-grown man!'

Jimmy groaned. 'I didn't grow overnight, Pa.'

'It felt like it,' his ma cut in. 'We were convinced you'd been standing in the manure heap.'

Jimmy rolled his eyes.

Everyone looked at the broad-shouldered, strapping lad, who sported the shade of a beard, a fine bone structure, and the makings of a handsome man.

'I reckon he's got those muscles humping hides about for Ben Pearson as Ben's assistant in the saddlery,' David said. 'Ben still can't do much at the moment; he's still recovering from that awful cliff fall incident he suffered last year.'

'Gosh, yes, Ben told me about it last week,' Josh said. 'He was thrown from that cliff up there, wasn't he?' He pointed to Poldhu Head.

'Aye. No one thought Ben would survive. Our Jimmy here witnessed the initial attack on him, and thankfully, justice prevailed, and the culprits were both hanged for their sins early this year.'

'It is hard to believe anything awful like that could happen here,' Josh added.

David pulled a face. 'The area has had its moments. Look at Maia's husband. Murdered in cold blood, and the culprit never caught.'

David had already told Josh about Henry's murder, but Josh had not broached the subject with Maia; she seemed not to want to speak about Henry much. All she had told him was that he had died a year ago. He glanced now at Maia, who had stiffened at the mention of Henry.

'*David!*,' his wife Alice berated. 'You should not bring that subject up; you'll upset Maia!'

David glanced sheepishly at Maia. 'Sorry, Maia. This is not a polite discussion for a Sunday tea.'

'It's fine, David.' Maia held her hand up. *She could never think of Henry and polite discussion in the same sentence.*

'Anyway,' David said, changing the subject. 'Jimmy insisted on coming here for a cream tea for his birthday, even though his ma has a larder full of food at home. We think he has his eye on a certain young waitress - haven't you, lad?' He nudged Jimmy.

Jimmy looked bashful, but he did not deny the fact.

Maia smiled. 'Ah, the lovely Fee. She is certainly a fine-looking young woman,' Maia agreed. 'The image of her ma,' she said, glancing at Ellie.

Ellie smiled gratefully. 'I shall get Fee to bring your order out then, Jimmy,' she said with a wink.

'Thank you.' Jimmy beamed from ear to ear.

'How are you settling in then, Josh? Or should I ask Maia that question?' David laughed.

'He's settling in very well. I simply could not do without him.' Maia smiled, and Josh gave her a grateful look.

*

Inside the tearoom, once Ellie had put the Trevorrow's order together, she called Fee over to take it out.

'Oh, just a moment,' Fee said, picking up another tray. 'I just have to take this order out.'

'No matter. I will take that one.' Ellie took the tray off of her, leaving Fee confused. 'I think a certain young man outside is looking forward to you serving him,' she explained.

'Really!' Fee's face brightened, thinking of Jago.

'Yes. Jimmy Trevorrow: I think he is rather sweet on you.'

Fee could not hide the disappointment on her face.

'What's the matter? Jimmy is a fine, upstanding young lad.'

Fee twisted her mouth to the side. 'I know, but he is only fifteen years old!'

'So are you!'

'Not for much longer!'

'Just go and have a look at him. He does not look fifteen.'

Fee sighed and picked up the tray. 'Well, he is still fifteen, whether he looks it or not!'

'Just go and say hello and make his day.'

Fee narrowed her eyes. 'Are you matchmaking?'

'I might be!' Ellie chuckled.

'Well, stop it, please. I shall find my own beau.' *In fact, I have already found him!*

15
Kitty 1881

Wearing her new dress, Kitty could hardly contain her excitement about her day out with Freddy.

'Oh, lordy me, Kitty! You do look a picture in that dress,' Sissy said, then lowered her voice. 'Freddy will be bowled over. Here, this is for you.' She passed her a muslin bag. 'I have packed you a small picnic. It's nothing much – just a couple of ham sandwiches and some apples, but it'll keep the hunger pangs at bay.'

'Thank you, Sissy.'

Kitty was just about to leave when Mrs Bligh entered the kitchen. 'Morton!' she roared. 'Where do you think you are going, all dressed up like a dog's dinner?'

Kitty felt stricken, thinking she was being refused her day out.

Kitty is taking some time off - time owed to her!' Sissy stepped in to answer.

'Well, she can't go because I have a job for her to do.'

'If I can spare her, *you* certainly can!' Sissy bristled. 'Off you go, Kitty.'

'Now, just wait a moment.' Mrs Bligh folded her arms. 'I say who can take leave in this house.'

'And you,' Sissy pointed angrily at her, 'agreed when I asked you a fortnight ago if Kitty could have today off!'

'Well, it must have slipped my mind. However, it is not convenient to let her go now.'

Kitty glanced in despair at Sissy.

'Poppycock!' Sissy argued with Mrs Bligh. 'Whatever job you need her to do, *I* will do it. Now, off you go, Kitty,' she said, shooing her through the door. Sissy turned, folded her arms, matching Mrs Bligh's stance, and said, 'Right, what is the job you want me to do?'

The housekeeper gave a short, sharp snort and backed down. 'It's nothing. It will wait.'

'I thought as much,' Sissy said with a huff.

*

Kitty ran up the drive as fast as she could, frightened that Mrs Bligh would send someone to fetch her back. She only slowed down when she made it past the granite gate posts. Freddy said they were to catch the ten thirty wagon to Mullion and had given her the price of the ticket in the last note he had passed to her. But when Kitty arrived at the wagon stop, Freddy wasn't there! Deflated, she feared she might cry. Everything seemed to be against her having this day off with Freddy, and she had so desperately looked forward to it. By the time the wagon had trundled up the road from the Lizard towards the stop, Kitty had decided not to board it. She was about to start walking back to the manor when she saw Freddy running out of Chypons Lane. He gestured for her to climb aboard and boarded moments after her, flopping down on his seat to catch his breath. As planned, they sat apart, though they surreptitiously glanced at each other as the wagon made its way through Cury and down to Poldhu.

The sight of Poldhu Cove as the wagon trundled down Poldhu Hill almost took Kitty's breath away. Sand dunes gave way to a long stretch of golden beach reaching down to a sparkling sea. Kitty had never seen a more spectacular sight - the sea looked turquoise and so crystal clear you could see down to the seabed. It was as though she was about to set foot in paradise.

Freddy stood up when the wagon stopped at the bottom of Poldhu Hill, so Kitty followed suit. Freddy stood at the wagon steps to help other passengers down, so taking his hand seemed acceptable for Kitty to do the same. They waited a moment while the other passengers dispersed before Freddy held his hand out again for Kitty. Tentatively placing her hand back in his, her heart gave a little dance of pleasure as he curled his fingers around her hand. It felt lovely.

'Kitty, you look beautiful in that dress.'

'Thank you. Sissy bought it for me, especially to wear today.'

'She is a very kind and special friend to you, isn't she?'

'She is indeed.'

'It's the same for me with Mr Bolitho. Come on, let's walk up to Poldhu Head. There's a splendid view right down towards Land's End from there. I think you will love it.'

To Kitty's delight, Freddy kept a hold of her hand as they walked up the steep coastal road, taking a diversion across the top of the great black cliffs.

'Oh, Freddy, this is beautiful,' she said when they climbed to the highest point.

'I knew you would like it – the view is especially lovely on a sunny day like this.' He stood close to her and pointed. 'That's St Michael's Mount, and beyond are Newlyn and Mousehole, with Land's End just around that far corner. Down there.' He pointed to the cove below. 'That is Church Cove, and that is St Winwaloe's Church nestled in the cliff – it is named the Church of Storms. Beyond that is Dollar Cove, named as such because bucketloads of silver dollars spilled out of a ship that wrecked there in the 17th century. I have never found any yet, and I have never met anyone who has!' He grinned.

Kitty turned to look at him. 'Do you go there a lot?'

'I used to, yes. I was born at Gunwalloe in the next cove, so this was my playground.'

'Lucky you.'

'Where were *you* born, Kitty?'

'A place called Gweek.'

'Ah, yes, I know of it. It's an ancient port, isn't it?'

'Yes, it's a very busy little village.'

'Mr Bolitho said you came from the workhouse.'

Kitty nodded.

'How did you end up there, if you don't mind me asking?'

'I don't mind telling you. Ma, Pa, and my sister Jean all died of consumption in 1875, and as I had no relatives who would take me in, I was sent to the workhouse.'

'Gosh, Kitty. I'm that sorry for you.'

Kitty smiled gratefully, but speaking of the memory caught her by surprise, and she had to sniff back a little tear.

Freddy put his arm around her shoulder to comfort her. 'I'm sorry, Kitty. I didn't mean to upset you.'

'It's all right, Freddy - it happens when I think about them.' Feeling that she could trust Freddy and speak about her parents to him, she showed him the locket she had hung around her neck. 'This was Ma and Pa. I don't have a photo of Jean because she was only a baby when she died.'

'What a lovely keepsake.'

'I nearly lost it. Joyce, the laundry maid, stole it, but I got it back.'

'She's an unpleasant girl, I must agree.'

'Well, I think we've curbed her thieving for a while,' Kitty mused.

'Oh yes?' He grinned and tipped his head. 'Might the mousetrap incident have something to do with you?'

'Maybe.' She laughed and then changed the subject. 'Do you still have family, Freddy?'

'I do. I am the oldest of six children. Ma looks after the little ones, and Pa fishes out of Gunwalloe Fishing Cove.'

'A fisherman! Did *you* not fancy being a fisherman?'

'Not likely. I like my feet on solid ground and my hands in the soil.' He lifted his hands. 'Hence the pitted dirt in them. I can't get them clean, sorry.' He grimaced.

'A stint washing up at Bochym would do the trick. It used to take me hours sometimes and make my hands look like prunes,' she frowned.

'No thanks.' He grinned. 'Anyway, let me continue to help you get your bearings. Over there,' he pointed south. 'That is Mullion Island in the distance, and beyond that are

Kynance Cove and Lizard Point. One day, I shall take you to see them all. Shall we sit and take in the view for a while?' He pulled a rug from his backpack and spread it on the ground.

Without shyness, Kitty sat down and settled next to Freddy. They had an easy way with each other, even though they had never spent much more than a few short minutes speaking before. Kitty always felt they would have a good relationship, and being here with him now confirmed that.

'Thank you for coming today, Kitty. I have wanted to ask you for so long, but I held back because you are so young.'

'I'm fifteen! Besides, I don't think it matters how old you are to be friends.' She smiled.

'Well, I am nearly eighteen, and friends or not, people might talk.'

'We are not doing anything wrong, so there is nothing to speak about, is there?' she huffed.

Freddy's eyes lowered.

'I do hope you didn't think we would do anything wrong, Freddy Hubbard?'

Freddy blanched. 'Of course not! I'm not that sort of person to take advantage.'

'I'm pleased to hear it.' She smiled and bumped his arm playfully. 'So, we can have a jolly old time, knowing that we are not doing anything we shouldn't!'

'I promise I will never compromise you,' he said ardently.

She smiled warmly at him. Bringing her knees up to cradle them, she lifted her face to the sun. 'Oh, this is blissful.' She glanced down at the sea, creeping slowly up the beach. 'It looks so inviting, but I can't swim - in fact, I have never been to the seaside before.'

'We can dip our toes in the surf later if you want. I've brought a towel to dry our feet. The wagon back to Cury Cross Roads is at three thirty, so we have lots of time.'

'Oh, well, yes, Freddy. I would love to do that.'

'Then we will. We can do anything you want to do!'

Kitty's eyes travelled along the cliff edge, watching the sand martins flit in and out of the sandy cliff.

'Goodness, but that cliff looks terribly soft. It's a wonder that the house above it hasn't slipped into the sea.'

'Ah, that is Penn als Cottage – Pa says it means house on the cliff head. It has been perched precariously on that cliff since Pa was a boy. Holding on by its fingernails, Pa used to say, when he and Grandfather fished off the cove.'

'Gosh! I'm not sure I would like to live there! Does anyone live there?'

'It belongs to the Penhallows. It was built at the turn of the century by Jack Penhallow, and not without some speculation. My grandfather said people would bet with Jack that his house would slip down the cliff whenever we had a storm. Jack Penhallow always won the bet because Jack had secretly had iron rods bored into the granite rock to secure the foundations when he built it.'

'So, will it always be there?'

'Who knows, the boreholes may make the cliff unstable one day.'

Kitty shuddered. 'I would not like to live there, just in case.' She rummaged in her bag. 'Look, Sissy has made us a sandwich.' She unwrapped the muslin cloth.

'Oh, delicious. Perhaps later, after we have dipped our toes in the sea, you will let me take you to the teashop on the beach for tea and cake.'

'But...?'

'Don't worry. I shall say that you're my sister. The owner will never know you're not, will she?'

'Oh, Freddy, fancy us going out for tea together. You are spoiling me today.'

'I hope you let me spoil you again someday because this is just the start of our adventures.'

*

After drying their frozen toes with the towel after their paddle, they slipped their shoes back on and climbed the wooden steps to the veranda surrounding the teashop, surprised to find that nobody was about.

'Is it closed?' Kitty asked disappointedly.

Freddy tried to peer through the glass. 'It doesn't say so on the door.'

Kitty glanced back down the beach towards the sea. 'Wouldn't it be nice to sit out here and drink tea while looking at the sea?'

'Indeed, it would - if they had tables and chairs,' Freddy mused as he turned the handle on the door.

A bell tinkled above them to herald their arrival, and a rotund woman bustled out from the back of the tearoom and eyed them suspiciously.

Recognising the look on her face, Freddy quickly said, 'Good afternoon to you. My sister and I were just saying how lovely it would be to sit outside drinking tea on such a day.'

The owner bristled. 'Why, what's wrong with the inside of my tearoom?'

'Oh, nothing at all. It's, erm… it is quite charming,' Freddy said, glancing around at the dour furnishings. 'I was just saying.'

The woman shook her head. 'Who in their right mind would want to sit outside in that draughty breeze? There is always a chill wind coming off the sea. Folks would freeze, and the tea would be cold in seconds. No. That is a ridiculous idea – sitting outside – what a notion.'

Freddy bit down on his lip. 'You're probably right,' he said, not wanting to engage in any argument with this formidable woman. 'So could we have a table for two, please?'

'Oh! I am sure I can accommodate you and your…*sister*,' she said, narrowing her eyes at Kitty. 'Take your pick.'

Freddy helped Kitty off with her coat and gestured to the seat at one of the many empty tables.

'We would like a pot of tea for two, please,' he said, settling down.

'Anything with it? We have some Dundee cake or scones.'

Freddy glanced at Kitty.

'Dundee cake, please,' she answered.

'Make that two slices, then.' Freddy smiled at the owner who was still eyeing Kitty with suspicion.

The owner served the tea and cake, still with a sceptical look in her eyes, but when they bit into the cake, they grimaced, returning the rest of their slices to the plate to be left uneaten.

'Gosh! She can't have had many customers these last few days - this cake is stale!' Freddy whispered, washing it down with a sip of tea.

'I know,' Kitty agreed, glancing around at the dark brown painted walls, tables, and chairs. 'I'm not surprised about the lack of custom - the décor does not exactly say welcome, does it?' Dark green tablecloths covered at least three of the tables. 'It looks as dark and uninviting as that cave we have just seen on the beach!' Kitty wondered if the owner ever had full occupancy of the teashop. 'If this teashop were mine, I would paint everything white, put gingham tablecloths on, and place a vase of flowers on each table. And I would put tables and chairs outside!' she added with a definite nod.

Freddy smiled. 'Do you fancy running a teashop then?'

'Well, I could certainly make a better cup of tea and cake than this!' she whispered.

'We will find somewhere nicer next time we go out.' He winked.

Kitty bit down on her lip. 'I feel awful now for saying bad things about it, as it was your treat.'

'Don't feel bad.' Freddy chuckled. 'I totally agree with you.'

When the owner came to clear the table, she raised an eyebrow at the uneaten cake on their plates.

'Very filling,' Freddy said, patting his tummy, then added, 'You're very quiet here today.'

'It's quiet every day. I don't know why I bother opening some days. You are my only customers today, well, all week if the truth be told!'

Freddy and Kitty exchanged unsurprised glances.

'Have you run the teashop long?' Freddy enquired.

'Nearly a year - so too long by my estimations. I will be glad to leave once the lease is up in September. God help anyone else who takes it on. I'll wager that no one will ever make a go of this place! Nobody can bake cakes like I do, but you can be the best baker in the world, and the customers still don't come here.'

Kitty pulled her mouth into a tight line.

'No. A tearoom near the sea is *not* what people want! Who wants to come to the sea and get all sandy? Not me, and that is a fact! I am planning on leasing a café in Helston High Street. I am going to give that place, Bumbles, a run for its money,' she said, folding her arms.

Kitty lowered her head to hide her mirth. She and Sissy had enjoyed a wonderful cup of tea and delicious scone there only last week.

'Well, I wish you luck,' Kitty said, trying not to sound sarcastic, as they retrieved their coats to leave.

'Brother and sister, you told me!' the owner said. 'And where did you say you were from?'

'We didn't. Come, sister, dear. Good day to you,' Freddy said as he ushered Kitty through the door.

*

Later that night, Kitty lay in bed, smiling from ear to ear. Despite the stale cake and disgruntled teashop owner, Kitty had had a lovely day out with Freddy. He had promised to take her to Lizard Point next time, though Lord knows when that would be. More often than not, her days off were cancelled at short notice if the family decided to entertain at the last minute. Still, nothing could take away the lovely feeling she had inside – it was as though every time she thought of Freddy, her tummy did a little somersault.

16

Maia and Josh walked back to Wild Cliff Farm after they visited the tearoom, and Maia said she would leave Josh to his own devices as she had some work to do in the studio.

Josh smiled because he had his own special task to do that day.

Wiping the sweat from his brow, it had taken brute strength for Josh to move the leaky trough to a prominent position in Maia's rose garden before he could fill it with soil. A few days ago, he stumbled across a glorious carpet of sweet camomile at the edge of a barley field. The barley field belonged to the Bochym Manor Estate, so he had spoken to the saddler, Ben Pearson, who was married to Lady Emma Dunston from Bochym Manor. He had asked for permission to dig and roll up a sizable patch of camomile. He had no plan at first as to what to do with it, but he thought Maia might like a small camomile lawn laid within the rose garden. It wasn't until Maia had commented that the old leaky trough would go to waste that he had the idea of making a camomile seat for her.

With a spade in hand, he walked the perimeter of her land to find a patch of field that he could dig up to collect topsoil for the trough. In a far corner, Josh found a shady patch of land without much grass and began to dig for soil. He had not dug more than two spadefuls when he found something buried in a cloth. At first, Josh wondered if he had unearthed the grave of an animal, but curiosity got the better of him, and he pulled the cloth from the hole. After inspecting the find, he surmised that for whatever reason Maia had buried these items, it had nothing to do with him, so he replaced everything where he had found it and buried it again. He moved further down the field to dig for soil and tried to put what he had seen out of his mind. It took the best part of the afternoon to ferry enough soil to the trough to fill it and then roll the camomile turf over it. He brushed his hands and stood back to admire a job well done. He wouldn't water it yet so that Maia could sit on it and enjoy the beautiful apple-like fragrance as she did.

*

On Sundays, the Poldhu Tea Room closed early at two 'o clock, so Fee Blackthorn had the rest of the afternoon to herself. Discarding her black waitress uniform, she slipped on her best Sunday dress. It was a pale blue linen shift dress that Ma's friend and Fee's namesake, *Sophie* Trevellick, had made for her.

On her day off last Monday, Fee had been to Helston to purchase lipstick from the chemist, and now she stood by her mirror, smoothing down her dress and pouting her lips. The lipstick certainly made her look older. If Jago had doubts about her youth, maybe she could dispel them.

She grabbed her cardigan and planned to sit on the beach, where she could see Jago coming and going from his house.

'I'm just going out,' she trilled as she passed through the Blackthorn's cosy kitchen, but her pa put down his newspaper and stopped her.

'Just a minute, young lady. What have you got on your face?'

'Leave her be, Guy,' Ellie said, glancing up from writing her letter.

Ignoring Ellie, Guy said, 'Come here.' He beckoned Fee closer and scrutinised her face. 'I thought as much. Why are you wearing lipstick?'

'Ma wears lipstick!' she countered.

'Ma is older! You're too young to wear that stuff.'

'Guy,' Ellie warned again. 'You've just called her a *young lady,* and that's what she is now.'

'She's not yet sixteen, Ellie!' he argued. He turned back to Fee. 'You're still the baby of this family.'

'Oh, Pa!' Fee moved towards him and kissed him on the head, quickly rubbing away the lipstick mark she had left there. 'You'll have to let me grow up sometime. I've been working for the last two years!'

Guy folded his arms. 'Where are you going anyway?'

'Just to the dunes.'

'You're wearing lipstick to go and sit in the dunes!' he mused.

Fee just shrugged.

'Who are you meeting?' Guy asked.

'Guy! Leave her be! Off you go, Fee, and have a nice afternoon,' Ellie said, shooing her out of the kitchen before Guy could interrogate her further.

*

When Maia arrived in her vegetable garden with her wicker basket to pick up some beans and peas for their meal, she was met by Josh, who was in high spirits. He always had a happy disposition, but today, something seemed to delight him. Maybe the walk had filled him with euphoria; it had certainly made *her* happy. It had been lovely sharing some of the things she loved to do with him.

Having picked the vegetables needed for the meal, Josh called her over to the flower garden. 'Before you go. I want to show you something I've made for you.'

Maia felt a flutter of delight. 'You've made something for me!'

He nodded and led her over to the rose garden. 'Now close your eyes.'

She tipped her head and smiled. 'You said you wanted to show me something; I can't do that with my eyes closed.'

'I want you to experience it. Close your eyes. I will guide you.' At the seat he had made, he turned her around. 'Now sit. I'll hold you until you're seated, but keep your eyes closed for a few seconds.'

'Oh! It's spongy!' she said in delight before taking a deep breath. 'My goodness. What is that fragrance?' She breathed in again. 'It smells like apples.' Her fingers ran across the soft seat. 'Is it camomile?' She opened her eyes and looked down at the seat beneath her. 'Oh, Josh, I've always wanted a camomile seat.' She stood up and ran her hands over the delicate flowers. 'It's beautiful. Thank you.' She took hold of his hands and squeezed them. 'That is the most wonderful thing anyone has ever done for me, Josh.'

Josh smiled softly. 'I wanted to make something lovely for you because you are so lovely, Maia.'

'Oh, yes! What the hell is going on here then?'

They both spun around at the grating sound of Jago's voice as he barrelled across to them with a bunch of flowers in hand.

Maia dropped Josh's hands and thumped her fists into her hips. 'Why are you here, Jago? What do you want?'

Jago dropped his voice to a low hiss. 'It's what *he* wants more like, and he looks like he's getting it.'

'Don't be so ridiculous. I was thanking Josh for doing something for me.'

'I don't recall you ever holding my hands when *I* did jobs for you!' Jago sneered. 'So, what *is* going on?'

'Nothing that concerns you, Jago. Now, why are you here?'

He struggled to tamp his anger down before replying, 'I've come to tell you that I've booked rooms and a table for dinner for us at The Royal Hotel in Truro for next Friday.'

She gasped incredulously. 'You have done what?'

'It's to commemorate Henry. It's just been over a year since he died. I was too busy last week, but I thought a nice dinner in a classy hotel would be right up your street. We could toast the memory of Henry. Here, these are for you.' He thrust the bunch of flowers towards her.

Aghast, Maia stepped back from him. When she found her voice, she hissed at him, 'I don't want flowers off you; why would I? And you must be completely deluded if you think for one moment that I would want to toast a single memory of that drunken, nasty brute of a man.'

Jago scowled. 'Hey,' he said savagely. 'That's my brother, you're disrespecting.'

'He might be your brother, but he was my hateful husband, whom I loathed with every fibre of my body and for every single moment that I endured him!'

'That's no way to speak of someone who saved you from ruin! He didn't have to marry you, you know. He could have left you to bear the shame of being a fallen woman.' He surreptitiously glanced at Josh to check his reaction to this revelation, and frowned when Josh seemed unfazed.

Deep anger rose inside Maia, and her eyes blazed with fury. 'Oh, how I wish I'd had the choice not to marry him,' she spat back at him.

'And now, I suppose you're spreading your legs for *him*.' Jago glared again at Josh.

'How *dare* you!' She said through clenched teeth. Out of the corner of her eye, she could see the anger building in Josh.

'If you think I'm going to stand back while this... bastard, whoever he is, covers you and takes my brother's farm, you have another think coming, Maia.'

'For the last time, this farm is mine! The courts have ruled on it. Now please leave – and never come back here again.'

'I'm going nowhere,' Jago snarled. 'Until this one has gone.' He glared at Josh. 'Go on, sling your hook, or shall I kick you off this land?' he threatened.

'Jago!' Maia snapped. 'You have no authority here to order any of us about.' She glanced anxiously back at Josh, but she could see from his stance that he had held back long enough and was about to defend their right to be here.

Josh locked eyes with Jago and took a large intake of breath, almost swelling in front of their eyes. Seemingly keeping his anger under control, he began to roll up his sleeves, revealing muscles and strength he could easily defend himself with. Muscles pumped from five years of hard work on a ship.

Josh stepped towards Jago, flexing his muscles and balling his fists, while Maia stood wide-eyed and held her breath.

'You have insulted us both long enough,' Josh said in a low, threatening voice. 'I will give you ten seconds to leave this farm, as Maia asks.'

Maia noted, for once, a flash of uncertainty clouding Jago's eyes, and realising he had met his match, he turned to her. 'This is not the end of the matter, Maia, so don't think it is.'

'Enough of your threats.' Josh stepped menacingly forward, making Jago stagger back slightly.

Glancing between Maia and Josh, Jago threw the flowers down and ground them into the earth with his heel before walking away.

Maia slumped down on her camomile seat, allowing the apple fragrance to calm her frayed nerves.

'Forgive me, Maia, for my threatening behaviour,' Josh pleaded. 'I'm not a violent man, but I could not stand by and watch him insult you like that.'

Maia reached out her hand to him, and he took it willingly, and she guided him to sit beside her.

'No need to apologise, Josh. I'm so grateful to you; truly, I am.' A quiver of desire passed through their joined hands.

'I just hope I haven't made your life more difficult.'

'Josh. Please know this.' She looked deep into his eyes. 'You have made my life happy again!'

Face-to-face, they were so close. Maia wondered if Josh would kiss her. But he didn't; he just smiled gently at her. She rose to go and start the evening meal, leaving Josh on the camomile seat. As she walked across the field to the farm, a frisson of pleasure coursed through her veins – perhaps a kiss would come another day – another day soon.

*

Fee had been on the beach for over an hour when she spotted Jago driving too fast down Poldhu Hill. Here was her chance to get him to take her somewhere in the car today. She got up, dusted the sand from her dress, and ran past the tearoom towards the access to the road leading to Jago's house. Panting with exertion, she managed to get there just before he turned the car into his road. Patting her hair tidy, she stepped out and waved, giving him her best smile.

'Get out of the way, you stupid bitch,' Jago shouted as he drove past at speed.

Fee's breath caught in her throat as she stepped back in shock. Tears pricked behind her eyes as she watched him bring the car to a halt. She had a sliver of hope that Jago would realise his blunder and come back to apologise, but he just jumped out of his car, opened the door to his house, and slammed it shut behind him.

Hurt and humiliated, she bit down on her bottom lip to stop it from quivering and quickly glanced around to make sure no one had witnessed his rebuff of her. With the back of her hand, she wiped the lipstick from her lips, glad to be rid of it because it had felt unnatural on her. Making her way dejectedly back to the dunes, she cradled her arms around her knees and nursed her wounded heart.

*

Jago threw his keys on the table. Furious at what had happened at Wild Cliff Farm. *How dare that nobody, that bloody incomer, threaten me off my farm like that? How dare he think he can step in and take what is mine!* He kicked a chair out of the way and paced the room like a caged lion. He would own that farm and Maia, one way or another. But first, he needed to get rid of Josh Harding.

*

On Monday morning, Maia made the first of her trips to Bochym that week with a tray of pots carefully packed with straw, ready to be fired.

These new pots, in particular, felt special. They reflected her happiness at having Josh around the farm. He made her feel calmer, which showed in her work.

As she pulled up outside the shed where the kiln was situated, she was delighted to see Viscount William Dunstan walking up the path from the steward's cottage.

'Good morning, my lord,' Maia said. 'Are you home from university for good now?'

'Indeed, I am, and am ready to be let loose on the running of this estate, albeit with a great deal of help from Papa and Mr Pearson – the latter, I suspect, may take a little persuading that I can do the job,' he said with a wink.

Maia smiled. 'Mr Pearson has been your papa's right-hand man for many years!'

'You're right, but I am willing to take his lead. So, Maia, I trust you are well – you look well?'

'Thank you. I'm very well.'

'Are you here to see Mama?'

'No, just to fire my pots today.'

'Here, let me help you unload.' He began to roll his sleeves up to help. Maia hesitated, but he smiled and assured her, 'I promise I shall be careful. I know they are precious cargo.'

There was an ease between the two young people – there always had been. Maia and her brother Alec had moved in a similar social sphere to the Dunstans, as they had been brought up by local gentry Lady Martha Jefferson, so they had often played together as children.

Maia noted that William, fresh out of university, seemed to have a vitality about him that had been missing on the few occasions she had met him during his visits home. It was good that he had renewed energy and a desire to buckle down to life on the estate. It would ease his papa's burden enormously.

'How are you managing at the farm? Papa said you've taken on a farmhand.'

'Yes. His name is Josh Harding. He's not from around these parts but would like to settle here. He has taken a lot of the burden off my shoulders.'

'I suppose that will put Jago's nose out of joint!' he enquired tentatively. 'I remember when I spoke to you last, at my sister's wedding, Jago was helping you a little, though I got the impression you were not too enamoured with him coming around.'

Her face became serious. 'How perceptive of you, but you're right. Jago wants more than to help,' she said spikily.

'Oh dear!' He looked taken aback.

'He still thinks he has a claim to the farm because he is Henry's brother.'

William frowned. 'I thought Papa sorted that out for you?'

'Yes, he did. Thank goodness.'

'But Jago will not accept it?' He tipped his head.

'It seems not - he is becoming a nuisance.'

'Maia, I *will* intervene if he gets out of hand. Just say the word. We Dunstans have some clout with the law, you know.'

'Thank you, my lord.'

He laughed heartily. 'Now, no more of this, *my lord* business, Maia. We have known each other for a long time. You always used to call me William in private, so please do so again.'

She broke into a broad smile. 'Thank you…. William.'

*

As Maia went about her business, William watched her for a while. Every time he saw her, her beauty struck him afresh. He liked Maia - he always had done – it was a shame she had got caught up with the Penhallows. With her bohemian lifestyle, unconventional clothes, and wild, untamed, fiery red curls, she was enough to make any man's heart palpitate. It did not surprise him that Jago coveted her. If he was truthful, deep down, he found her fascinating as well.

A slap on the back made him jump, and William turned and smiled at his new brother-in-law, Ben Pearson.

'Welcome back, Will, and congratulations on your excellent results at university. When did you get home?'

'Last evening, and I am raring to get started on my new role on the estate. How are things with you and my sister, as if I need to ask?' He nudged him playfully.

'Utterly blissful,' Ben said dreamily. 'Em's teaching me to drive so I can get myself to the saddlery workshop, and Em can get on with writing her novels. I still can't walk very far yet, you see.' He tapped his legs.

'Are your legs still giving you pain?'

'They are, even though it has been almost a year since I was injured.' He shook his head as though to rid himself of the demons of that time. 'Still, I never thought in those terrible dark days that followed that I would ever walk again, let alone be married to the most beautiful woman in the world.'

William cleared his throat. 'Perhaps Emma might be the second most beautiful woman,' he mused and glanced over to where Maia was chatting with one of the other Arts and Crafts Association members.

'Ah, I see the gorgeous Maia still has you in raptures.'

William gave a wry smile. 'She enthrals me, Ben. I have thought a lot about her since she became a widow.'

'As a potential wife?'

'Well, she does have aristocratic blood in her veins!' He gave a slightly crooked smile. 'And we have always got along well with each other.'

'I feel a *but* coming on.'

'You're right, there is a *but*. I'm not sure my parents would accept a widow as the next Countess de Bochym, because that's what she would eventually become if she married me.'

'Oh, I don't know.' Ben beamed. 'Stranger things have happened. Look at me and your sister, the fair Lady Emma. Who would have thought that I, a lowly saddler, would have ever had a chance to be her husband? Yet here I am, living on this grand estate, eating with the Earl and Countess de Bochym, and married to - and I have to overrule you on this - *the* most beautiful woman in the world.'

'Well, I am happy for you, my friend. Alas, I must choose a wife from the cream of society.' He sighed and glanced wistfully back at Maia. 'But, my goodness, I do not think any woman will evoke the same feelings in me as Maia does - she moves me! I think I will invite Maia to a few social soirees. Let society see her with me, then we will see how the land lies.'

'Ah, well, Maia has a new farmhand, you know?'

'Yes, she was just telling me. What has that to do with anything?'

'Well.' Ben bit down on his bottom lip. 'He is a handsome chap. I've met him a couple of times. Strangely enough, he looks a bit like you.' He arched an eyebrow. 'And David Trevorrow has seen them out together - he said they made a nice couple.'

'Oh!' William's shoulders slumped. 'Well, thank you for bursting my bubble, Ben. I can't pursue Maia, but my doppelganger can!'

'Sorry, my friend, but I thought I had better warn you.'

17
Kitty 1881 – 1882

Over the next few months, Kitty and Freddy managed to get away on three more occasions. He took her to Kynance Cove, and she was astounded at the rock formations, caves, and clear turquoise sea. The day was sunny, but a chill wind kept most people away, so they had the cove all to themselves. They had taken a picnic that Sissy had secretly made up for them without Mrs Bligh knowing - nothing grand, cheese and pickle sandwiches, and a couple of apples. So, they sat on the golden sands, wrapped up warm, and even had a paddle in the sea! On another day out, he took her to Lizard Point, the most southerly point in Britain, where, to Kitty's joy, she saw seals bobbing up and down. At first, she thought they were people; they looked so lifelike. One seal had even climbed into a fishing boat. Hoots of laughter came from the other fishermen as they watched the boat owner try to shoo it out of his vessel. The seal would not budge and kept snapping at the fisherman - until another fisherman came alongside and tempted it out by tossing a couple of mackerel near the side of the boat!

There was no need to take a picnic at the most southerly point because Freddy had heard that there was a tiny café there, and they enjoyed a much fresher piece of cake than the one at Poldhu.

'Mr Bolitho tells me that a lady called Betty Trerise has taken over the teashop at Poldhu. It is now called the Poldhu Tea Room. He also said he had heard that she had put a couple of tables and chairs on the veranda, and her cakes were delicious. So, we might go back there next time.'

'I'd like that, Freddy, but you shouldn't be spending all your money on me.'

'I've no one else to spend it on. I send half of my wage home to Ma, but she insists I keep the other half.'

'Yes, but, Freddy, I don't mind paying my way sometimes. Especially as I get paid now!'

Freddy frowned. 'Did you not get paid before?'

'Not since October. Mrs Bligh said I had ruined an expensive rug when I spilled a bowl of water on it. She docked my wage for nine months until Sissy found out that I was not getting paid for my work. Sissy went to inspect the rug, found that it hadn't been damaged, and demanded that Mrs Bligh pay me and backdate all she had held back.'

'Good for Sissy! Oh, but that flipping woman! Mr Bolitho hates her, you know?' Freddy fumed.

'Everyone hates her - except Mr Carrington and Mr Lanfear. They are all as thick as thieves.'

Quite unexpectedly, Freddy put his arm around Kitty. 'I'm sorry you have to put up with all that unpleasantness. It won't always be like that, you know. One day, you will have your own kitchen to run and won't have to take orders from anyone.'

'I don't mind taking orders from Sissy, but it would be nice to think I wouldn't have to dodge Mrs Bligh's wrath.'

'One day, you won't have to, Kitty.' Freddy squeezed her hand affectionately.

*

It was after their return visit to Poldhu to sample Mrs Trerise's tearoom that Freddy first declared his love for Kitty. They had had a wonderful day paddling in the surf, even though it was October, before taking the wagon home, sitting apart as they always did for decency. When they got off and walked down Chypons Road, they stopped at the Bochym tradesmen's gate. There, Freddy reached into the bushes to retrieve a red rose he had cut earlier and wrapped in a wet cotton cloth.

'I hid it in the bush to give it to you on our return. I thought you could put it in a glass by your bed tonight.'

Kitty stood back and shook her head. 'I can't take a rose indoors, Freddy. Mrs Bligh will skin me alive. She'll think that I've picked it myself from the garden.'

Freddy looked downcast. 'Sorry, I never thought about that! I'll put it in a bottle in the greenhouse for you so that when you pass to collect the eggs, you can see it and know it is for you.'

Kitty tipped her head. 'Why are you giving me a red rose, Freddy Hubbard?'

'Why do you think?'

'Roses are for love, are they not?'

'Yes, they are, Kitty.' His eyes twinkled.

A half smile formed on Kitty's face, and Freddy was just about to lean in for a kiss when the clock in the clock tower chimed four, and Kitty realised she was late to help with dinner.

'Gracious, but I'll have to go. Mrs Bligh was in a foul mood earlier.' She turned to leave Freddy.

'We have unfinished business, my lovely Kitty,' he shouted after her.

Kitty smiled to herself as she skipped down the drive.

*

A few weeks later, Kitty and Sissy were standing at the kitchen door, arms folded, looking upwards at the sky, which had first turned pink and then into a blanket of orange and red. There was going to be a rare sunset, by the look of it. Unfortunately, they couldn't see much because the rooftops and the clock tower obscured their view.

There was a lull in their kitchen duties, so they had a few minutes to take in the spectacle. Suddenly, Kitty spotted Freddy standing at the end of the kitchen courtyard. Was he beckoning her?

'I think Freddy wants you,' Sissy whispered, and then glanced around to see if anyone was in the kitchen. 'There's nobody about, so be swift and see what he wants.'

Stealthily, Kitty followed where Freddy was leading, which was to the door of the clock tower. The building stood next to the granite gates to the stable courtyard. Freddy beckoned her to join him quickly.

'Freddy Hubbard, you will get me dismissed,' she giggled.

'Hush! Do you think you can climb a ladder?'

'Yes.'

'Follow me then.' He slipped through the door of the clock tower and closed it after them.

'What are we doing?'

'Climbing to the top. Mr Bolitho has given me the job of winding the clock, so I am allowed to be here.'

Kitty's eyes widened. 'Well, I'm not!'

'It's all right.' He placed his hand on her shoulder. 'Nobody will know. Come on, up you go.'

Kitty walked to the bottom of the ladder and looked up with a gasp.

'What's wrong?'

'You asked me if I could climb a ladder. There are at least three up there.'

'It's all right. I'll follow you so you don't slip. Up you go, quick before we miss it.'

'Miss what?'

'Hurry.'

Kitty turned and began to climb, slowing considerably by the time she reached the bottom of the last ladder.

'I'm pooped, Freddy,' she said, dabbing her forehead with her handkerchief.

'Just climb one more, quickly.'

Her legs felt leaden, but once she reached the top and lifted the trap door, she looked up in awe at the fabulous evening sky.

'Step onto the roof. It's quite safe,' Freddy called up from behind her.

No sooner than she had stepped up, she gasped again. She could see for miles.

Freddy was by her side in an instant. 'Isn't it wonderful? I thought it was the perfect place to watch the sunset with the girl I love.'

Kitty turned to face him, her eyes glistening with happiness. The sunset was forgotten for a moment. 'Oh, Freddy. I love you too.'

'Good. So, may I kiss you now?'

She nodded and closed her eyes. His kiss was soft and warm, and Kitty could not help but smile while his lips were on hers. When they parted, he was also smiling, and he reached for her hand before they turned to watch the remains of the day together.

*

Throughout the winter, Kitty and Freddy had little time to themselves. The family entertained almost every weekend up to Christmas and well into the New Year. Sissy and Kitty never seemed to stop cooking. Kitty only managed to snatch the odd half hour off to meet Freddy in the hothouse, where he was nurturing the tender plants ready to plant in the flower borders later in the spring.

They had secretly met there one morning when they both turned on hearing a giggle outside. They turned and saw Hilda, one of the chambermaids, take the hand of the lad who delivered the meat from the Helston butcher and disappear around the back of the stables with him.

Freddy shook his head. 'That one has a right reputation. Mr Bolitho said she was around the back of the other greenhouse with the milk churn delivery lad last week – the girl has no morals, meeting lads like that.'

Kitty's brow furrowed. 'I'm here meeting you,' she said cautiously.

'That's different. We love each other, and we only ever steal a kiss. It isn't right to do more until we're married. According to Mr Bolitho, Hilda was doing more than just kissing. She's a damn fool – no decent man will want her now that she is ruined!'

*

It was Valentine's Day. The family had been in London for a month but were due back later that day. The house was spick and span, ready for their return, and many of the servants were enjoying the last few hours of time off before the household became a hive of activity again.

Sissy and Kitty had prepped everything needed for all the meals that day, and Kitty had wrapped up warm to take a walk with Freddy, albeit secretly, while Sissy put her feet up by the stove.

It was about two hours later that Kitty breezed into the kitchen in a heightened state of excitement, and as there was no one else about in the kitchen, she danced up to Sissy and gave her a big hug.

'Well. What's all this then? It looks like someone's happy.'

'Oh, Sissy. The most wonderful thing has happened.' Kitty could hardly contain her excitement. 'Freddy has proposed to me today.'

'Proposed, has he?'

'We're to wait until I'm sixteen in April, and then we will have the banns read. He gave me this as an engagement present.' She showed Sissy a four-leaf clover set in copal resin.

'Oh, how pretty, Kitty.'

'Freddy said it had been in his family for years and is a good luck charm.'

'I'm so happy for you, Kitty. You belong together, but I will miss you terribly. You know you cannot carry on working once you are married. What on earth am I going to do without my assistant?'

Kitty grimaced. 'I don't want to leave you either, but I suppose June will move up to my position then.'

'Aye, if I can prise her away from her beloved chamber pots.' She grinned. 'Whoever takes the job will not be able to fill your shoes - and that's a fact! So, where will you live?'

'Well, that is what has prompted Freddy to ask me. Mr Bolitho is retiring when Freddy turns eighteen next month; his lumbago is stopping him from doing heavy work now. Mr Bolitho is going to Falmouth to be near his grown-up children but will live with his widowed sister, so the gardener's cottage will become vacant. Her Ladyship has asked Freddy if he will take over the role as head gardener – in fact, the only gardener because they will not take on another lad.'

'He's a capable lad. Freddy will fare well alone, I'm sure.'

'Oh, Sissy, I am so happy I could burst.' She did another little dance.

Sissy laughed. 'I'm very happy for you too, Kitty. Now, shall we have a celebratory cup of tea? There is still some fruit cake left over from Christmas that I've hidden from Mrs Bligh in the larder, so bring some of that too.'

*

Standing in the corridor outside the kitchen, Joyce had heard the conversation. She scowled angrily. That little bitch, Kitty, had all the luck. First, she got to be Cook's assistant, and now she was getting married to the best-looking lad on the estate. Well, she would see about that! If Kitty had been meeting Freddy secretly, that would mean instant dismissal once her aunt found out, and she would find out, because Joyce would tell her! Joyce gifted herself with a smile. Kitty would be banished and, therefore, never be able to live on the estate with Freddy. She tiptoed across to the housekeeper's room and was just about to tap on the door when she heard a conversation between her aunt and Albert Lanfear, the Earl's valet. Glancing around to make sure no one was about; she pressed her ear closer to listen.

*

Mrs Bligh rolled her eyes as Albert Lanfear informed her that another maid was in the family way.

'Another one! I have only just got rid of Hilda for getting with child by one of the delivery drivers.'

'Well, this one wants money to get rid of it. She is threatening to tell everyone who has put that babe there.'

'Is she now!' Mrs Bligh folded her arms. 'Well, she will get nothing from the household purse.'

Lanfear shrugged. 'That's what I told her.'

'You'd better send her to me immediately. I'll send her packing with a warning before she starts bleating to the other maids.'

'Who shall we use next? His Lordship is back today, and will expect someone in his bedchamber tonight?'

'My God! But that man has an insatiable appetite for young girls.'

'Yes, and he likes them pretty, remember!' Albert Lanfear smirked.

'He'll get what he is given! Now, I'll have to request another girl from the workhouse. I'm having to recruit a new maid every few months now!'

Lanfear picked his teeth with his fingernail. 'I'm sure the workhouse has loads of young girls they need rid of.'

Mrs Bligh pursed her lips. 'And most of them end up back there in disgrace. Do you think His Lordship can ease off for a while? If I recruit another maid, I need to get some use out of her after training her before she ruins herself.'

'I'm afraid not. His Lordship likes to exercise his needs every night. So, you'd better think of someone sharpish.'

*

Joyce stepped back from the housekeeper's door when she realised Mr Lanfear was coming out. She scuttled back into the shadows. A few minutes later, he returned, dragging the chambermaid, Eileen Dawson, by the scruff of her dress into the housekeeper's room. Joyce waited, and a couple of minutes later, Eileen emerged from the housekeeper's room in deep distress, followed by Mrs Bligh, who escorted her upstairs to pack. Within five minutes, Mrs Bligh marched Eileen through the laundry to the backyard.

'If you breathe a single lie about how you have ruined yourself or if you try to bring this household into disrepute, you will regret it *bitterly*. I will personally make sure everyone knows what kind of girl you are. Now get off this land.'

Mrs Bligh shoved Eileen hard, making her fall to her knees in the dirt. She waited a moment until Eileen scurried away sobbing, before turning to walk briskly back through the laundry room, brushing her hands as though Eileen had soiled her.

'Can I have a word, Aunty Joan?' Joyce asked.

'Make it quick.'

'Can we go into the housekeeper's room?'

Joan Bligh sighed heavily. 'If we must, but I am very busy.'

Ten minutes later, Joan Bligh sought out Albert Lanfear.

*

It was ten thirty that night when Kitty lay in bed, her book discarded, too excited to read. She truly believed nothing could take the smile off her face and could hardly contain her excitement at her forthcoming marriage. She was about to extinguish the light when her door opened, and Mrs Bligh entered.

'You're needed,' she said briskly. 'Come quickly.'

'What is it?' Kitty asked.

'Be quiet, or you'll wake the others.'

'Let me just get dressed.'

'No. Follow me now. It's urgent.'

Thinking Sissy needed her in the kitchen for something, or perhaps a late visitor had arrived who needed a spot of supper, Kitty grabbed her shawl and followed Mrs Bligh.

They descended the stairs from the attic until they came to the floor, where the family slept.

'Wait here, and *do not* move,' Bligh ordered.

Kitty watched as Mrs Bligh walked back upstairs to bed. Glancing down the gloomy corridor, Kitty pulled her shawl closer to ward off the February chill and waited anxiously.

A door opened somewhere along the corridor, and footsteps approached. From that moment on, Kitty's world changed forever.

18

On Tuesday afternoon, Maia steered her horse and cart down the long drive at Bochym as she drove Josh to his meeting with Mrs Blair.

'My goodness, what a place this is!' Josh said in wonderment.

'It is rather spectacular!'

'Have you ever been inside?' he asked.

'Yes. I have on several occasions. The Arts and Crafts Society sometimes has drinks parties there, but also as children, Alec and I played with the Dunstan children.'

'Gosh, lucky you. So, this was your playground?'

'Sometimes, yes.'

Maia steered the horse to the back of the manor, pulling up near Sissy Blair's cottage. At the cottage door, Maia knocked and waited.

When Sissy opened the door, she gasped and clasped her hand to her chest when she saw Josh. 'Oh, lordy me. You look, you look...' She glanced in the direction of Maia and changed tack. 'You look like Kitty.'

Josh smiled. 'Yes, it has often been said there is a likeness. I am very pleased to meet you, Mrs Blair. Thank you for giving up your time to speak to me.'

'It's my pleasure, my dear boy. Come in; the tea is brewing.'

They stepped into the cottage, which was so cosy that it seemed to wrap its arms around them.

'Take a seat. I've made a cake for us.'

'Mrs Blair makes the best cakes in the district,' Maia remarked. 'I'll wager they even surpass anything Ellie Blackthorn at the Poldhu Tea Room makes, and that is saying something, but don't tell Ellie I said that!'

Sissy smiled at the compliment.

Josh gratefully took a slice of Victoria Sandwich, and Sissy observed him with interest as he took a bite.

'Goodness, this is delicious, Mrs Blair. My grandma said you were a brilliant cook and baker.'

Sissy smiled wistfully. 'She wasn't too bad herself – even if I did train her. Kitty was my right-hand girl. She was quick to learn and could do almost anything in the kitchen.'

'Ah, that's nice to know. My grandma spoke fondly of you. I think she looked on you as a mother figure.'

Sissy's eyes watered slightly. 'I was only five years older, but I admit, I did mother her. Oh, Mr Harding, I cannot tell you how happy I was to hear that Kitty is still alive. I have always wondered how she fared.'

Josh cleared his throat. 'She always said she regretted not writing to you. She wanted to, but for some reason, Grandpa, although a wonderful man, forbade her to write. She would never say why.'

Sissy nodded knowingly.

'Grandma told me that she would be forever grateful for what you did for her. I understand you gave her two pounds, a basket of food, and arranged for someone to take her to a boarding house where she could stay until she decided what to do. That was an awful lot of money, Mrs Blair.'

Sissy sighed. 'I needed to give her the best chance of surviving out there after losing her job.'

'Was that the last you heard of her?' Josh enquired.

'No. The boarding house belonged to my sister, so I knew she was safe. She worked there for a while, and then my sister told me that Kitty met someone who was staying at the boarding house, and that was the last we both heard of her.'

'That was probably Grandpa. Grandma said they met in Falmouth.'

'He must be a remarkable man, your grandpa,' Sissy said with a smile.

'He was, in many ways. Grandma always said she would have liked to have come back to see you and pay you back, but again, Grandpa would not let her.'

'I understand why. I know that Kitty told the man she met – the man we now know was your grandpa - the circumstances of her dismissal, so I can understand his reluctance to let her keep in touch with anyone at Bochym.'

'Can you? So, why was she dismissed, Mrs Blair?'

'It's not my secret to tell. If Kitty has never told you, then it is not for me to divulge.'

'I see. I would be very grateful, though, if I could pay back the money that she owed you.'

'Goodness, no.' She shook her head. 'I won't hear of it. I gave it to Kitty; I did not loan it to her.'

'Well, thank you from the bottom of my heart.' Josh placed his hand on his chest. 'Thank you for being so kind to her.'

There was a knock at the door, and before Sissy could get to it, it opened.

'Sissy. It's only me, Freddy. Can I have your list of vegetables you want me to dig up for dinner?' He glanced at Josh and touched his cap. 'Goodness, sorry, my lord...' He stopped short and glanced between Josh and Sissy, gave an embarrassed laugh, and shook his head, realising his mistake. 'Goodness, I thought for a moment...'

'I just have a couple of guests for tea, Freddy,' Sissy interjected. 'Maia has brought her new farmhand, Mr Harding, to meet me. He is the grandson of an old friend of mine. Mr Harding, this is Freddy Hubbard, the head gardener at Bochym.'

Josh stood up to greet him.

'Oh, I see.' Freddy wiped his hands down his jacket and shook hands with Josh. 'My, but you look familiar. I honestly thought you were...' He laughed. 'No matter. I'll be off then. Nice to meet you. Sorry to disturb you all.' He touched his cap.

When Sissy showed him to the door, he whispered to her, 'Christ, but he is the image of Lord William! I very nearly made a fool of myself in there. And he is related to a friend of yours, is he?'

'He is, yes.'

'Anyone I know?'

'Erm, I'll speak with you later, Freddy.' She ushered him out. 'I need to get back to my guests.'

'Of course. Sorry, Sissy. I'll catch up with you later.'

*

While Sissy was seeing Freddy out, Josh turned to Maia, his expression giving way to realisation. 'That gardener called me my lord.'

Maia hummed in her throat noncommittally.

'Both you and your friend Ellie said I reminded you of someone. Do I look like the lord of this manor?'

Maia nodded cautiously. 'A little – you have startling blue eyes - similar to the Dunstan men.'

'Oh!' he said quietly.

*

Freddy set about his business for the afternoon, gathering the produce that Sissy had asked him for. She would be back in the kitchen by five, to finish preparing the dinner for the family, but Vicky, the cook's assistant, would need the produce to prepare everything.

Even after all these years – forty one to be exact - Freddy always hoped that one day he would walk into the kitchen at Bochym and find his darling Kitty working there again.

Freddy had never got over her loss. He often thought that if she had died, he would have had some closure and been able to forge a new life – maybe even fall in love again and marry. But Kitty's disappearance weighed heavy on his mind. Always in the back of his mind, he thought that she was somewhere out there and would come back or get in touch. He wanted so much for her to explain why she needed to leave him, and then maybe they could have worked something out and had a chance to be together as planned. He could not understand her disappearance or the fact that Sissy did not know where she had gone, especially as they had been so close. At first, he feared that Kitty had been murdered on the road the night she left, or worse, she had been kidnapped and taken abroad – a pretty girl like that – it could have happened - he had read about such things in the newspaper. All he knew was that wherever she was, something or someone was stopping her from contacting him. The worst scenario popped into his head occasionally: that Kitty had been false with him, had strung him along, and had found someone she liked better. He even briefly wondered if the *serious misdemeanour* she had allegedly committed and been dismissed for – as the housekeeper, at the time, had accused her of – was something to do with Kitty being caught with another man. Had they run off together in the night? He shook that thought from his head, not wanting to entertain wicked thoughts of Kitty. It was impossible for Kitty to have been seeing another man, because in his heart of hearts, he knew she had loved him as much as he had loved her. No, he was sure there had to be a good reason for her leaving him.

Vicky must have seen Freddy walking across the kitchen courtyard because she had opened the door to let him in.

'Cook's order for you to start on, Vicky.' Freddy smiled.

'Thank you, Mr Hubbard. Mrs Blair will be back at five, so I had better get cracking. She has a visitor today.'

'Yes, I called on her earlier.' He laughed. 'I almost mistook her visitor for Lord William; he had the same blue eyes.'

'I think he is a relative of a good friend who used to work with Mrs Blair many years ago.'

Freddy's breath caught short. 'Did Mrs Blair say who this friend was?'

'No,' Vicky said, pulling the veg out of the box so that Freddy could take it away with him.

Freddy bade goodbye to Vicky and returned to the potting shed to deposit the box, a curl of unease manifesting in the pit of his stomach. Freddy had known Sissy for a long, long time. She had had many kitchen assistants, and though she always got along well with them, it was only Kitty she had been really close to. Sitting on an upturned bucket, he rubbed the roughness of hours-old bristles on his chin in thought. Deep down, he knew - he just knew -that man was somehow related to his darling Kitty.

Trying to focus on a spider grabbing a fly from the tangle of its web to stop his mind from working overtime, Freddy could not help but wonder why Mr Harding looked like a Dunstan. He suddenly felt very sick in the pit of his stomach.

*

Maia and Josh were saying their farewells to Sissy when a loud knock came at the door.

'Lordy me, who on earth is trying to break down my door?' Sissy patted her heart.

Freddy stood breathlessly on her doorstep - his face florid. 'Sissy, sorry to bother you again, but...' He looked over her shoulder. 'Is your visitor still here?'

Sissy saw the look on his face and felt suddenly anxious. 'Yes, Freddy, he is.'

'Is he...?' He swallowed hard. 'Is he... Kitty's relation?'

Josh heard his grandma's name and stepped forward with a smile. 'Yes, I am. I'm Kitty's grandson.'

Sissy took a great intake of breath as Freddy visibly staggered. She quickly reached out to grasp his sleeve.

'You... are Kitty's grandson!' Freddy gasped.

Josh nodded.

Freddy looked stricken and paled significantly. 'Excuse me, I erm...' He turned to leave. 'Sorry, excuse me.'

Josh watched Freddy's swift retreat and glanced at Sissy questioningly.

'Oh, dear!' Sissy twisted her mouth. 'Kitty was Freddy's sweetheart. She was going to marry him before being dismissed.'

'Oh, dear, I see.' Josh plunged his hands into his trouser pockets.

'Did Kitty never mention him?'

'No. But I could never understand why Grandma had an affinity for this place when something clearly upsetting had happened here.' Josh frowned. 'It seemed my presence upset Mr Hubbard.'

Sissy nodded, trying to think on her feet for a reason. 'I suppose, in the back of his mind, Freddy always wondered if Kitty had another sweetheart and had run away with him. He probably thinks your grandpa was the one who enticed her away,' she said unconvincingly.

'So, Mr Hubbard is unaware of the reason behind Grandma's dismissal or why she went away?'

'I'm afraid so.'

Josh raised his eyebrows. 'You never told him?'

'As I said. It's not my secret to tell, and it would have caused repercussions.'

'Then I need to speak to Mr Hubbard and put some of the story straight.'

Realising that Freddy would be putting two and two together now that he had seen Josh and likened him to a Dunstan, Sissy knew what she must do now. 'No, Josh. It is I who should put the story straight. I have kept Freddy in the dark too long, and rightly or wrongly, I think you need to know Kitty's secret too now.'

*

When Freddy opened his cottage door to them, his hair was stood on end, as though he had raked his fingers through it.'

'Freddy, may we come in?' Sissy asked.

'Why, to rake over old coals – to dredge up the hurt again? Why, Sissy? Why do you want me to meet this man, who should have been *my* grandson? His eyes watered, and he quickly looked away to wipe the tears with his handkerchief.

'I need to speak to you, Freddy; I need to tell you something.'

Eventually, Freddy recovered himself, sighed, and looked up at Josh.

'Kitty's grandson. Eh?' His eyes swept over Josh. 'You do sort of look like her.'

'Yes, people have said that.' Josh cut a smile to Sissy.

'Has she been happy?' He said spikily. 'I mean, did she have a good life after she left here?'

'I believe it was hard for her initially, but Grandpa looked after her well.'

Freddy lowered his eyes. 'Oh, I see! So, she did leave me for someone else?' He looked to Sissy for confirmation.

'No, Freddy, she did not!' Sissy answered softly.

'Well, she definitely left me!'

'She had to, Freddy.'

Freddy shook his head, laughed bitterly, and addressed Josh. 'We were going to be married just as soon as she was sixteen.' His face creased with the pain of long-suppressed hurt. 'But then, phut! She'd gone, vanished into the night without a word or letter, just gone. Left me here with my broken heart.' He looked up at Josh apologetically for speaking ill of his grandma. 'Why did she leave me then?' he asked, fearing that he knew the answer.

'Freddy, sit down,' Sissy said. 'I think it is time I told you what happened.'

19
Kitty 1882

It was only by chance that Mr Bolitho entered the barn early that morning, intent on gathering some straw for his pineapple beds, when he stumbled upon Kitty cowering in the corner in great distress.

'Oh, good, God, Kitty!' He rushed up to her. 'What on earth has happened? Look at the terrible state you are in! Goodness me, what will Freddy say when he sees you?'

Panic clouded Kitty's tear-stained, bruised face. 'No, no, no, Mr Bolitho. Please do not tell Freddy.'

'But, Kitty,' he gasped.

'Can you get Sissy to come to me? But please do not tell another soul that I am here. I've been dismissed; I should not be here.'

'Dismissed!' He shook his head in astonishment. 'Whatever for?'

'Please, Mr Bolitho. I need Sissy to come to me.'

John Bolitho could hardly catch his breath, so upset with her predicament. 'Of course, I'll go and get her.' He ran to the kitchen and grabbed Sissy by the arm. 'You must come, quick!' he whispered, refusing to take no for an answer.

'Wherever are we going, John?' Sissy picked up her skirts so she could run after him. 'I do not have time for this. I have the servant's breakfast to make, and Mrs Bligh just informed me that Kitty has gone! She claims that she went last night. Gone where? I asked her, but she refused to say. I cannot understand it.'

Mr Bolitho stopped at the barn, glanced around him to see if the coast was clear, and lifted the wooden latch.

'What are we doing here, for goodness' sake?' Sissy demanded.

Inside, John Bolitho nodded to Kitty in the corner.

Sissy's mouth dropped. 'Oh, lordy me,' she gasped as she fell to her knees to cup Kitty's battered face with her hands. 'What happened to your lovely face? Who has done this?'

'Oh, Sissy.' Great, fat tears trickled down her face, wetting Sissy's hands. 'I've been dismissed. Mrs Bligh threw me out last night. I have no wages or references, and none of my clothes,' she sobbed broken-heartedly.

Sissy frowned. 'Mrs Bligh told me you had left but said nothing about a dismissal. Why have you been dismissed?'

Kitty glanced mournfully over to Mr Bolitho. 'I cannot say what happened in front of Mr Bolitho.'

Taking his cue, John said, 'Sissy, I will be outside if you need anything.'

'Thank you, John.'

'Please don't say a word to Freddy, Mr Bolitho,' Kitty pleaded again.

John looked uncertain.

'Please, I beg you.'

He nodded reluctantly. 'You have my word, Kitty.'

As soon as he had gone, Sissy turned back to Kitty. 'Now, tell me everything that has happened.'

Tears of humiliation and anger started to stream down her face.

'Come on now, tell me,' Sissy said, handing her a clean handkerchief.

Furiously wiping her eyes, Kitty started her story:

'Last night, Mrs Bligh came to my bedroom and said I was needed urgently. So urgently, she would not let me get dressed. I thought you needed me, Sissy, to help make supper for a late visitor or something.' Kitty's lip trembled, and a sob caught in her throat.

Sissy squeezed her hand for her to continue.

'We went to the first-floor landing, and Mrs Bligh told me to wait and not to move, and then she went back to bed. I was shivering in that gloomy corridor, and I pulled my dressing gown closer to ward off the chill while I waited. A door opened along the corridor, and footsteps approached.'

Her face crumpled again as more hot tears ran down her face, so Sissy hugged her. 'Take your time, Kitty. I need to know what happened.'

'When Albert Lanfear approached, I stepped back into the shadows, hoping he would not see me, but...' she dropped her head, 'but he walked right up to me – he was clearly expecting me to be there.'

Sissy felt her breath catch.

'Mr Lanfear hissed at me that I was to follow him and told me not to make a sound. Oh, Sissy, my heart was hammering. I didn't know what was going on. We stopped outside His Lordship's bedroom, where Mr Lanfear knocked, grabbed me by the arm, and dragged me in.'

Kitty stopped talking and baulked as though she would be sick, as the memory of that unpleasant smell of cigars, whisky, and sweat in the room flooded back.

'Carry on, Kitty,' Sissy urged, fearing the worst now.

Kitty's mouth turned down, and her lip trembled. 'There was a movement behind the room divider and the sound of someone relieving themselves. I turned to Mr Lanfear to ask why I was there. He told me to shut up. The sound of breaking wind preceded His Lordship emerging from the divider. He was wearing a dressing gown that was flapping open, and...' Kitty shuddered alarmingly, 'little else.'

'Oh, dear God!' Sissy hugged Kitty tighter, knowing and fearing what was coming next.

'His Lordship walked towards me and ran his eyes over me. His stare made me tremble like a leaf. I knew something terrible was about to happen to me, so I began to move back towards the door to escape, but Mr Lanfear grabbed me. His Lordship asked if I was clean, and Mr Lanfear answered, "Aye, and as pure as driven snow." Then His Lordship said...he said...,' a sob caught in her throat '...he said, "Well then, my beauty, let me see you in the flesh. Take off your clothes." I grabbed hold of my shawl and held it tight to my body. Then His Lordship told

Mr Lanfear to strip me. I tried to fight Mr Lanfear's hands off, so he smacked me across the face to stop me from resisting. The smack stunned me, and Mr Lanfear hissed that I was to do whatever His Lordship said, as he was the one who paid my wages. Then he grabbed my shawl and wrenched it off my shoulders so hard that I staggered backwards. His Lordship yelled, "Come on, come on, Lanfear. Strip her. I haven't got all night." Mr Lanfear grabbed me again, and I started to cry and told them I was to be married! But Mr Lanfear grabbed my nightgown and ripped it off, leaving me completely bare in front of both of them. I started to scream for my life, but Mr Lanfear gave me such a blow to the side of my head that he silenced me, and then my knees gave way. I scrambled towards the window wall, crouching by the curtains, trying to cover my body with them. I knew what was to come when Mr Lanfear grabbed me by my hair and dragged me towards the bed. I curled myself into a tight ball, but he kicked me on the buttocks so that my legs would unfold. He grabbed me around the waist, picked me up, and threw me onto the bed. Oh, Sissy,' she sobbed, 'I tried - I really tried to scramble to the other side of the bed to get away, but Mr Lanfear caught me again by the hair and dragged me back. I screamed again, but this time, Mr Lanfear grabbed me by the throat, almost choking me until I stopped. He warned me that if he heard one more peep out of me, I would not live to see another day.'

Kitty paused and lifted her bloodshot eyes to Sissy. 'I wish he had killed me because I do not want to live another day with this shame.'

'Oh, my poor girl,' Sissy crooned as she pulled her back to her chest.

Kitty closed her eyes, enjoying the comfort of Sissy's arms as she gathered her strength to complete her story. 'His Lordship discarded his dressing gown and climbed onto the bed.' Kitty's lip curled in utter distaste, remembering those last few moments of innocence. 'His

Lordship told Lanfear to hold me down until he had "mounted me", as he did not mind me bucking when I was safely under him.' Kitty fell silent as she gathered herself to continue. 'Oh, Sissy. I thought my lovely, handsome Freddy would be the only man I would ever lay with. His Lordship was horribly fat and sweaty – he stank of brandy and cigarettes. I could feel my heart hammering in my chest. I knew he was going to ruin me, so I pleaded for him not to do it. I so wanted Freddy to come and rescue me, so I started to shout for Freddy over and over, for him to come and help me, but Lanfear put his hand to my mouth to stifle my cries. I remember hearing His Lordship say, "Who the hell is Freddy?" When Mr Lanfear told him he was the gardener's apprentice, His Lordship laughed and said, "At least he won't have the trouble of breaking you in then." Then he pushed my legs apart, and all I could feel was a searing pain as he tore through me.'

'Oh, Kitty, Kitty, my love.' Sissy squeezed her tighter and cried with her.

'The pain was terrible, Sissy. I knew he had ruined me, but I managed to free one of my hands that Mr Lanfear was holding down, and I scratched His Lordship several times down his face. I drew blood, and I am glad of it! He punched me in the face and burst my nose to stop me from scratching him, but I was determined to fight him, so when he had finished with me, I kicked him hard between his legs. I kicked him *real* hard, Sissy, because he squealed like a stuck pig. I think Mr Lanfear must have beaten me senseless then because I woke up on my bedroom floor, naked, cold, and bleeding, with Mrs Bligh standing over me. She threw my coat at me and ordered me to get up and leave the manor immediately. She said I was an absolute disgrace. I could barely walk, but Mrs Bligh forced me down the stairs and out of the laundry room door. She threw a pair of boots at me and then slammed the door on me. I wanted to come to you, Sissy, but I couldn't walk far because of the pain. Everything hurt so much, and it still does. I managed to crawl to the barn, hoping that you would come to collect the eggs on the way to work and find me. You don't think Mr Bolitho will tell Freddy, do you?'

Sissy sat back. 'Freddy will have to know.'

'No!' She cried, her eyes wide and tearful.

'You will need his help. You could go somewhere far away and start again.'

'No, Sissy. Freddy will not want me now!'

'He will not spurn you for this. It wasn't your fault.'

'I know how he feels about ruined women. This is something we cannot overcome. Do you remember what Freddy said about Hilda before she fell pregnant? He said, "She's a damn fool - no decent man will want her now that she is ruined!"'

Sissy vigorously shook her head. 'Hilda was a very different kettle of fish - she was promiscuous and got what she deserved. You have been violated, and you did not consent to it. Freddy loves you dearly. He will understand!'

'No, I say,' Kitty shrieked. 'Freddy will take his revenge on His Lordship and most probably kill him. Then Freddy will hang. I cannot have that on my conscience.'

'But Kitty....'

'No, Sissy, I insist. He must never know. I need to get away from here before he comes looking for me, but I need some clothes. I have nothing on under this coat.'

Reluctantly agreeing not to tell Freddy, understanding that there was no point in ruining two young lives, Sissy said, 'Give me some time. I will gather together everything you need.'

Kitty fell back into Sissy's arms. 'Thank you,' she sobbed.

*

Outside the barn, John Bolitho was standing guard. He shot Sissy a grave look when she came out to join him.

'What happened to her?'

'Oh, John. It's so horrible, I cannot share it with you. But do you think you can help me?'

'Just say the word.'

'We need to get Kitty away from here later this evening, but first, I need to get her some things, and she needs some warm water to bathe her injuries.'

'I'll fetch the water from the scullery,' he said. 'Then I'll fetch the cart later tonight and take Kitty where she needs to go.'

'Thank you, John. Will you be able to keep this from Freddy today?'

John nodded. 'He's got the day off to go and see his parents in Gunwalloe. He won't be back until first thing tomorrow. He was going to share his good news with his ma and pa,' he added sorrowfully.

'Oh, lordy me! What a mess this has all turned out to be!'

They walked forlornly back to the kitchen to be met by Mrs Bligh.

'Mr Bolitho, kindly burn these, will you?' She pushed a pile of Kitty's clothes into his arms as he made for the scullery. 'And you, Mrs Blair. I would have thought that with Morton going, you would have been rushed off your feet trying to make breakfast without her.'

Sissy clenched her teeth, feeling the rage growing inside her.

'Get out of my kitchen,' Sissy snapped. 'I do not want to speak with you.'

Mrs Bligh stood back, astonished. 'I beg your pardon.'

'You heard me. I said, Get out of my kitchen and keep out of my sight, or the next knife aimed at you will *not* miss.'

'You…you…,' Mrs Bligh stuttered, '..you cannot speak to me like that.'

'I just did!' Sissy spat the words at her and then narrowed her eyes. 'And we *both* know why.'

Mrs Bligh swallowed hard and backed out of the kitchen.

Sissy grabbed the vinegar and the first aid box and left the kitchen once again, telling June, the scullery maid, to abandon the chamber pots, wash her hands, and start slicing the bread for the servant's toast. 'I'll be back in ten minutes to make the porridge. If anyone asks, I have just popped out, but you don't know where.'

'Where *are* you going?' June said anxiously.

'If I told you, then you would know. Now get on with slicing, and don't slice the bread too thickly!'

*

John Bolitho had carried the pile of clothes and the bucket of warm water to the barn, arriving at the same time as Sissy.

'Thank you, John. I will see to Kitty now.'

'Very well. I'll call at the kitchen later to make arrangements.'

'Thank you.' She placed her hand on his sleeve gratefully.

Kitty scuttled into the corner of the barn like a startled fawn when Sissy opened the door.

'It's all right, Kitty. It's only me,' she said gently. 'I have your clothes...'

Kitty scrambled forward and started searching through the pile of clothes Sissy had brought, as if looking for something.

'What is it, Kitty? What do you need?'

Kitty found what she was looking for and started to cry. 'It's my locket and the lucky four-leaf clover Freddy gave me yesterday,' she sobbed. 'I thought I had lost them forever, but they are still here - in the pocket of my drawers, thank goodness! She rocked backwards and forwards, clutching her treasures to her heart.

Sissy's mouth twisted slightly - little luck that four-leaf clover had brought her—but she kept her counsel.

'Kitty,' she said gently, 'I have some warm water here too, so you can wash yourself. Once you have cleaned yourself up, soak vinegar in this muslin and insert it inside you. It will sting, but it will hopefully stop a babe from coming.'

'A babe!' Kitty gasped and looked wide-eyed at Sissy. 'Oh no!'

'Kitty, listen to me. Do as I say, and pray that it works. I'll have to go. Here, my lovely, I brought you a piece of jam and bread. Later, I'll bring a bag for your clothes and some more food, and then Mr Bolitho has offered to take you away from here.'

'But, Sissy, where shall I go?' she cried.

'I will make sure he takes you somewhere safe.' She took her into her arms again. 'My poor girl. I'm so sorry this has happened to you. I swear, I'll never forgive those who have done this to you.'

*

While back in the kitchen, Sissy's ears pricked at hearing the voices of Mr Carrington and Mrs Bligh speaking in the servant's dining area. Pulling her pans off the stove so that nothing would burn, she moved a little closer to listen in.

'Goodness, Mrs Bligh!' Mr Carrington said. 'You should have seen the state of His Lordship's face this morning - covered with scratches he is! Mr Lanfear says that a cat climbed through His Lordship's window and attacked him last night. Apparently, His Lordship had the devil of a job fighting it off. He banged and hurt himself in the process, so much so that His Lordship says it hurts to walk. He'll be staying in bed. He'll take all his meals in his room today. Would you tell Howarth to inform Her Ladyship when she attends her this morning, Mrs Bligh?'

Sissy stood at the threshold of the dining room, folded arms and stony-faced. 'His Lordship must have done something dreadful to have been attacked like that!' Sissy said accusingly.

Mr Carrington and Mrs Bligh turned to look at her, though Mrs Bligh quickly lowered her eyes ashamedly.

'Well, whatever he did to defend himself, the cat seems to have gotten the better of him, so we need to find the cat and kill it,' Mr Carrington said with a nod.

'It'll be the scullery cat!' Mrs Bligh said, knowing full well Prudy the cat was liked and looked after by Sissy and June.

'Don't be so ridiculous!' Sissy countered, staring Mrs Bligh down. 'Prudy is as soft as a kitten. She never comes into the manor and is far too fat to climb the wall to His Lordship's bedroom! So, I think we both know that it was *not* Prudy who did that to the Earl. Don't we, Mrs Bligh? So, you had better leave Prudy alone - unless you want to be overrun with rats again.'

Mrs Bligh shuddered at the thought, remembering when she found a rat nesting in her linen cupboard, having eaten through the wainscot in the housekeeper's room.

'Well, perhaps it was not the scullery cat then,' Mrs Bligh said, backing down.

'Goodness me, but the household is at sixes and sevens this morning. Is it true that Morton has run off?' Mr Carrington asked all of a fluster.

'Yes, it is,' Mrs Bligh said, smoothing down her dress with her hands. 'She left in the middle of the night.' Mrs Bligh dared not meet Sissy's accusing eyes.

'Well, someone will have to assist Cook in the kitchen. Who do you suggest, Mrs Blair?' Mr Carrington turned to Sissy.

'I don't care,' Sissy said cuttingly. 'I just want the plainest girl you can find.'

The butler frowned. 'Plain, you say! Why? Do plain girls make better cooks?'

'Let us just say they have a fighting chance of lasting longer in the role than the pretty ones,' she said tartly in Mrs Bligh's direction before storming back to the kitchen.

A maid was duly sent to help Sissy - Nora, a small, mousy-looking girl who flashed a gappy smile at her promotion to assistant cook.

'You will do nicely,' Sissy said shortly, and she set Nora to task with a large bowl of potatoes to peel.

20
Kitty 1882

Sissy was so angry that day that no one dared say a word to her for fear of getting their heads bitten off. The servant's meals were slammed down in front of them, making their cutlery bounce, but Sissy could not help but give a wry smile when she presented Joan Bligh and Albert Lanfear with their dinners. She had laced them with a small, equal amount of castor oil and senna extract and done a similar thing to His Lordship's meal as he was eating alone in his room. It was not enough for them to detect while eating, but enough to keep them on the pot with stomach cramps for several hours later that day. They would not be able to pin it on Sissy because everyone else in the household would be unaffected. They would think they had picked up a bug from somewhere. She pitied poor June, the scullery maid - her joy of scrubbing chamber pots may wain by the end of today. But needs must. Sissy would never forgive any of them for what they did to poor Kitty.

*

Over the course of that day, Sissy managed to gather a basket of food for Kitty's journey. She had written a letter for Kitty to take to Effy, her sister, whose boarding house in Falmouth Sissy was sending her to, as she knew Effy would take Kitty in. John Bolitho had kindly offered to take Kitty there just as soon as darkness fell. Fortunately, or unfortunately, in Mrs Bligh's case, after several swift trips to the privy, the housekeeper had confined herself to her room with a bucket and an upset tummy, so at least she was out of the way and could not witness Sissy and John helping Kitty to her new life.

*

Sissy was about to finish in the kitchen that evening to go and prepare Kitty for her journey when Mr Carrington, the butler, rushed into the kitchen.

'Mrs Blair, have you, by any chance, seen Mr Lanfear this evening? His Lordship was ringing for him, and as I could not locate him, I had to go in his place. His Lordship appears to have an upset stomach now, on top of his injuries. I have had to send the maids up to change his bed!' he said with a short cough of disgust. 'I pity Joyce, the laundry maid today,' he added.

Suppressing a smile, Sissy thought of the smirk Joyce had worn all day - a bundle of foul-smelling sheets should wipe that off her face. Sissy did not doubt that that little madam had some hand in Kitty's downfall, and when she found out what it was, Joyce would be sorry.

'I really need to find Mr Lanfear,' the butler urged.

'I believe he is in the privy – he has been there for quite some time! Nobody has been able to use it because of him,' Sissy answered.

Mr Carrington swept past her, went through the scullery, and out to the privy yard. Moments later, he returned. 'Good lord, but Mr Lanfear appears to be quite unwell. He says it must be something he has eaten, and of course, Mrs Bligh has been ill all day with a similar affliction, and now His Lordship - perhaps it *is* something they ate,' he said accusingly.

Affronted, Sissy countered, 'Well, it's nothing I have cooked. You ate the same meal, Mr Carrington, as did the rest of the staff, and no one else is ill, are they?'

'Well, no.'

'Then I suspect whatever bug Mrs Bligh contracted, she has clearly passed it onto Mr Lanfear, who in turn passed it onto His Lordship! So, I would give them all a wide berth if I were you.'

'Oh, dear! I shall confine Mrs Bligh and Mr Lanfear to their rooms until they can control themselves.' He shook himself and cleared his throat, uncomfortable with this conversation. 'However, I shall have to see to His Lordship.' He grimaced.

'Well, good luck,' Sissy mused.

With Mrs Bligh and Mr Lanfear out of the way and Mr Carrington busy upstairs with His Lordship, Sissy gathered everything she needed to send poor Kitty on her way to a very different life.

*

In the barn, Sissy and Kitty shared a tearful farewell. They clung to each other as though their lives depended on it.

'Now, Kitty, hopefully, if you have done what I told you, there will be no baby.'

'Yes, I did, and it stung like heck.'

'Better to be safe than sorry. Keep doing it for a few days.'

'I will.' Her bottom lip trembled. 'Oh, Sissy, what will I do?'

Sissy hugged her again and let her cry on her shoulder. Presently, she said, 'When you are feeling better, you must find the courage to start again somewhere. I have a letter for you to give to my sister, Effy. She has a boarding house in Falmouth. She will look after you until you feel able to find work. Mr Bolitho, very kindly, will take you there in his cart. It is best that you don't write to me, Kitty. You know Mrs Bligh steams letters open if she gets to them first. I shall write to Effy, and she will find a way of letting me know how you have got on without mentioning your name.

Under the cover of darkness, John Bolitho helped Kitty onto his cart. She had with her a bag of clothes, a basket of food, and a flask of water, and Sissy had given her two pounds.

'I've written you a glowing reference, Kitty. I forged Bligh's signature, so you should be able to secure another position somewhere.'

Kitty reached out to Sissy, tears streaming down her face. 'I'm going to miss you so much.'

'And I will miss you too,' Sissy answered, her voice breaking with sadness.

'It is breaking my heart to leave you and Freddy. Oh, poor Freddy, whatever will he think when he finds I am gone?'

'Leave Freddy to me,' Sissy said, though she had no idea what she was going to say when he found out.

*

It was late when John Bolitho pulled up at the address Sissy had given him. The house was in darkness, but Sissy had told him to knock on the door, as her sister Effy was used to travellers arriving late.

The door opened, and a woman, who could have been Sissy's twin, peered out at the couple on her doorstep.

'Can I help?'

'Sissy Blair has sent us. She said you would help,' John explained.

'Oh, I see.' She stepped back into the hall and beckoned them in.

Kitty sniffed the strong smell of lavender polish in the air; it reminded her of her parents' house.

John put his hands on Kitty's shoulder. 'Give the lady the letter that Sissy wrote for you.'

*

Effy took the letter from Kitty's trembling hand. Now that they were under the hall light, Effy could see that Kitty was in a poor state.

'Come through to the parlour.' She gestured for Kitty to sit, which she did, but John remained standing as Effy read the letter.

My dearest, Effy.

I have a huge favour to ask of you, and knowing your kindness, I am sure you will help me. The young girl who gave you this letter is my good friend, Kitty Morton. We have worked together for a couple of years, but she has unfortunately fallen foul of 'you know who' – I have spoken about him before to you.

Effy's heart fell. She knew exactly what Sissy meant, having heard on many occasions about the terrible goings on at the manor and the shocking use of the maids by the Earl.

I beseech you to take her under your wing. Kitty is a practical girl and a good cook, and she will help you in the boarding house. You will see she has been terribly hurt after putting up a brave fight, and she has been used as well as abused. I pray no baby comes from this dreadful incident, but if it does, let me know, and I will enclose more money to care for her and the baby. I have enclosed enough money to cover her first two months of bed and board. Kitty has some money of her own, and hopefully she will be able to pay her way, either by working for you or, if you have nothing for her, you could perhaps help her find suitable employment as soon as she is well enough. I have written and enclosed a reference for Kitty, though I will get dismissed if Bligh finds out.

I implore you to let me know how she fares in the future. Remember not to mention her by name in any letter you send me, as her whereabouts are to be kept secret.

We shall have to arrange to meet one day soon, perhaps halfway between Helston and Falmouth. I long to see my big sister again.

Thank you again, Effy. I know I can rely on you.

Your loving sister, Sissy.

Effy Blair looked down at Kitty's bruised and battered face. The man who accompanied her stood stoically by her side, clearly not wanting to leave her until he knew she would be safe. Effy folded the letter and knelt at Kitty's feet to gather her into her arms to hug her.

'Come on, Kitty, love. Let me run you a nice hot bath and then settle you into bed.'

Kitty's eyes welled with tears as she turned to Mr Bolitho.

'Off you go with the kind lady, Kitty.'

Kitty stood and threw her arms around Mr Bolitho's neck, clearly not wanting to let go of her last link to Freddy.

'Thank you for everything, Mr Bolitho,' she sobbed gently.

'You're welcome, Kitty. You take care of yourself now. I promise I will take care of Freddy.'

Kitty's mouth quivered. 'Poor Freddy,' she wept. 'You won't tell him, will you?'

'I won't tell him, Kitty. I promise.'

*

By the time John Bolitho had deposited poor Kitty at the Falmouth boarding house and returned to Bochym, it was gone three in the morning. He had been upset by Kitty's constant gentle weeping on the journey to Falmouth, so much so that when he had fallen exhausted into his bed early that morning, he could not sleep at first for worrying about her. He had not been privy to what had happened to Kitty, but he had a good idea. He had heard of a few young girls leaving the manor after being dismissed at some ungodly hour, walking forlornly with a stomach swollen from an unwanted baby. He had heard about the Earl's wicked ways and his insatiable appetite for young girls. From Kitty's poor state, it did not take a genius to know what had happened to her, and it certainly had not been consensual. The poor girl had put up a brave fight if the terrible cuts and bruises on her face and arms were to go by. The fact that both he and Sissy had sworn to her that they would not tell Freddy about the distressed state they had found her in, only confirmed to John that she had been used and abused and was no longer a maiden.

*

After the emotional goodbye, Sissy had barely slept that night and had been on tenterhooks, dreading seeing Freddy that morning and having to tell him that Kitty had gone. Sissy very nearly jumped out of her skin when a knock came at the door as she was getting ready for work.

'Oh, lordy me, thank goodness it is you, John, and not Freddy,' Sissy said, holding her hand to her heart as she observed John's tired, unshaven appearance.

'Sorry, Sissy, I just wanted to come and tell you before Freddy comes back to work that we got to Falmouth safe and sound, and your sister was very kind to Kitty.' John reached over and put his hand on Sissy's shoulder. 'I know you haven't said anything to me, but if what I think has happened to the poor girl, and although it goes against the grain to lie to the lad, it is probably best that Freddy never knows the truth, I fear he will take his revenge.'

Sissy nodded. 'That is what Kitty feared. Thank you for understanding, John, and for all the help you gave us last evening.'

'It is the least I could do for the girl. I just feel so sorry for Freddy. To have love snatched away from him like that when they were planning to marry. I know how it feels to lose someone you love. I lost my dear wife, Ethel, twenty years ago and I have never got over it.'

Sissy sighed. 'I am dreading telling Freddy that Kitty has gone. God forgive me for lying to the lad.'

'It is for the best, Sissy, it really is.'

21

When Sissy finished that part of her story, silence ensued, other than the sound of the ticking clock. Freddy was sitting with his head in his hands. Everyone in the cottage watched Freddy as he began to tremble.

'No.' He shook his head and said tremulously. No, no! How could this have happened to my lovely Kitty?' He lifted his head to narrow his eyes at Sissy. 'And you! You knew all this time! You have watched me grieve all these years for my Kitty, and you never said a word!' He bared his teeth. 'Mr Bolitho too - I cannot believe it – I thought you and he were my friends, but you both lied to me!'

Sissy was stricken. 'I am so sorry, Freddy.'

Freddy shook his head, stood up, and pointed to the door. 'I would like you to go. *All* of you.'

Without question, everyone rose to leave.

Sissy put her hand on Freddy's shoulder. 'Freddy ..…'

'Just go, Sissy,' he choked. 'I do not want to speak to you just now.'

*

With everyone gone, Freddy could not settle. He paced the front room distractedly before he could no longer bear its confines. He needed to be outside to think about and process what his poor darling Kitty had gone through and how much he had been lied to by Sissy and Mr Bolitho. His thoughts took him back to that day, that awful day that was seared into his mind as though it had been branded there – the day he had found out Kitty had gone.

It was the 16th of February 1882 - he had been so happy that day as he walked down the drive towards the cottage he shared with Mr Bolitho. Although he had taken the first wagon out of Gunwalloe that morning, he was nearly an hour late to start work. He was sure Mr Bolitho would not mind too much. Fortunately, he was an easy-going man. Freddy was in high spirits that morning. He could not wait to tell Kitty that his parents were over the moon with the news of their forthcoming marriage. They had invited her over for tea the next time she had a day off.

At the cottage, he pushed the door open and was aghast to find Mr Bolitho still there - and only just getting shaved and ready for work. It was seven o'clock! Mr Bolitho was normally up and about at six every morning.

'Goodness, Mr Bolitho. Have you slept badly? It is not like you to rise late,' Freddy said, then added. 'Now we are both late to work, so I don't feel so guilty.' He grinned. 'Shall I put the kettle on to make a cup of tea for us?'

Freddy remembered how quiet Mr Bolitho was as he drank his tea, and now he knew why.

It wasn't until Freddy walked into the kitchen with a box of vegetables and a beaming smile on his face that he noted Sissy's distress, and then he saw the new girl assisting her in the kitchen, and the world that he knew collapsed around him.

He frowned. 'Where is Kitty, Mrs Blair? I have some news for her.'

Sissy's eyes watered, and Freddy frowned again.

'Mrs Blair. Where is Kitty?'

'She's gone!' Nora, the new kitchen assistant, piped up. 'I am doing her job now.' She flashed a gap tooth grin at him.

'Nora!' Sissy snapped. 'Go into the scullery now, and do not come out until I tell you to.'

'But...' Nora glanced at the chopping she had to do.

'Now!' she shouted.

The girl scurried away, and Sissy turned to Freddy.

'Gone!' Freddy said, aghast. 'Gone where?'

Sissy bit down on her lip as though trying to find the courage to answer him.

'Mrs Blair. Where has Kitty gone?'

Just as Sissy opened her mouth, a voice behind her answered.

'Morton has gone, dismissed for a serious misdemeanour,' Mrs Bligh said authoritatively as she breezed into the kitchen. 'Now, get out, boy. You're not allowed to linger in this kitchen.'

Freddy stood stock still as Sissy rounded on Mrs Bligh.

'I say who stays in my kitchen, Mrs Bligh, and I believe I told *you* to keep out of it!' She bellowed at the housekeeper. 'Especially as you have had a bout of diarrhoea!'

Mrs Bligh blanched, not only at being berated in front of a lowly gardening assistant but also at having her bodily malfunction brought up in front of him. 'How dare you, Mrs Blair? I will not have you speak to me in this fashion.'

Sissy thumped her fists into her sides. 'I *will* speak to you as I like. I run this kitchen. Now *you*, get out of it - before you spread your germs.'

'Well!' Mrs Bligh bristled. 'I am not standing for this. I shall report your behaviour to Mr Carrington for this.'

'Do so. I am up for the fight,' Sissy raged.

Suddenly, Mrs Bligh grasped at her stomach and fled down the laundry corridor, shouting at Joyce, 'Get out of the way; I need the privy!'

Freddy noted that despite Sissy's anger at Mrs Bligh, she also looked amused at the housekeeper's swift retreat, but Freddy was in no mood to inquire about the joke. He tipped his head, waiting for answers to his questions.

Sissy cleared her throat and called Nora back in to keep an eye on the dinner. Putting her arm around Freddy's shoulders, she walked him into the kitchen courtyard.

'What is going on? Is it true that Kitty has been dismissed?'

'I'm afraid so, Freddy. That's why I'm so angry with Mrs Bligh. Kitty was dismissed and sent away in the middle of the night.'

'Well, where is she? Where did she go?'

'I can't tell you, Freddy. She just vanished into the night.'

'Vanished!' Freddy moved from disbelief to anger. 'She can't have just vanished! Did she not say anything to you?'

Sissy shook her head. Lying to Freddy was breaking her heart.

'What is this *serious misdemeanour* Kitty has allegedly committed?'

'I don't know. They will not tell me.'

'This is ludicrous?' Freddy stood up and paced the courtyard. 'What on earth could my lovely Kitty have done that would be deemed so bad?'

Sissy shook her head and shrugged, not knowing what to say.

'Mrs Blair,' he lowered his voice and then spoke to her as a friend, 'Sissy. You know her better than anyone. Where would she have gone? She has no family, as far as I'm aware.'

'I'm at a loss as to what to say, Freddy. I'm sorry.'

'You must know, Sissy. You are her friend!' His voice rose in anger.

'Hey! Hey! What is all this racket?' John Bolitho walked across the kitchen courtyard, glancing anxiously between Freddy and Sissy.

Freddy turned to John. 'Kitty has gone! Dismissed, they tell me, and Mrs Blair will not tell me why or where she has gone.'

'I'm sorry, Freddy. I can't tell you anything,' Sissy reiterated, her voice full of pain.

Freddy remembered that Mr Bolitho had feigned shock at the news.

'Now, now, Freddy,' he said. 'Mrs Blair is clearly upset about this as well. If she says she can't tell you anything, you must believe her and not press the matter.'

Freddy's anguish turned his voice into a high-pitched whine as he argued, 'But, Mr Bolitho. Kitty could not have just disappeared. We're getting married!'

'Perhaps Kitty will send word to you when she settles somewhere,' Mr Bolitho said to appease.

Freddy felt his lip quiver as he struggled to keep the tears at bay. 'I just cannot believe she would have gone without leaving a note - for any of us!'

Unable to bear it any longer, Freddy cupped his hands to his face and broke down in tears, but when Sissy tried to comfort him, he pushed her away and ran off.

The endless days and weeks that followed Kitty's disappearance weighed heavily on Freddy's heart. Long, drawn-out bouts of melancholia almost cost him his job as he stumbled his way through his working day, waiting for word that never came from her. Mr Bolitho made excuses for his malaise to Lady Lucinda. He covered for Freddy when his depression engulfed him to the point that he could not get out of bed. Eventually, Mr Bolitho served him a meal of tough love and gave him two options. Firstly, he could carry on like this and lose his job, as well as Kitty, because Mr Bolitho would have to let him go, as he needed someone reliable to help him in the garden. Secondly, Freddy could get up, fight this depressive state into submission, and dig deep within to find the spiritual strength that would help him to go on living a productive life without Kitty. Just as Mr Bolitho had had to do when he lost his wife twenty years previously, he'd told him.

After leaving him to mull over his options, Freddy had cried in self-pity for the next half hour and then got up, dressed, and returned to work - albeit a shadow of his former self.

*

That had all happened forty-one years ago. In truth, Freddy's heart had never properly healed, despite the constant sympathy from Sissy and Mr Bolitho. Now, after all these years, he knew the truth behind their sympathy - it had all been to mask their lies. The two people he thought he could trust had lied to him!

Despite being outside in his garden, breathing in the fresh air, a heavy weight lay on his chest. There was more to Kitty's story, but his anger had gotten the better of him, and he had ejected Sissy from the house before she could explain more. Freddy knew as he tried to suppress his terrible anguish that deep down in the pit of his stomach, an icy chill had formed, remembering his initial reaction to seeing Sissy's grandson. If his poor Kitty had been used and abused by the Earl, he squeezed his eyes shut to the reality that, when he had mistaken Josh for Lord William, it had probably not been a faux pas. Because now it was as clear as day that Josh was the product, of that old salacious bastard, Lord Randolf Dunstan, The Earl de Bochym, albeit once removed.

'Oh, God!' Freddy sat down and buried his head in his hands again. His mind was a whirl, trying to imagine what became of his Kitty after she left there.

22
Kitty 1882

After saying an emotional goodbye to Mr Bolitho that night, Kitty sat in the bath, shivering despite the warm water. Every fibre of her body felt sore. Large purple bruises covered her arms and legs; even her hair hurt. She could hardly touch her broken nose because the pain was intense. She had not looked at herself in the mirror yet, but she knew from touching the swollen skin around her eyes and cheeks that they would be black and blue. The warm water eased the cuts and rawness deep inside her, but nothing could ease the unfathomable, penetrating pain in her heart at the loss of Freddy. Her cuts and bruises would heal in time. Her heart, she feared, would never recover.

Silent tears trickled down her face as Effy helped her out of the bath and wrapped her in a towel. Like a mother would a daughter, Effy dabbed Kitty's sore and swollen skin gently dry. She helped her dress in a clean nightdress, three sizes too big for her, and tucked her into bed, leaving a glass of warm milk and a pile of handkerchiefs on the bedside table.

'Try to get some sleep, sweet girl,' Effy said with a gentle smile.

*

For the next two weeks, Effy looked after Kitty, making sure she slept and ate properly. She could not have been kinder. Kitty's bruises began to fade to yellow, and her nose hurt less as every day passed. Slowly, her body was mending, but despite administering a vinegar-soaked plug deep inside her, a week later, Kitty and Effy's worst fears came to fruition. Her monthlies never showed; her desperate administrations had failed to prevent the seed planted from growing.

'Are you sure you have the right date, Kitty?'

'I'm as regular as the moon,' she said sadly.

'It may be just the trauma you have endured, but if not, then there is nothing to be done. What will be, will be. I will tell people that you are my niece and that you have lost your husband and have come to live with me.'

Kitty's face crumpled. 'You and Sissy have been so kind. I feel terrible that you all have to lie for me.'

'That's what friends are for. Now, you mustn't worry. It will be best if you keep busy now that your bruises have healed. I have plenty of work for us both to do.'

'Thank you, Effy. Just tell me what you want me to do,' she said gratefully.

*

Over the next few weeks, though reticent and in despair of her ongoing predicament, Kitty proved popular with the guests staying at Effie's boarding house. In particular, there was an older man named Hugh Walsh, a gardener who annually visited Falmouth for a week every April in order to visit his mother's grave. He was a tall, broad-shouldered, good-natured man who was kind to Kitty and even voiced his concerns when he saw how sad she looked on occasions. Kitty was always courteous to him but could never divulge why she was so unhappy.

Without wanting to, Kitty saw a lot of Hugh. With him being a regular guest, Effy invited him to sit with them in the evenings and share a sherry in the boarding house's cosy parlour. He spoke of his work as a gardener, but with every mention of the word, Kitty felt a pang of sadness for the gardener she had left behind. Hugh told them he was taking up a position in Portsmouth as head gardener at a fine house. The position also offered a tied cottage, which was his until his death. Laughingly, he hoped that would be a few years away!'

The day Hugh checked out after his week-long visit, he lingered, as though he wanted to say something. When he realised his train wouldn't wait, he left with a cheery goodbye and a warm smile for Kitty.

As Effy waved him off, she realised from the way he had looked at Kitty that he had taken quite a shine to her. It was a great pity that Kitty was with child. She suspected that Hugh could give Kitty a good life and perhaps make her forget her former love, Freddy.

*

On the 7th of May, a letter arrived for Effy at breakfast. Kitty was entering her third month of pregnancy, though as yet she was showing few signs that she was with child, what with her being so slim and having little appetite. She watched Effy's facial expression as she read the letter with interest.

'Oh! You had better get the sea view bedroom aired, Kitty. Hugh Walsh has written to say he is visiting again,' she announced. 'How strange; he has only ever visited in April before—on the anniversary of his mother's death!'

'When is he coming?' Kitty asked.

'Tomorrow! Gosh, that's short notice. Thankfully, the post was on time, or we might not have been ready for him.'

Hugh duly arrived at half past twelve the next day and asked Effy if he could speak privately with Kitty.

'May I ask why?' Effy answered warily.

'I would like to ask her something.'

Effy knew this could only mean one thing. She opened her mouth to speak, but closed it again. It was not Effy's place to tell him of Kitty's predicament.

Kitty walked into the parlour, smiled, and smoothed down her apron. Hugh had been standing at the window, his hands clasped behind his back, when he turned and smiled warmly back at her.

'Hello, Kitty. Can you guess why I'm here?'

'No, Mr Walsh,' she answered in all innocence.

He tipped his head. 'Hugh, call me Hugh.'

'Oh! But I couldn't. It's not fitting to call guests by their Christian name.'

'Well,' he said, extending his hands towards her, 'I'd like to think I am more than just a guest to you.' He beckoned her to sit.

Kitty sat tentatively on the edge of her seat and placed her hands on her lap.

'Kitty, I am here to ask you to marry me.'

'Pardon?' she baulked. Shocked and taken aback by Hugh's proposal, Kitty stood and shook her head. 'I can't.'

Hugh held out his hands to calm her. 'I know we haven't known each other long, Kitty, and I am twenty-five years your senior, but I like you a lot, and I want to make you happy again.'

'I can't,' she said. 'I just can't.'

A deep frown appeared on his brow. 'Why can't you?' He looked pleadingly at her. 'I can give you a home and a good life. I'll look after you. Do you not like me at all? Am I too old for you?'

'Yes, I do like you, and no, it's not your age, but...' She shook her head violently, feeling panic rising in her chest. 'I cannot marry you.'

'Kitty, I understand this has come as a shock - it came as a shock to me too how ardently I want you. I thought I would be a bachelor all my life! I have grown very fond of you. I would like you to do me the honour of becoming my wife. After all, you said yourself that you like me, which makes me more determined to make you mine,' he said softly.

'I'm sorry,' she said. 'Excuse me.' She fled from the room and into Effy's arms, who had been waiting outside the parlour door.

'Kitty, whatever has happened?' Effy looked through to the parlour at Hugh, who looked mystified.

'He wants to marry me, Effy. Tell him, please, tell him why I can't.'

Holding her at arm's length, Effy was puzzled. 'You want me to tell him the truth! But...?'

'Please, Effy, make him understand. Hugh is adamant that he wishes to marry me. You must tell him the truth because I cannot speak of it – I'm too ashamed,' she cried and ran upstairs to shut herself in her room.

A few minutes later, the front door banged shut, and when Kitty looked out into the street, Hugh was walking towards the harbour.

'Kitty?' Effy knocked on her bedroom door and entered.

'Has he gone?' Kitty asked.

'Yes, he's gone out.'

'Did you tell him?'

'I did.'

'The truth about everything? My shame?'

'Everything.'

Kitty nodded sadly. 'Will I have to leave here now that my shame is known?'

'No, Kitty. You won't have to leave until you are ready to go,' she said, gathering her in her arms.

'But what if Mr Walsh tells people?'

'He won't.'

*

Neither Effy nor Kitty knew if Hugh Walsh would return that day. He missed teatime, and Kitty began to relax and pray that he had gone forever and that she would not have to face him again. But at eight-thirty, the front door opened, and Kitty and Effy exchanged an apprehensive glance. Kitty panicked, but there was no escape from the room when Hugh knocked and entered the parlour without waiting for consent.

Kitty noted Hugh looked grey and troubled as he apologised for his intrusion. He wrung his hands, gave a thin smile, and settled his eyes on Kitty's tummy.

'I wonder. May I speak again with Kitty alone?' he asked.

Effy glanced at Kitty, who shook her head.

'Could I speak with you if Effy stays then, Kitty?'

There was no way out of this. Kitty closed her eyes to the inevitable condemnation he was about to inflict on her. She nodded, just wanting to get it over with.

'You will know that Effy has told me of your troubles,' he said softly.

'Yes,' she said, unable to look at him.

'I cannot tell a lie. I was shocked when I heard your story. Truly shocked!'

Kitty dropped her head lower in shame.

'I have been walking for many hours, and after a great deal of soul-searching and deliberation, I have finally concluded that you are the victim in all this, and you should not suffer the consequences alone. The child you are carrying is the burden of the dreadful events that have taken place. I am willing to share your burden, Kitty. I'm still willing to marry you.'

'But I'm sorry, I don't love you. I love Freddy!' She blurted it out before she could stop herself.

Silence ensued for a few moments before Hugh nodded. 'Effy has explained that you have a sweetheart, but that *he* would not have taken kindly to your predicament.'

Tears streamed down her face; she could not argue with that.

'I can give you a new start in life. The baby will bear my name; the child will never know how it came about. Your secret is safe with me.'

'Why?' she cried, wiping her tears with her hand. 'Why do you want someone disgraced?'

'Because, sweet girl, the more I see you, the more I want to look after you.'

Hugh glanced at Effy for help.

Effy put her arm around Kitty's shoulders. 'Why don't you sleep on it, Kitty?' she said, thus giving her a little breathing space.

Kitty nodded sadly and fled from the parlour, forgetting to say goodnight to either of them. In her bedroom, she kicked off her shoes, lay on the bed, and stared into the abyss of life without Freddy.

Effy brought her a cup of cocoa an hour later and sat beside her bed.

'It's a good offer, Kitty.'

Kitty did not respond.

'Hugh is a good and kind man.'

Still, Kitty remained silent.

As Effy turned to leave, Kitty said, 'Do you think I should accept him then?'

'The decision is yours, Kitty.'

'But *you* think I should?'

'You may never get another chance like this. Hugh can give you a good life, a home, security, and.... respectability.'

'But I love Freddy!' she cried.

'I know, I know,' Effy soothed. 'But I think we both know that Freddy has gone from your life forever, so you need to do some soul-searching and give Hugh's offer serious thought. It's not easy bringing up a babe alone, even if you have friends around you to help. Having said that, if you decide to decline Hugh's offer, I want you to know that you will always be welcome to stay here with me.'

Kitty slept little that night, and when dawn broke, she had made her decision. For better or worse, she knew what she must do.

*

Kitty and Hugh were married at the Falmouth registry office on Saturday, the 14th of May – the day that she and Freddy had chosen for their wedding day! Kitty had no say in the date; it was a fait accompli when Hugh presented the special wedding licence to her.

As Kitty took her wedding vows and watched Hugh slip a thin gold band on her finger, her young heart yearned for Freddy and what could have been.

*

With her bags packed, Kitty stood at her bedroom window, her hand resting on one of the cold panes.

'Freddy,' she whispered. 'I know you are somewhere out there, but know this. I may have married someone else, and I know it is terrible to admit after Hugh has been so kind to me, but I will always, always, love you.'

After a sad farewell to Effy, they boarded the train to Portsmouth. As they crossed the Tamar and left Cornwall behind, Kitty turned to say goodbye to Freddy and Cornwall forever.

'Kitty.' Hugh's voice jarred her back to the present. 'From this moment on, you must never look back, and you must forget *everything* that went before – that includes Freddy.'

Kitty's lip trembled slightly.

'He is in the past and must stay there, I insist,' he said sternly. 'Now that we are to start a new life together, It will be best for you to sever all ties with Effy and anyone you knew before. You will make new friends, and I will care for you and the baby, and we will be a family.'

Kitty cast her eyes downward and nodded sadly.

23

After being ejected from Freddy's cottage, Maia, Josh, and Sissy reconvened outside Sissy's cottage, and although the air was warm, the trio felt chilled after reliving Kitty's tragic tale.

'Well!' Josh raked his fingers through his hair. 'I understand now why he mistook me for Lord Dunston.' Josh's jaw tightened as he looked at Sissy. 'I take it my grandma fell pregnant after the attack?'

'I'm afraid so, Josh. My sister wrote to tell me the terrible news, but fortunately for Kitty she met your grandpa at Effy's boarding house.'

Suddenly, realisation dawned on Josh. 'Oh, goodness, then he wasn't really my grandpa then?'

'I'm afraid not,' Sissy answered.

Maia put a comforting hand on Josh's arm.

'I wonder if Grandpa knew what had happened to Grandma then?'

'Oh yes. After Hugh proposed marriage to Kitty, she insisted he knew the full facts. Hugh was shocked but was still prepared to marry her anyway and give the child his name. As I said, that was the last I ever heard of her. From looking at you, Josh, and your resemblance to the Dunstans, it's clear that Kitty went full-term with the baby. Did she have a boy or a girl?'

'A boy - my father - and now I know where Father got his unpleasant traits! Grandma always said he was an awkward baby, and she admitted once that she had never really bonded with him. I think she had a difficult birth, so much so that she never had any more children. My father's persona did not improve with age. Grandma would shake her head in disgust at how he treated me and Ma.'

'Is your ma still alive, Josh?'

'No, she died just over five years ago. My father knocked her around a lot - more so when he got home from the war. I came home one day, and Father told me that Ma had fallen, cracked her head open, and died! I think he did it to her! I left home shortly after that.' Josh omitted to mention that he had been forced into the Navy by him. 'I severed all ties with him.'

'Thankfully, you are nothing like your father, Josh,' Maia said, squeezing his arm.

'And thankfully, neither of the Dunstan men show any of the old Earl's traits either,' Sissy added.

Josh's eyes narrowed. 'I take it the old Earl died. Damn his eyes!'

'He did, Josh. He died in 1892 and is hopefully rotting in hell for what he did, not only to Kitty but to numerous girls before and after her.'

'Amen to that!' Josh bared his teeth. 'Gosh, but this makes me so angry!'

Sissy shot a worried glance at Maia at Josh's reaction.

'Josh, you're not going to make trouble here, are you, now that you know?' Maia asked anxiously. 'I know this has been a shock, and what happened was terrible, but if you do cause trouble, you will not be welcome in my home anymore,' she warned. 'The Dunstans are lovely people and have been inordinately kind to me.'

'Yes, they're a good family now,' Sissy interjected. 'Sarah and Peter Dunstan, the Earl and Countess de Bochym, cut out the rot within the staff when they took over the manor twenty years ago; I will not have you upset them.'

Josh put his hands out to calm them. 'I promise I will not cause trouble. In fact, I don't want them to know about me. If Father ever got wind of this, he would come shouting for compensation, without a doubt. Do you think Mr Hubbard will keep this secret?'

'I'll speak to him, Josh,' Sissy said. 'Well, that's if he'll ever speak to me again!'

'Mrs Blair,' Josh said sincerely. 'I am so sorry this has blown up like this. All I wanted was to say thank you on behalf of Grandma. From what you told me, you went far above and beyond what most people would have done.'

'I don't regret any of it, Josh. I would do it again tomorrow if I had to. I'm just so sorry that it hurt Freddy in the process. He never got married, you know. He always thought Kitty would come back to explain. He would have forgiven her anything, even though Kitty thought not.'

'Oh, dear, that poor man.' Josh sighed.

'Will you tell your grandma that I have broken my promise not to tell a soul about what happened?' Sissy said anxiously.

'No, Mrs Blair, the secret is safe with me.'

Sissy nodded. 'Perhaps Kitty may contact me again one day; I will probably have to confess to her then. Now, I hope you will both forgive me, but I must leave you. The kitchen beckons.'

She bustled off while Maia and Josh clambered aboard the cart.

'Are you all right, Josh?' Maia placed her hand on his sleeve. 'This has all been quite a shock, I suspect!'

'I'm all right, yes. I'm obviously deeply saddened to learn of Grandma's troubles. No, what troubles me is how guarded I must be. It brought it home to me when I said to Mrs Blair that I would not tell Grandma about the broken secret. I would give anything to contact Grandma again, but by now she will have been told that I am dead – drowned after jumping ship! None of this sits comfortably on my conscience, Maia.'

'I'm afraid needs must, Josh. Maybe it's best not to fret about it.'

'Yes, but I know that Grandma would love to contact Mrs Blair again, and if Grandpa *has* passed away - God rest his soul - she might just do that! If Grandma did write, Mrs Blair would surely write back to tell her that she had met me, and then she would know I was alive, and the cat would be really out of the bag.'

Maia cupped her hand over Josh's to comfort him, but his heart sank at the prospect that his residence here in Cornwall might be tenuous.

*

Freddy had had a terrible night, and it took all of his reserve to face Sissy in the kitchen that morning. He was still so angry with her that he had decided he wouldn't speak to her. He would just deliver the day's vegetables and leave, but when he saw her, he could not hold back his anger.

'Why did you not tell me before?' He slammed the vegetable box down and shouted at Sissy.

'Everyone in the kitchen stopped and stared at Mr Hubbard, whom they had never heard raise his voice before.

Sissy quickly wiped her hands down her apron, set Vicky to watch the pots on the stove, and ushered Freddy outside where they could have a conversation in peace.

'Well?' Freddy demanded, regarding her reproachfully. 'Why did you lie to me?'

'Freddy, I'm so sorry.' Her voice was filled with sadness. 'You know why. I told you yesterday. Kitty made me promise not to tell. She was so ashamed of what you would think of her, and she feared you would take your revenge on the Earl and most probably kill him. She didn't want you to hang, and you would have if you had harmed the Earl. Kitty didn't want that on her conscience as well.'

Freddy could not deny that he would indeed have taken his revenge. 'And Josh – Kitty's grandson - he's a Dunstan! Isn't he?'

'I'm afraid so.'

'Oh, God!' Freddy clasped his head as though it hurt. 'Why is he here, stirring up terrible memories? What is he after? Money, from His Lordship?'

'No, Freddy. Josh wants nothing. He didn't even know what the Earl had done to his grandma until yesterday. He is adamant that no one must know of his connection. He asked me to tell you to keep his secret.'

'Why? He could make a pretty penny in compensation! There's no bloody doubting who his grandfather was!'

'I just know that Josh is not that sort of person. Yes, he may have come from the lineage of the Dunstans, but he is Kitty's grandson through and through. I only spent a couple of hours with him yesterday, but it was clear that he shares her sweet temperament.'

Freddy's eyes filled with fat tears. 'Oh, my poor Kitty. How on earth did she manage with a baby all by herself?'

Sissy took a deep breath and answered, 'She wasn't alone. She met a man shortly after leaving here. He married Kitty to give her respectability, and so the babe would have a name.'

Freddy hung his head in shame, to think his unguarded comment about Hilda's ruin had forced his Kitty to flee and settle with another man. He could have bitten his own tongue off for the harm it had caused.

Sissy reached forward and took him in her arms. 'Freddy, I am so sorry; please forgive me. John Bolitho and I did not lie to you lightly.'

Freddy's body heaved with wracking sobs in her arms, and then he pulled away and rushed off.

*

With tears in his eyes, Freddy stumbled blindly into the gardens and sat on the first seat he came to. Despite the smell of the sweet grass, the sound of bumblebees humming from flower to flower, and the heady fragrance of the rose garden, nothing could calm Freddy's despair. Burying his face in his hands, he wept until a voice startled him and made him look up.

'Mr Hubbard, are you quite well?' Lady Sarah Dunstan asked.

'Yes, my lady.' He sniffed and quickly wiped away his tears. 'Dreadfully sorry,' he said, a sob catching in his throat.

'Please, Mr Hubbard. There is no need to apologise. Can I help in any way? I fear you are in a state of deep distress.'

'No, my lady.' He shook his head. How could he tell her that her late father-in-law was the cause of his distress? 'I...I'm sorry. I just need a moment or two if you don't mind.'

'Of course I don't mind, and you're very welcome to sit here as long as you need to. I'll come and speak to you later – it was nothing of any importance - it will keep. But are you sure I cannot help you with anything?'

This time, he just shook his head - too grieved to speak.

'Very well.' She smiled sympathetically and left him to his woes.

As he tried to gather himself, all he could think of was the crypt where the Dunstan family's bones lay locked up and mouldering. Freddy would have taken great pleasure in desecrating the 4th Earl de Bochym's grave if he could have gained entry to it.

*

Two days later, Freddy Hubbard knocked on Wild Cliff Farm door. Maia and Josh had just finished supper, so Josh took himself off to the studio while Maia answered the door. It would not do for it to get out that they were eating meals together. Josh could hear a male voice but could not recognise it as anyone who had called previously, and then Maia came into the studio and called him through.

Freddy stood awkwardly in the kitchen, kneading his hat in his hands anxiously.

'I'm sorry to bother you both, but...' He looked around, not knowing how to continue.

'Mr Hubbard, please take a seat,' Maia invited, and without asking him, she poured him a cup of tea.

'How can I help you, Mr Hubbard?' Josh asked. 'Maia said you wished to speak to me?'

Freddy took a large intake of breath before he spoke. 'I'd like to know something.'

Josh nodded and waited.

'I understand from Sissy that Kitty married soon after she left me!'

'Yes, she did. My grandpa. Grandma told me they had met in Cornwall, but I didn't know until Mrs Blair told me the other day that they met in that boarding house she stayed in when she left the manor.' Josh laughed softly and shrugged. 'I had no idea he wasn't my real grandpa!' he added.

Every muscle of Freddy's tensed. 'Believe me, you would not have cared for your true grandfather,' he said caustically.

'No, I don't believe I would have,' Josh answered curtly.

Josh and Maia exchanged glances, wondering where this conversation was going.

Freddy clasped his hands together as though in prayer. 'Has your grandpa been good to her?'

'Yes.' Josh's face softened. 'He was a lovely man.'

'Was?' A spark of interest flashed in Freddy's eyes. 'Has he died? You spoke about him in the past tense.'

Josh shot a furtive glance at Maia.

'He was very much alive when last I saw him,' he answered evasively.

'Oh, I see.' Freddy's shoulders drooped. He cleared his throat. 'May I have Kitty's address?'

Josh shook his head. 'I'm afraid not.'

'Why not? I just want to tell her I understand. To put the record straight that I do not think badly of her. You heard what Sissy said. Kitty thought I would denounce her.'

'I'm sorry, Mr Hubbard, but I cannot give you her address. It may cause a great deal of upset for Grandpa in particular, especially if an old flame of Grandma writes to her - you must understand that!' Josh stood up to indicate this conversation was over. 'I'm sorry, but I can't help you further.'

Deflated, Freddy hung his head, nodded, and then put his palms on the table to wearily push himself up. 'I'm sorry to have bothered you.'

After Maia showed Freddy out, she found Josh standing at the kitchen window, staring out into the evening.

'God, Maia. I think I've opened a whole can of worms now. I should have kept my mouth shut and not gone to see Mrs Blair. I hate all this lying, and now I've upset that decent chap.'

'No, Josh.' She laid her hand gently on his shoulder. 'Freddy was being a little too forceful and demanding.'

He shook his head. 'I don't think he will leave things there. He seemed determined to find Grandma again. What if he goes looking for her? Then my family will know I'm still alive. Oh, God. Just when I felt safe here.'

'Freddy will not go looking for Kitty. How could he? Nobody knows you originate from Portsmouth. Besides that, Mr Hubbard has not been further than Truro all the time I have known him.'

'I do hope you're right.'

*

When Freddy walked across the kitchen courtyard the next morning, he knocked on the kitchen door.

Vicky answered it and frowned. 'You don't normally knock, Mr Hubbard.'

'Who is it, Vicky?' Sissy shouted.

'It's Mr Hubbard, Mrs Blair.'

Sissy was at the door in an instant.

'Have you a minute or so to spare, Sissy?'

Sissy looked uncertain. 'As long as you're not going to shout at me again.'

'No,' he said sheepishly. 'But I do need to speak to you.'

'Very well.' She wiped her hands down her apron. 'Vicky, watch the pots and keep stirring that custard.' She ushered Freddy out to the bench in the courtyard.

When he sat, he told her where he had been.

'Josh will not tell me where Kitty lives, Sissy. I just want to write to her. I want to tell her I know and understand now why she left me. What am I to do?' Freddy's eyes watered.

'Oh, sweet man. I'm sorry I have stirred up painful feelings with this, and I'm sorry that I've hurt you deeply. But I honestly think there is nothing we can do. I understand that the man Kitty married did not want her to contact me. I suspect he was worried that I might have told you where she was.'

'Why?' Freddy straightened his shoulders. 'Do you think Kitty told him about me then?'

'I do, yes. My sister Effy told me that Kitty told Hugh everything - she wanted to be truthful with him if he was going to marry her.'

Freddy looked downcast. 'He sounds like a jolly good sort to do what he did. Though I can't help feeling jealous of him,' he grumbled. 'The way Josh spoke about his grandpa indicated that he may have died now.'

'Well then, perhaps, and this is a very long shot, perhaps if he has died – for I know he was forty when he married Kitty - that would make him eighty-one now, Kitty might contact me.'

'Do you think?' His face, animated, brightened.

'She might, or she might not. Don't get your hopes up, Freddy. Look at old Mr Bolitho; he is ninety-six and still going.'

Once again, Freddy felt deflated. He nodded resignedly. 'If Kitty does write to you, you *will* tell me, won't you? You won't keep it a secret, will you?'

Sissy placed her hand on his. 'Of course, I'll tell you. I promise, no more secrets.'

'Oh, Sissy, I am that grieved at what happened to her. Especially when you said how badly beaten she had been.'

'I know, Freddy. It was an awful thing to witness at the time. Though she put up a brave fight that night.'

'Good! That bastard deserved it. Begging your pardon for swearing, Sissy,' he said sheepishly.

'Believe me, I have called him a lot worse.'

24

It was Sunday, the 1st of July, and the Poldhu Tea Room was buzzing with customers despite the westerly winds that had whipped up, ruffling the sea and moving the sand around Poldhu Beach in swirls.

Maia and Josh sat at their reserved table on the veranda, trying to dodge the occasional dusting of sand that the wind kept whipping up and threatening to spoil their cream tea!

After the revelation of Kitty's story, Maia and Josh heard no more from Freddy Hubbard that week, and Josh prayed that all interest in his grandma would die down now and he could start to feel more settled.

It felt wonderful to be out with Maia again, and he felt heartened that she wanted him to join her for a walk and tea at the tearoom. Their relationship had fallen into a happy routine of working together in the gardens and sharing the chores with the livestock. Meals were happy occasions, and since Maia had lent him some books to read, they had long discussions about favourite authors.

As they enjoyed their tea, Josh could not help but notice that Maia was watching Fee quite intently. When he asked her why, she answered, 'Fee hardly raised a smile when she served us. I think something is amiss. I do hope that Jago hasn't anything to do with it. I know she has her eye on him - maybe he has rebuffed her.'

When Maia mentioned it to Ellie, she just rolled her eyes.

'She is just so moody at the moment,' Ellie whispered. 'I know at their age they can be, but I never had a moment's moodiness from Agnes when she was Fee's age.'

'Is anything bothering her?' Maia asked.

'Not that I know of. If I ask, she clams up.'

Maia put her hand on Ellie's arm. 'Don't worry. It'll no doubt pass.'

'I hope so, and quickly. It isn't like Fee to be moody.'

'Perhaps that young man over there will put a smile on her face.' Maia nodded to Jimmy Trevorrow, whom they had seen arriving on the beach a few moments earlier. He was sitting in the dunes, possibly, they thought, waiting to see Fee when she finished work.

Ellie glanced over at Jimmy. 'Mmm, I think not,' Ellie answered dryly. 'Young is the operative word there. He is only fifteen, and with Fee fast approaching her sixteenth birthday, she thinks he is too young for her.'

'Oh dear,' Josh interjected. 'Well, I feel sorry for Jimmy. I think he is smitten with Fee. I popped into Ben Pearson's saddlery the other day, and Ben was teasing Jimmy about being lovestruck. Jimmy was taking it all in his stride.'

'Oh dear. I hope he doesn't get his heart broken by her then,' Ellie mused as she left them so she could clear tables.

'Poor Jimmy.' Maia frowned. 'Young love, eh?'

'It's a brave man who declares his love for a lady. Especially if he is unsure if his sentiment will be reciprocated.' Josh smiled at Maia, holding her gaze with unsaid words.

*

After the euphoria of thinking that Jago was interested in her, Fee had sunk into a disgruntled mood since he had bawled at her to get out of the way and called her a "silly bitch" a week ago! She knew her moodiness made her ma angry, but Jago had humiliated and bruised her pride; she would never forgive him.

When they closed the tearoom later that afternoon, Fee did not run home this time to put her best dress on or apply lipstick as she had the previous Sunday in the vain hope of tempting Jago to take her out. She laughed without mirth at the thought of her foolishness.

Sitting forlornly on the beach, with her back to Jago's house so she did not have to see him if he ventured out, she kicked off her shoes, buried her feet in the sand, positioned a parasol behind her to shield herself from the blown sand, and began to wallow in self-pity.

'Hello,' a voice behind her made her jump.

She turned to find Jimmy Trevorrow smiling at her. Unable to hide her annoyance at being disturbed, she snapped, 'What is it?'

'Nothing. I'm sorry. I can see you don't want company.' Wounded by her sharpness he began to move away.

Realising she had just treated Jimmy with the same contempt that Jago had treated her, a pang of guilt made her call him back.

'Jimmy.'

He waved his hand and continued to walk. 'It's nothing.'

'No, Jimmy, I'm sorry. That was very rude of me. Please come back and sit with me. Though I warn you, I'm poor company.' She patted the sand.

Warmed by her invitation, he returned to her side. 'You could never be poor company, Fee.'

'I have a lot on my mind,' she said with an apologetic smile.

'A problem shared?' he asked hopefully.

She shook her head. 'It's very private.'

'Well, if you change your mind, I can always lend an ear.'

She giggled. 'You would look funny with only one ear.'

He laughed gently at her joke. 'I was wondering...?'

She tipped her head questioningly.

'I was wondering If you would like to go for a walk or something, perhaps to Polurrian Beach?'

Fee shot him a wary sidelong look.

'Oh, I don't mean to walk out. You know, like sweethearts do!'

'Good!' She said a little more acerbically than she had meant it to sound.

Jimmy dropped his eyes to pick up a pebble from the beach.

'Sorry, Jimmy, I didn't mean to sound mean. It's just that you're only fifteen.'

'As are you,' he countered.

'I'll be sixteen on the 21st of this month.'

'I see. I suppose you'll be looking for someone older. Someone like Jago, perhaps,' he said tentatively.

'Jago!' She flashed her eyes angrily at him. 'Why do you mention *him*?' she said sharply.

Jimmy shrugged. 'Well, I know all the girls like him – with his money, fancy car, and things.'

'Well, you can be sure that I don't!' She answered huffily.

Jimmy's shoulders relaxed. 'That's good to hear. Pa said he is not to be trusted, and I reckon Pa is a good judge of character.'

Fee turned away and looked into the distance to hide her watering eyes.

'I know I'm too young for you; in that way, I just want us to be friends, and there is no age limit to being friends, is there?' He asked hopefully.

Fee turned back to him and smiled gently. Jimmy was quite handsome on closer inspection and looked older than his fifteen years. 'No, of course, there isn't.'

'So, shall we go for a walk?' he asked.

She shook her head as she slipped her shoes back on. 'Not today, Jimmy. As I say, I am poor company.'

*

As Fee left Jimmy sitting on the beach, Ellie, who had been watching from the tearoom window, sighed. She walked out onto the veranda just as Jimmy stood up to brush the sand from the seat of his pants.

'Don't lose heart, Jimmy,' she said.

Jimmy turned and gave Ellie a thin smile.

'Just give her time.'

He nodded sadly, but he was very much afraid that in time, Fee would find someone more her own age, and then his poor heart would be crushed.

*

On Monday morning, Joe Treen was handing out the mail to the staff in the Bochym Kitchen.

'One for you, Mrs Blair.'

Sissy smiled, taking the envelope from Mr Treen and recognising her sister's handwriting. She had written a couple of days ago to tell her that she had met with Kitty's grandson. Effy often said in her letters that she wished she knew how Kitty had fared.

My dearest sister, Sissy.

What a lovely surprise to get your letter telling me you had met with Kitty's grandson and that he told you Kitty is well and happy. However, I did think it strange that you called him Josh Harding, for, if you remember, Hugh's surname was Walsh.

Sissy put the letter down, puzzled. Yes, she remembered now; it was Hugh Walsh, but his name had cleanly gone out of her mind. Now, why was Josh going by another name? Something did not quite add up. She would ask Maia if she knew the reason why Josh was using the name Harding the next time she saw her.

*

During those first days of July, the westerly winds battered the coast and buffeted Maia's rose garden, stripping the newly opened blooms of their petals. Maia was beginning to despair. She wouldn't have any roses left if these winds didn't abate soon. However, after the 4th of July, the weather turned and became extremely hot, making it uncomfortable for her to work outside for any length of time. Her fiery hair and pale skin made her susceptible to sunburn; even a minuscule amount of time spent in the sun made her skin blister and itch. More often than not, she spent the hot summer days dressed in high-necked, white cotton dresses with long sleeves, topped off with a large-brimmed straw hat.

For the last couple of days, Josh and Maia ate their evening meal, picnic-style, outside in the rose garden under the shade of the rose arch. After the winds, the rose garden had recovered quickly and surrounded them with a glorious fragrance of newly opened blooms baked in the fierce sunshine. As neither wanted their usual hot meal, they picked from a plate of cold meat, bread, cheese, and pickles, washed down with Maia's refreshing elderflower cordial.

After supper, Maia returned to the house to finish the pots she had thrown earlier. Even now, early in the evening, the heat made sitting with the heavy leather apron on uncomfortable. Reluctantly leaving her work, she went to her bedroom to swill her face with water and sat by the open landing window to try and get some air and cool her damp body down.

*

Josh swilled his body with cold water and settled shirtless on the steps outside his hut to enjoy the twilight. The birds were in the trees, still twittering as they began their roost. The thermometer inside the hut was reading 90 degrees F – he didn't think it would drop much during the night. He suspected sleep would be nigh on impossible again. He ran his fingers through his hair. For some reason, his head ached – perhaps he had worked too long outdoors today – although he had kept his shirt on and always wore a hat!

He glanced up at the farmhouse and found all the windows flung wide open. Maia must also be feeling the heat.

Dabbing the beads of perspiration from his forehead it struck Josh that the only relief from this heat was to go down to the sea to take a dip. The icy waters of the mighty Atlantic felt suddenly very appealing! He pulled on his shirt and boots, grabbed a towel, and set off to the cove.

*

Maia watched with interest as Josh walked past with a towel slung over his shoulder. She knew where he was heading - she'd had similar thoughts herself. Though she was no swimmer, a paddle in the sea started to feel enticing.

Earlier that evening, Maia had noticed that Josh looked tired while they shared supper. He passed his tiredness off with a wave of his hand, blaming broken sleep the night before. She toyed with the idea of offering a bed in the farmhouse, as she knew the hut must be stifling, but somehow held back from offering it to him - after all, she had only known him for a few weeks. She was also unsure if she could trust herself if they slept under the same roof. She felt sorry for him now – he was clearly uncomfortable. Why else would he be setting off for the sea?

Although the moon was waning and in its last quarter, the light was bright enough to see Josh as he walked down the hill in front of her. By the time Maia reached the beach, Josh had shed his clothes and walked into the sea. She held back slightly, allowing him to walk far enough in to cover his modesty before kicking off her shoes and hitching up her skirt to walk barefoot in the surf.

She watched him plough through the water, and then he turned and must have realised someone was watching him.

'Is that you, Maia?' He called out.

'Yes, sorry, I don't want to disturb you. I just want to dip my legs in the sea for a moment, and then I'll leave you in peace.'

'No need to go on my account,' he said, standing up to wade through the surf. 'Come on in – it's wonderful.'

'I can't swim.'

'A dip then.'

'I don't have a costume on.' *In fact, she had nothing on under her dress.*

'No matter, it's almost dark, and I'll turn around until you get in. I promise I won't look.'

Glancing about to make sure no one else was watching, the thought of stripping to dip naked in the sea thrilled her.

'Come on, it's lovely,' he beckoned.

'All right.'

Once he had turned away from her, Maia discarded her dress and waded in.

'Are you in yet?' he called.

'Yes, but I'm frightened to go too far, so you won't have to avert your eyes too long.' She swished the water onto her hot body until she felt deliciously cool before turning back towards the beach. She rubbed her salty skin vigorously and pulled her dress on, though it stuck alarmingly to her damp skin.

'Right, I'm decent,' she called out. 'I'm going back to the farm.'

'No, wait!' He was making his way up the beach, quite unabashed that he was naked in front of her.

She turned and felt a shiver of desire - he looked magnificent and still did nothing to cover himself. She saw him smile when he caught her looking at him.

'You don't seem to be at all concerned about your state of undress in front of me,' she said, folding her arms.

'Forgive me, Maia, but I reckon you have seen me like this before,' he teased.

Maia laughed lightly. She could not deny that she had watched him from her window. 'Well, you are inclined to strip and wash in my line of view,' she countered.

'Touché.' He grinned as he wrapped the towel around his waist and sat down beside her. 'I don't mind if you watch me,' he nudged her playfully. 'I quite like it. It makes me wonder if you want me,' he whispered.

Maia felt her breath catch. She turned to face him and smiled but did not answer.

'Do you want me, Maia?'

She took a deep breath, but before she could answer, a flash of lightning lit the sky, followed, in quick succession, by several more flashes. Seconds later, thunder boomed so loudly that it made them both shudder.

'Goodness!' Josh said. 'I did wonder if we would have a storm. I've had a headache all day. That's why I thought I would take a dip.'

'Oh dear. I'm sorry that I disturbed your dip.'

'You most certainly did not. You're very welcome company.'

Another flash lit up the beach, and thunder boomed again. Almost immediately, great fat raindrops fell, and they both jumped up.

'Come on, we need to get back,' he said, pulling his trousers up his damp legs.

She held his towel while he dragged his shirt on, then he grabbed her hand, and they ran laughing up the beach, wet sand splattering them as torrential rain hit the ground. They were soaked to the skin when they reached the farm, laughing but exhausted.

'At least we won't need to swill the salt water and sand off us.' Maia laughed as she opened the door. 'Do you want to come in?' she offered, aware that the question he had asked her before the storm had broken was still unanswered.

Josh paused for a moment and smiled gently. 'I'll come in for a headache powder if you have one, but then I'll go back to the hut and lie down until this headache abates.'

'Little chance of that happening with this noisy storm,' she answered as she mixed a powder in a glass of water at the sink.

'Nevertheless.' He took the glass and smiled warmly at her through his dripping hair. 'I'll see you tomorrow, Maia. Maybe you can answer my question then?'

'Maybe I will.' She smiled back.

*

Maia closed the door on him, pulled the bolt across, and then stripped off her sodden clothes.

Josh was so easy to be with - she felt safe with him. She knew what her answer would have been if the storm had not broken. So, it was with a light heart that she set off to bed while the magnificent thunderstorm raged overhead.

*

Jago stood at the window of Penn als Cottage and watched the storm over the sea. He was seething angry. He'd been out inspecting his ever-decreasing front garden as it crumbled slowly down the cliff when he'd heard voices carrying up from the beach.

Returning indoors, he had turned his telescope towards the beach, and by the light of the moon, he'd seen Maia and Harding laughing in the surf – both quite unabashed with each other's nakedness. He had watched that bastard take Maia's hand and run up Poldhu Hill in the rain. They were clearly lovers now, and that made his blood boil.

25

Maia was up with the lark that morning. The storm had not cleared the air, as she had hoped, but had left it humid and overcast. She saddled Shadow and rode down to the beach to collect any interesting finds that would give her inspiration for her pots.

On her return, and after milking the goats - as it was her turn - Maia decided to make the most of the dull day and spend some time in the garden tending her crops. Glancing around, Maia looked for Josh. It was unusual for him not to be out and about. The shepherd's hut door was closed, but the windows were open. Only when the pigs became vocal did Maia realise something was amiss. The pigs only set up a racket when hungry, which was rare nowadays as they were well looked after. Getting off her knees, Maia brushed down her skirt and walked over to the pigsty to find their trough empty! Quickly rectifying the situation and topping up the water trough, Maia felt a curl of irritation that Josh had left the animals wanting. She could only assume he had slept late after last night's trip to the beach. With a sharp knock on the shepherd's hut door, Maia stood back, arms folded, feeling the warm glow of last evening spent with him ebbing away. She would not tolerate her animals suffering from Josh's lack of care and would tell him so. When he did not appear, Maia knocked again and opened the hut door to find Josh on the floor, sweating profusely and shivering. Falling to her knees, she cupped his face, alarmed at his clammy skin.

'Josh, what is it? What's wrong?'

'Maia. I'm so sorry,' he said breathlessly.

'What's amiss?'

'I'm afraid it's malaria,' he gasped.

'Malaria!' She moved back. 'Is it contagious?'

'No, no. I promise it isn't.'

'Oh, thank goodness for that!' She moved back to him and gently touched his brow. 'You're burning up. Can I help you back to bed?'

'I can't stand. I've tried, but I can't.' His body shuddered involuntarily.

'Right, I'll go for help. I'll be back in a few minutes.'

Picking up her skirts, she climbed the stile and ran like the wind across the fields to find David Trevorrow at Polhormon Farm.

Her anxiety must have registered with him immediately because David grasped her arms to calm her. 'Maia, what is it?'

'It's Josh. He's collapsed in the shepherd's hut. I need help to get him to the house, but I also need to fetch the doctor.'

On hearing the commotion, Jimmy Trevorrow appeared behind his father and said, 'Ben has had a telephone installed at the saddlery workshop, Pa. I'll call the doctor from there, and then I'll follow you. You'll need me to help lift him.'

'Good lad. Come on, Maia.'

They ran across the meadow, knee high with wild flowers, though the beautiful spectacle escaped them in their haste to help Josh.

At the hut, they both observed the raging fever that had gripped Josh, and David stepped back slightly. 'Good God, what's wrong with him – is it the flu?'

'No, he said it was malaria.'

'Malaria! Isn't that a tropical disease?' David asked.

'I believe it is.'

'Where the hell has he got that from then?'

Jimmy joined them, breathing heavily from the run. 'The doctor is on his way,' he said.

'Good, grab his arms, Jimmy.' They pulled Josh to his feet, hooked his arms around their necks, and carried him towards the house. Maia ran ahead to open the doors, directing them to a bedroom, where they could lay him.

Josh was drenched with sweat and moaning incoherently as they rolled him onto the bed.

'Christ, he looks done for!' Jimmy uttered.

'He's deteriorating fast,' Maia said in a panic. 'Would one of you mind removing his clothes while I get a bowl of water and a sponge to cool him down?'

When Maia returned, Josh was bare-chested, his modesty covered only by a sheet, which was already staining damp from his sweating body as he began to thrash about in the bed.

David and Jimmy glanced at Maia in dismay. 'How are you going to cope with him, Maia?' David asked anxiously.

'I don't know,' she whispered fearfully, sponging his forehead to try and calm him. 'I really don't know.'

'Hello, Hello, doctor calling?' A voice came from the bottom of the stairs. David went to the landing to beckon him up.

Josh was shaking violently, and the doctor took one look at him and asked Maia gravely, 'Have you any idea what has brought this on?'

'No, except that he had a terrible headache last evening, and when I found him this morning, he had collapsed in his shed, though he was lucid enough then to say that he thought it was malaria.'

'Malaria! How the devil...?' The doctor shook his head and checked his temperature, then his pulse. 'I will give him something to cool and calm him for now, but he needs quinine. I'll need to go to the hospital in Helston for that.' With an injection administered to Josh, the doctor turned to Maia. 'Keep him cool. He may fight you for a while, but it's just the fever!'

'I'll stay with you until the doctor returns, Maia,' David said, and she nodded gratefully.

The injection calmed Josh slightly, but he still fought the covers, and twice, his dignity was compromised, causing Maia to avert her eyes as David covered him again.

'How on earth did he catch malaria, Maia?'

'I don't know, David,' she answered, not daring to disclose that he had been in the Navy.

'Has he not spoken to you of his travels?'

'No,' she lied.

David scratched his head. 'My pa served in the army during the Boer War, and he told me that some of his friends came down with malaria. Once they get it, it reoccurs,' David said gravely.

Maia's mouth tightened. 'Can you die of it?'

'Yes, it can be fatal if not diagnosed and treated quickly, but it was lucky that you found him, and he was able to tell you what it was.'

'Yes, thank God,' she sighed.

David reached over to cup Maia's hand. 'Don't worry. The doctor didn't seem too concerned with his condition. He knows how to treat Josh, so he is in good hands.'

Maia's eyes watered as she nodded.

*

Jimmy had to return home shortly after the doctor's visit, but before leaving, Maia asked David and Jimmy to keep Josh's illness to themselves.

'I don't want folks to know Josh is ill enough for him to reside in my house. I'm a woman alone here, and you know how people talk!' she said.

'You can depend on us, Maia,' David promised.

It was over an hour before Dr Martin returned with the quinine, though administering it was another matter. It took both Maia and David to hold Josh steady while the doctor administered a measure of quinine.

Josh coughed and choked and tried to spit out the bitter medicine, but the doctor persevered and managed to get most of the measure down his throat.

'It'll be easier to administer once the fever breaks,' the doctor assured them.

'How soon will that be, doctor?' Maia asked with a tremble in her voice.

'He should rally within twenty-four hours, but he will have to be treated with quinine every day for seven days.'

Maia baulked at the thought of the cost.

'He may vomit and lose control of his bowels – sometimes that does happen with this disease.' He glanced anxiously at Maia. 'I understand he is your farmhand?'

Maia nodded.

'Are you able to care for him, Maia, or should I arrange for a nurse?'

'A nurse will not be necessary. I'll care for him,' Maia lowered her eyes diffidently.

'Very well. I suggest you cover the bed with towels or blankets – something that will wash easily should Josh soil the bed,' he advised.

Maia nodded and ran to the linen cupboard for several towels, and after they tucked them under Josh's damp body, they all stood back, wiping away beads of perspiration at the exertion. The still and humid air had not helped with their task!

Another thunderstorm began to rumble in the distance – hopefully, it would cool the air this time, Maia thought.

'It's going to be a trying time for you, Maia,' the doctor said as he picked up his bag.

'I'll be fine,' she answered more confidently than she felt.

When she had seen the doctor out, David asked, 'Forgive me for asking, Maia, but can you afford all these doctor's visits?'

'Yes, I think I can, David. I am making some money now selling my pots through the Arts and Crafts Association. And, of course, I haven't got Henry drinking all our profits now!' She arched an eyebrow.

'Indeed!' He smiled. 'And nursing Josh, are you sure you can manage?'

'Well, someone has to,' she said softly. 'I think Josh would rather have me tending him than a stranger.'

David smiled broadly. 'And I know for a fact that he would rather have you looking after him than anyone else.'

Maia lowered her lashes shyly.

'You're a good woman, Maia. Josh is a lucky man to have you care for him.' David got up. 'Now, I shall leave you, but I will check in with you later today to see if you need anything.'

'That's very kind of you, David. Thank you. I may need someone to sit with Josh while I see to my livestock.'

'I'd be happy to help.'

*

No sooner had Maia shown David out and locked the door than she heard Josh vomiting. Racing back upstairs, she quickly turned him on his side so that he would not choke.

'Oh, you poor thing,' she said, grabbing the bowl she had been using to sponge him down and quickly began to clean him up. Pulling the soiled towel from under him, she replaced it with a clean one, but Josh would not stay on his side. He rolled onto his back and tossed his head violently from side to side, fighting some inner demon.

Cupping her cool hands to his hot face, she whispered, 'Stay calm, Josh, and all will be well. I'm right here by your side.' He whimpered slightly, and his eyes flickered open momentarily before they rolled back into his head. 'Hush now.' She took the soiled towel to soak in the bathtub; she had no doubt there would be more soiled linen before long. With a clean bowl of water, she began to sponge down his body, and now that David had gone, she could deal with him without embarrassment. Josh was taller and broader in the shoulders than Henry had been - his stomach was toned, and so too were the muscles on his arms, which looked powerful and pronounced as he tensed them during his ongoing anguish. Once again, he kicked away the sheet, exposing Maia to the rest of his body. Although she had seen him naked at the beach the previous evening, it seemed wrong in this situation, so she averted her eyes as she covered him again and quickly tucked the covers tightly under the mattress to secure the bottom half of the sheet. Before David had left, they had considered dressing Josh in his underclothes, but with the constant risk of incontinence, it would have been futile.

Finally, after fighting against her constant cooling sponge for several hours, Josh relaxed. Thankfully, without losing control of his bowels! Small mercies!

*

It was just after four when a knock came on the front door. Checking her visitor from the bedroom window, she was relieved to find David Trevorrow at her door.

'How is he?' he asked, following her up the stairs.

'Settled a little, thank goodness.'

'Do you want to get on with anything?'

'Yes, please. I need to feed the pigs and milk the goats.'

'Take your time, Maia. I'm in no rush.'

Maia sighed exhaustedly. 'Thank you. I'll lock you in if that's okay. I don't want Jago to know what is happening.'

David frowned. 'Has he been bothering you again?'

She nodded. 'We had a slight altercation a few days ago. He has accused Josh of trying to wheedle his way into my affections and the farm, which Jago still thinks should be his by-rights. He is jealous of Josh, though he has no reason to be,' she added quickly. 'Unfortunately, jealousy makes him dangerous. He got it into his head that he could pick up where Henry left off, and not, I might add, just with the farm!' She grimaced at the thought.

'What the devil does he want the farm for? He has a perfectly lucrative car business!'

'I don't know, David. He must have some scheme up his sleeve. I saw him measuring the width of my farm gate a few weeks ago. When I confronted him, he said it needed widening, as he'd nearly scraped his car coming in! But frankly, it had been perfectly wide enough for him before that, and he has the largest car hereabouts!'

'Damn the man!' David folded his arms. 'I'll speak to him if you want?'

'Well, after our last argument, I told him not to come here again, but you know Jago – he does what he pleases.'

'Just give me the word if he calls again, and I'll sort him out once and for all.'

*

The pigs were agitated when Maia approached, as though they knew something was amiss. Josh had cared for them these past three weeks, and they had become used to him. Maia gave them all some extra feed and tickled as many piglet ears as she could. After milking the goats, she put the hens to bed, fed Shadow in her field, and returned to the farmhouse, just as Dr Martin had driven into the yard.

'How is the patient?'

'Settling,' she said, unlocking the door. 'He was sick three times, so I suspect he lost the medicine you gave him, but the vomiting stopped about three hours ago. David Trevorrow kindly offered to sit with him while I dealt with the farm business.'

After a quick check on his temperature, the doctor got David to hold Josh's head steady while he poured another measure of quinine into his mouth. This time, most of it went in.

'Will he be sick again?' Maia asked.

'I hope not. We need to keep the quinine down to make him better. How soon after I administered the last lot was he sick?'

'Within minutes of you leaving, I'm afraid.'

'I will wait a while then, just to make sure.'

'How long will it take before he gets better, doctor?' Maia asked anxiously.

'As I said earlier, he should rally within twenty-four hours, but the episode will have knocked the stuffing out of him. I have only seen a few cases of malaria; they seem to follow a similar pattern: fever, sickness, disorientation, sweating, and headaches – the latter lasts a few days. You will still have your hands full, but his symptoms will lessen as the days progress.'

'When would he be fully back to health?' She asked, watching Josh closely for any sign of vomiting.

'Once the fever breaks, he should recover completely in two weeks.'

Maia's heart sank. How would she ever cope?

Seeing her dismay, David reached out to her. 'Don't worry, Maia. I'll make sure you get all the help you need until Josh is better.'

'Thank you,' she said, relief washing over her.

'Do you know how he has contracted malaria?' The doctor asked Maia.

'No, doctor.'

'Malaria is a disease caused by a parasite that spreads to humans through the bites of infected mosquitoes. It is normally found in tropical countries. Has he mentioned that he has been travelling?'

She shook her head.

'Sorry, Maia,' David said as he got up and donned his jacket to leave. 'I'll have to go, but I'll pop back after milking in the morning to free you up for a while. I'll see myself out.'

'Thank you, David. Your help is very much appreciated.'

Maia and the doctor stood over Josh for fifteen more minutes, and when Josh showed no signs of vomiting this time, the doctor also took his leave.

*

As darkness fell, another thunderstorm rumbled in, though much more violent this time, with sheet lightning and booms of thunder that shook the farmhouse windows. It felt as though the world was ending.

Eventually, the storm passed, and Josh fell into a deep sleep, enabling Maia to rush downstairs to do some essential indoor chores - her pottery would have to wait a while. After pouring some milk into a saucer for Prudence to lap, she put the rest of the goat milk into a large bowl and set it aside to make cheese, though Lord knows when she would find time to take her cheese to Mrs Blair. Grabbing a bite to eat, Maia took a mug of tea upstairs and settled down to sit with Josh. Her eyelids were heavy, and with the heat of the evening and sheer exhaustion, she dozed in the chair until the storm returned with a vengeance. The lightning was spectacular over the sea, but the thunder had upset Josh again. He was moaning incoherently and sweating profusely again, so Maia set to and began to sponge him down until the storm had passed and he settled once more.

Believing Josh would not become lucid for many hours, Maia lay on the bed beside him and closed her eyes in exhaustion. She was woken in the early hours by an audible gasp and glanced at Josh, who looked wide-eyed and disorientated.

'It's all right, Josh. Settle down. You're going to be fine.'

He seemed alarmed to find her beside him, but his mind was on more pressing matters. 'I need, I need to...' he grasped himself.

'Oh, I see! Just a moment.' Swiftly running around the bed, she grabbed the bucket she had in place in case he vomited again and strategically placed it in his hands before quickly leaving the room to give him some privacy. Hearing an audible sigh of relief from him, she returned to the room just in time to stop the bucket from falling to the floor. Josh had once again closed his eyes, his mouth had slackened, and he was breathing deeply back into a slumber.

She looked down at his handsome face and smiled. If he could control his bladder, perhaps the worst of the crisis was over.

26

Over the next couple of days, David, true to his word, arrived to sit with Josh, bringing with him his soon-to-be daughter-in-law, Jane, to milk the goats for Maia.

'My milkmaids have noticed that Josh hasn't been around these last few days, so I told them that Josh has the flu and is lying incapacitated in his hut.' David winked. 'I told them to keep quiet about it because if Jago gets wind that Josh is out of action, he'll begin to bother you again with his unwanted help. They understand that you're uncomfortable with Jago visiting Wild Cliff Farm. They'll keep their counsel, of that, I'm sure. Despite Jago thinking he's desirable to all women, none of the young girls who work for me think well of him.'

'Jago would be wounded to know that!' Maia quipped satirically.

David laughed. 'Anyway, the milkmaids were practically fighting over who could come with me to help with the goats. In the end, I brought Jane. She, for one, will not try to knock on the shepherd's hut door to see if Josh is well. She only has eyes for my eldest son.' He smiled gently.

'I'm so grateful to you all,' Maia said, pulling on her gum boots to see to the pigs. 'I'll be as quick as I can.'

*

Jago was running late for a meeting with a client that morning. As he pulled his car to a halt at the junction at the bottom of his road, despite being late, he stopped to take the time to eye the young Blackthorn girl as she ran across the road to the Poldhu Tea Room. Jago marvelled at her pretty face, pink from running, and her long, dark, glossy hair shining in the summer sunshine. He would have to bide his time there, having been informed that Fee was only fifteen years old! Though folks hereabouts thought Jago was a cad, there were rules about young girls to abide by. He smiled inwardly - he would not have to wait long. He had had it on good authority that she would turn sixteen later this month, and that happy thought gave him a frisson of pleasure.

A car approached down from Mullion Road, and seeing that it was Dr Martin driving the Ford Model T that Jago had sold to him a couple of years ago, he let it pass. The Ford Model T was a sturdy, reliable workhorse, built for practical rather than aesthetic reasons. Not like this beauty! Jago caressed the steering wheel of his Alvis 12/50, knowing his car was the envy of everyone hereabouts.

With nothing else on the road, he followed the good doctor up Poldhu Hill, easing back when he realised the doctor was turning into Wild Cliff Farm. *Was Maia ill?*

He pulled up just a little out of sight from the farm, but still with a visual of the farm's back door. To his astonishment, he saw David Trevorrow answer the door! David let the doctor in, and then a few seconds later, he saw David leave the farm to walk towards Polhormon Dairy. *What the devil had Trevorrow been doing there?* Jago waited as long as he could, but when the doctor seemed in no hurry to leave the farm, he cursed to himself. He couldn't wait any longer; he needed to be in Helston. The client Jago was meeting had booked an appointment to view one of his more prestigious cars, and as it was his assistant Sidney's day off, Jago would have to go. As he started the car up again, he thought that he would damn well find out what was going on later that day.

*

The doctor was pleased and relieved to hear that Josh was in better control of his bodily functions after Maia told him that Josh had woken up a couple of times and asked to use the bucket.

Josh woke upon hearing the doctor's voice but was terribly drowsy, barely able to keep his eyes open.

'Josh, if you can hear me, I need you to stay awake long enough to sip this quinine,' the doctor said.

Josh nodded sleepily, grimacing at the bitterness of the liquid.

'Have you had malaria before, Josh?'

'Yes,' he murmured, 'three times.'

'Where on earth did you pick it up from?'

Maia stood behind the doctor with her fingers crossed that Josh was lucid enough not to disclose that he had been in the Navy - that would really give the game away. Fortunately, Josh drifted back into slumber without revealing more.

The doctor smiled at Maia. 'I'll ask him again when he's less sleepy. I shall check back this evening, and if all is well, I'll leave you with the quinine. If you can administer the medicine, it will save you money on my visits. Do you think you can manage to do it?'

'Yes, doctor. Thank you.' The longer she could keep the doctor away, the more time they had to come up with a feasible story of how Josh had contracted malaria.

*

David was pleased to find that Josh was more settled when he arrived later to help Maia. With Jane, the milkmaid, helping with the goats again, David only had to spend half an hour in vigil that day. When Maia had finished her chores, she let David out of the door and locked it after him, smiling when she heard a knock on the door a couple of minutes later, thinking David had returned.

'Have you forgotten something?' Maia laughed as she unlocked and opened the door to find Jago on her doorstep!

'Jago! What do you want?' she snapped.

'A fine way to greet someone who has only called to see if all is well.'

'Of course, all is well,' she said irritably. 'Why wouldn't it be?'

'Then why was the doctor calling, and why is David Trevorrow in and out of your house?'

Maia flushed with irritation. 'Are you spying on me?'

'No, I saw the doctor and David this morning as I drove past. I've just seen David again as he was leaving. So, what is going on? Are you ill? You don't look ill!'

'What is wrong is of no concern of yours, Jago.'

'Why do you need a doctor?'

'For personal reasons,' she snapped. 'David is just helping us out at the moment.'

'So, you bring another outsider in to help instead of calling on family.'

'Jago, you are *not* my family anymore,' she insisted.

Before he could answer, a car drove into the yard. Jago turned, and Maia's heart fell when she saw it was Dr Martin.

Jago stepped back to let the doctor pass.

'Good afternoon, Mr Penhallow.'

Jago nodded. 'Doctor.'

'Good afternoon, Maia.' The doctor doffed his hat at her. 'How is my patient faring?'

Maia cut a glance at Jago and answered tentatively. 'Improving slightly, thank you.'

'Ah, that's good news,' Dr Martin said, stepping into the kitchen. When Maia saw Jago about to follow him in, she quickly closed the door on him and bolted it. A sudden kick to the door clearly expressed Jago's annoyance at the exclusion.

Dr Martin turned and raised a questioning eyebrow.

'I do not want anyone to know about Josh's illness or the fact that he is residing here – especially with me being a woman alone here. Jago can be quite indiscreet at times,' she explained.

Dr Martin gestured that he understood.

*

Later that evening, Jago was drinking at The Old Inn. Despite closing a deal for one of his most prestigious cars earlier that day, Jago was seething into his glass of ale at being excluded from Wild Cliff Farm so rudely.

When Tom Pilgrim, one of the inn's regular customers, joined him, he noted Jago's poor mood. 'You look like a bear with a sore head,' he joked.

'I feel like one.' Jago answered irritably. 'Something's amiss at Wild Cliff Farm, and Maia will not tell me what it is.'

'How do you mean amiss?'

'The doctor has called twice today, and David Trevorrow has been visiting, helping out, I'm told! The thing is, Maia doesn't look ill. She looked fine when she answered the door to me. If something is amiss up there, I should be informed. It is my farm by rights.'

The conversation died when David Trevorrow walked in and ordered a glass of ale.

Jago could not hold back. He sidled up to stand beside David. 'So, are *you* going to tell me what you're doing at Wild Cliff Farm so regularly?'

David shot Jago a look of contempt. 'Minding my own business, as you should be,' he growled.

'It is my business. It's my late brother's farm; I have a right to know.'

'I think not!' David snapped.

'Is Maia ill?'

'If she is, that is her business and none of yours.'

'Well, if she is incapacitated somehow, it seems that Maia has employed a wastrel in Josh Harding if he cannot manage the farm without *your* help! You must tell her to get rid of him immediately, and I'll send someone around who can manage without her having to call on you. I'm sure you have enough work at the dairy. In fact, I have just the person in mind: Graham Treloar, who is looking for farm work. I shall bring him to the farm in the morning.'

David slammed his glass down on the bar. In an instant, he grabbed Jago around his throat and pinned him to the wall. Everyone in the bar stood back in shocked silence.

'*David.* I don't want any trouble in here,' the landlord warned, but David kept his grip around Jago's neck.

'I shall tell you this only once, Jago,' David snarled. 'Maia does not want your interference. You will stay well away from Wild Cliff Farm, Maia, and Josh if you know what is good for you. Do you hear me?'

Jago's eyes widened, but he did not speak.

'*Do you hear me?*' he reiterated, banging Jago's head against the wall.

'Ow!' Jago yelped. 'Yes, yes.'

'Good. If you set one foot on that farm ever again, I shall deal with you most severely. That farm is Maia's, not yours or your late brothers. It belongs to Maia! Understand?'

Josh bared his teeth.

'*I said, do you understand?*' David knocked Jago's head against the wall again, and this time Jago nodded.

'Good, now *leave* her be,' he growled.

Jago slithered down the wall to sit in an untidy heap when David released his grip on his neck.

David drained his glass of ale, slammed it on the bar, and left the inn.

Tom Pilgrim reached down to help Jago, but Jago shrugged his help away.

'I've been thinking,' Tom whispered to Jago. 'You said the doctor visited twice today!'

'What of it?' Jago answered, rubbing his throat where David had grasped him.

'Well, I'm not sure if this is relevant, but...' Tom scratched the stubble on his chin. 'Our Sadie's eldest works at the Helston Hospital as a porter. He mentioned that our good doctor was at the pharmacy picking quinine up on Saturday. He overheard the doctor say to the pharmacist that he had a patient with malaria and needed to administer quinine every eight hours for a week.'

'Malaria!'

'Aye, and by all accounts, it's a tropical disease, so the chances are that it isn't Maia he is visiting – if you know what I mean. Because, as far as I know, Maia has never left Cornwall to travel abroad - unless you know any different?' Tom raised his eyebrows.

Jago shook his head and took a sip of his ale as he digested this snippet of information. He narrowed his eyes - that could only mean it was Harding who was suffering, and if that was the case, where had he been to contract it? Maia had told him that Harding had come from Exeter. He laughed disdainfully. Harding might be from over the Tamar, but as sure as hell, that wasn't the tropics. There was obviously more to Josh Harding than met the eye, and for some unknown reason, they were keeping his past a secret. He was determined to find out one way or another.

*

At Wild Cliff Farm, the next couple of days followed much the same pattern. Josh had periods of disturbed sleep and drenching sweats, and when he did open his eyes, he could not stand the light due to his ongoing headaches. The doctor left Maia to administer the quinine and had told her he would return on Friday, when hopefully Josh would be able to explain how he had contracted malaria. Thankfully, Maia had no more visits from Jago either. David had told her he had given him a final warning to stay away.

It was on Wednesday evening – five days after falling ill - that Josh turned a corner in his illness and started to pull through. He slept more but was able to deal with any toilet needs himself, though they did have one accident, which mortified Josh momentarily, though he soon fell back into slumberland and the incident was forgotten. With Josh sleeping longer, Maia had more time for her outdoor chores without the help of David or Jane, the milkmaid. She had even decorated a couple of pots, though a trip to the Bochym's kiln was still out of the question until Josh had complete control of his bodily functions.

*

At Bochym, despite the disruptive July heat and storms and the Treen's noisy new baby on the premises, a period of near normality had settled on the household staff, though everyone still felt the loss of little Loveday keenly.

With the past very much in the forefront of her mind since Kitty's grandson Josh had visited her, Sissy could not help but be thankful that Peter and Sarah Dunstan, the kindest of employers, were now the custodians of the manor instead of the old Earl and Countess. But then, no, Sissy reprimanded herself. Lady Lucinda Dunstan, the Dowager Countess, now residing in France with her daughter, had been a fair mistress and should not be tarred with the same brush as her odious husband, the old Earl. The thoughts of the previous senior Bochym staff, Albert Lanfear, Joan Bligh, and John Carrington, made Sissy shiver with disdain. She wished Kitty could come back and see what a happy place it was to work now.

It was Thursday morning, the 12th of July. Sissy was serving the staff breakfast while Joe Treen doled out the mail he had just sorted.

'One for you today, Mrs Blair,' Joe said with a smile.

'Me?' Sissy said in astonishment, glancing at the unfamiliar handwriting – it was certainly not from her sister, Effy! Who on earth could be writing to her? Checking that everyone had all they needed for breakfast, she flipped her tea cloth over her shoulder and opened the letter.

From Mrs Kitty Walsh
42 Cubb's Alley
Portsmouth
My dear, Sissy.

I have no idea if you are still at Bochym Manor or if that nasty Mrs Bligh is still reading everybody's mail, so I shall keep this missive short and sweet.

If you are there, please let me know, as I would love to hear from you. I apologise that I have been unable to contact you before now. I do so wish to catch up with you after all these years.

Love, Kitty.

'Well, I never.' Sissy sat down heavily on a chair by the servant's table; it was as though she had conjured Kitty out of thin air.

'Are you quite well, Mrs Blair?' Joe Treen asked anxiously.

'Yes, quite well. Thank you, Mr Treen,' she said, pushing the envelope into her apron pocket. 'Just a voice from the past in my letter.'

'Hopefully, it's nobody who will cause you upset?'

'On the contrary. It's a shock, but a nice one.'

Later that evening, Sissy sat at her table in her cosy cottage and wrote a short letter back to Kitty.

My dearest friend, Kitty.

How wonderful to hear from you! Yes, I am still here, making meals for the Dunstans! As expected, there have been many changes over the last forty-one years at Bochym. Bligh and Carrington got their marching orders in 1902, and you'll be pleased to know that the old Earl is dead and rotting in hell, and so too is Lanfear - hung for murder!

Sissy tapped her teeth with her pen - something stopped her from telling Kitty that she had met Josh, her grandson – that could come later. Sissy also decided that she would tell Kitty in a later letter how she had gotten rid of Joyce, the laundry maid, and smiled, thinking back to that day. It had all come about a couple of days after Kitty had been dismissed. Sissy and June, the scullery maid, had noticed that Joyce seemed elated at Kitty's dismissal.

Joyce, though, had made the fundamental mistake of confiding in June, boasting that she was glad about Kitty's banishment from the manor.

'Of course, we all know what the serious misdemeanour was that Kitty committed!' Joyce boasted proudly as she pegged the washing out.

'Oh yes, and what would that be?' June had asked.

'Kitty has been fraternising with Freddy, the gardener's assistant. I overheard her say they were getting married soon, so she must have been loose with him! Mrs Bligh does not stand for loose morals in this household, so she rightly banished her as soon as she found out,' Joyce giggled.

As soon as June relayed the conversation to Sissy, it was clear that Joyce had informed Mrs Bligh of Kitty's intention to marry because nobody else had known about it, and this had set in motion the dreadful events that followed.

The very next day, when Joyce put Her Ladyship's silk underclothes to soak and loaded the dolly tub with the family's crisp white linen bedsheets, she found to her horror that everything turned yellow and was ruined. No amount of scrubbing on Joyce's part brought them back to white. As Joyce received her marching orders on the instructions of Her Ladyship, Sissy placed her pastry brush and pot of turmeric back on her cooking shelf.

Putting a nib to paper, Sissy continued to write.

I also have so much to tell you, Kitty, but I will let you tell me your news first.

I shall look forward to hearing from you very soon.

With love, Sissy.

She sealed the envelope and looked forward to Saturday and seeing Maia when she dropped her fortnightly box of goat cheese off. She could not wait to tell her the good news about Kitty.

27

It had been over two weeks since learning about his darling Kitty, and Freddy could not get what had happened to her out of his mind. He was suffering from bouts of melancholia, and tears would spring forth without any warning. Several times over the last fortnight, Her Ladyship had questioned his unhappy disposition, even suspecting that Freddy might be ill and insisting he should share his burden with her so she could help. Time and time again, he apologised for bringing his low mood to work. Eventually, he told her that he was not ill but was dealing with something very private and personal, which he had to work through in his mind.

His disturbed sleep was not helping his situation. He constantly laid awake, thinking about Kitty. Now that he knew she was still alive and somewhere out there, he was desperate to see her again. If only that damn grandson of hers would tell him where she was! He would make sure she was alone before he spoke to her, not wanting to cause her any trouble with her husband *if* he *was* still alive.

He thanked the Lord that someone had been kind enough to come along and offer her marriage, and he certainly did not blame Kitty for carving a life out with someone else. Oh, but he was so jealous of Kitty's husband and could not stop the uncharitable thought that he had died! It was driving him crazy to think that until he did die, Freddy could not see Kitty and apologise to her for his behaviour and unguarded words about ruined girls. He so wanted to tell her that no matter what had happened to her, he still loved her dearly after all these years. For now, though, he must try to put Kitty out of his mind and focus on the busy job of getting the gardens pristine for the annual Bochym Manor garden party in August. He owed it to Her Ladyship for the patience and compassion she had shown him these past couple of weeks.

*

On Friday, seven days after he fell ill, Josh was still abed and sleeping for most of the day. Over the week, whenever Josh woke, he was totally disorientated and complained of a terrible headache. The pain meant he could barely keep anything down and had eaten nothing much. His skin and the whites of his eyes had yellowed – it was all part and parcel of malaria; the doctor had told Maia.

'Will this happen again, doctor?' She asked when he made his next visit.

'It could, yes, but as soon as he feels any symptoms coming along, we need to get quinine into him so that it does not take hold like this. If, as he says, he has had this before, I am at a loss to know why he did not seek my help sooner.'

Maia had a good idea why. From now on, she would ensure that if Josh stayed with her, they would get help quickly should it arise again.

The doctor glanced down at Josh, who was sleeping soundly. 'I will not disturb him – he needs this rest. Has he been lucid enough to tell you how he contracted it?'

'No,' she lied.

Maia had been pondering a story they could spin about where he had contracted malaria. A scenario quite different from his being in the Navy. But before Josh could stay awake long enough to absorb the information, she had to try and keep the doctor at bay.

'I will send word to you as soon as Josh is able to speak to you,' she said. 'Then you don't have a wasted journey.'

'I would appreciate that. I had to inform the Ministry of Health of his condition; it's compulsory. The ministry is keen to know if he has been in the Armed Forces or on a merchant ship abroad.'

'I see,' she breathed.

'I will look forward to hearing from you,' the doctor said as he took his leave.

Maia closed the door after him and leant against it – they must put a watertight story together to put the Ministry of Health off Josh's case. Maia's most pressing concern was delivering her goat cheese order to Mrs Blair at Bochym the next day. With Josh still so disorientated when he woke, Maia was reluctant to leave him, but the cheese was ready and waiting - she had to get it to Bochym one way or another.

Once again, David came to her rescue. When he came to see how Josh was faring that morning, he said he would ask Ben Pearson, the saddler, to pop in and collect it on his way home from work that evening.

'Now that Ben lives on the Bochym Estate, I'm sure he will oblige.'

'Thank you, David. You are heaven-sent.'

David grinned. 'I've been called many things in my time, but never that.'

'Well, you have been a star this last week. I don't know how I would have coped without you.'

'So, how is the old lazy bones today?' David joked.

'I think we may have him back in the land of the living by the end of the weekend.'

*

Maia heard the car pull up in the yard later that afternoon and froze, thinking it was Jago. She glanced at Prudence - a good indication of whether the visitor was friend or foe - she had pricked her ears but seemed unconcerned.

Peeping out the window, Maia was relieved to find Ben Pearson walking to her door. 'It's all right, Prudence; no spitting is required.'

'I do hope I haven't inconvenienced you too much, Ben,' Maia said, handing him the cheese as Prudence wound affectionately around his legs.

'Not at all. It's no bother, Maia. I know you have your hands full at the moment with Josh having the flu. I'm glad to help. I hope Josh feels better soon and is up and about again.'

'Thank you. He's on the mend. Please tell Mrs Blair I will collect the plate the cheese is on when I next see her. Would you also be so kind as to tell Her Ladyship I am behind with my ceramics? I'm afraid there will be a delay of a week.'

'Consider it done.'

*

Ben Pearson breezed into the Bochym kitchen that evening. His marriage to Lady Emma gave him no airs and graces; therefore, the staff greeted him, as they had always greeted him, with a cheery, 'Hello, Ben.'

'Special delivery from Maia, Mrs Blair!'

'Oh!' Sissy wiped her hands down her apron as she inspected the cheese. 'Maia normally brings it on a Saturday – tomorrow. Is she ill?'

'No, but Josh is incapacitated at the moment.'

'Goodness, whatever is wrong with the poor lad?' She smiled inwardly, realising the affinity she felt now with Kitty's grandson.

'He has the flu, so Maia is extra busy on the farm. David Trevorrow has been helping her.'

'Oh, lordy me! Well, if you see her again, send my regards to them both and tell her...' Sissy smiled, thinking of Kitty's letter: '...Tell her I have some news for her and to pop in and see me when she can.'

*

On Saturday, at the motorcar showroom, Sydney had had to keep his head down all that day – Jago had been in such a bad mood. The atmosphere in the showroom was so unpleasant that Sydney feared it was putting customers off. He glanced at the clock – it was nearly time to close for the day, but he was damned if he was going to put up with another day like today.

'Right, come on, spill the beans. What is eating you now? Maia again?' Sydney demanded.

'If it is, I shall not be taking any more advice from you on that matter! Your last suggestion that I take her flowers and arrange to take her for dinner went down like a tonne of bricks.'

Sydney twisted his mouth. 'You need to give up on her, Jago – you'll give yourself a heart attack being so angry all the time!'

'Just shut up! Anyway, it's not about Maia – it's that bastard who lives there – he's getting his feet too far under Maia's table.'

Sydney tipped his head. 'What about him?'

'They are hiding something about his past. *He* is hiding something! And in my books, you only hide something if you've done something wrong.'

Sydney raised an eyebrow, *and you would know*, he mused. 'How do you know he's hiding something?'

'We've heard that someone in the Mullion area has malaria.'

'Really!'

'Yes, and I've seen the doctor going in and out of Wild Cliff Farm. I think it's Harding. If it is, I want to know where the devil he has contracted it, because it sure as hell is not here in England! So, where has he been, eh? And why has he been so secretive about it?'

'How do you know he is being secretive?'

'There are very few strangers who come into our midst where we don't find out everything about them and why they are here – otherwise, they're not accepted. Harding has said nothing about being abroad to anyone – something like that would have got out.'

'Isn't malaria contagious?' Sydney said, scratching his chin.

Jago straightened his shoulders. 'I don't know. Is it?'

'It sounds like it!'

Jago tightened his lips. 'It had better not be. Bloody David Trevorrow has been visiting Wild Cliff Farm, and David has been drinking in The Old Inn! He was in there the other night. He had me pinned to the bloody wall he did when I questioned what was going on up there.'

Sydney surreptitiously moved away from Jago. 'Bloody hell, he might have given it to you!'

Jago paled at the thought.

'If I were you, Jago, I would go and speak to the doctor about it.'

Jago did not need telling twice. He swiped his car keys from his desk and drove like a maniac to Mullion. He didn't go to the doctors - he went straight to The Old Inn.

'Usual?' the landlord asked when he walked through the door.

'Not yet.' He turned to address the other men drinking there. 'Look here, everyone. I have it on good authority that we have someone in our vicinity with an infectious disease, and I know who it is! Josh Harding – that *up* countryman who has come into our midst. Not only that, but David Trevorrow has been visiting him, and we all know that David has been coming in here, spreading the infection around and no doubt contaminating the milk we all drink. I reckon we might all come down with it soon if we're not careful.'

His audience had stopped drinking and looked aghast.

'How do you know it's infectious?' someone asked.

'All tropical diseases are!' Jago countered. 'I think we should all go and see Dr Martin about this. He's the one treating Harding. We should ask him outright if Harding has brought disease into our community, and if he has, we must all insist that he be sent back to where he came from!'

The crowd looked at each other and nodded in agreement.

'Who is with me then?'

Half of the drinkers drained their glasses in readiness to leave, much to the displeasure of the landlord.

Jago smiled. 'Right, you lot, go and get your wives. We'll have a better chance of outing the bastard if we go en masse.'

*

Dr Martin's housekeeper, Mrs Sadler, opened the door and stood back in shock to find an angry crowd of people on her front lawn.

'What do you all want? Shoo, shoo. Get off my lawn this instant,' she squeaked.

'We want to see the doctor,' the crowd shouted in unison.

'What? All of you! You'll have to make an appointment.'

'We're not leaving until we see him. Now!' Jago stepped forward.

'Mrs Sadler, what on earth is going on out here?' Dr Martin gently moved his housekeeper to one side as he addressed the crowd. 'What is the meaning of this?'

Jago folded his arms. 'We know you've been treating Josh Harding for malaria, and we want him removed from our community immediately. He has no right bringing an infectious disease into our midst.'

Dr Martin rolled his eyes in annoyance. 'Mr Penhallow I have no intention of discussing *any* of my patients' conditions with you, or any of you, for that fact. How would you like it if I discussed that I was treating a boil on your backside to all and sundry?'

The crowd behind Jago laughed heartily, and someone shouted, 'Is that why you always stand at the bar in The Old Inn, Jago? Is it painful?'

'I don't have a bloody boil on my backside!' Jago snarled and glared at the doctor.

Dr Martin folded his arms. 'No, you don't, but you take my point now.'

Jago ground his teeth angrily. 'This is different. We have it on good authority that you are treating someone hereabouts for malaria and as you have been frequently visiting Wild Cliff Farm, we believe it is Josh Harding. You have a duty to tell us how and where he contracted it. We insist on knowing where he has been. Damn it, man! We could all catch it and die,' Jago shouted.

'Mr Penhallow, I do not have to tell you anything, and you seem ignorant of the fact that malaria, *if* anyone were to suffer from it, is a common infection that many, many men brought home from war. There will be few people here on my lawn who have not had a family member suffer from it if they served abroad. Malaria is an infection that is difficult to treat. But, I might add, *not* contagious. Now, please vacate my property before I call the police.'

'It's Harding who has it though, isn't it?' Jago insisted.

'Good day to you, sir.' Dr Martin ushered his housekeeper inside the house and slammed the door in Jago's face.

When Jago turned to the crowd, they were all deeply disgruntled at him for wasting their time.

'Keep your vendettas to yourself in the future, Jago,' someone muttered as they made their way back from whence they came.

28

As Maia predicted, it was Sunday afternoon when Josh became completely aware of his surroundings. The quinine treatment had ended, though the past week had been a whirl of pain and confusion for him. Now fully awake, he glanced about the unfamiliar room, spotted a glass of water on the bedside table, and drank thirstily from it to rid himself of the sour taste in his mouth. He smiled when he saw his good luck charm - the four-leaf clover in copal - which his grandma had given him, sitting next to where his water had stood. Again, it had helped him through a difficult time.

He needed to relieve himself quickly. He pushed the covers away, shocked to find himself completely naked. Pulling the sheets back to cover himself, he remembered that between bouts of unconsciousness, Maia had been in the room with him, and if he was not mistaken, David Trevorrow had too. He vaguely remembered speaking to a doctor, and that worried him. Had he given away his secret and told them where he had contracted malaria?

It was no good - the urgency to pee was at the forefront of his mind, so wrapping his sheet around him, he moved his legs over the side of the bed and tried to stand, falling hard to the ground as he did.

*

Maia was in the studio when she heard the thud from above. Without discarding her splattered apron, she ran up the stairs to find Josh wrapped in a sheet, struggling to get up.

'Goodness! What's happened? Did you fall out of bed?'

Josh looked up at Maia in alarm. 'No. I appear not to have a functioning pair of legs,' he said, trying desperately to cover himself.

'Oh, dear. The doctor said you would be as weak as a kitten for a while. Let's get you back up. Can you try to help me to help you.' Hooking her arm under his, he grabbed the mattress, and with whatever strength he could muster, together they heaved him back on the bed.

She looked down on him sympathetically; he looked pale from the effort. 'Can I get you anything?'

'I'm really sorry, but I need to relieve myself.'

'Here.' She grabbed the bucket and pushed it into his hands.

He frowned. 'I err, I can't do it in this - you would have to take it away!'

Maia's smile broadened. 'And who do you think has taken the bucket away to empty all this week?'

'Oh!' He felt himself flush with embarrassment.

'I'll leave you to it.' She waited on the landing for a couple of minutes and found, on entering the bedroom, the bucket tucked under the bed out of sight.

'I might get enough strength back in my legs to empty it myself later,' he said anxiously.

Maia nodded. 'We'll see. I must say, it's so good to see you back in the land of the living. It was a worrying time for us all.'

'All?'

'The doctor came every eight hours for the first three days, and David Trevorrow sat with you while I saw to the livestock for the first four days you were ill. Even one of his dairymaids came over to milk the goats for me. We put out a story that you had the flu and were laid up in your hut. She grinned again. 'Apparently, the dairy maids were fighting over who could come and offer you help. I told you that you'd made a big impression on them.' She raised an eyebrow.

'Alas, it isn't the dairymaids I want to impress,' he said softly.

Maia suppressed a smile.

'Maia.' Josh reached out for her hand, which she gave willingly. 'Thank you for all you have done for me. I may have been drifting in and out of consciousness, but I was always aware of you by my side – sometimes beside me in bed, if I am not mistaken.'

Her eyes twinkled. 'It was more comfortable than the chair.'

'I'm sorry you have seen me at my very worst.'

'Remember, I've seen you at your very best as well.' Her eyes twinkled. 'I'm just glad I was here to help you through this.' She pulled her hand away. 'Is there anything else I can get you? Do you think you can stomach food – a little soup perhaps?'

'Sounds lovely. Could I impose on you to get my toothbrush from my shed, and perhaps a shirt and underclothes? I appear not to be wearing anything,' he said, his cheeks pinking again.

'You're only in a state of undress because you have been very sweaty and incontinent.'

'Oh no, I haven't! Have I?' The pink flush on his cheeks turned fiery.

'Nothing to worry about.' She assured him. 'I'll go and fetch what you need and put some soup on for us. Don't try to get up today. Just rest.' With that, she whipped the bucket from under the bed before he could protest.

*

When Maia opened the shepherd's hut door, it smelled hot and musty, so she flung open the windows to freshen the place. She already had Josh's underclothes and shirt at the farmhouse, the ones they had taken off him when he fell ill. She had washed and ironed Josh's clothes, finding an unexpected pleasure in doing so. Laundering Henry's clothes had repulsed her; his personal hygiene had often been lacking. She gathered Josh's toothbrush and tin of toothpaste from near his washing bowl and then picked up the book he had been reading from his bedside table. Then something interesting caught her eye - it was a pile of drawings. Placing everything she had collected for him on the table, she flicked through the drawings, feeling her breath catch - they were all of her, and of superb quality.

How had he done these without her knowing? From memory? He had captured her image perfectly. She placed them back where she had found them; he clearly wasn't ready for her to see them yet.

*

Half an hour later, his breath freshened and modesty restored, Josh gratefully took the tray of soup from Maia, his stomach groaning hungrily at the smell.

'Thank you. I didn't realise how hungry I was until the aroma of your cooking drifted upstairs from the kitchen.'

Maia returned a few moments later with her own tray of soup. 'Do you mind if I sit with you? I have missed us eating together. Well, I mean, I *have* sat here and eaten with you, but you have been poor company.' She smiled.

This heartened Josh. He had wondered if she could still like him after what he had put her through. 'I would like that very much. I shall try to offer more scintillating conversation from now on.'

He savoured a spoonful of soup with a satisfied sigh and then asked, 'I suspect the doctor wondered where I had contracted malaria.'

'He did. He asked you at one point.'

'Oh, no!' He frowned. 'Did I mention I had been in the Royal Navy?'

'No, just that you'd had malaria three times. Josh, it is imperative that we get a story together about how you contracted malaria. The doctor said he has had to inform the Ministry of Health of your condition. Apparently, it's compulsory to report it! They'll need to know if you have been in the Armed Forces or on a merchant ship abroad.'

Josh put his spoon down in his soup, feeling his appetite waning. 'What am I going to say? How could I have caught this disease if not on deployment?'

'Well, where *did* you catch it?'

'Africa - Mombasa to be exact.'

Maia's face brightened. 'I might just have a solution then. My aunt and uncle spent some time living in Africa.'

'Where abouts in Africa?'

'Nairobi. My aunt lived in a fine house there. She often told us stories of opulent balls and soirees in the Government House while Uncle Clarence took off on shooting parties for days, sometimes weeks. You could say you were out there working on something like that. My aunt told me there were many Englishmen working out there.'

Josh bit down on his lip. 'I know nothing of Nairobi and shooting parties. I only ever visited the port of Mombasa.'

'Well, I believe Nairobi is about four hundred miles from Mombasa. When my aunt and uncle went out there, they sailed to Mombasa before taking the four-hundred-mile train journey to Nairobi. I have my aunt's diaries and books on Nairobi if you want to read them. She was a prolific diarist - it might just save you.'

Quite unexpectedly, Josh started to cry.

'Oh, my goodness, Josh!' Maia discarded her tray of soup and rushed to cup her hands to his damp face. 'Don't cry.' She wiped his tears with her thumbs.

Clasping his hands over hers, his breath caught. 'Maia. You are an angel, and no truer word has been spoken.'

'No, Josh. I'm no angel - believe me,' she answered. 'I just want you to be safe.'

Their faces were so close, lips swelling at the intimacy - a kiss seemed imminent, but Maia pulled back, smiled, and said, 'No more tears, Josh. Onwards and upwards now,' she said, breaking the spell. 'I'll bring you my aunt's books and let you read through them. Perhaps we can make something of them.'

*

Josh looked up from his books when Maia knocked later that evening. She entered and flashed him a dazzling smile, which made his stomach flip.

'I've brought you a cup of tea. Can I get you anything else?'

'No, thank you. I already feel terrible that you are doing all the work while I just lay here.'

'It's fine. I'm in a routine now. How long are you normally laid up for after malaria?'

He gave a dismissive laugh. 'Last time, I was ordered out of my hammock three days after I stopped having a fever. I could hardly walk, but they dragged me to the captain's room, where he called me a lazy wastrel. I received ten lashes of the cane, one for every day I was laid up. I had to crawl about to do my duties for the next three days - my legs were so fatigued.'

'Good grief – that man was a monster. Did no one help you?'

Josh shook his head wearily. 'They couldn't - they too would have been punished if they offered me any help. Occasionally, one man in particular would help me - Harry Flintman– the one who pushed the lifejacket into my arms before I was thrown overboard. Goodness, but he took a great risk in doing so, but he'd been punished too in the past for a slight misdemeanour and held a real grudge against Captain Wright. He was also looking forward to the end of his service and getting off that ship once and for all.'

'Well, Josh. You are not returning to work until you are completely fit and well. That's an order.'

'Aye, Aye, Captain.'

'How are you getting along with my aunt's diaries and books?'

'I think I am gleaning what it was like to live out there. Fortunately, there are many letters from your uncle to your aunt. They described in great detail how they lived on their shooting parties and how one or two of them had come down with malaria.'

'Splendid. Josh, I was wondering. The doctor has been treating you with quinine – did they not dole out quinine while you were abroad? I mean, how did you contract it in the first place?'

'They do dole it out, yes. But while we were in Mombasa, a few of us contracted a stomach bug and couldn't keep anything down for days, including the quinine. We all came down with malaria afterwards. It's dreadful when it takes hold. I don't think I have ever felt so poorly.'

'You certainly looked dreadful. I must admit, David, Jimmy, and myself all thought you were a goner when we found you.'

'Thank the Lord you did.'

'Now then,' she said, changing the subject. 'I've brought your book from your bedside table if you need a change from my aunt's diaries.'

'Thank you. Reading is a luxury I had never had before I came here. There were no books on the ship.'

Maia sighed. 'Henry didn't agree with me reading, either. He said they filled my head with fanciful ideas.' A shadow crossed her face at the mention of him. 'God knows I needed something to take my mind off my predicament. Anyway,' she shook her head, 'enough about horrible thoughts. Now, I normally sit and read downstairs before bed. Would you mind if I sat and read here with you?' Maia turned to pull the chair closer to the lamp.

'I don't mind at all. But you might be more comfortable on here.' Josh patted the bed beside him.

Without embarrassment or hesitation, she moved to the bed and settled beside him.

'What are *you* reading? he asked.

'Anna Karenina, by Leo Tolstoy. It tells the story of Anna Karenina, trapped in a loveless marriage, and her passionate affair with Count Vronsky.' Maia smiled. 'I do love a romantic tale,' she said, snuggling down into a more comfortable position.

The thrill of her being so close almost took his breath away. 'You used to lie here when I was ill, didn't you?'

'I did. I wasn't sure if you were aware or not. You were very agitated. I wanted you to know that someone was close so you would feel calm.'

'It was lovely. Thank you.' He reached down and squeezed her hand. She didn't pull it away until she needed to turn the page. Even then, she moved her hand back to his and curled her fingers around it. Soon, Prudence joined them, and her gentle purring added to the peace of the room.

Occasionally, Josh glanced at Maia, lost in her book, and felt a wonderful feeling of calm settle over him. He was about to start another chapter when he heard a soft thud of Maia's book as it fell to her chest. Her eyes were closed, and her lips parted slightly – she looked just as beautiful asleep as she did awake. He put his book down and turned to watch her at rest. How he longed to take this woman into his arms. 'I love you, Maia, with every fibre of my body,' he whispered. He smiled when she began to snore gently, and he loved how relaxed she was with him and how she fell asleep. Suddenly, she grunted, and her eyes snapped open. She licked her lips and smiled.

'Was I snoring?'

'No.' He smiled.

'I do believe you're telling me fibs. I always snore on my back,' she said knowingly as she swung her legs over the side of the bed. 'I must leave you now.' She put the book she was reading on the bedside table – a gesture that said she would return to this spot again.

'Do you need anything before I go?'

He bit down on his lip.

'Ah, I sense the bucket is needed.' She grinned. 'Let me help you sit up.'

She pulled the sheets from his legs, hooked her arms under his, and helped him to a seating position. 'Are you all right?'

'A little dizzy.'

She handed him the bucket. 'I'll be back in a moment.'

This time, he left her the bucket and had managed to lie back down, albeit his face pinking from embarrassment.

She returned with it from the privy and kissed him on his hot cheek.

'If I can snore in front of you, you can let me see to your needs. All right?'

He nodded and then caught her hand before she moved away. 'Maia. Thank you for everything.'

Her eyes twinkled. 'I'll see you in the morning.'

29

Josh woke as dawn broke and was deeply aware of the stale smell of his body. Maia had brought him a bowl and cloth the previous day, which he managed to clean himself down with, but the constant sweating – a residue of malaria – made him feel wretched. His hair, in particular, felt dreadful. If he pushed his fingers through it, they stopped dead, unable to rake through the mat of greasy curls. The fact that he had swum the night before he fell ill and had not had a chance to rinse the salt from his hair did not help.

Moving his legs to the side of the bed, Josh managed to sit up without being too dizzy, which meant he could go to the toilet without calling for help. He could hear Maia moving about now – getting ready to start the day, so he pushed the bucket out of view, hoping that he could walk today and deal with it himself. One way or another, he wanted to ease Maia's burden of looking after him; she had enough to do with all her other chores.

As Maia passed his bedroom, she knocked and opened the door slightly. 'Are you decent?' She grinned.

'More than I have been,' he parried.

She laughed gently. 'I see you are sitting.'

'I'm going to try to walk a little. I can feel the ground under my feet today – I couldn't do that yesterday, so that's an improvement.'

Maia held her arms out to him. 'Come on, then, let me help to see if you can stand.' Supporting him under his arms she helped him to his feet. His body shook, and the dizziness returned, making him lean into her.

'Forgive me, Maia. I'm not as fragrant as I could be. In fact, I feel downright wretched.'

She pulled away from him slightly, though still supporting him and asked, 'Do you think you can manage a bath today then?'

'I could, but I can't let you hump water up the stairs.'

'Nonsense. I'll put the buckets of water to warm in the range. They should be ready by the time I've done the outside chores.'

'No, Maia. Please don't go to all that trouble.'

'It's no trouble. Besides, if I am to hold you in my arms while you learn how to walk again, I would rather you smell a little fresher.' She winked at him. 'Now, I'll hold you while you try to walk.'

Very tentatively, he took four steps towards the window and inhaled the fresh air blowing in from it. He looked at his shepherd's hut, briefly abandoned for now. The pigs were snuffling in their pens, and the sun shone brightly on the morning dew across the fields to the Polhormon Dairy Farm.

'Back to bed, now?' she asked.

He nodded and turned slowly. This time, he walked with his arm around Maia's shoulder.

Once he settled back on the bed, she said, 'I'll be with you in a while.'

He smiled and shook his head. 'It was a lucky day I found your stable to hide in.'

'Josh.' Maia smiled sweetly and placed her hand on his shoulder. 'The luck runs both ways.'

A knock came to the back door, which made them both still.

'I hope that isn't the doctor,' Maia said fearfully. 'I said I would contact him when you were lucid enough to speak to him.'

'I hope not as well. I've barely skimmed the surface of your aunt's diaries. I'm not sure I can give a convincing story of my life in Africa yet!'

'Don't worry, I won't let him in.' Maia glanced out of the window and smiled. 'Oh, it's all right. It's only Ellie from the tearoom. Oh goodness!' She slapped her forehead. 'I clean forgot to cancel my table for yesterday – I have completely lost track of the days.'

*

Maia opened the back door to Ellie, apologising profusely about the table.

'Oh, gosh, don't worry,' Ellie said, flapping her hand. 'Jimmy Trevorrow told us yesterday that Josh had the flu, so I suspected you might be too busy to come. Is he any better?'

'Yes, he is, thank you.'

'Bless the Trevorrow lad,' Ellie smiled. 'He waits every Sunday to say hello to Fee after she finishes work, but she seems oblivious to his attention. Anyway, I had no problem giving your table reservation to someone else. Speaking of Fee, I'm here with a birthday invitation! It's Fee's 16th birthday on Saturday, and we're having a party at the tearoom after we close. I wondered if you and Josh would like to come - that's if Josh is better by then. Sarah and Peter Dunstan will be there, as will Sophie and Kit Trevellick from Gweek. Sophie Trevellick delivered Fee, you know, back in 1907!' She smiled, remembering the incident. 'Kit had brought Sophie to visit us for the first time when my waters broke quite unexpectedly. So, I had only known her for a few hours before the poor woman was forced down to the business end to help deliver my baby!'

Maia chuckled.

'It certainly cemented our friendship, and we called Fee after her – though we rarely call her Sophie now - unless she's in trouble for something.' She winked. 'Goodness, but it seems like only yesterday. So, will you come?'

'Thank you, Ellie. Hopefully, we'll both be there, all being well.'

*

An hour and a half later, Josh watched in dismay, unable to help, as Maia lugged the tin bath into his bedroom.

'Right, I'll go and get the buckets of water so we can get you bathed and back in the land of the living. Oh! And we have just had a party invitation from Ellie, so we need you ship shape before Saturday.'

'Enough with the nautical connotations, please – you'll bring me out in hives,' he joked. 'And do you know you look dirtier than me - your face is splattered with mud?'

'Is it!' She wiped her face with her hand and inspected the mud. 'One of the naughty piglets escaped. I had to try and catch it. It managed two circuits of the garden before I threw myself at it.' She laughed. 'It squealed alarmingly because I damn near squashed it! I might have to get in this bath with you,' she teased.

Josh's face brightened at the prospect and the gestured did not go unnoticed by Maia.

After pouring two buckets full of water into the bath, Maia helped Josh off the bed. He had discarded his underclothes but kept his shirt on to cover his dignity. Holding on to Maia for dear life, he let her steady him as he stepped into the water. He began to tremble as he tried to lower himself into the bath.

'Relax, Josh. I'll stay until you're seated.'

His legs felt like jelly, and despite her holding him, his knees buckled so that he sat with a splash.

'Oh, God. I'm so sorry, Maia.' Seeing the water pool around the bath.

'No matter, it will mop up.'

She turned away as he pulled his shirt off and wiped the perspiration from his face. He was going to place the shirt strategically over his privates, but then thought, *What the hell* and dropped it over the side of the bath. Feeling the clean water wash over him, he closed his eyes and sighed.

Once Maia heard him settle, she said, 'I'll go and get a jug of clean water to wash your hair. Are you fine with me coming back into the room?'

He looked up at her and tipped his head. 'Maia, I do believe I have nothing you haven't seen before.' His eyes twinkled. 'If *you* don't mind, *I* certainly don't.'

*

When she returned, armed with a jug of water, a couple of towels, a clean shirt, and underclothes, Josh shifted as far forward as his long legs allowed while Maia wet his hair and gently massaged lavender-infused soap into his scalp. As she rinsed his hair with clean, warm water, he gasped in ecstasy - nobody had washed his hair since his mother when he was a child. He could safely say that this was probably the most intimate gesture he had ever experienced in adulthood.

Maia smiled as she squeezed the water out of his hair. 'You're clearly enjoying this.'

'Gosh, Maia.' He sighed. 'I admit, it feels wonderful.'

She passed him the soap. 'I'll leave you for a few minutes. Call me when you need to get out.'

*

Getting out of the bath proved to be more problematic than getting into it, as it was clear that Maia could not lift him from it.

'Right. If I sit on one side of the tin bath, could you manage to heave yourself up onto the edge of the other?' she suggested,

'I'll try.' After two attempts, his trembling arms gathered enough strength to lift himself from the water.

With her eyes averted, she asked, 'Are you settled?'

'Yes,' he gasped, and she passed him one of the towels she had slung over her shoulder. 'Wrap this around your middle, and I'll try and help you up from where you are sitting now.' Rising tentatively from where she sat for fear of the bath tipping, she quickly hooked her arms beneath his wet body and helped him stand. He quivered in her arms as she supported him while he stepped from the water. Slowly, she helped him walk to the chair by the window, where she handed him the other towel to dry himself.

He buried his head in the towel in dismay. 'My God, I feel so useless. I'm like a newborn.' He dropped his guard and gave her a desperate look.

Maia knelt at his feet and cupped his face with her hands. 'You've been ill, Josh. Please don't be so hard on yourself - this will pass.'

Another sharp rat-a-tat-tat came to the front door, and they exchanged another anxious glance. Again, Maia went to the window and relaxed when she saw it was David Trevorrow.'

'It's David. Shall I let him in?'

'Yes, I'd like to thank him for all he has done.'

'Shall I get him to wait downstairs until we get you dressed?'

'No, it's fine. Let him come up. I'm too exhausted to get dressed yet!'

David doffed his cap when she opened the door. 'Morning, Maia. It's hot again!' he said, wiping his damp forehead with his shirt sleeve. 'How is the patient, and can I do anything for you?'

Oh, if only you had come ten minutes ago, she mused. 'He's on the mend. He's just had a bath. I wonder if you could help me move the bath later; it's full of water.'

'Of course.'

'Just a minute. I'll see if he is decent now.' As she turned to climb the stairs, she missed David's amused smile.

*

David entered the bedroom with a smile still engrained on his lips. Josh was rubbing his hair dry.

'You're up then?'

'I am. Sorry about the state of undress. Could you help me get back to bed? My legs seemed to be made of jelly at the moment.'

David hooked his arm under Josh's, alarmed at how unsteady he was. 'How the hell did you manage a bath?'

'Maia helped me in.'

Again, David wanted to smile but managed to suppress it.

'Could you pass me that shirt from the sideboard? It might give me a modicum of decency while I talk to you. I fear that Maia has seen more of me than is decent for any woman outside of marriage.'

'You'll have to marry her then!' David joked, noticing Josh wore his own smile.

'She has been an absolute angel, you know!'

David occupied the chair just vacated by Josh and folded his arms. 'I know; I witnessed her nursing you when you were bad. So, malaria then!'

Josh nodded.

'Where the hell did you contract that?'

Josh took a deep breath and told him he had been in Africa, which wasn't a lie.

'What the devil were you doing out there?'

'Oh, this and that,' he answered evasively. 'They run a lot of shooting parties out there and big game safaris.' Again, this was not a lie, because they did. He was just giving David a variation of the truth. It did not sit well with him, but needs must.

'Gosh, what a life you've lived! I'm surprised you never told us any of this before now.'

Josh smiled weakly and shrugged. 'It wasn't a happy time for me.'

'I see. So, you thought you would come home and make your fortune here?'

'Something like that,' Josh said cagily.

David tipped his head as though he knew Josh was keeping something close to his chest. 'You know, you can always talk to me if you need to.'

'Thank you, David. I might, one day.'

'Anyway, how long before you're up and about then?'

'Soon, I think. I couldn't walk at all yesterday. I reckon I might be able to go back to work in a few days.'

'Splendid. Right then!' David slapped his hands on his thighs to get up. 'I'll leave you for now. It was just a quick visit. I'll just fetch Maia, and we'll remove the bath from the room, and remember, if you need anything - anything at all - just let me know.'

'Thank you, David.'

*

Over the next few days, Josh started to improve immensely. The day after the bath, Josh managed to get up and walk a few steps unaided to sit in the chair and read the books and diaries Maia had given him on Nairobi. When he felt he had gleaned enough information to offer a convincing story about his life on the African plains, he allowed Maia to send for the doctor. He needed to get it over with, as the worry was hanging over them both like a dark cloud.

*

Maia cleared all the books and diaries of Africa away from Josh's bedroom in readiness for the doctor's visit and stood in silent fear as Josh told the story of how he had contracted malaria.

'You told me you had had it three times before. Why did you not seek help as soon as it started to take hold?' The doctor asked sternly.

'I misread the signs. I thought my headache was down to the oncoming storm,' he lied. It worried him that he was becoming a proficient liar. His poor departed mother would turn in her grave if she could hear the fibs he was telling folk – she had always brought him up to always tell the truth.

'Well, from now on, when you get the first indication that the symptoms are returning, you must take this vial of quinine and call me at once. At least then you won't have it so severely next time.'

'Thank you, doctor, for all your help.'

'You might not think that when you get my bill!' he mused.

*

After the visit from the doctor, a period of calm settled over Wild Cliff Farm. Now that Maia could leave Josh, she packed her boxes into her cart and took her pots to Bochym. After collecting her bisque-fired pots, which had been waiting almost two weeks for her, she loaded up the kiln again before setting off to see Mrs Blair. Ben Pearson had told her that Mrs Blair wanted to see her about something. Unfortunately, when she called at the Bochym kitchen, Mr Treen informed her that Mrs Blair was unavailable as she was in Her Ladyship's parlour busy planning the food for the annual garden party. Whatever news Mrs Blair wanted to tell her; it would have to wait.

30

By Friday, Josh had managed to feed the pigs, but milking the goats and cleaning the pigsty was just out of the question, and he had to sit that job out on the steps to his hut.

'I'm sorry, Maia. Give me half an hour, and I should be able to gather my strength to help a little more.'

Maia pretended to jab him with her pitchfork. '*I* will do it. Don't run before you can walk. What you *have* done today has really helped.'

He sat in the shade and reluctantly watched Maia work. The heatwave had abated, and the temperature had come down, bringing welcome relief. Since emerging from his illness, Josh had relished this last week. Though confined to his room until two days ago, Maia had spent a great deal of time with him, reading, eating together, and just talking about everyday matters. He didn't want the intimacy to end.

Watching as she toiled, he smiled to himself. Despite her being dressed in a man's shirt, trousers, and gum boots, with her hair tied back with a green ribbon, she had never looked lovelier. Her face was rosy with exertion and splattered with mud from cleaning out the pigsty, but nothing could mar her beauty. He felt the urge to sketch her again. If he had the paints to hand, he would paint her portrait. Maia had a rare beauty; he wanted to capture it for eternity. He turned and glanced around at the interior of the hut he was due to move back into that night. A pile of freshly ironed bedding sat on his mattress, and a duster had whisked away the spiders who had commandeered the hut in his absence. Thinking of painting Maia, he remembered that his sketches of her were still on his bedside table – Maia must have seen them! It was strange that she hadn't mentioned them. He bit down on his lip – he would have to confess to them now.

His thoughts turned to his return to the hut – he didn't want to move back here. On several occasions this week, they had almost stepped over the threshold from being friends to lovers, though, in truth, Josh was grateful they had not – his physical strength had not, until today, been up to par. More than anything, he wanted them to take that next step, but only when Maia was ready. He was sure Maia felt the same attraction as him, but he would wait. He sighed deeply. Would moving back to the hut sever that invisible gossamer thread pulling them together? He dearly hoped not.

*

When Josh sat down to supper that evening, he noted that Maia was dressed rather beautifully in a silk embroidered gown - the image of her rather took his breath away. Her hair was still piled atop her head from her bath, but her demeanour was rather reticent, which made supper around the kitchen table that evening feel a little strained. They spoke, but there were periods of hesitancy throughout the rather stilted conversation. It crossed Josh's mind that perhaps he had truly outstayed his welcome in the house. So, as soon as he had helped her with the dishes, he suggested that he should get settled back into the hut. He had moved some of his clothes back earlier and had only a small bag of essential items with him now.

Maia got up to go to the door with him and grasped the handle first. He waited, but she did not turn the handle. She just stood facing the closed door. Still, she didn't speak, but he was aware of her deep breathing.

'Maia?' he whispered.

She turned, and they both felt the heat of their proximity.

Lifting her eyes to his, she whispered back. 'I love you being here.'

Josh's lips twitched into a smile. 'Are you saying...?'

She nodded. 'That I love you being here in this house with me. I don't want you to go.'

'Oh, Maia.' He sighed and gently slid his arms around her waist, pulling her close. His lips, warm and yielding, kissed hers.

When they pulled apart, she whispered, 'When we were on the beach that night, you asked me if I wanted you.'

'I did.' His eyes sparkled.

'This is my answer.' Maia turned to lock the door, reached for his hand, and led him up the stairs. Bypassing the room where he'd spent the last two weeks, she invited him across the landing into her bedroom.

He stood at the threshold and glanced around a sumptuously furnished room! There was a richly embroidered satin spread on the bed. A large wicker chair held matching cushions, and a deep pile rug lay beside the bed – the whole room emulated Maia's personality.

Maia untied the side belts to the beautiful silk embroidered wrap-around dress she was wearing. She smiled as the dress fell open to reveal her body, naked but for white stockings tied with green ribbons.

'Oh, my!' Josh sighed as his hands, soft from lack of manual work, slipped the dress off her shoulders. Her skin, like porcelain, shimmered in the reflected light of the sunset through the window as he softly kissed her neck.

'You are so beautiful, Maia.' He murmured, pulling his shirt over his head to discard on the wicker chair before stepping out of the rest of his clothes. Gently releasing the pins from her hair, a waterfall of fiery red curls cascaded down her back. Caressing her face with his fingers, he kissed her on her lips, now swollen with desire, before gently enveloping her body with his arms. Skin on skin, they wrapped their love around each other, and as he lay her on the bed in a cloud of soft goose down, they made love as the sun set over Poldhu Cove.

*

When dawn broke, Maia's eyes opened. Disorientated for a moment as she was sleeping on the opposite side of the bed she usually slept on, the warm presence of Josh snuggled close behind her made her smile, knowing this love was real and forever. It was the dawn of a new future for them! His arm was draped over her, so his hand lay gently on her tummy. She cupped her hand over his, her touch waking him. He snuffled into her hair and kissed her neck.

Turning to face him, he smiled at her. 'Good morning, beautiful,' he whispered.

'Good morning.'

'Are you happy?' he asked.

'I don't believe I have ever been happier.'

The goats could be heard through the open window, bleating their demand to be milked.

'I think we are needed downstairs,' she said reluctantly.

'Can they just wait a while longer?'

Maia smiled as he moved ever closer to her. 'I think they might have to,' she whispered.

*

By the time Maia and Josh got to the milking shed, the goats were very cross, but they both agreed it was worth their displeasure.

'Are you feeling strong enough to attend Fee's birthday party?' Maia asked as she carried the jug of goat milk to the larder.

'I would like to, but I'm not sure I will make it down and back up Poldhu Hill.'

'I'll take the horse and cart if you wish.'

'Very well, but I warn you, I will not be able to hide my feelings for you in front of everyone, Maia.'

'I'm not sure I want you to,' she smiled and kissed him.

He wrapped his arms around her waist. 'I just want to hold you in my arms forever more.'

'And I will be very happy to be in your arms forever more.'

'I wish I could marry you because people will start talking soon. They will wonder if I'm living with you in the farmhouse.'

'I know.' She tapped her lip with her finger. 'Perhaps we could open and close your curtains in the hut and leave a lantern on in case of prying eyes.'

Josh nodded. 'David said I should marry you,' he said wistfully.

Maia raised an eyebrow. 'Did he?'

'Yes. I think he can see how the land lies between us, but of course, it's impossible under the circumstances.'

'Maia nodded and lowered her eyes sadly.

Josh took her hands in his. 'I know it's a hypothetical question, but would you marry me if you could?'

'Yes, Josh, I would marry you in a heartbeat.'

He gathered her into his arms and hugged her as though his life depended on it. 'Maia, my Maia,' he whispered into her hair. 'I want to shout from the rooftops that I love you. Because I have loved you from the moment I saw you.'

'Hence, the sketches of me?'

He laughed softly. 'I guessed you would have seen them, but you never said.'

'I felt as though I was prying into your personal things, but they are lovely. You've got a rare talent there.'

'I have a beautiful subject.' He touched her face gently, and the gesture sparked a desire within them that they could not ignore.

Maia laughed as they ran up the stairs together. 'We are meant to be getting ready for a party.'

'If the goats can wait, then so too can the party,' Josh said, smothering her protests with kisses.

*

When they boarded the cart to go down to Poldhu an hour later, Josh flinched and blinked, almost blinded by a bright light coming from the direction of the cove.

'Goodness, whatever was that?' He covered his eyes. 'All I can see is a bright yellow light now - even with my eyes shut!'

Maia squinted to see where the light was coming from and sighed. 'It's coming from Jago's house. He has a telescope, and it's not always pointing out to sea. I've seen the sun reflecting on it before.'

'You mean he spies on you?'

'Without a doubt!'

'How dare he encroach on your privacy,' Josh uttered angrily.

'As I have said before, Jago thinks he owns everything here.'

'Damn the man. If only we were married – that would stop him once and for all, wouldn't it?'

'It would, but we can't,' she answered wistfully.

'Well, I've been thinking about that.'

'Really?' She smiled. 'I thought you were otherwise engaged this last hour.'

'I certainly was.' He reached over to squeeze her hand. 'But I was thinking - we could pretend that we are married. Whose to know we haven't really?'

Maia turned and regarded him for a moment as she digested this.

'We could pretend we have obtained a special licence and go off for the day to have a handfast ceremony of our own. You could become Mrs Harding by the end of next week.' He smiled. 'Though, by rights, you should be Mrs Walsh.'

'Or Dunstan,' Maia said jokingly.

'Oh goodness! Don't say that. I don't think Grandma would like to be associated with the old Earl, and neither would I, now that I know his character. I hope it never gets out, Maia. Christ! But if my father found out he was the son of an Earl, he would cause an awful lot of trouble for the Dunstans.'

Maia dropped the reins for a moment as she digested his proposal.

Josh tipped his head. 'So, what do you think?'

'I think you should get down on one knee and ask me properly,' she laughed.

'Your wish is my command.' Josh jumped down, lifted Maia from her seat, and kneeled on one knee. 'Maia, will you be my wife?'

'I will, yes.' She flung her arms around him, and he swung her around joyously.

*

At Penn als Cottage, Jago swiped the telescope away in disgust. If he was not mistaken, that bastard Harding had just proposed to Maia!

*

At Poldhu, Fee was relishing the attention of being the birthday girl. Lots of her school friends had joined in the celebration. There were also many of her parent's friends there, including Kit and Sophie Trevellick, her godparents, an honour bestowed on them due to the latter helping to deliver Fee sixteen years ago.

The party spilled out of the tearoom onto the beach as the day was fine and sunny, and for once, to Jimmy Trevorrow's delight, Fee welcomed him into her close circle of friends.

Guy and Ellie stood on the tearoom veranda, watching their children celebrate together. It was rare nowadays to gather the family in one place. Fee's brother, Zack, who was carving out a glittering career as a pianist in London, had come down to celebrate with her, and Agnes, their elder sister, wore a bloom on her face that Ellie thought could mean more good news very soon. If that were to be the case, Ellie and Guy would become grandparents soon. Ellie sighed wistfully. *Gosh, where did the time go?*

Sarah Dunstan joined Ellie and Guy on the veranda; the Earl, Peter Dunstan, had been called away on urgent business and was unable to attend.

'Who is that with Maia Penhallow?' Sarah asked.

Ellie, who had been watching with interest the body language between Maia and Josh, said, 'That's Josh Harding. He's Maia's new farmhand.'

'Ah, yes, Peter did say that she had help. Are they, you know...?' Sarah asked questioningly.

Ellie laughed gently. 'I was just thinking the same.'

'That will be nice for Maia if she has found someone to love, especially after that awful business with her husband.'

'I couldn't agree more.'

'He looks familiar,' Sarah said, tipping her head.

'I know. We all think the same, but Josh is not local. He's from Devon. He has one of those faces that makes you think you know them. Shall I introduce you to him?'

Sarah nodded enthusiastically.

Maia and Josh were in deep conversation. When Ellie and Sarah approached them, they practically jumped apart.

'Sorry to interrupt,' Ellie said, amused. 'But can I introduce you, Josh, to Lady Sarah Dunstan, the Countess de Bochym?'

'I am very pleased to make your acquaintance, my lady.' Josh bowed his head.

'And I, you, Mr Harding. How are you settling in at Wild Cliff Farm?'

'Very well, thank you.' He beamed.

Sarah looked deep into Josh's eyes and gave a short laugh. 'Forgive me, Mr Harding, but now that I look at you closer, you do look very familiar.'

Josh shifted uncomfortably and smiled but did not answer.

'Ellie tells me that you're from Devon, so I must be mistaken in thinking I know you.'

'Yes, my lady,' Josh answered tentatively.

'Are you interested in the arts, Mr Harding? Maia will have told you she is part of our Arts and Crafts Association.'

'I am interested, my lady, and yes, Maia has told me.'

'Josh is an artist; his sketches are beautiful,' Maia said proudly.

'Really! How wonderful. I am in excellent company then. I also wield a paintbrush from time to time. What is your medium?'

'I have only ever painted with watercolour, though I would love to paint with oils one day, but I mostly sketch with pencil.'

'Splendid.' She smiled and turned to Maia. 'Maia, you must bring Mr Harding to the garden party at Bochym.'

'Thank you, Sarah. I will.'

'I will bid you a good day then,' Sarah said, then shook her head again. 'It's quite uncanny how familiar you are, though!'

31

Jago was in a bad mood; nothing was going right. He had argued with his assistant, Sydney, blaming him for his humiliation at the doctor's house, and now Sydney threatened to leave, stating he'd had enough of Jago's bad moods. Another thing bothering him was that another part of his garden had slipped quietly over the cliff edge, forcing him to consider moving if any more of it decided to break away. He folded his arms. And if that wasn't enough, he had been trying all week, without success, to bump into the Blackthorn girl now that she had turned sixteen. He'd been watching the Blackthorn's house through the telescope, and when he'd seen her leaving the house to go to work, this had prompted him to walk down the road to meet her. Twice, he had called out to her, but she seemed not to hear or notice him; it was as though she was avoiding him. He couldn't understand it – she had seemed so keen a few weeks ago. Damn her eyes if she was avoiding him - he could have done with her on his arm – to rub Maia's nose in it now that she was flaunting herself at bloody Harding! The thought of Harding made his blood boil. After watching for several days through the telescope, he knew without a doubt that he was living with Maia in the farmhouse, and he was determined to drag their names through the mud to all and sundry.

*

On Friday, July 27th, Maia and Josh were up early to tend to their livestock, leaving David and his soon-to-be daughter-in-law to look after things on the farm later that afternoon while they took a day off. All they told David was that they had something important to do. David had just smiled and nodded, happy as always to help.

They took the wagon to Helston and stopped off to buy the essential items needed for that day. They caught the train first to Penzance and then another train to take them to St Ives on the most scenic train journey Josh had ever witnessed. They had thought long and hard over the last few days about where to spend their special day, eventually deciding to go to the North Coast, far enough away from everyone they knew. Maia wanted Josh to see the tiny fishing village, so famed for its light and so loved by artists. They had chosen the day perfectly after consulting the barometer for the weather, which had set 'fair to very dry'.

They got off the train at St Ives to a picture-perfect scene: a calm, azure sea, golden sand, and palm trees!

'Oh, my goodness!' Josh breathed. 'I think we have landed in paradise.'

Maia laughed gently, remembering a similar reaction all those years ago when her aunt had first brought her here on a day out.

Dressed in a cream lace dress and wide-brimmed straw hat, as befitting the day, Maia took Josh's hand as they wandered through the maze of narrow cobbled streets towards the busy harbour. The tide was in, and so were the many fishing boats. They walked along Smeaton's Pier, careful to keep out of the way of the busy fishermen as they loaded their catch into baskets.

After watching the bartering of fish for a while, they walked to the end of the pier to St Leonard's Chapel.

'My aunt brought me and my brother here many years ago. She told us that since mediaeval times, fishermen have prayed in this chapel before heading out to sea.' From where they stood, Maia pointed up to the top left of the town. 'Up over there is the huer lookout hut, where the huer would watch for pilchard shoals arriving in the bay. When he saw one, he would raise a hue-and-cry of "Hevva, hevva!" and guide the fishing boats to the right place. Pilchards were a big part of St Ives, but by the late 1800s, the industry was in decline, and now, sadly, it has all but died out.'

As they stood and gazed over the pretty town, Josh noticed the church on top of a hill.

'Shall we go over to where that church is - it looks quite grassy – we could eat our picnic there,' he suggested.

It took a while to negotiate the many tiny alleyways, often emerging onto yet another little beach, until they finally found a snicket that led them to the island. After scrambling up the grassy hill to the church at the top, Maia laid out a simple picnic of ham, cheese, and bread on a tablecloth. As they sipped elderflower cordial, Josh sighed contentedly. 'I can certainly see why artists visit,' he said, surveying the beautiful scene before him.

Slipping her hand in his, Maia said, 'I do believe that it was back in 1811 that J.M.W. Turner spent a few weeks here, producing scenes depicting St Ives. Then, the introduction of the railway to this part of Cornwall in 1877 made it so much easier to come here. It was this, with the added allure of what they call St Ives' unique natural light, that more and more artists came to visit. I don't doubt that many more artists will do so in the future; I do hope they don't spoil its character,' she added wistfully. 'Does it make you want to paint?'

Josh nodded. 'But first, I want to put a ring on your finger.'

Maia turned towards the little church named St. Nicholas' Chapel. 'Why don't we do it in here? It's a perfect place for our handfast wedding. I understand St. Nicholas is the patron saint of sailors.'

'I was a very reluctant sailor,' he mused.

'He saw you safely to shore, though, and then to me.'

'He did, but I also put that down to Grandma's four-leaf clover,' he patted the pocket in his underclothes where he kept it.

'Well, let's hope it brings us luck in our future together. Come on.' They packed away the picnic, and then she led him into the chapel.

The interior was simple and whitewashed, with a high beamed ceiling, a low round-headed niche in one wall, and a small piscina – a shallow basin, under a pointed arch in the east wall. There was no altar, just a lectern holding the Holy Bible. A single window looked out over the rocks towards the north of the island, and they turned to each other, smiled, and said in unison, 'Perfect'.

With both of them feeling a little nervous, they faced each other, holding hands and wrapping a silk scarf around their wrists as if to bind them together. They had decided to make this ceremony special by saying a few words to each other.

Josh cleared his throat and squeezed her hands.

'My darling, Maia. There is an old Indian proverb that asks, 'Is it love that makes the impossible possible? I say yes. Your love for me makes everything possible. I was once lost. But with you by my side, I now know where I am going.' He leaned forward and kissed her softly on the lips. 'I love you.'

With tears in her eyes, Maia replied, 'Josh, my love, my life. From this day forward, I promise to walk with you hand in hand through life. I need your arms wrapped around me at the beginning and end of each day. You're the one I want to love completely and forever. So, in the words of Robert Browning, "Grow old along with me; the best is yet to be."'

Josh nodded, his blue eyes brighter from the emotion building in them. He brought the thin gold band from his pocket, lifted Maia's left hand first to his lips, and answered, 'We may not be married in the eyes of the law, but here, before God and St. Nicholas, in this tiny chapel, will you take me as your husband and be my wife from this day forward?'

'With all my heart, I will,' she answered as he slipped the gold band on her finger to seal their love.

*

When Josh and Maia arrived back at Wild Cliff Farm, they found a sprig of myrtle tied to their doorknob.

Josh picked it up to find a label tied to the sprig with twine, which just said, *from David*. He looked questioningly at Maia, who smiled.

'Myrtle flowers represent good luck in marriage,' she said. 'I think he guessed our secret.'

'Good. Because I no longer want to keep my love for you secret,' Josh said, scooping her into his arms to carry her over the threshold.

*

On Saturday morning, Josh and Maia walked to Polhormon Farm to see David.

David smiled when he saw them and lifted Maia's hand to inspect the wedding band.

'Ah, just as I thought, Josh. You have made an honest woman of Maia,' he said, kissing Maia's cheek softly and shaking Josh's hand.

Josh grinned. 'As you well know, I think I had to.'

'Well, congratulations. I hope you'll both be happy, though my milkmaids will be devastated and probably cry a river of tears when they find out. Was it a special licence wedding?'

'It was special, yes,' Josh said evasively.

'I'm very happy for you both. That should put paid to Jago's pursuit of you, Maia,' David added.

'Yes, hopefully,' Maia answered.

'And his denouncement of you,' David added.

Maia looked at him, puzzled.

'I've heard that Jago has told folks in The Old Inn that you are living in sin.'

Maia sighed. 'We know he has been watching us with a telescope from his window.'

David shook his head incredulously. 'Has that man got nothing better to do? As I say, because of him, there have been a few rumbles of condemnation in the village, but when I've heard anyone speak of it, I have silenced them. You could bring a charge against Jago with the police for that, especially now that you are married. That is defamation of your character.'

Maia swallowed hard. *That would mean proving we are really married.* She shook her head. 'I don't want any more trouble from him. Hopefully, he will leave us alone now.'

*

Maia delivered her fortnightly cheese order to the Bochym Kitchen to be greeted by Joe Treen, the butler.

'Is Mrs Blair around, Mr Treen?'

'I am afraid not. Mrs Blair has gone to Helston shopping.'

'Gosh! She is proving elusive at the moment. I keep missing her. She sent me word that she had some news for me. No matter, I'll catch up with her eventually.'

'Mrs Blair did leave a request with me, Maia, should you call in,' he added. 'She said to ask if you could bring two pounds of goat cheese next Saturday in time for the garden party – and as much onion marmalade as you can spare.'

Maia nodded. 'I think I can manage that.'

'Splendid,' he said with a smile. 'We are all rather partial to Mrs Blair's goat cheese and onion marmalade tarts.'

'I agree, they're rather delicious,' Maia answered, licking her lips.

*

The next place they visited together was the tearoom on Sunday. Being her closest friend, Maia especially wanted to tell Ellie that they were married. They sat at their usual table, but before Maia could order, Ellie had noticed the wedding band on Maia's finger and grabbed her hand.

'Oh, Maia, Josh! You've married!'

Maia smiled. 'We have made a commitment to each other, yes.'

Ellie gathered her into her arms to kiss her before doing the same to Josh. 'How wonderful. Congratulations to you both. You've obviously done it in secret. Are you telling people?'

'We're just going to let people find out in their own time, but we wanted you to know.'

'Oh!' Ellie put her hand to her heart. 'You make me feel very special. You know, I did wonder if you were about to marry. When you came to Fee's birthday party, I noted that you were quite engrossed in each other. I'm so happy for you. Now, what can I get you today? It's on the house.'

*

In the Bochym Manor kitchen on Monday, July 30th, Joe Treen handed out the letters at the staff breakfast.

'Another letter for you, Mrs Blair.' Joe said.

Sissy smiled. 'Thank you, Mr Treen. I've been waiting for this.' She pushed it deep into her pocket to read later, and it would be later, for the manor was a hive of activity at the moment. A party of six adult guests, along with three children and their nanny, were arriving the next day. They would be staying for a week to incorporate the Bochym garden party into their stay. There were dinner parties to prepare, along with extra breakfasts and lunches - nothing that fazed Sissy, though she wasn't as young as she was.

At eight thirty that evening, an exhausted Sissy flopped in the chair and put her aching feet up on the stool. She fished in her pocket for Kitty's letter and began to read.

Friday, July 27th, 1923.

Dearest Sissy,

I'm sorry to have taken so long to write back. The address on the letter you sent me got wet, making the ink run, so the letter went astray for a while. What joy to hear you are still at Bochym Manor, and things have improved considerably. I hope you have kept well all these years.

I suspect your sister, Effy, told you that despite our efforts with the vinegar, I found myself with child after that dreadful attack. I was three months gone when a kind man came to stay at the boarding house. His name was Hugh Joshua Walsh. He was a gardener, would you believe? We became friends, and he asked me to marry him. I could not accept without telling him of my shame, but bless the man, he did not reject me as I thought he would. He said I was blameless in a dreadful act of brutality. I also told him I had a sweetheart, Freddy, but I'd had to leave him behind. This news he did not take so well, and I thought he would forsake me. In the end, he made a pact with me. We would become husband and wife, and the baby would have his name, but the condition was that I would never contact anyone from my past life. It was in case you, or Effy, told Freddy where I was, and he came looking for me.

We moved to Portsmouth after the wedding, and Hugh became a gardener at a large country estate where we lived in a tied cottage. I've had a good life with Hugh. He was a good and kind man, a lot older than Freddy, but I have no regrets. My baby - a boy, Jacob, came into the world angry and shouting, and his temperament never changed as he grew. He was, without a doubt, the Earl's son. I am ashamed to admit that I could not warm to the child – though it wasn't his fault how he had come about - but that probably shaped his disagreeable character in adulthood.

Jacob married Jenny, a lovely girl, but she suffered at Jacob's hands, as he too had a cruel streak and was handy with his fists. They had a son, Gideon! What a dreadful name, isn't it? Hugh and I hoped he would be called Joshua after his grandfather, but Jacob wouldn't hear of it. However, we always called our grandson Josh whenever he was staying with us, which was quite often, as life at home for the lad was brutal.

Sissy, I must tell you that writing about Josh has brought me to tears because tragedy has struck our family in the last few years. First, Jenny 'fell' and died, and then Hugh died in March of this year after a long illness, but the worst was yet to come. Two months ago, we had the shocking news that Josh, who had been in the Navy, had gone overboard and is assumed to have drowned.

Sissy stopped and re-read the last sentence. What on earth did Kitty mean? Josh was here, alive and well! She must write back, tell her, and put her mind to rest.

I would have written to you shortly after Hugh died, but I had to move from the tied cottage. Jacob moved me to 42 Cubb's Alley, a dark and dingy little house in an awful part of the city. I hate it, but

I am trying to make it habitable. Fortunately for me, Jacob has taken up with another woman - God help her - and has moved away, so I have little to do with him anymore. So, I am now my own woman. Although Hugh left me with a little pot of money to live on, I intend to get some work and try to find a better house to live in as soon as possible.

I long to hear all your news, Sissy, and though I have no right to ask - as I am sure Freddy is settled with his own little family now - I'd love to hear that he got over my desertion of him. I have never forgotten him. Although Hugh was good to me, and I loved him, I am ashamed to admit that I have only truly ever been 'in love' with Freddy.

I look forward to hearing from you. It's so lovely to be in touch again.

Your dear friend, Kitty.

Sissy put the letter down; it would take her a while to write the letter that she wanted to, so it would have to wait, but at the moment, the garden party and all that entailed were at the forefront of her mind. Oh, but Kitty will be so happy to find out that the rumours of Josh's demise were untrue. Suddenly, an uncomfortable thought struck her. If Josh had been in the Navy and gone overboard, then surely he was a sensible enough man to understand that his family would have been notified of the incident. Yes, she knew he didn't get on with his father, but why on earth had he not been in touch with Kitty, at least, to stop his grandma from worrying? Folding her doughy arms, Sissy leaned her head back against the antimacassar and thought again about Josh going by the name of Harding – something was amiss here and didn't add up. Perhaps she could find the time to pen a short note to Kitty– if only to put her mind at rest about Josh.

32

Maia and Josh spent the next few days at Wild Cliff Farm in blissful happiness. There were stolen kisses between farm and gardening jobs, and Maia sang happily while she moulded her pots from clay, and each night, they fell into bed together to make love.

Their news, it seemed, had not reached the gossips of Mullion yet; David and Ellie had obviously been discreet with their knowledge. But when Clem, the ice delivery man, arrived at Wild Cliff Farm early on Friday and noted Josh sitting at the kitchen table and Maia wearing a shiny new gold band on her finger, Maia knew it would only take a few hours for the news to whip around like wildfire.

*

Sure enough, when Maia popped into the Bochym kitchen the next day to deliver the goat cheese and onion marmalade as requested, she was greeted by a chorus of congratulations from the Bochym staff, who had been reliably informed of her marital status by Clem when he had delivered the ice there.

Maia laughed. 'Good news travels fast. Is Mrs Blair not around, Mr Treen?' Maia glanced around the kitchen. 'I'm starting to think she doesn't work here anymore!' she joked.

Joe Treen smiled. 'Alas, I'm afraid Mrs Blair is busy with the housekeeper, arranging the final details of the garden party preparations. Though I understand she is keen to speak with you as well.'

'Ah, no matter. I might have a chance to speak with her tomorrow at the garden party.'

'However,' Mr Treen added, 'Her Ladyship asked if you could join her in the Jacobean drawing room. I believe she wants to speak with you.'

Maia thought Sarah Dunstan looked resplendent in a pale green and cream drop-waisted dress when she stood to greet her. Though Maia was also well dressed, her attire was almost two decades out of date. Nevertheless, she was still stylish.

'Hello, Maia. I'm glad Mr Treen caught you. I feared I would not have time to speak to you properly tomorrow if I missed you today. Do sit down.' Sarah beckoned Maia to one of the sumptuous red sofas flanking the large open fireplace. 'May I get you some refreshments?'

'No, thank you,' Maia said, thinking about how stretched for time the kitchen staff were.

'Now, I understand congratulations are in order?'

'Yes, thank you.' Maia smiled happily.

'I have a little gift for you. A Fortnum and Masons hamper, which Mr Treen will load onto your cart when you go home. I arranged for it to be sent down by train yesterday when we heard the news.'

'Goodness.' Maia clasped her hands to her face. 'Thank you so much, Lady Sarah. What a wonderful gift.'

'You're very welcome. I hope you and Josh will be very happy. Now, I also have good news for you. Liberty London is very interested in your ceramics. I don't know if you're aware, but although founder Arthur Lasenby sadly passed away a few years ago, his magnificent dreams of an emporium in Great Marlborough Street, London, will come to fruition next year. As you know, they specialise in beautiful wares, selected from the world's greatest craftspeople, and one of their buyers saw your work last week when he came to peruse our workshops. They would like you to supply them!'

Maia felt her mouth drop slightly and closed it again quickly.

'I see from your reaction that you are shocked.' Sarah laughed gently. 'Would you be interested in speaking with the buyer?'

'Oh, yes, thank you. I would.'

'Splendid. The buyer would like to come back down on Tuesday. So, if it is convenient for you, we could meet him then. We have a selection of your work here waiting to go up to our other outlets, but if you have more, please bring them along.'

'Thank you for this opportunity, Lady Sarah.'

'You're the one who makes the beautiful objects; I just have the contacts. I think it's time you had some good luck, and 1923 looks like it will be your year.'

*

Back home, having placed her bisque-fired pots in the studio ready for decorating, Maia filled the kettle to make tea, and as it boiled, she watched Josh from the kitchen window as he worked on the land. She still liked to secretly watch him, even though she was privy to the delights of his wonderful body each night. Maia loved him; she loved every bone in his body. He was her soulmate, and she never wanted to part from him. Unfortunately, in the back of her mind, there was always that uncertainty that if anyone ever found out his true identity, he would be arrested and taken from her. Goodness knows what punishment he would endure if that happened. It was something she could not begin to contemplate.

Maia took the tray of tea out into the garden, eager to share her good news with Josh about Liberty London.

Josh took her in his arms and swung her around before planting a passionate kiss on her lips. 'You deserve this, Maia. You deserve every good thing that is happening to you now.'

'You are the best thing that has ever happened to me, Josh,' she said, returning the kiss. 'Oh, by the way, thanks to Clem, our secret is out.'

'Yes, I know. David has just been over to inform me that when Jago found out we had married, he was drinking in The Old Inn and apparently smashed his glass of ale in a rage. The landlord has banned him from the inn. Serves him right – flipping hothead.'

*

It was Sunday, the 5th of August, the day of the Bochym Manor garden party, and Maia was still buzzing from her wonderful news. They had opened a bottle of champagne from the luxury hamper and shared a meal fit for a king the previous night.

The weather that morning did not look favourable when she and Josh had risen, but Josh read the sky and said all would be well later that day. Maia rushed to finish the chores, but Josh seemed reluctant to share her enthusiasm about the day out.

Eventually, he said, 'I am not sure I should go to Bochym, Maia. What if one of the family members recognises me as a blood relative? You saw how Freddy and Lady Sarah reacted the other week.'

'They will have to meet you one day, Josh. You're my husband!' She kissed him on the lips. 'If anyone says anything about the likeness, just laugh it off. Besides, I still think the beard is a good disguise.'

He sighed and scratched his chin. 'I would give anything to get rid of it.'

*

Sure enough, as Josh predicted, the weather brightened, and though not bathed in glorious sunshine as many of the garden parties had been before, at least there was no rain.

The Bochym Manor garden party was an open invitation for local people in the area to picnic in their beautiful gardens. A large marquee was set up near the entrance to the garden, serving complimentary tea and cordials for the visitors.

Meanwhile, a champagne reception was in the French drawing room, and white linen-clad tables adorned the front lawn for family members and VIP guests only.

Maia and Josh stood on the drive, which separated the house and the formal gardens. Maia, as a member of the Arts and Crafts Association, would normally be admitted to the front lawn, but because Josh was with her - and though he was her husband - she did not want to take it for granted that he too would be allowed in. That area was only for friends of the family.

'Let's have a cup of tea,' she suggested. 'Then we can walk around the garden. The fragrance from the beds is intoxicating.' But as they made their way to the tea marquee, Maia suddenly felt her skin prickle when she saw Jago glaring at them. She hoped he would keep his distance today and not decide to make trouble for them.

*

While the Earl and Countess mingled with the villagers in the long borders of the garden, Lord William, Lady Emma, and her husband Ben Pearson, were sat at one of the tables on the front lawn, enjoying the delights of smoked salmon sandwiches and Mrs Blair's speciality goat cheese with onion marmalade tarts.

'Have you seen Maia's new husband, Will? They're standing over there by the garden gate,' Ben said.

'Husband!' William looked shocked as he turned to follow the direction Ben was looking.

'Yes, I am reliably informed that she married Josh, her farmhand, last week. I kid you not, Will - he is the image of you!'

William squinted towards them. 'I haven't got a beard!'

'It's his eyes. Go and introduce yourself; it will be like looking in a mirror!' Ben urged.

William gave him a sceptical look but put his champagne glass down and walked over to where Maia and Josh were standing.

'Hello, Maia,' he said.

Maia smiled broadly at William and dropped him a small curtsy. 'Hello, Lord William,' she said, reverting to propriety while people were around.

Josh, who had just had his attention diverted by someone in the garden, turned when Maia touched his arm.

'Josh, there is someone here I would like you to meet.'

Josh felt his stomach flip at being faced with someone who could easily have been his brother.

'Josh, this is Viscount William Dunstan,' Maia said. 'Lord William, may I introduce Josh Harding, my husband?'

'I am very pleased to meet you, Lord William,' Josh said sheepishly.

'Good grief!' William stated. 'Ben said you were my doppelganger, and he was not wrong. I'm pleased to meet you too, Mr Harding, and congratulations on your marriage to the lovely Maia. You're a very lucky man.'

'I am indeed,' Josh answered happily.

William laughed heartily and looked again at his almost mirror image. 'I must say the resemblance, apart from the beard, is quite uncanny. I understand you're from Devon!'

'Yes, my lord.'

'Thank goodness you are not from around here; otherwise,' he lowered his voice, 'I might have thought that Papa had been sowing wild oats hereabouts.' He laughed at his own joke.

Josh cleared his throat and could do nothing else but laugh along with him.

'I am so glad that Maia has found someone to love. This past year has been very difficult for her. I trust that you will look after her.'

'You have my word, my lord.'

William watched the loving glance between Maia and Josh and could not help but feel a slight pang of jealousy. 'I also understand you had some good news yesterday, Maia. Mama tells me that Liberty London is to buy work from you.'

'Yes. It's a dream come true.'

'Everything is going well for you, Maia, and I am happy for you both.'

'Thank you. I believe it is, yes.' Maia's eyes glistened with happiness.

'Well, I hope you both enjoy the day. Do take advantage of the champagne reception, won't you?'

'Thank you, Lord William. I did not want to assume.'

'Nonsense, Maia. You know you are one of us, and we also welcome your husband into the fold.'

William stopped to speak to several other guests before he returned to Ben and Emma.

Ben grinned at him. 'Well?'

William nodded. 'You're right. I can see the similarity. Damn it, but Harding is a lucky man to have married Maia.'

Ben nudged him playfully. 'Do I detect a hint of jealousy there, Will?'

'Perhaps a little, but as we said before, Maia was probably not for me, and he seems a nice enough chap,' he said almost reluctantly.

'I didn't know you had taken a fancy to Maia,' his sister Emma mused.

William smiled tightly. 'I always liked her, but I am not sure I knew how much until someone else took a liking to her,' he answered resignedly.

'I think she would be slightly too bohemian for you, dear brother.' Emma placed a comforting hand on his arm.

'Yes, I know. My destiny is to marry some well-heeled aristocrat, but mark my words, I, like you, dear sister, will choose whom I marry, and it will be for love.'

They all raised their glasses to that.

'I understand Jago is not too pleased about Josh,' Ben added. They both turned to look at Jago, who seemed to be eyeing up Fee Blackthorn, Guy and Ellie's youngest daughter, though thankfully Fee was ignoring him.

'That man is a predator. I wouldn't trust him as far as I could throw him,' Ben said. 'I saw him walking along the boundary of Polhormon Dairy Farm and Wild Cliff Farm the other day, as though he were assessing the land from Maia's property to David Trevorrow's. Lord knows what he is up to.'

William took a sip of champagne. 'Well, he can't touch Wild Cliff Farm now. Papa's lawyer secured the land for Maia; nothing can alter that. I'm glad she has remarried; I believe she was a little frightened of Jago. Hopefully, he won't bother her any more.

*

Fee Blackthorn had not left her parents' side. She knew Jago was watching her but was determined not to look in his direction or allow him to approach her. Fee was aware that Jago had been trying to meet her. She had heard him call out her name on occasions, but she had not forgiven him for his rudeness towards her, nor would she.

*

Jago clenched his teeth, seething at the young Blackthorn girl. The little minx seemed to be ignoring him! He frowned, puzzled by her slight. He was sure she had quivered with excitement when he offered to take her out in the car the other week. His eyes travelled the length of Fee, noting that she was a trim, pretty little thing. He smiled as he imagined her sprawled naked on his bed. Perhaps her reluctance was due to being with her parents. If he could get near her, maybe he could beckon her away from them.

Glancing at the champagne being drunk by the people milling about in front of the manor, Jago walked with determination towards the gate to the front lawn.

'Your pass, please, sir,' the gateman said.

Jago patted his pockets. 'I must have mislaid it.' He started to walk forward, but the gateman blocked his way.

'No pass, no entry, sir.' He smiled thinly at Jago.

Jago pursed his lips. How dare he deny him entrance and class him as one of the commoners? He, who had a successful motor company! 'Do you know who I am?' he demanded.

'I do, sir. You are someone without a pass.'

He narrowed his eyes in annoyance. He could see Maia flaunting her new husband to all and sundry, drinking champagne with him on the lawn. Damn it, he should be the one invited to the VIP area among the elite, not bloody Josh Harding - a jumped-up farmhand!

Resigned to being left out, he stalked off around the outside of the high garden wall. Where the wall adjoined the conservatory, he leaned against it and lit a cigarette to calm his anger.

*

Maia's relief was palpable now that they were in the VIP area, as she knew that Jago could not approach them there.

It was quite by chance that Maia spotted Mrs Blair emerge through the back door of the conservatory to check on the buffet tables.

'Look, Josh, Mrs Blair is over there. Let's see what she wanted to speak to me about.'

'Oh, Lordy me! But am I glad I've seen you two at last!' Sissy said, eyeing Josh cautiously. 'We seemed to have missed each other every time you came to the kitchen, Maia. Now. Have I got some news for you! Your grandma, Kitty, has been in touch, Josh - or should I say, Gideon!' Sissy raised her eyebrows. 'Now, now,' she berated, 'I am not sure you have been a hundred per cent truthful with me, have you!' She put her hand on Josh's shoulder.

'Pardon?' Josh visibly paled at this news.

'Kitty said that your name was Gideon Walsh, not Josh Harding - though she did say you prefer the name Josh – and I must say I don't blame you,' Sissy added. 'I have had a similar dilemma all my life – I was christened Persephone, but I much prefer Sissy as a name.'

Shocked, Josh whispered, 'How... how did she get in touch?'

'By letter. I am sorry to tell you, Josh, but I can confirm now that your grandpa Walsh *has* died. His death enabled her to contact me at last, so she sent a short letter to see if I was still working here.' She beamed.

'When was this?' he asked seriously.

Sissy tapped her head. 'Let me see. She wrote to me about three weeks ago now. I would have told Maia, but as I said, I kept missing her, and I understand you were poorly for a while, Josh. Are you all right now?'

Josh nodded, but he could hardly keep the anxiety building in his throat from choking him. 'Did you... did you write back?'

'Of course!'

Josh reached over and grasped the back of a chair to steady himself. 'Did you tell her that you had seen me?'

'No, not in the first letter, but when she wrote again. She told me she had moved from her tied cottage, and your father found her another house to live in – though it sounds like she does not care for it much! But Josh, the worst thing is that your family thinks you are dead! Kitty said you were in the Navy, and they had reported that you went overboard and drowned! If what Kitty said was true and you did go overboard,' she pursed her lips, 'why on earth have you not at least informed your grandma that you are safe and well? She is going out of her mind with grief.'

Josh struggled to speak, so Maia stepped into the conversation. 'Mrs Blair, I must ask you, have you written and told Kitty otherwise?'

'Yes, but…'

'Mrs Blair.' A maid approached, in need of Sissy's immediate attention. 'We need you to open the larder again. We've run out of tea!'

'Forgive me. I need to go. Come and see me in the kitchen later, and I will tell you more,' Sissy said, then turned to follow the maid.

Noting his distress, Maia grasped Josh by the hand. 'Josh, stay calm. If the worst happens, we shall get you some help.'

Josh tried to swallow, but his mouth seemed devoid of any moisture. 'Oh, my God, Maia. I will have to leave you. Once Father learns that I am alive - well, you know what will happen – they'll come looking for me.'

'What happened to you was criminal, Josh! Surely, a court will look favourably at you. Come. We'll speak to

Mrs Blair again to find out exactly what she has told your grandma. Then we'll take it from there.'

*

From where Jago was standing, smoking his cigarette, he had heard every word spoken through the open conservatory window. *So, they will come looking for you, will they?* Jago now had all the information he needed to have this cuckoo removed from Wild Cliff Farm. A malevolent smile formed on his lips – this garden party was turning out to be advantageous after all.

*

Maia led Josh through the conservatory and out of the back door to the courtyard. The hustle and bustle of the garden party faded, though Josh's ears were ringing with panic.

'Goodness, are you here already?' Sissy exclaimed. 'Just give me a moment to sort these maids out.'

When she returned, Sissy looked at their anxious faces and frowned.

'Mrs Blair.' Maia stepped forward. 'We need to know. Have you told Josh's grandma that you have seen him?'

'In the letter, yes. I thought it would put her mind at rest. Why? Surely you don't want Kitty to fret any longer than necessary – that is cruel!'

Maia grasped Josh's hand again. 'When did you send it?'

'I haven't yet. I haven't quite finished it, what with the garden party to see to.'

This time, Josh stepped forward beseechingly. 'Oh, Mrs Blair. I beg you. Do not tell Grandma.'

Sissy pursed her lips. 'Why?' she said sternly.

'It is a dreadfully long story, but if you have time, I will tell you everything, but you must promise to keep my secret and not say a word. Especially to Grandma. If my father finds out that I'm alive, I could be imprisoned.'

Sissy stepped back in shock. 'Why? What on earth have you done? Maia, who have you brought into our midst?'

Maia put her hands up to calm Sissy. 'Mrs Blair. I can assure you that Josh has done nothing wrong. But he has been wronged and will be wrongly charged if his whereabouts are known.'

Sissy glanced at the clock to see if she had time to listen. 'Well, then, Josh, you had better sit down and tell me your story.'

33

When the last of the public had left the manor, Freddy Hubbard helped the estate steward, the gamekeeper, and the grooms clear away the tables, chairs, and any other debris left behind. The marquee would stay in situ until the company that supplied it came to take it away the next day. Freddy set off down the garden to check all was intact, as the odd member of the public did tend to uproot the occasional plant that took their fancy, even though they had set up a plant stall for people to purchase young plants. All seemed to be in order this year, although the lower boughs of the apple trees in the orchard seemed depleted of fruit. Ah, well, such is life, he sighed. Freddy had been in the garden all day, so his presence might have deterred the odd plant thief. It was not the only reason he had been down here all day—he'd been avoiding Maia and Josh. Freddy was still smarting at Josh's reluctance to give him Kitty's address. All he wanted was to see Kitty - to tell her that he knew what had happened and how very sorry and sad he was that she thought he would denounce her. He thought it was terribly unfair of Josh to keep her address from him.

Ever since he found out about what had happened to Kitty and why she had left him, the urge to go and find her now that the garden party was over was ever higher on his priorities.

He looked up when Her Ladyship approached and took his cap off.

'Well done, Mr Hubbard. Your garden has been a triumph again.'

'Thank you, my lady. It's all down to your help, too. You have the vision; I only do the groundwork.'

'Nonsense. The garden would flounder without you at the helm. I do hope you have no wish to retire yet.'

'Not yet, but I will need to train another gardener one day soon.'

Sarah tapped her lips. 'I suppose you will. Do you have anyone in mind?'

'I thought perhaps, young Denny Travail. He's almost eleven now and spends a little time with me in the garden when he's not walking the estate with Mr Pearson and His Lordship.'

Sarah nodded. Peter had already told her that Denny had an affinity for the land.

'Perhaps he could work a few hours with me at the weekends for a small wage. I could train him over the next three years, and he could perhaps join me as an apprentice when he is fourteen,' Freddy suggested.

'What a good plan. So, now that the garden party is over, you must go and put your feet up for a while. Take some time off. I don't think you take enough time off.'

'I might just do that, my lady.'

*

Back at Poldhu, Jago sat at his window and glanced over at Wild Cliff Farm. He was pondering who to tell about what he had heard about Harding, or Walsh, as was his real name. He had decided not to go to the local police; they might think it was sour grapes and not take his allegation seriously. No, he would go higher, to the Metropolitan Police. They would know if anyone was looking for a fugitive called Gideon Walsh. He tapped his teeth with his fingernail, casting his mind back to remember the date Josh had first arrived at Maia's farm. The date might help, and he had to get all the facts right. If Maia were harbouring a fugitive, the consequences for her would not be pleasant, so he might be able to remove both cuckoos from his brother's farm with one stone!

*

William joined his papa in the Jacobean drawing room for a pre-dinner drink before the others came down.

'Here's to another successful garden party, Papa!'

Peter raised his glass to William's.

'Did you, by any chance, see Maia's new husband, Josh Harding?' William asked.

'Only from a distance, why?'

William took a sip of whisky. 'It is just that Mr Harding bears an uncanny resemblance to the Dunstans. It was like looking in a mirror. I would have sworn you had been sowing your wild oats hereabouts.' He chortled.

Peter slammed his glass down on the table. 'I'll thank you not to say such things – even in jest. I have never sown wild oats!'

'I'm sorry, Papa. I didn't mean anything by it.' The apology seemed not to have any effect because his papa was clearly angry.

Peter refilled his glass. 'I was nineteen when I had to take over the running of this estate when my father died. I had no time to myself, but if I had had time, I would *not* have sown my wild oats - as you call it. I was determined to love only one woman—your mama.'

William bit down on his lip and sat down to nurse his drink, sorry that he had said anything. He watched his papa stand by the window.

'Your grandfather, my father, was a horrible letch. He was cruel, and he drank too much.' Peter took a sip of whisky, shook his head, and placed his glass back on the drinks table. 'By all accounts, my father used many maids here for his own pleasure.' He paused and sighed heavily. 'There were stories – rumours - that bubbled to the surface and it was Father's downfall in the end, but that's another tale. He had a valet, Lanfear, who selected young girls from within the household for him.' Peter grimaced at the thought of him. 'I inherited the scoundrel when Father died, though I did not know of his murderous ways then.'

'Murderous!' William sat up straight.

'Oh, yes, Lanfear went too far one night and killed one of the maids. He covered his tracks for many years, but then he tried to kill another woman, someone who used to live here when she was a child, when she brought the incident to light. Lanfear was convicted and hanged for his crimes in 1902. It was a bad time for the Dunstans. My father and Lanfear's actions sullied our family name almost beyond redemption. I was determined to cut out the rot in this household. Your mama and I sacked everyone who had helped in the act of debauching those poor girls. I vowed that I would never act promiscuously and was adamant not to be tarred with the same brush as Father!'

'Papa, I didn't know. I'm really sorry—it was a poor joke.'

Peter picked up his glass again and took a long drink from it. 'Yes, well, let's have no more talk of sowing wild oats. Your mama will be down soon. But I trust I can depend on you to keep our family name pure from now on.

'Of course, Papa.'

*

Later that evening, when Sissy finally sat down in her comfy chair, she picked up the letter she had been writing to Kitty. What she had heard from Josh today was absolutely shocking. Sissy had promised both Maia and Josh not to tell Kitty that he was alive. She tore the letter to shreds; she would have to write another now.

*

At Wild Cliff Farm, Josh lay in bed, unable to sleep that night. Although Mrs Blair had promised that she would not tell his grandma that he was alive, he could not settle.

Maia slipped her fingers into his hand. 'Try not to fret so, Josh. All will be well. I'm sure it will.'

Josh breathed a long, low sigh. He wished he could share her confidence. He had been so happy with his life since his arrival here, but now he feared his life was about to unravel. Now that he knew Grandpa had died, he very much feared that Grandma would come down to Cornwall looking for her old love, Mr Hubbard. Josh knew Mr Hubbard was disgruntled with him over his refusal to tell him where Grandma lived. If Grandma told Mr Hubbard about losing her grandson, he would have no qualms about putting the record straight. It was only a matter of time before his secret would be out. His head told him to run, but his heart was so embedded here, with his darling Maia, that he couldn't leave her voluntarily – even to save his own skin. He squeezed Maia's hand and then turned over, and for the first time since exchanging vows, they did not make love.

*

The next morning, Fee Blackthorn waited patiently for the Helston wagon to collect her from Poldhu, but it was over an hour late. She was en route to shop and bank the week's takings for her ma. Monday was the only day that the Poldhu Tea Room closed, and with the sun hot and high in the sky today, she thought that there would be a few disgruntled customers wanting a cup of tea and not being able to have one.

Fee was the natural successor to taking on the management of the tearoom when her ma stood back from her duties – of course, that would not be for some time yet, but she had put it to her ma that they should employ more staff so that they never had to close, except perhaps for Christmas Day. There were few days, except really stormy days, when Poldhu Cove was without visitors. It seemed silly to close at all. She smiled inwardly – even at sixteen, she was turning into a proper businesswoman.

Fee looked up sharply when she heard Jago's car start up further up the hill. A prickle of annoyance washed over her. How on earth could she avoid him now that she was standing here waiting for the wagon to take her to Helston? Her infatuation for him had certainly diminished the second he called her a stupid bitch. Glancing around, she looked to see if she could dip out of sight but found she was too late, as his car appeared around the corner and came to a halt.

Hooking his elbow casually on the door, he raised his eyebrows, revealing eyes bright with interest.

'Well, hello there. Want a lift somewhere?' Jago said with a confident smile.

'No, thank you.' Fee stared him down.

Jago frowned. 'I thought you liked me and my car. You were keen to go for a drive the other week.'

Fee folded her arms. 'That was before you called me a stupid bitch.'

Ruffled, he said indignantly. 'I did no such thing!'

'Yes, you did! I was on the path up towards your house the other Sunday, and you told me to get off the road and called me a stupid bitch.'

A realisation dawned on his face. 'Oh, no, was that you? He got out of the car, and Fee stiffened as he walked over to her. 'Fee. It is Fee, isn't it?' he asked, his eyes clearly appreciating all he saw before him.

She nodded curtly.

'I apologise profusely for any distress I've caused you. I do remember saying it – I cannot tell a lie, but I was so angry at something that had happened. I'm afraid I saw red, and unfortunately, you must have been in the firing line, though I honestly didn't know it was you. I am profoundly sorry for any offence I have caused.'

Fee took a deep breath.

'Please, Fee. Forgive me.' Jago held his hand to his heart.

Before she knew it, the words were out of her mouth. 'Very well. Apology accepted.'

'Good. Now, let me give you that lift. I have to go to the showroom to make an important phone call, and then perhaps we could take a drive somewhere so I can make it up to you.'

'I have shopping and banking to do,' she said firmly.

'Afterwards then?'

Fee glanced around to make sure no one was around and nodded.

'Hop in then.' He opened the door and let her slide onto the sumptuous leather seats.

Feeling shy now that she was sitting in the car, she turned her legs slightly towards the door. They had to drive past her parents' house, so she wriggled down, deep into the seat, hoping that her ma had not seen her.

At the top of Poldhu Hill, she sat up straight again and glanced at Jago.

He grinned and reached over, patting her on the leg and leaving his hand there long enough to tell her she was the object of his desire.

*

At Wild Cliff Farm, Josh had just popped back upstairs to collect a handkerchief when he glanced out of the window in time to see Jago's car pass, and to his dismay, he could see Jago had his hand on Fee Blackthorn's lap! A split second later, Jago glanced up at where Josh stood and removed his hand from Fee's thigh.

When Josh relayed what he had seen to Maia, she folded her arms and asked, 'Are you absolutely sure?'

'I am.'

'Oh, God! He is not to be trusted. What on earth is Fee thinking? I need to speak to Ellie. Fee's on dangerous ground with Jago.'

*

Jimmy Trevorrow was in the car with Ben Pearson, returning to the saddlery having just picked up a roll of leather from the tannery. He felt his heart sink when he saw Fee, hair blowing in the wind, sitting in Jago Penhallow's car with him as it drove past them at speed. Suddenly, all his hopes that she would one day become his girlfriend, albeit next year when he was sixteen, had been dashed instantly.

*

At Bochym, Freddy Hubbard delivered his box of vegetables as he always did in the morning. Whereas he and Sissy had been firm friends for over forty years, their relationship felt strained at present. Sissy missed his jolly banter, but she had done him a great disservice, no matter how well meant it was.

Sissy smiled at Freddy and thanked him for the vegetables. He, in turn, just nodded and said, 'I've a box for you too.'

'Thank you, Freddy. My cottage door is open if you want to drop it in?'

He nodded again and left the kitchen.

Sissy so wanted to tell Freddy that she had heard from Kitty and that she was widowed. It had initially crossed her mind that now that all was out in the open and they were both free, maybe they might have a chance to be together, as they should have been all those years ago. But now she dared not say anything - this new information about Josh gave Sissy a real dilemma. If she told Kitty that Freddy had never married, Kitty might write to Freddy, and he, in turn, might give the game away about Josh. Perhaps Josh needed to tell Freddy his story; she would put it to Maia the next time she saw her.

'Are you quite well, Mrs Blair?' Joe Treen asked. 'You look terribly pensive there.'

'Oh, erm, yes, fine. I'm fine, thank you, Mr Treen.' She turned to busy herself with the staff dinner and shook her head at the many, many secrets she had to keep.

*

Freddy duly took the box of vegetables to Sissy's house. He was sad when he crossed the threshold that he no longer felt that he could come here to share a cup of tea and a slice of cake with her. He humped the box into the kitchen and cursed softly when a potato rolled out onto the floor. As he picked it up, he noted the remnants of a torn letter scattered in the log basket. His heart missed a beat when he saw Kitty's name on part of the letter. He quickly gathered another piece of the letter until he had her full name and address. He slumped down on the kitchen floor, the wind taken out of his sails.

'Oh, Sissy. How could you keep this from me?' he whispered. 'I will never speak to you ever again for withholding this.'

34

Jago pulled up on Coinage Hall Street in Helston, jumped out, and opened the door for Fee.

'How long will you be?' he asked.

'An hour at the most.'

'Meet me here then, at eleven thirty, and I'll take you for a little drive.'

Jago left her to do her shopping and drove to the car showroom. It was Sydney's day off, so he thought he wouldn't be disturbed and went to his office to use the telephone.

Jago sat on the chair with his feet on the desk as he called the operator. He was going to enjoy this.

'Can you put me through to the Metropolitan Police, please?'

A few seconds passed as the operator connected him. Jago lit a cigarette and could hardly keep the smile from his lips.

'Met Police, how can we help?'

'I have some information about a possible fugitive,' Jago said, drawing on his cigarette.

'Go on.'

'He goes by the name Josh Harding, but it's a pseudonym. His real name is Gideon Walsh. I believe he was in the Navy and could have recently jumped ship and pretended to have drowned. You can find him living at Wild Cliff Farm, Cury, near Mullion, Cornwall.'

'I see,' the officer said, 'do you have a description of this man?'

'I do!' Jago said with relish. 'He is approximately six feet tall. He has sandy blond hair and a beard, and he has very blue eyes. I reckon he weighs about twelve stone. He told us he was from Exeter, but it could be another lie. He arrived at the farm around June 14th. We all thought there was something strange about him – that he was not who he said he was!'

'And how have you found out to the contrary?'

'I overheard a conversation yesterday which exposed his deception.'

'And you are?'

'Jago Penhallow of Mullion, Cornwall,' he said proudly.

'Thank you, Mr Penhallow. We will pass this information on to the Admiralty.'

Jago replaced the receiver and folded his arms. 'Oh, sweet revenge.' Today was turning out to be better with every hour that passed. He glanced at the clock and felt a stirring in his groin. Another half hour, and he would have his arm around young Fee Blackthorn.

*

With her shopping basket full of everything Fee had come to Helston for, and after banking the week's takings and enjoying a cup of tea at Mrs Bumble's tearoom to check on the competition, Fee stood waiting for Jago. When she saw his shiny new car approach, despite herself, her stomach did a tiny somersault.

Like a gentleman, he got out and opened the door for her, taking her shopping to put on the backseat. When he got behind the wheel, he gave her a cheeky wink and set off at a speed that almost took Fee's breath away.

They drove through the countryside and out to the coast at Rinsey Head, where they parked overlooking the magnificent St Michael's Bay. He reached his arm over the back of Fee's seat and rested his hand on her shoulder.

'So, am I forgiven?'

She glanced at his hand as it squeezed her shoulder. 'Perhaps.' She gave him the hint of a smile.

'So, what is a nice girl like you doing in my car?' His fingers started to move slightly down from her shoulder.

Fee could see his eyes were dark but full of mischief, and suddenly felt uncomfortable with his manner. Not wanting to encourage him in any way, she moved forward, away from his hand, and touched the dashboard. 'I was interested to know what it was like inside such a car. I might buy one someday.'

He gave a disparaging expression. 'Not one like this! Not on a waitress's wage, I'm afraid.' He smirked.

'The tearoom will be mine one day,' she countered.

'Will it now!' He raised an eyebrow. 'A regular little businesswoman. Eh?'

'Yes, I am.'

He reached forward and pulled her back so he could rest his hand again over her shoulder. 'So, it's the car, not the driver you're interested in?' He teased and squeezed her arm. 'What shall I do to change your allegiance?' He raised his eyebrows suggestively.

Fee felt her skin crawl and began to feel like this jaunt was a big mistake. 'Why would you want me to change allegiance from the car to you? It would be a waste of time, would it not?' She watched the frown forming on Jago's forehead. 'I mean, do you not have your sights set elsewhere?'

He snorted. 'And where might that be?'

'I understand you have interests at Wild Cliff Farm, and everyone knows that you only have eyes for Maia, or you certainly did before Maia got married!' She locked eyes with him to see his response.

Jago pulled his arm from the back of her shoulder and put his hands on the steering wheel. His knuckles whitened, and Fee realised she had hit a nerve with him.

'My interest in Wild Cliff Farm is purely professional.'

'Oh!' she shrugged. 'If you say so.'

'I do say so!' he snapped.

Fee could see he was visibly angry, and she wondered if she had gone too far.

Much to Fee's relief, Jago took a deep breath and said, 'I think it's time for me to drive you back home. But first, I need to make a detour back to the showroom.'

'Then you can drop me off in Helston, and I'll catch the wagon home, thank you,' she said in relief.

As they pulled up at the showroom, he said, 'Stay here. No need to catch the wagon; besides, there isn't one for a couple of hours. I'm heading back to Poldhu soon. I just have another phone call to make, and I need to pick up some paperwork. I shall leave you here for a few minutes to look at my impressive car display. Seeing that is all you seem to be interested in,' he said stiffly.

Fee nodded curtly. After about ten minutes of waiting, she glanced around where she was sitting and found an envelope under the dashboard with papers in it. Glancing at the showroom to confirm Jago wasn't coming, she pulled the papers from the envelope and scanned the document.

It was a bundle of correspondence between the Tehidy Minerals Limited, Camborne, to the Somerset Oxide and Ochre Company Limited and appeared to be a draft indenture - dated 10th of October 1923! Fee frowned in puzzlement - it was only August 1923!

With her interest piqued and having nothing better to do while she waited, she decided to read through it. The document was written in legal jargon and stated that - *Tehidy Minerals Limited had granted permission to the Mullion United Mines Cornwall Limited and the Somerset Oxide and Ochre Company Limited to work serpentine rock and metallic minerals around Mullion!*

'What!' She gasped and read a couple more paragraphs. One of which stated, *'This absolute discretion as to place of erection and machinery is tantamount to revocation. Grantors usually have power to disallow works on specified land of exceptional value or convenience to their estate; but leases have full rights to search and discover; and having discovered minerals, must have complete liberty to erect buildings and machinery on the place or places to win, work, raise, manufacture, and transport their discoveries without let or hindrance.*

Puzzled, Fee read on:

This gives complete liberty to erect works and machinery at all places of discovered minerals, or at convenient places to dress, manufacture and transport them. And should contain powers to construct roads, tramways, or other means for convenience of the minerals and requirements of the work.

Fee frowned - she didn't like the sound of this - and then looked at the other document and gasped. It was a map of Mullion, covered with several large, shaded areas. She noted that one area was situated at the back of her parents' house, bordering Maia's farm and David Trevorrow's dairy. She saw a handwritten note in bold pencil that said, *'Essential and financially beneficial access to the mining area is here!* And there was an arrow pointing to the entrance of Wild Cliff Farm. Glancing back at the draft indenture and then at the map, Fee suddenly felt her stomach turn. Not being schooled in such matters, she thought she was reading this wrongly, but no, this company, the Somerset Oxide and Ochre Company Limited, had been given access to mine their beautiful countryside! She reread the top line from the first paragraph: *This absolute discretion as to place of erection and machinery is tantamount to revocation.* From what she could tell, this document was supposed to be a secret. She wondered why Jago Penhallow had it in his possession. Quickly returning the documents to their envelope, Fee shifted uncomfortably in her seat, knowing she must tell her pa about the plans, but how? He would want to know how she knew. It was a split-second decision when Fee retrieved the documents and pushed them deep into her shopping basket a few moments before Jago returned to the car. But what would she do with them now that she had stolen them? Perhaps she could leave them on the front door mat for her pa to find, as though someone had posted them through the letterbox.

Unable to contain her guilt at the theft of the documents, she felt herself colouring up when Jago got back into the car.

He gave a knowing grin when he saw her blush. 'Ah, I see my presence has some effect on you at last!'

Fee glanced at him and gave a weak smile — she just wanted to get home and out of this car before he discovered what she had done.

*

At half past one that afternoon, Jago dropped Fee off at the top of Poldhu Hill at her request. She had already taken a risk getting into his car, and now, having gotten the measure of him, she was determined not to let anyone see her getting out of his car. There was one thing for certain: Fee would never get in it again! She didn't trust Jago as far as she could throw him.

Jago was pulling his car to a halt outside his house on the cliff when Fee rounded the corner to her parent's house. What a fool she had been to be so fascinated with him - he really was a disagreeable character. As Fee approached home, her step faltered, noting that her pa's wagon was parked outside. She knew he was thatching a cottage in Mullion that week, but he never came home for midday dinner! She hoped all was well.

'Hello, I'm back,' Fee called out as she opened the door, but when she walked into the kitchen, she found Ma and Pa, stern-faced, waiting for her.

'What is the matter? What has happened?' Fee said, placing her shopping on the table.

'Where have you been?' Guy snapped.

Fee felt a shock wave run through her body. Pa rarely raised his voice to her. 'Helston, shopping.'

'With whom?'

Fee swallowed down a lump that had formed in her throat. 'On my own.'

'Do not lie to us, Fee. You were seen in Jago Penhallow's car earlier this morning.'

'He, he gave me a lift into Helston. I was waiting for the wagon, but it didn't turn up.'

'And did he bring you back?' Guy demanded.

Fee could not tell a lie. 'Yes, Pa,' she answered, casting her eyes down.

'Have you been with him all the time?'

Fee couldn't help but think this interrogation was unnecessary. After all, she was sixteen! But she thought better of railing against his questioning.

'Have you? Answer me.'

'No, Pa. He dropped me off in Helston, and I went to the bank. I had a cup of tea in Bumbles tearoom and bought the groceries for Ma.' She placed the basket on the table.

'And then what? You have been gone ages!'

'Jago took me for a drive to Rinsey Head.'

Guy's anger burst forth. 'For God's sake, Fee. You know the man's reputation. Do you want to be tarred with the same brush? You will never, do you hear me, never, get in his car again!'

Ellie reached out and touched Guy on his arm to calm him.

'Nothing would possess me to do so, Pa, I promise.'

Ellie stepped forward. 'Why, darling? Did he touch you? Are you hurt in any way?'

'No, Ma. I quickly got the measure of him, and when he realised I wasn't interested in him, he brought me home.'

Guy was incandescent with rage. 'What on earth possessed you to get in the car in the first place?'

'Guy, calm yourself,' Ellie said. 'You heard Fee – the wagon was late, and she was wise enough to see him for what he is.'

Ellie took Fee into her arms. 'We were just so worried about you, darling. You're so beautiful. Your pa and I don't want your reputation spoiled by the likes of him. You deserve a much better man when the time comes.'

'I know I do.' As the cat was *out of the bag,* so to speak, Fee decided to hand over the documents she had found in the car rather than leave them randomly on the doormat.

'I have done something very wrong, though!' she admitted.

Guy raked his fingers through his hair in desperation at what she was about to admit.

'I took something from Jago's car – some documents!'

'Documents! Why?' Guy demanded.

'I thought you needed to see them, though I admit I didn't know how to get them to you. I think Jago is doing something underhanded. Something that will spoil our lovely village, and I don't know for sure, but I think Maia has some part in it.'

Guy and Ellie exchanged curious glances. Unbeknownst to Fee, it had been Maia who had told them she was driving around the countryside with Jago.

'Where are these documents?'

'In my basket.'

With the map and draft document laid on the table, it seemed like an age that her parents spent as they poured over them.

Eventually, Guy stood up – his face drained white. 'They mean to mine all this beautiful land! I'm taking this to Tobias Williams to show him. We need to call an extraordinary meeting of the parish council.'

'Pa.' Fee said fearfully. 'Can we somehow get this envelope back into Jago's car? Otherwise, he will be angry when he finds out what I've done.'

Guy cupped his daughter's face and kissed her on the nose. 'You have done the correct thing by bringing this to our attention. Don't worry about Jago Penhallow. We will deal with him.'

*

Later that evening, the parish council members gathered at Tobias Williams' house to discuss this matter.

'Gentlemen,' Tobias started the proceedings, 'I've read this document from end to end, and apparently, The Somerset Oxide and Ochre Company Limited has been given full and free liberty to dig, work and search for decomposed serpentine rock or green or other coloured earth in, under and throughout the fields or enclosures of land situate in the parish of Mullion. They have given the company a term of 21 years from 25th March 1923.'

'Why have we not heard about this before?' Guy asked.

'From this draft document, they were going to present it to us as a fait accompli on the 10th of October. They mustn't have wanted anyone to get wind of it before they had.'

'Can you imagine what this means to our village? We are going to be surrounded by quarries!' The head of the parish council, Bill Rowe, said in dismay.

'Yes, and the impact will be devastating to the people who own the land the mining will encroach on,' Guy added.

'Imagine what it will be like to be subjected to pollution, noise, traffic, smoke, and dust! Not to mention the damage, loss of land, deterioration of the water quality, and having to live with an eyesore of the damage to the landscape and the environment. The village will change beyond recognition!' Tobias added.

'Is there anything we can do to stop this?' Guy asked.

Bill Rowe shook his head. 'I'm afraid not - this is a done deal.'

'I wonder how long Jago has known about this?' Tobias added.

'And Maia!' Guy interjected. 'From this note, they plan to push a road through her farm to one of the sites.'

'Well,' Bill said, standing up to bring the meeting to a close, 'I suggest we go and see her tomorrow. See what she has to say for herself.'

'What about Jago? When shall we confront him?' Tobias asked.

'When I've been over to Camborne to the Tehidy Minerals Limited. I want to know how long Jago has known about it and if we could have done something to stop it if we'd known sooner.'

*

As they sat down to their evening meal at Wild Cliff Farm, Maia noted that Josh had relaxed a little, much to her relief. She did not like this unhappy, quiet version of him. He had been busy all day, taking the larger share of the outside work to give Maia time to collate and wrap her pots, ready to show the buyer from Liberty London in the morning.

He helped, as always, to dry the dishes after she washed them, and when they finished, he wrapped his arms around her and kissed her.

'Sorry about last night.'

'Nothing to apologise for,' she said, nestling her head in his neck.

'I am so worried they will find me one day and take me away from you, Maia.'

'Well, let's hope for the best.'

'I'm worried about Mr Hubbard - he might not let sleeping dogs lie. He might try to find Grandma – especially now Mrs Blair knows where she lives - and that she's a widow.'

'When I go to my meeting in the morning, I'll ask Mrs Blair if she's said anything to Mr Hubbard, and if she hasn't, I will beg her not to do so.'

'Oh dear, more lies and secrets,' he said, flopping down on one of the chairs. 'Even our marriage is a lie.'

'No, Josh, it isn't a lie. We just had an unconventional marriage – no different from the handfasting that used to happen.'

'My understanding is that we should marry legally within twelve months of handfasting, but I fear we'll never be able to make our union legal.'

Maia sat on his knee and ran her hand softly down his face. 'I will always belong to you, and you, my darling, will always belong to me. That will suit me for eternity.'

35

After a very successful meeting with the buyer from Liberty London and an assurance from Mrs Blair that she would not give Mr Hubbard Kitty's address, Maia felt she could relax. All her money worries were over, and Josh was safe.

Maia was busy cooking dinner while Josh was finishing off in the vegetable garden when the knock came to the door. Wiping her hands down her apron, she glanced at Prudence, who had arched her back – not a good sign. Running to the window, half expecting to see Jago, Maia frowned to find the Blackthorn's wagon in the drive. She opened the door only to be confronted by the three stern faces of Bill Rowe, Tobias Williams and Guy Blackthorn.

'May we come in, please,' Guy said stiffly.

Puzzled at the hostility in Guy's voice, as she had always had a good relationship with him, she said, 'Of course.'

She let the three, clearly angry men into the kitchen and watched as they cleared a space on the table and slapped some papers and a map down. Even more confused now, she said, 'What is this?'

Guy grunted at her response.

Maia's eyes cut questionably to Guy - he had never been hostile towards her before. As she began to study the map, her eyes settled on the large, shaded areas. Stepping back, she asked, 'What is this shaded area that borders my land?'

Guy pushed the draft document for the proposed mining under her nose. 'Read this.'

After scanning the document, she looked up at the men. 'They're proposing to mine the area!'

'Correct.' Guy said coldly. 'So, Maia, what do you know about this?'

'Me?' She looked astonished. 'Nothing, why?'

'This.' Guy stabbed his finger at the handwritten note, pointing to the entrance of Wild Cliff Farm.

Maia read it: *Essential and financially beneficial access to the mining area is here!* She looked up, puzzled.

Guy folded his arms. 'We can tell you now that this document was in Jago Penhallow's possession. What has he said to you about this? Are you in cahoots with him on this scheme to make a profit?'

Maia felt a bubble of anger form. It was rare for her to get angry, but when she did, her eyes blazed with a fiery temper that matched her red hair. 'How *dare* you suggest such a thing?' she yelled. 'I know *nothing* of this document!'

All three men in the room stepped back from her fury.

'Then why is this pencil marking the entrance to your farm?' Bill Rowe interjected.

'You know, as well as any man in this village, that Jago believes this farm is his. He has tried everything to gain possession of it. I even had to get a court order to say it was mine!' She laughed without mirth. 'And now I know why! He obviously has big plans for *my* farm. Well, he has another think coming. And as for you lot!' She picked up the documents and pressed them hard against Guy's chest. 'I would like you to leave my property and never dare to suggest that I could be privy to something as evil as this. Don't you know how much I love this area? Do you really think I want my land churned up with wagons going back and forth? Get out, go on, get out, all of you.'

*

Josh was walking into the yard whistling as the three men climbed back into the Blackthorn's thatching wagon. When he entered the kitchen, he found Maia in tears.

'Oh, my love. What has happened? What did those three want?'

After relaying the conversation to Josh, she wept again. 'Oh, Josh, they're going to dig up our beautiful village. I'm going to have a deep quarry between my land and David's. It's going to be such a scar on the landscape.'

'Is it definite they're going to do it?'

'It seems so.' She sniffed back the tears. 'I don't want to live here if they do this!'

'We'll cross that bridge when we come to it, Maia,' he said, gathering her into his arms.

*

No sooner had the trio left Wild Cliff Farm than they paid a visit to Jago.

Bill Rowe folded his arms. 'The Tehidy Minerals Limited were very interested, and I might add, quite alarmed to know that you had a copy of a secret draft document of the proposed mining at Mullion. Apparently, it was private and confidential.'

Jago narrowed his eyes and countered, 'And how pray do you know I had such a document if it was so private?' *His mind was rapidly going over where he had left the documents - and how the hell these three men had found out about them.*

Ignoring Jago's feigned innocence, Bill Rowe said, 'How long have you known, Jago? We might have stopped this if you had divulged this information sooner.'

Jago smirked and shook his head. 'You couldn't have put a stop to it. It's progress. Why would you not want this? It'll bring in so much work and revenue.'

'We've told Maia, you know, what you were proposing to happen at her farm, and she was very angry with you. We will all fight you tooth and nail to stop you from bulldozing through her farm. So, your little business venture will fail if you are banking on making money via access through Wild Cliff Farm.'

'Maia has no right to that farm – it was my brother's farm, so I *will* bulldoze through her farm when this project takes off, whether you or Maia like it or not! I'll mow that bitch down in the process if she tries to stop it.'

'Will you now!' Tobias said. 'I shall be logging that threat with the police, and rest assured, if you try to carry out that threat, you will be punished.'

Jago could have bitten his own tongue off as he had clean forgotten that Tobias had once been a policeman. 'Maia is irrelevant anyway because she and her *new husband* will be in jail by then.'

'You're talking nonsense now,' Tobias said sharply.

'Am I? We'll see. I know that Maia is harbouring a criminal. Because Josh Harding is not who he claims to be!'

'Enough of this, Jago. I shall also log your defamation of Josh and Maia's character with the police. We all know of your jealousy towards Josh, but as a widow, Maia has every right to happiness with another man. What she does is of no concern to you, and as for the farm, the court has already ruled in her favour. You can't touch it.'

Jago laughed sardonically. 'But you don't know the half of it, you see. I overheard Harding and Maia talking at the garden party. Harding was worried that someone might have found him out. From what I gleaned from the conversation, he'd been in the Navy but absconded, and I might add that Josh Harding is not his real name. Speak to your police friends in London, Tobias. I've reported Harding to them.'

Tobias glanced at Guy, unsure of what to make of the allegations.

Guy prodded Jago in the chest. 'You're the bloody criminal here, and you don't deserve to live in this village if you're happy with the destruction this mining company will wreak. We are going to make this information known to everyone in the village now, and I'll also make sure that everyone knows that you were looking forward to profiteering from it.'

The three men left, slamming the door behind them and making the house timbers creak alarmingly.

In a rage, Jago cleared the table of its contents with his hand and then went to stand at his window, glowering over at Wild Cliff Farm. Damn the person who took those documents. He scratched his chin, trying to remember where he had left them and how anyone could have gained access to them - and then it dawned on him – they were in the car! That sneaky little bitch, Fee Blackthorn, must have taken them. He felt another bubble of rage rise in his chest – the same chest Fee's father had just prodded as he damned him to all and sundry. Well, Miss Blackthorn, you had better watch your step from now on - because with theft comes consequence.

*

In Portsmouth, Kitty was busy scrubbing the black mould from all the window frames. It was a chore she had to do every week, but it still returned. This house was so damp that Kitty needed to air her bedsheets outside every day and make her bed afresh every night; otherwise, it was like climbing into a damp sock! She had complained to her son Jacob when he came around earlier that week, but he seemed uninterested in her plight.

'You have a roof over your head - what more do you want? I can't provide you with a better house,' he snapped. 'Especially now that I'm getting no wage from the admiralty. Nor am I getting any bloody compensation from them, because they're now saying that that wastrel Gideon jumped ship!'

Kitty's mouth tightened. Jacob had no right to collect her grandson's wage in the first place. Poor Josh had told them, when he had come home on leave two years ago, that he was only given a pittance for his naval service. Josh had told them his father had arranged with Captain Wright that the lion's share of his wages was to go straight to Jacob – to feed the family. Hah! None of the family had seen anything of these so-called wages. Jacob had kept every single penny of it and drunk it away!

Kitty shook herself from her angry reverie when Jacob started to speak again.

'Besides, I'm to be married again next month!' Jacob said. 'And we'll have a babe to feed in the New Year. So, you'll have to fend for yourself from now on.'

Kitty felt sorry for his bride-to-be. When Jacob brought her round to meet her a couple of weeks ago, the poor girl was already sporting a black eye. Now that the girl was pregnant, there would be no escape for her. Poor lass!

The thought of her dear grandson, Josh, brought tears to her eyes. She climbed the stairs and glanced through the landing window, where she could just about glimpse the sea. Where are you, Josh? Are you somewhere out there? Drowned, they said, jumped ship! Kitty shook her head. Surely Josh would not be so foolhardy as to do such a thing, but neither could she believe that he had drowned. When Jenny, his mother, gave birth to Josh in 1900, it had been what they call an 'en caul' birth - when the baby comes out still inside an intact amniotic sac. Folklore said it was a lucky omen because those born with an 'en caul' would never die of drowning. Kitty held onto this fact as the only shred of hope that he was still alive because the thought of losing Josh didn't bear thinking about.

Returning to her scrubbing, after several minutes, Kitty wiped the perspiration from her forehead, put down her scrubbing brush, and checked her doormat to see if there was another letter from Sissy yet – but still, there was nothing. It had been almost a fortnight since she had written to her, and Bochym Manor had been on her mind for some time now. How would she feel if she were to go back there again, she wondered? She longed to see Sissy again and needed to know if Freddy had gotten over her desertion of him. In the last letter Sissy had written, she said that none of the horrible old staff was still at the manor, and with the old Earl long dead and mouldering in his grave, the urge to go back there was getting stronger by the day.

Glancing around her musty house, she knew she needed to get out of there – if just for a short while. She wouldn't tell Jacob she was going. She would leave him a note saying she was out visiting a friend. The last thing she wanted was for Jacob to know who his real father had been. She would die of shame if he ever went to Bochym Manor to demand his birthright! After wiping the mould off her suitcase, Kitty packed a few things. Then she put on her hat and coat - even though the day was hot and sunny - walked to the bank and withdrew enough money to cover her train fare to Cornwall and to find board and lodgings somewhere.

*

Just after breakfast on Wednesday morning, Maia opened the door to find Guy and Tobias standing on her doorstep. Folding her arms, she tipped her head questioningly, determined not to invite them inside this time.

'Maia, we need to speak with you.'

'I have told you this mining business has nothing to do with me. I know nothing about it.'

'We know that now, and we're here to apologise.'

'Apologies accepted,' she said, and she began to close the door on them.

'Maia.' Tobias put his hand up to stop the door from closing. 'Something else has come to light, something you need to be aware of. Can we come in?'

She sighed heavily. 'As long as you don't accuse me of anything else.'

'We're not accusing you of anything, we promise,' Tobias assured her.

'Well, I suppose so then.' She stepped back reluctantly as they walked into the kitchen, but she did not offer them a seat.

'Maia, where is Josh?'

Immediately on the defensive, she narrowed her eyes. 'Why?'

Tobias took a deep breath. 'When we confronted Jago about the draft document, he made some allegations about Josh.'

Maia's mouth twitched. 'What sort of allegations?'

'That Josh is not who he claims to be. Jago reckons you are harbouring a criminal.'

Maia began to shake visibly. 'So, you are accusing me of something?'

'No, we are here to warn you that Jago has spoken to the police about Josh.'

Maia's mind was in a whirl. She had to think of something quickly. 'Are you surprised? Jago would do anything to defame Josh's character. He's jealous of him!'

'That's as maybe, but I've spoken to my police colleagues,' Tobias said, 'and yes, the Metropolitan Police are taking the report seriously.' Tobias took another deep breath. 'Apparently, Jago overheard a conversation at the Bochym garden party and gleaned that Josh Harding is not his real name and that he had absconded from the Navy.

Maia felt suddenly lightheaded as a gasp emptied her lungs of air.

*

Outside, Josh looked up from collecting the eggs to find David Trevorrow climbing the stile.

'Morning, Josh,' he shouted. 'I'm just here to speak with you and Maia about this awful business of them mining the area.'

'Yes. She's terribly upset about it all. Especially as the parish council thought she was in cahoots with Jago over access to one of the sites via this farm. As if that could be possible, that Maia would collude with that scoundrel!'

'Indeed. Jago has a lot to answer for. And if I know this village, they'll make their annoyance known, good and proper.'

'I hope they do and drive him out of this village. Now, just let me finish collecting these eggs, and I'll come in with you.'

As they rounded the farm building, Josh slowed when he once again saw Guy Blackthorn's wagon in the drive.

'Well, I hope they've returned to apologise to Maia,' he said to David.

Josh breezed into the kitchen with a clutch of eggs in his hands and felt a sudden curl of dread when everyone turned to look at him.

He glanced at Maia's stricken face and felt his heart sink. 'Has something happened?' he asked tentatively.

36

At Bochym, Sissy returned from a quick meeting with Mrs Johnson, the housekeeper, to find two boxes of vegetables waiting for her.

'Oh!' She frowned. 'Why has Mr Hubbard left two boxes?' she asked Vicky, her assistant.

'He said he's taking a couple of days off.'

'Is he!' Sissy said astonished. 'Mr Hubbard never takes time off!'

'He *is* entitled!' Vicky said in his defence.

Sissy bristled. 'I know he is! It's just that he never normally takes time off. Did he say where he was going?'

'Erm.' Vicky looked skyward, searching her mind to remember what he said: 'Somewhere up country. I can't remember what he said now. Plymouth, or was it Portsmouth?' She laughed.

'Oh, Lordy me!' Sissy's hands flew to her face. That could only mean one thing. He had gone to look for Kitty, but how on earth had he found out where she was?

*

At Wild Cliff Farm, Josh slumped down on one of the kitchen chairs after learning that he had been reported to the police. Josh had no option other than to tell them all his story – if only to keep Maia from being implicated in harbouring him.

'Well!' Tobias looked astonished after hearing the tale. 'From what you've told us, you've clearly been wronged.'

'The Admiralty might not think so.' Josh sighed. 'Captain Wright told me that if I survived and was caught, then I would be court-martialled for jumping ship.'

'How long has it been since you were thrown overboard?' Tobias asked.

'It was the 1st of June.'

Tobias did a mental calculation. 'You need to be absent without leave for four and a half months to be court-martialled. Shorter absences are dealt with at a summary hearing. You might get a better result if you try to bring a prosecution against your captain in a hearing rather than a court martial, though you would need a good lawyer!'

Josh slumped lower in the chair. 'How can I afford a lawyer?'

Everyone stopped speaking when a car pulled up outside, and when Prudence stood, arched her back, and hissed, Maia looked through the window and gasped.

'Oh, God, Josh! I think they're here. There are two men in military uniform getting out of the car!'

Josh glanced at Tobias. 'Damn you!' he shouted at him. 'You've trapped me, haven't you? You've trapped me!' He got up in a panic but didn't know what to do.

Tobias also stood. 'I promise you, Josh. I have not trapped you. I just came to warn you.'

Maia looked stricken faced at Josh. 'Do you want to run – get away out of the scullery door?' she asked.

'It will be better if he doesn't,' Tobias warned.

'Better for whom?' Maia cried.

'For Josh. He needs to stop hiding and tell them what he told us.'

Josh was breathing hard now. 'They won't believe me!'

'I will stand as a character witness for you if need be.' Tobias offered.

'And I,' Guy said.

'Count me in,' David added.

Josh looked frantically between the men. 'But you all hardly know me! I have lied to you all!'

'With good reason,' Tobias answered. 'Now, I think I can speak for everyone here, but if Maia trusts you, you must be a good man.'

Although they were waiting for it, a loud rap on the door made them all jump. Maia glanced frantically at Josh, who nodded to let them in.

Their manner was swift and brusque. As soon as they established that Josh's real name was Gideon Walsh, Josh was arrested, handcuffed, and cautioned.

Without the chance to say their goodbyes, they marched Josh out of the farmhouse.

'No! No! No!' Maia screamed and ran after Josh, grabbing him back by the arm, but one of the arresting officers pulled her away and pushed her backwards.

'Leave her be,' Josh shouted in despair.

'Shut up.' The officer warned him as they bundled Josh into the back of the waiting car.

'Where are you taking him?' Maia cried, trying desperately to fight her way back to Josh.

The officer shoved her away again. 'To Portsmouth to be tried and convicted. Now step away from the car, Madam.'

As the car drove off at speed, Maia ran after it, tripping and falling to her knees. She looked on in despair as Josh turned for one last look at her from the rear view window. 'Josh. Josh,' she screamed as the car turned the corner out of sight.

*

Maia sat on the road in a cloud of dust and exhaust fumes until Guy and David ran to pick her up. Her body felt limp, like a rag doll, as though all the life in her had drained away with the loss of Josh. Tears streamed down her face as they helped her back into the kitchen, where Tobias had pulled out one of the chairs for her.

'Josh. Oh, God, Josh.' She slumped on the table and wept brokenheartedly. Her skirt was ripped, and blood was oozing through her dress from cuts to her knees and elbows.

'Maia,' Tobias said gently. 'If Josh tells them the truth, just as he told us, he will not be punished.'

Maia lifted her head, her face dirty with dust and tears, and her eyes swollen with sorrow. 'He will. You know he will. Josh never had any intention of going back.' She glanced wide eyed at everyone. 'We were happy.' Her lip trembled and more tears fell. 'We love each other! Now I'll never see him again,' she wailed.

'Damn Jago for his bloody meddling,' Guy snarled.

'Rest assured, Jago is going to get his comeuppance,' David said. 'This mining matter has caused quite a rumpus, and now this – he will not be able to live here for much longer.'

All the men agreed.

'Josh will need a good lawyer, Maia,' Guy said seriously. 'Can he afford one?'

Maia shook her head and then suddenly stood up, sending the chair crashing to the floor. 'I must go.'

'Go where? Portsmouth!' Guy asked in surprise.

'Maia, you won't be able to do anything there,' Tobias warned.

Ignoring their protests, she pushed past everyone and ran to fetch Shadow's saddle from the stable. *There was only one person who she knew could help Josh, and she needed to go to him now.* They followed her down to the paddock as she saddled her horse, pleading with her to stop.

'Give me a leg up,' she demanded.

'But where are you going?' David shouted.

'To get Josh the help he needs,' she said, as she rode out of the yard and past the trio.

*

Jago felt joyous as he drew up outside his car showroom that morning. He had been lucky enough to see the military police arrive at Wild Cliff Farm when he passed that morning. At last, he had removed that bloody cuckoo from the nest. He sincerely hoped that Josh Harding would go down for a very long time for being absent without leave. However, his removal had come a little too late for him to work on Maia about gaining access to the new mining sites. He knew that his involvement in the scheme was causing a few ructions in the village. Though he had not been in The Old Inn since being banned, he fully understood the measure of his fellow villagers' anger at how he had planned to profit from the destruction of their village. When he went into the local store to buy food, he found that they wouldn't serve him. Then, on his exit from the shop, an old man, whom Jago had known all his life, spat at him. He shrugged. What the hell did he care? He would be moving elsewhere soon anyway. His house on the cliff was creaking and groaning alarmingly. He reckoned it would be unsafe to live there for much longer. Good riddance to the village of Mullion. It was going to be a bloody mess soon, anyway!

When Jago walked into his car showroom, his self-satisfied smile dropped as he found Sydney, stricken-faced, standing in the destruction and debris of all Jago's beautiful cars. Windscreens and lights had been smashed, hammer marks covered the car bonnets, and all the leather car interiors had been cut with a knife. An acrid smell filled the room from a pool of oil, growing by the minute as it seeped from every damaged sump, and not a single tyre had evaded being punctured with a knife.

'What the....!'

'I've called the police. They'll be over dreckly,' Sydney said. 'Whoever did this must have gained entry through the back window.'

Jago narrowed his eyes. 'You must have left it open then!' he said accusingly.

'They smashed it to gain entry, for your information!' Sydney snapped, trying, without success, to keep his temper at being accused of allowing this to happen. 'So, Jago.' Sydney folded his arms. 'You tell me - who did this? To whom have you been nasty this time?'

'Oh, shut up and clean this place up.' Jago stormed off to his ransacked office.

Sydney followed and threw his resignation letter at him. 'Clean it up yourself – I quit. Your angry, dark moods make it impossible for me to work with you anymore. You're a nasty person, and this is what happens to nasty people. I have no idea what you've done for this to happen, but I am not staying here to be tarred with the same brush as you. Besides, your business is in tatters now, and it bloody well serves you right.'

'Get out then!' Jago threw a book at Sydney, smashing the only window left whole in the office door. He swiped the debris off his chair and slumped down. He was seething with anger, but Sydney was right - his business could not recover from this because he wasn't insured. He was sure this had something to do with a revenge attack for his part in the Mullion mining contract. So, what should he do? He had money in the bank and an expensive car, which he would have to sell to fund a new life, but where would he go? He tapped his teeth with his fingernail for a moment and then picked up the phone – relieved that it was still connected - and rang the operator.

'Put me through to Southampton docks,' he barked. He would go to America and rebuild his empire, but first, he had a few more scores to settle.

*

The trip to Bochym on horseback felt like the longest ride Maia had ever taken. When she arrived, she jumped down without securing her horse and rushed into the Bochym kitchen, her face still streaked with dust and tears.

'Oh, lordy me, Maia! Whatever's the matter?' Sissy shrieked when she saw the state of her.

'Oh God, Mrs Blair,' she cried. 'I need to see His Lordship urgently. They've taken Josh.'

'Goodness me, whatever is going on in here?' Joe Treen demanded as he rushed in to see what all the commotion was.

'Oh, Mr Treen.' Maia practically fell on him. 'I need to see His Lordship urgently.'

'May I ask why?'

'I need his help, Mr Treen. I need him to help free someone who has been wrongly arrested.'

Joe's face blanched; he had also once been wrongly arrested, and the memory still made him shudder. 'May I ask whom?'

'Josh.' Her face crumpled. 'It's my Josh.'

Sissy was by her side with a comforting arm around her shoulders.

'Please, Mr Treen,' Maia said, and both women looked at him beseechingly.

'Very well,' Joe said gently. 'I shall see if His Lordship is free to see you.'

*

At Helston Train Station, Freddy felt as nervous as a kitten as he sat on a bench after arriving too early to catch his train. Better too early than too late, he thought. He felt like a fish out of water today, as he very rarely travelled anywhere - his life was with his flowers at Bochym Manor.

The station master blew his whistle and shouted, 'Plymouth train due in two minutes.'

Freddy stood. 'Is this the one I need to catch to get to Portsmouth?' he asked the station master.

'Aye, but you'll catch it on its way back. It's bound for Penzance first, but when you do board, you'll need to change at Plymouth to get to Portsmouth. I reckon you have about an hour and a half to wait, I'm afraid.'

'Oh, I see.' Freddy sat down, deflated. After deciding to go and find Kitty, he wanted to be off and on his way. At this rate, he wouldn't get to Portsmouth until late in the afternoon. He would definitely have to find somewhere to stay that night. He settled down resignedly. All he could do was sit, wait, and watch the world go by.

The signal down the track changed, and with great puffs of steam, the train approached the station. It came to a stop, doors opened and closed, and clouds of steam obliterated the view of the platform. Ghostly figures loomed large, wafting away the cloud to see where they were walking. Freddy counted about twenty people who got off and walked past him, all scurrying away to wherever they were going. As the steam cloud lifted, Freddy glanced at a woman dressed in black, who, in turn, glanced back at him as she walked by. There must have been a moment of mutual recognition because no sooner had Freddy stood than the woman backtracked and stood open-mouthed before him.

After a few seconds of stunned silence, Freddy spoke.

'Kitty!' His breath caught in his throat.

Kitty gasped and, in a soft voice, whispered, 'Freddy Hubbard! Is that really you?'

37

As Maia followed Joe Treen to Peter Dunstan's study, she met with Sarah, who was coming down the stairs.

'Goodness, Maia!' Sarah looked horrified as she took in Maia's appearance. 'Whatever has happened?'

'Oh, Lady Sarah,' she answered distraught. 'The very worst thing has happened. Josh has been arrested on a false charge. Please forgive my appearance; I fell running after him when they took him away.' She spread her arms to reveal the full state of her attire. 'His Lordship has kindly agreed to see me. I desperately need his help.'

'I see. Of course.' Sarah nodded.

Peter Dunstan stood by the window in his study, his stance stiff and his hands clasped behind his back, when Maia entered. He had no idea how he could help her, but because it was Maia, he must at least give her his time if nothing else. He was shocked at her distressed appearance. Her beautiful face was streaked with tears, her blood-stained clothes clung damply to her skin, and her mass of fiery curls were wildly tangled from the ride over.

'Maia. Do sit down.'

'Thank you for seeing me, my lord,' she said tremulously.

Another knock came to the door, and Sarah popped her head around. 'Forgive the intrusion, but I met Maia in the hall. May I sit in on this meeting?'

Peter glanced at Maia, who nodded in agreement, and Sarah settled on a chair in the corner of the room. Peter knew that if Sarah was giving some credence to this matter, this might not be as straightforward as a chat.

Peter turned his attention to Maia, and concerned for her wellbeing, he asked, 'Can I ring for some refreshment – water perhaps?'

Maia shook her head. 'No, thank you.'

'I understand from Treen that your husband was arrested?'

'Wrongly arrested, my lord, by the admiralty for desertion.' Her voice cracked as she uttered the last word.

Peter frowned. 'Maia, I appreciate how distressing this is, but I don't know how I can help you!'

'He needs a good lawyer, my lord.'

Peter sat down and steepled his fingers. 'Maia, I understand that you have recently married this man, but lawyers cost a great deal of money. I would gladly help an old friend in need, as we did with you over the farm deeds, but to be frank, none of us knows the first thing about Josh. He has only been among us for a few weeks, and it seems he has hidden his true character, even from you.'

Maia shook her head violently. 'Oh, but I do know his true character. He told me everything the day I met him. I can vouch that he is a good man who has been severely wronged.'

Peter twisted his mouth. 'Or so he says.'

Maia got up and started to pace the room in agitation.

Peter watched her anxiously. 'Maia, I know he is your husband, but...'

'Yes. He is my husband, but Josh is also a Dunstan, my lord!' She interjected before he could say more.

Sarah shifted uneasily in her chair, and Peter felt a strange sensation wash over him.

'I beg your pardon?'

Returning to her seat, Maia said, 'Josh is the grandson of a maid called Kitty who was used and abused by the old Earl in 1882. I don't know if you saw Josh at the garden party, my lord, but Lord William did and commented that it was like looking in a mirror. Josh is most definitely a Dunstan.' She turned to Sarah. 'You have seen him too, Lady Sarah; you must have seen the resemblance?'

'I did, Maia. Yes.'

Peter clenched his fists, trying to contain his feelings.

Maia then relayed the whole story of what had happened to Kitty Morton.

'Mrs Blair will verify what I have said - she witnessed the aftermath of the attack and helped Kitty away.'

'Goodness!' Sarah gasped. 'And you say that Kitty was going to marry Mr Hubbard before the attack?'

Maia nodded.

'And does he know what happened to her?'

'Yes, but he has only just learned of it.'

'I see. Now I know why Mr Hubbard has been so upset these last few weeks,' Sarah said gravely.

Peter stood up abruptly and walked to the window. 'Is that why Josh came to this area - to claim kin?'

'No, my lord. Josh only found out himself a month ago, when he met with Mrs Blair, and they put two and two together. I can assure you that Josh did not want you or your family to know. He will be deeply upset that I have told you. But now, oh goodness, now that this awful thing has happened, he needs help quickly. Will you help him, my lord?'

Peter knew his odious father's reputation perfectly; he did not doubt that Josh was an illegitimate offspring and could only feel contempt towards his parent. 'But they must have some evidence that he deserted his ship; the Admiralty does not arrest people without reason,' he stated.

'Please, my lord. Let me now tell you exactly what has happened to Josh.'

Peter took out his pocket watch, checked the time, and took a deep breath. 'Very well, Maia.' He sat down again.

Maia explained about Josh's time in the Royal Navy, how cruelly the captain had treated him, and how and why he had had Josh thrown off the ship to his potential death.'

Peter expelled a low breath. 'This is a grave story indeed, Maia. Tell me, how did the Admiralty find out where Josh was?'

'Jago Penhallow informed them. I understand he overheard a private conversation between Mrs Blair, myself, and Josh. We were foolishly discussing Josh's tenuous situation at your garden party.'

'I see.'

Maia's eyes watered again. 'I fear for Josh, knowing Captain Wright's character. He will twist Josh's story, and they won't believe him. I'm terrified they will convict Josh for a crime he did not commit. Please, my lord, Josh has suffered enough.'

Peter stood again to glance out of the window.

'Please, my lord,' Maia begged.

'Where have they taken him?'

'Portsmouth.'

Peter turned, caught the beseeching look from Sarah, and nodded. 'I cannot promise anything, Maia, but I will do what I can.'

'Oh, thank you for your kindness, my lord,' she sobbed. 'If it will help, Tobias Williams, Guy Blackthorn, and David Trevorrow have offered to give character references. Josh has only lived here a short time, but people know that he is a good man.'

Peter nodded.

Sarah got up and put her arm around Maia. 'Come, my dear. We'll take tea in my parlour while Lord Dunstan does what he needs to do.'

'Thank you, Lady Sarah, but I really need to get back to my animals.'

*

At Helston Railway Station, after the initial startled acknowledgement, Kitty and Freddy had simultaneously stepped towards each other, arms automatically lifting to embrace. Suddenly, both halted awkwardly, remembering the circumstances of their parting all those years ago. For a good few seconds, time stood still.

Freddy spoke first. 'Kitty,' he breathed. 'My goodness. I cannot believe it's you!'

Kitty's eyes searched his face for recriminations. 'Freddy, I don't know what to say to you. I am so sorry, I...'

'No.' He shook his head and placed his finger near her lips. 'You have nothing to be sorry about.'

'But, but I left you over forty years ago. without a by-your-leave.'

He saw the tragic look in her eyes and smiled gently. 'Hush now. I know why you had to leave me.'

Kitty paled. 'You do! How?'

'Sissy told me.'

Closing her eyes to the shame, Kitty said softly. 'I'm so sorry, Freddy. I pleaded with Sissy not to tell you. I cannot believe she broke my confidence, and now, here you are - standing in front of me!'

'But Kitty...'

She shook her head. 'Oh, Lord.' Her glove-covered hands covered her stricken face. 'I never expected to see you again. I hoped only to see Sissy on this visit, and now... oh goodness, me.'

'Kitty!'

'I'm so ashamed of what you must think of me,' she cried, turning away from him.

'Kitty, listen,' he said, gently pulling her hands from her face. 'Do not distress yourself. The shame belongs to only one person, and that person is dead and buried.'

Kitty, unable to meet his gaze, asked, 'But why did Sissy tell you? I hoped and prayed that you would never find out. Oh, goodness. All these years, you must have despised me.'

'No, Kitty. I could never have despised you, and I only found out what happened about a month ago. Your grandson came to Bochym to thank Sissy for helping you.'

Kitty's eyes widened. 'My...my grandson!' She gasped and almost staggered backward.

Alarmed at her response, Freddy caught her arm and quickly led her to the bench to recover.

Kitty looked up at Freddy in astonishment. 'Josh! Are you telling me that you've seen Josh in the last month?'

'Yes. He was taking tea in Sissy's cottage when I happened upon him.'

'But, but....' She shook her head.

'But what, Kitty?'

'You can't have seen Josh! He was reported to have gone overboard from his naval ship and drowned!'

Freddy sat back suddenly. 'Well, I can tell you, he was very much alive the last I saw of him, which was only last Sunday, at the Bochym garden party.'

Bemused, she asked, 'Are you sure it was my grandson?'

'Positive. Sissy confirmed it, and then when I set eyes on Josh, well, it was like looking at His Lordship, and I put two and two together - he was obviously a Dunstan. It was then that I forced Sissy to tell me what had happened to you.'

'So, does Josh know about the Earl too?'

'Yes.'

'Oh, goodness! Hugh and I kept it a secret all these years. My son, Jacob, Josh's father, never even knew. How did Josh take the news?'

'Much the same as I. He was shocked and deeply saddened for you.'

Kitty lowered her eyes as tears streamed down her face again – this time they were happy tears. 'Oh, but thank goodness Josh is alive! I thought I had lost him forever.' She quickly dabbed her face. 'Did he look well?'

'He did.'

'Did he... did he mention anything about being in the Navy?'

'No. But thinking about it, he was rather reticent about giving much away about himself. When I asked about you, he told me that you had married a good man and had been happy with him. I had the impression that Josh spoke of his grandfather in the past tense, but he would not say more when I pressed him for information. I'm afraid we had high words because he refused to give me your address, even though he knew I was desperate to see you again. He said it would cause a great deal of upset, especially for his grandfather, if I, an old flame, contacted you. But, Kitty, I only wanted to put the record straight with you - that I did not think badly of you - even though I said those things about Hilda. I could bite my tongue off for those comments now.'

Kitty put her hand on his sleeve to indicate that she understood his sentiment. 'I am sorry you have argued with Josh, Freddy, but Josh was right - Hugh would not have taken kindly to your appearance.'

'You too seem to be speaking about your husband in the past tense. Are you widowed then?' Freddy asked gently.

'I am. Hugh died in March.'

'I am sorry for your loss,' he said, more with relief than sincerity.

'And you, Freddy, do you have a wife and family?' She asked with a slight tremble in her voice.

'No, Kitty. I never married.'

'Oh, Freddy. That makes me feel very sad for you.'

He shrugged. 'You are the only woman I ever loved, Kitty, and I suppose I always hoped you would come back to me one day.'

Kitty lifted her tearful eyes to meet his – those eyes she loved so much and had dreamed about for so long. 'And now you still wanted to find me – even knowing my shame? Another tear trickled down her cheek.

'Oh, Kitty. Don't cry.' Freddy took her hand in his. 'I have told you the shame was never yours – the shame is on that evil man who used and abused you. I hope he is rotting in Hell.'

Kitty answered tremulously, 'I wish for the same every day.'

Freddy squeezed her hand. 'And yes, despite what Josh said, I still wanted to come and find you. I was going to seek you out and try to speak to you alone, so that I would not upset your husband. I was just about to get on a train to Portsmouth to come and look for you!'

'Really?' She sniffed and dabbed her eyes.

'Yes, and here you are, as if by magic.' He smiled gently.

'And as I said, I was just coming to see Sissy. We've exchanged a couple of letters recently, but I never received an answer from my last one, so I thought I would come and see her in person.'

Freddy's shoulders drooped dejectedly. 'So, I was right - Sissy has been writing to you?'

'Only over the last month. It was I who contacted Sissy first, after Hugh died. My husband was a good man in all other things, having taken me in even though I was a fallen woman, but he had always forbidden me to write to the manor. He knew about you and that you were my first sweetheart. He was worried you would come and claim me back.'

'I see,' he sighed. 'I just can't understand why Sissy didn't tell me she was writing to you — she knew how much I wanted to find you.'

'Tell me, Freddy, if you didn't know about the letters we had exchanged, how did you know where to come looking for me?'

'Ah, well.' His cheeks pinked guiltily. 'I was delivering a box of vegetables to Sissy's cottage and found a torn-up letter she was going to send you. I got your address from there.'

'A torn-up letter!' Kitty frowned. 'I wonder why Sissy decided not to send it. Oh, dear, perhaps she has decided to let sleeping dogs lie and not renew our acquaintance. I hope she won't be angry at my dropping in on her like this.'

'I'm sure she will be delighted to see you again, as am I.' This time, it was Freddy's eyes that were watering. 'All these years, Kitty and I never knew what had happened to you. I thought the worst, you know! When we learned that you had been dismissed and thrown out into the night for a serious misdemeanour, I could not comprehend what you might have done. When you left me no word, I wondered if you had been caught in a compromising position with another man and had run away with him. I am so ashamed to say that now.'

Kitty blanched, wounded by this theory.

'I'm sorry, Kitty.' He squeezed her hand and grimaced. 'Sissy refuted my theory quite vehemently and berated me for even thinking that was possible.' He lowered his eyes. 'Then, for some time after, especially as no word came from you, I feared that you might have died, been murdered, or kidnapped even, the night you were sent away.'

'Oh, Freddy, my sweet, sweet man. It broke my heart to leave you without a word. But rest assured, I have never forgotten you. Never!'

They gazed at each other's ageing faces, and Freddy brought her hand to his lips and kissed it tenderly. 'You're still my beautiful Kitty.'

'And you're still my handsome Freddy.'

This time, nothing could stop them from coming together as they shared their first kiss in over forty years.

'Thank you for forgiving me, Freddy.'

'There is nothing to forgive, my love. Now, should we head back to Bochym to see Sissy? Though I must tell you, Sissy and I have not been the best of friends since I learned the secrets she had been keeping from me!'

'I beseech you, Freddy. Please do not blame Sissy. I put her in a terrible situation, and I am truly sorry for all the hurt it has caused.'

'Ah, well, she has certainly been a good friend to you. I have never known a woman keep such secrets for so long.'

As they got up from the railway bench to go and catch the Mullion wagon, Kitty turned to Freddy. 'Did you say that Josh is living nearby?'

'Yes, just down the road from the manor, on a farm. When you have had your reunion with Sissy, I'll take you to him.'

'Thank you, Freddy. I long to see Josh again; I still cannot believe he is alive and well.'

'He got married last week by all accounts - to Maia, who owns the farm.

'Oh!' A tiny, pained noise escaped her throat, and she began to cry again at the thought of missing Josh's wedding.

'I'm sorry, Kitty. I should have let him tell you the news himself.'

Placing her hand on his arm, she smiled. 'As long as he has found happiness - that is all that matters.'

'Are you planning on staying for a while? I should think Maia and Josh will happily put you up at Wild Cliff Farm if you do.' He looked deep into her eyes. 'Will you... stay a while?'

Reaching up to gently touch his face, she kissed him. 'Yes, Freddy. I think I will.'

38

Maia's distress over Josh had shaken Sissy that morning, but when Maia returned to the kitchen after her meeting with His Lordship, she seemed calmer, though her eyes were brimming with tears. Having told Sissy that His Lordship had promised to help, she returned home to Wild Cliff Farm to await news.

It was just before the staff's midday meal when a couple walking across the kitchen courtyard diverted Sissy's attention from serving dinner.

'It looks like Mr Hubbard hasn't gone away after all!' Vicky said.

Sissy looked over her glasses and frowned. 'No. It seems not.' She wiped her hands on her tea cloth, looked again, and gasped.

'Mrs Blair. Are you quite well?' Vicky asked in concern.

Sissy did not answer but left the kitchen and ran with open arms towards the woman walking with Mr Hubbard.

'Oh, lordy me. If it isn't my little Kitty!' Sissy gathered Kitty in her arms, squashing her against her ample bosom. After embracing for several seconds, Sissy held Kitty at arm's length, looked her over in disbelief, and laughed through her happy tears. 'But how are you here? Oh, is it because of Josh?'

'Well, now, not exactly. I have only just found out about Josh from Freddy. It's just that I couldn't wait another moment for a letter from you, so I thought I would come and meet you. I hope you don't mind?'

'I don't mind at all, but...' She looked between Kitty and Freddy and asked, 'How have you two got together?'

'Not with any help from you,' Freddy muttered.

Kitty nudged Freddy on the arm to quieten him. 'We met quite by chance on the railway platform at Helston. I was coming to see you, and Freddy was on his way to find me!' Kitty beamed, and then a frown formed, and she tipped her head. 'Freddy told me that my grandson is here and alive! If you remember what I said in my letter, we all believed him dead. Why did you not reply straight away and tell me otherwise, Sissy?'

Noting a slight accusation in her tone, Sissy reached out for Kitty's hand. 'Oh, Kitty, forgive me. It was just another secret that I had to keep. Josh was here hiding from the authorities, you see.'

'Was he?' Freddy asked in astonishment.

'Yes. It's a long story. I did write to you, Kitty, but didn't have time to send it, and then when I told Josh you had been in touch, Josh was forced to explain his situation to me, so I'm afraid I had to discard the letter I'd written to you. As I say, I'll tell you all about it soon, but I am afraid our secrecy has all been in vain. Someone found out about Josh being here, alerted the authorities, and he was arrested this morning and taken to trial in Portsmouth.'

'Arrested! Why?' Kitty paled.

'For desertion from the Navy. They believe he jumped ship, but he did no such thing; he told me the whole story.'

They all turned when Joe Treen came to the back door and called Sissy.

'Mrs Blair. The staff are waiting for their midday meal!'

'Oh, lordy me! I clean forgot I was in the middle of dishing up. Mr Treen, is it all right if my friend Kitty comes in? She used to work with me forty years ago.'

'Of course, of course, but come, make haste.' He gestured them indoors.

'Come in and take a seat,' Sissy said as she rushed back to her work. 'I'll just sort the meals out, and perhaps you'll both take a bite to eat with me in the kitchen. That's all right, isn't it, Mr Treen?'

'It's your kitchen, Mrs Blair. Who am I to say otherwise?'

Vicky, the kitchen assistant, stood open-mouthed as she watched Mr Hubbard walk in, holding hands with the lady visitor. 'Is Mr Hubbard in love with that lady, Mrs Blair?' she whispered.

'Never you mind, Vicky. Stop your gawping and take this dish of potatoes through,' Sissy said, smiling at seeing Kitty and Freddy together at last.

*

Kitty sat down in the kitchen she had worked in all those years ago and watched Vicky help Sissy dish out and serve the staff meal in the staff dining room, just as she had once done.

'Gosh! I never thought I would return here, Freddy.'

'It must hold some horrible memories for you,' he answered, cupping his hand over Kitty's.

Kitty shook her head. 'Not the kitchen. I was really happy here, working with Sissy, and looking forward to you and old Mr Bolitho coming in with the box of vegetables for the day.'

'Hey, enough of the *old*. I'm older than Mr Bolitho was then.'

Kitty looked up into the face of the man she had fallen in love with all those years ago. 'You don't look it,' she said, touching his weathered face.

He squeezed her hand. 'I think maybe you need spectacles.'

'I take it Mr Bolitho passed away?'

'Actually, no. He was 96 in July and now lives in Falmouth with his youngest son. We correspond regularly, but, I admit, I haven't been in touch with him since I found out he took part in spiriting you away from me,' he said guiltily.

'Oh, bless that man. He and Sissy were so kind to me that dreadful night. Please, Freddy, do not fall out with them or blame them for keeping my secret.'

Freddy sighed heavily. 'I just wish you had trusted me to help you.'

Kitty lowered her lashes. 'I didn't know how you would feel about me - whether you would despise me – because of what had happened.'

Freddy's eyes watered. 'Sissy told me the reasons, and as I said, I rue that day in the greenhouse when I denounced Hilda, for that alone led to you fleeing from me.'

'It wasn't just that, Freddy. I didn't want you to take revenge for what happened, and you would have! You would have hung for it, and I did not want that on my conscience.'

He squeezed her hand again.

'Freddy,' Kitty said in earnest. 'I know I said I would stay a while, but I think I should return home. If they have taken Josh to trial, it will be in Portsmouth.'

'I understand.' He glanced up at the clock. 'But I'm afraid there won't be another train today.'

Kitty cupped her hands to her face. 'Oh, my poor Josh. He had a terrible time growing up with his father. Jacob was cruel beyond belief, and now this! Josh is a good lad; he would not do anything that would get him into trouble. I'm sure of it!'

Freddy pulled her hands from her face and held them tightly, but his kindness could not stem Kitty's tears.

When Sissy returned from serving the staff dinner, she noted Kitty's distress and glanced at Freddy. 'Whatever's the matter?'

'She is worried about Josh.'

'Ah, well, Mr Treen tells me that His lordship has got his lawyer onto the case. Maia came and pleaded his plight to him this morning.' She lowered her voice. 'She told him that Josh was a blood relative.'

'Really!' Kitty was shocked. 'And he was still willing to help?'

Sissy nodded. 'Oh yes. Lord Dunstan is a very different man from the old Earl – very different indeed!'

Kitty dabbed her eyes. 'Maia sounds lovely to care about our Josh. Freddy tells me they're married.'

'Yes, and very happy they were, albeit for the short time they were together.'

'Oh, well, thank goodness she spoke up for our boy.'

'Where are you staying, Kitty?' Sissy asked.

'Well, Freddy was going to take me to where Josh lives now – a farm, I believe!' She glanced at Freddy for confirmation. 'But I'm not sure now. Maia sounds like a very caring woman, and I would love to meet her, but I would not want to impose on her distress.'

'I think Maia would welcome the company, especially as you are Josh's grandma,' Sissy said, placing a hand gently on her friend's shoulder. 'She was dreadfully upset this morning. Now, forgive me. I will have to make a start on the family luncheon, and then before you go to Maia's, we can sit down and eat, and I'll tell you all that has happened.'

'Are you going to tell *me* as well?' Freddy asked wryly.

'This time I can, Freddy.' Sissy put her hand on his sleeve.

*

After the family luncheon, William followed his father into his study after Peter announced he was going to Portsmouth the next day with his lawyer, Mr Sheldon.

'You didn't say why you were going to Portsmouth, Papa. Is it something I should know about?'

Peter sighed heavily. 'Sit down, William. I need to speak to you.'

William's mouth dropped as Peter explained all that had happened.

'Papa. You cannot be serious about this!' William was beside himself as he stood and paced the length of Peter's study.

'The man needs help, William.'

'Not at the cost of our good family name!'

'William. Josh has Dunstan's blood in his veins. I feel that I must help him if I can.'

'Is that why he came to the area? To claim kin!'

'No. I asked the same question, but Maia told me he found out about his bloodline quite by accident when he arrived here. He did not want us to know that he knew.'

William folded his arms and grunted sarcastically. 'How many more of my grandfather's bastard offspring will crawl out of the woodwork?'

'Thank you, William. I do not think we need that sort of language here.'

William sighed heavily. 'And if you get him off, what then? Are you going to invite him into our family fold? Are we to share a dinner table with him? I mean, what would he be to me – half cousin?'

'I am sure he will not want that, but nevertheless, I feel I must help him. This is a special case, and I will help him, whether you agree with me or not. I had hoped you would have had more compassion. I pride myself that I am nothing like my father; I trust you're nothing like him either?'

William's lips tightened. 'Do not tar me with the same brush as grandfather.'

'Then do not judge Josh. He sounds like a decent man.'

'Does Mama know?'

'Yes, of course. But it stops there. The fewer people know about his relationship to us, the better. I do not want it mentioned near the staff. I shall not claim kinship with him unless he is convicted; my name may lessen his sentence, but I assure you, the revelation will only be between myself and the judge. It's the least I can do for him after the way my father treated his grandmother.

*

After the mid-day dinner, Sissy had managed to take a little time off to catch up with Kitty that afternoon, so Freddy left them to it and went back to work for a couple of hours. As he potted up a few cuttings, he felt a bubbling of boyish excitement - he felt eighteen again! Being with Kitty had peeled away the forty-year gulf between them, and as with all true love and friendship, it now felt as though they had never been apart. They had shared a couple of chaste kisses and held hands a few times, so he was hopeful that their relationship would develop again, as it had done once before. With the worrying news about Josh sparking Kitty's early return to Portsmouth in the morning, he knew he only had a finite time to tell her how he felt. He would speak to her when he took her to Maia and tell her how ardently he still loved her.

*

On returning to Wild Cliff Farm after her meeting with Lord Dunstan, Maia stripped off her ruined dress and bathed her grazed knees and elbows. She stood in her bedroom and looked down at her bed, where she had spent many nights of passion with Josh these last few weeks. At the window, she leaned against the glass and looked out to sea – the same sea that had washed her beloved onto these shores and brought him to her.

'Josh, my love,' she breathed. 'Now it's me who is all at sea.' She glanced up the road, remembering Josh's stricken face as they drove him away. He was somewhere out there now, far away from her loving arms. 'Stay strong, my love. Stay strong until I can get you back where you belong.'

Turning away from the window, she found that her mind would not stop reeling, so she did the only thing she could do - busy herself with her farm work. It wasn't long before David came across the fields to see what had been done. He also had with him three letters bearing character references from Tobias, Guy, and himself to pass on to whoever was going to help Josh with his case. David also kindly agreed to look after the farm if and when Maia had to go to Portsmouth. 'He kept all that close to his chest, didn't he?' David said, sounding slightly put out, that Josh had not confided in him.

'The less people knew, the more chance Josh had of living a free life. Alas, it was all in vain. We were stupid enough to discuss his dilemma within earshot of Jago.'

'I could bloody strangle that man!' David fumed. 'There is talk that someone wrecked his car showroom overnight. They destroyed every single car he owned and, by all accounts, ruined his business. Quite frankly, he would do well to leave the area. People are angry. They can't fight the mining company, but they sure as hell can make profiteers like Jago pay.' David reached over and grasped Maia's hand. 'He will soon be gone.'

She nodded sadly. 'And so too has Josh.'

David ran his finger over her gold wedding band. 'If Josh is not who he said he was, how did you marry?'

Maia lifted her eyes to meet his. 'We're only handfasted.'

'Ah, I see! Hopefully, now that everything is out in the open and if Josh gets his conviction quashed, he can make an honest woman of you.'

'Oh, David. I hope you're right,' she said through tear-filled eyes.

*

After dealing with all the livestock needs, Maia, exhausted with fatigue and emotion, slumped down to cry at her kitchen table. Every time she thought of them taking Josh away and the look of fear in his eyes, she wept more. Prudence jumped up on the table, where she wasn't really allowed, and gently put her soft paw on Maia's arm to comfort her. As she stroked her fur, her purr settled Maia's heart.

When she heard a car pull up, Maia thought it to be His Lordship. He had said he would drop by when everything was in hand. Wiping her tears with the sleeve of her dress - her handkerchief already damp with tears—she flung the door open in welcome, only to find Jago on the doorstep. A prickle of fear shot down her spine as she tried to shut it again, but Jago put his boot in the door, pushed it open, and burst into the kitchen to loom over her.

Maia felt a stipple of gooseflesh cover her skin, realising how alone she was here. Anxiety brought a lump to her throat when Prudence arched her back, hissing at the unwelcome visitor.

Jago's dark eyes locked on the animal, and he bared his teeth, grabbed the cat by the neck, and flung her across the room and against the wall.

'Oh, no, Prudence!' Maia screamed and scrambled to the corner of the room to gather the limp and lifeless bundle of fur into her arms. Maia glared wild-eyed at Jago. 'You heartless bastard. Get out of my house.' She felt a chill run through her at Jago's cold laugh as he advanced towards where she was kneeling, cradling the injured cat.

'Your house,' he sneered, snorting indignantly. 'It should have been *my* house! But that is by the by now. I'm going away, you see,' he smirked, 'and I'm here to give you a parting gift. I don't want the farm anymore, you see - I have no use for it now, but I'm definitely going to claim something I've wanted for a very long time.'

She watched in horror as he began to undo the buttons on his trousers, clearly enjoying the look of apprehension on her face by the gleeful glint in his eyes. 'Don't you dare, *don't you dare*,' she said, her voice trembling.

'Oh, I dare,' he sneered, 'and you and that criminal, so-called husband of yours, can do absolutely *nothing* about it.'

Maia felt her bile rise and searched frantically around for something to arm herself with. Her chopping knife was on the table, and the poker was by the fire – both implements out of reach—but it was too late anyway. Jago was standing over her, clothes undone, intent on taking her. Prudence twitched and mewed in pain in her arms, and she clutched her closer to protect them both.

'I'll bloody finish that animal,' Jago growled.

Maia felt her mouth dry, seeing his eyes flash with malevolence. 'No,' she screamed as he drew his foot back and aimed an almighty kick at Prudence. Horrified, Maia turned her body away to save her cat and took the full force of his boot on the side of her face.

Maia howled in pain, Prudence fell from her arms, and Jago kicked the cat across the room. The blow to her face made Maia's eyes water and smart, and her heart contracted as she watched the life drain from her beloved pet. A low, painful moan escaped from her throat; a sharp metallic taste filled her mouth, and she spat blood onto the stone floor. Her hand cradled her jaw. Lightheaded and nauseous, she swayed alarmingly, and then suddenly her senses heightened as Jago grabbed her by the hair and yanked her head back.

'I'm going to show you what it feels like to have a real man between your legs. You won't be seeing Harding for a very long time. So, I want to leave you with a lasting memory that I, not he, was the last person to service you.' He tightened his grip on her hair, tearing it at the roots.

Fury fuelled some inner strength within her, and she balled her hand into a fist and thumped him hard in the mouth, rattling his teeth, bursting his lip, and knocking the smirk right off his face. Startled momentarily, Jago released his grip on her hair, and she took another swipe at him, this time clawing his face and digging her nails deep enough to draw blood.

He grabbed her, slammed her to the ground, and pinned her down with his hands. 'You'll bloody pay for that,' he snarled.

'If you touch me, I'll have you arrested for rape,' she cried, struggling to free herself from his grasp.

His lips curled into a cruel smirk. 'I told you – I'm going away, and no one will find me. Besides, no one gets arrested for servicing the local whore, and that's all I'm doing. I'm here to have fun with a loose woman, because that's what you are, Maia. Only loose women give themselves to men out of wedlock, and I know that Harding was not who he said he was. Therefore, you were not legally married, which, in my books, makes you a loose woman.'

Maia felt the colour rise in her cheeks.

'I'm rather partial to a whore now and then.' His eyes glinted with lust as he rubbed his groin. She struggled frantically to back away, but he pinned her tight to the ground. 'You weren't too proud to open your legs for the farmhand, were you? Or my brother before you were married, for that matter. Oh, yes, I know you have always had loose morals. I know you were pregnant when you married our Henry.'

'And did he tell you he forced himself on me to get me in the family way?' she yelled.

'He told me that you loved every minute of it – screamed for more, he said. You tricked him into marriage, and don't try to deny it – Henry told me all about it. But then you did something to rid yourself of that babe, didn't you? So, I might just put a Penhallow babe back in there, just to remind you of us.' He grinned salaciously. 'You know our Henry used to tell me what he did to you. He said you liked him to be rough with you before you complied.' He licked his lips. 'The thought of it whets my appetite for you.' He grabbed the front of her clothes and violently ripped them open, exposing her breasts to his leer.

She shrieked and tried again to scramble away, but he dragged her back and threw himself heavily atop her. Grabbing her by her painful jaw, he banged her head on the stone ground.

'You should have been mine, but you thought you were too good for me. So now I'm going to make sure you never forget me or what it feels like to have me inside you – and I guarantee it won't be pleasant.'

His breath was sour as he panted heavily over her, his brow beaded with sweat, and his eyes red with intent. Squirming beneath him, she clawed at his face again and screamed, 'Get off me.'

'Scream and squirm as much as you like – Henry said you used to, so the more you do so, the more I will enjoy this!' He held her down with one arm across her chest while he pushed his trousers down his legs.

As his hand crawled up her skirt to rip off her underclothes, Maia struggled for all she was worth, but when she felt his flesh on hers, her screams filled the room.

39

Freddy had requested the pony trap from Mr Treen to take Kitty to Wild Cliff Farm, but when he came to collect her, Vicky, the kitchen assistant, had asked if they could give her a lift to the top of Poldhu Hill. Being the gentleman he was, how could he refuse? Freddy resigned himself to holding back his declaration of love until the morning. He would tell Kitty how he felt when he took her back to the station.

Vicky was a lively young girl, full of life and vigour. She chatted constantly throughout the journey to the top of Poldhu Hill, so they had practically got her whole life story by the time they set her down to walk the rest of the way to the cove! Kitty and Freddy smiled and shook their heads as she skipped away.

'Oh, to be young again!' Kitty sighed.

'I agree. I would give anything to turn the years back.' Freddy answered as he steered the pony into Maia's yard, noting the fancy car parked there. It was then that they heard the screams within.

Leaving Kitty to get herself down from the cart, Freddy burst into the kitchen to find Maia pinned to the floor, her clothes array, kicking and screaming under a man who was trying to force himself onto her.

'Hey, hey!' Freddy roared. 'What the hell is going on here?' He grabbed Jago by the scruff of his neck.

Jago turned and swiped Freddy away, sending him reeling backwards, only just missing Kitty, who had arrived at the door.

Horrified at the scene before her, and with memories of the night of her attack flooding to the forefront of her mind, Kitty picked up the heavy bread bowl from the table and crowned Jago's head with it. Stunned for a second, Jago turned, baring his teeth at Kitty as she swung a chair at him, knocking him sideways.

Maia took this chance to scramble away from her assailant, pulling her clothes straight to give herself some dignity. She watched with astonishment as this strange woman wielded the chair at Jago, while Freddy Hubbard walloped Jago with a broom until he staggered out of the kitchen into the yard and to his car.

Freddy followed him. 'The police will hear of this,' he shouted as Jago sped off.

When Freddy returned to the kitchen, Kitty was sitting on the floor with her arm around Maia, who, in turn, was cradling the lifeless body of Prudence.

'Are you all right, love?' Freddy kneeled before Maia.

Maia nodded, albeit trembling with fear and adrenaline. 'Yes, thank you, thank you to both of you.' Maia looked up at the woman who was comforting her. 'I'm sorry. Do I know you?'

Kitty smiled warmly. 'No, but you know my grandson, Josh.'

'Oh, you must be Kitty, but how?' Maia looked to Freddy.

'It's a long story. Here, let me help you up,' Freddy said.

As he helped Maia to one of the chairs, she still cradled Prudence.

'Is your cat dead?' Freddy asked gently, but just as he said it, Prudence twitched.

'I'm not sure; she keeps twitching. Jago kicked her very hard.'

'Let me see?' Freddy lay Prudence down on the table, and she twitched again. 'She looks like she is quite badly hurt – her gums and tongue are pale with shock.'

'My poor Prudence.' Maia whimpered.

'Maia. I was going to ask if Kitty could stay with you until tomorrow. She's heading back to Portsmouth, having heard what has happened to Josh. But perhaps you might not want to stay here yourself now - not after this incident.'

Clutching her ripped dress to her breasts with one hand, Maia rested her other hand on Kitty's arm. 'Of course, Kitty can stay. As for leaving, well, I can't leave my livestock, and this is my home. I will not be scared of being here. I'll keep the doors locked in the future. But I must go and report Jago to the police. He cannot go unpunished for this, and I don't want him coming back here – locked doors or not!'

'I'll go and report the incident to the police for you,' Freddy offered. 'I'll get the constable to come and see you, and if you like, I can take your cat to Ryan Penrose while I'm in Mullion. I understand he has a way with animals; he may be able to do something for her.'

'Thank you, Mr Hubbard. That's so kind of you.' Suddenly, the shock of what had just happened, coupled with Josh's arrest, overwhelmed Maia, and she broke down in tears.

'Maia,' Freddy said gently. 'Did Jago...did he? ...... Do you need a doctor, or were we in time?'

Maia glanced tearfully at him. 'Thankfully, you were in time, and though my jaw feels terribly painful where he kicked me, I don't think it merits a visit from the doctor. It's the loss of Josh that distresses me most.' Maia's face crumpled again, and she let Kitty wrap her arms around her in a grandmotherly hug.

'Hush now, sweetheart. We have just come from Bochym Manor, and Sissy has told me that help is in hand, all thanks to you. Let's hope His Lordship can help our boy,' Kitty said softly.

'Right then!' Freddy said. 'I'll be off to the police station and the Penrose's house.' He gathered Prudence gently into his arms and kissed Kitty goodbye. 'I'll come back for you in the morning so you can catch your train,' he said.

When Freddy left, Maia smiled through her tears. 'How lovely that you have found each other again.'

'Yes. It's lovely to see Freddy again, and after all that has happened and all the secrets, we can still be friends. My journey is marred only by Josh's arrest, so I also feel your pain.' Kitty placed her hand on Maia's. 'Now, I understand you and Josh have married?'

Maia looked sheepish. 'In a fashion, yes.' Maia fiddled with her wedding band. 'Nothing is legal yet. We couldn't risk anyone knowing who he really was. Oh, Kitty. May I call you Kitty?'

'Of course.'

'I am terribly fearful of what will happen to Josh. I love him so much. He has been through such a dreadful time.'

Kitty nodded. 'Sissy has told me of Josh's terrible story, but surely the truth will prevail.'

'Oh, goodness, but I hope so!'

'It's heartening to know Josh has someone lovely like you in his life.'

'Oh, Kitty. I do not want to be without him. If he is convicted, he said he would get a prison sentence and then would have to serve another five years in the Navy – it seems that his father forged his signature on a new five-year contract.'

Kitty's mouth tightened. 'I cannot believe I gave birth to Jacob, Josh's father. Jacob is a monster, just like his father, the old Earl!'

Maia put her hand on Kitty's sympathetically. 'It's a real blessing that fortunately, Lord Peter Dunstan and his son William bear none of the old Earl's horrible traits. They are the nicest men you could meet.'

'Hopefully, the cruel streak ended with my son then. I will never forgive Jacob for this.' Kitty fumed. 'My husband and I had no idea Jacob had forced Josh into the Navy. Jacob told us that Josh had run away to sea. It almost broke our hearts. It was only when Josh came home on leave a couple of years ago that we found out that Jacob had practically pressganged him into the Navy and was claiming his wages.'

'Josh spoke very fondly of you and your husband – he loved you both very much. But I understand from Sissy that your husband has passed away.'

'He did - in March.'

'Is that why you're here? To connect again with Mr Hubbard?'

'No.' She laughed lightly. 'Seeing Freddy was a huge surprise. I came to see Sissy because I had waited weeks for her return letter.'

Maia bit down on her lip. 'It was our fault for the delay, I'm afraid. When we realised that Mrs Blair had been in contact with you and was about to tell you about Josh being here, we asked her not to. Not that Josh didn't want you to know he was safe and well, he did - it's just that he was fearful that his father would find out that he was still alive and would contact the Admiralty.'

'Yes. Sissy explained everything. Now, I apologise for breaking your bowl and one of your chairs,' Kitty said, picking up the pieces.

'No apology is necessary. You were magnificent.'

Kitty took a deep breath. 'I just saw red when I came in and realised what was happening to you – it brought dreadful memories back, you see. Now let me put the kettle on, and I will make you a nice cup of tea, and we can bathe your beautiful face.'

*

Jago had roared off in his car, angry at being thwarted by two *old* people! He had a splitting headache from where that stupid woman had crowned him, first with a bowl and then hitting him across his ear with the chair. He knew now that he must make himself scarce because that bloody man who had intervened had shouted that he would tell the police. No matter. He would be long gone from here before they came sniffing around. He just needed to collect a few personal belongings, and then he would be off to Southampton and onto America. The land of milk and honey was calling him.

As he drove, he shifted uncomfortably with the swelling in his trousers - the thought of Maia's bare breasts and her thighs wriggling and squirming beneath was still fuelling his desire. Damn that pair who had thwarted him from claiming his long-awaited prize! As he drove down towards Poldhu Cove, he spotted the Blackthorn girl making her way to the privy at the back of the tearoom.

He narrowed his eyes. Damn that bitch too; she had been the catalyst for his downfall. He was sick to the back teeth of these women getting the better of him! He drove to his house, parked the car, and set off walking back down the hill.

*

When Fee nipped out to the privy located behind the tearoom, she waved at her elder sister, Agnes, who was hanging the washing out on the line outside her beach cottage.

Fee smiled. She never imagined her sister would become domesticated. Agnes had always been 'just one of the boys' and had joined their father's thatching business as soon as she left school. Marriage to Jake Treen at Easter that year had brought out her nesting instincts, and though she still climbed the ladder every day, with the others, to do a full day of thatching, she had also softened with the love of her husband and a home of her own to look after.

Fee had noted Jago's car as it sped by, and fearful of being seen by him, she quickly ducked out of the way. At the privy door, she peered in, checking first for spiders lurking near the pot. When she was satisfied that it was clear, she entered and pushed the lock across the door behind her.

When she came back out of the privy, adjusting her skirt, an arm grabbed her around the waist, and a hand covered her mouth.

Feeling every fibre of her body prickle in alarm, she bit down hard on the hand covering her mouth. She heard Jago curse as she made him loosen his grip, and Fee began to scream at the top of her voice. Grabbing his handkerchief, Jago stuffed it into her mouth to muffle her screams, and he clamped his hand firmly back in place.

*

Agnes had just that minute waved at Jimmy Trevorrow, who had come down to the cove for a swim after work, when she heard Fee scream. She grinned at first, thinking Fee had encountered a spider, knowing that she hated them, but then felt a visceral feeling that the scream was more sinister and urgent than that. Dropping her washing back into her basket, Agnes ran to the privy, only to find the door swinging open. Stepping up onto the road, to her horror, she saw Jago dragging Fee, kicking and struggling into his house.

Like a bolt from a gun, she raced up the hill, suddenly finding Jimmy Trevorrow at her side.

'I heard the scream. What is it? What has happened?' He asked breathlessly.

'Jago has grabbed Fee,' Agnes cried. 'I think he's going to hurt her.'

Jimmy grabbed Agnes by the arm to stop her. 'Agnes. I'll go to Fee. You go back and get your pa and Jake to come and help.'

*

Jago threw Fee into the house, causing her to fall heavily against the table. He was highly sexually fired up again as he locked the door behind him - this time, no one would thwart him.

'Right, you little bitch. You've ruined me with your thieving little ways. I always believe in an eye for an eye, so get ready - I am about to ruin *you!*'

Fee scrambled to her feet in a panic. 'Don't you dare touch me! My pa will kill you if you so much as lay a finger on me,' she warned.

Ignoring her, Jago grabbed her by the arm and dragged her screaming up the stairs - her screams masking the thump, thump, thump of Jimmy's shoulders against the locked front door.

Upstairs, Jago threw her onto his bed and began to undo his trousers.

'Oh, no, you don't!' she screamed, scrambling from the bed, but he caught her by the foot, dragged her back on the bed, and crawled on top of her. Suddenly, the house creaked and shuddered violently, dust fell from the ceiling, and the lamp fell off the bedside table. Glass shattered somewhere in the house, and Fee's alarm at Jago's intent suddenly became coupled with the fear that this house was about to go over the cliff with her in it!

'Oh, my God!' She screamed again. 'Get away from me, you maniac - this house is going over the edge?'

'Shut up.' He smacked her resoundingly across her face, drawing blood from her lip.

With all the strength she could muster, she kicked him hard on the shin and jumped from the bed just as the bedroom wall began to crumble before her eyes. She screamed in terror as the wardrobe came crashing down on top of her, knocking her unconscious.

Jago laughed heartily. He grabbed her arms to drag her from where she was trapped, adamant he would have his way with her – conscious or not - until the realisation hit him that the house *was* going to go over the edge. Jago glanced again at Fee, there for the taking, then at the crumbling walls. He seethed, knowing he had been thwarted again, quickly fastened his trousers, and ran downstairs to collect what he needed for his journey - only to be confronted with Jimmy Trevorrow, who had smashed a window to gain entry.

Jimmy grabbed him by the neck. 'You bastard, where's Fee? What have you done with her?'

'Get out of my way.' Jago aimed his knee at Jimmy's stomach, sending him reeling backward down the stairs. Winded, Jimmy curled into a ball, clutching his stomach.

Jago stepped over Jimmy at the foot of the stairs and shot a look at his living room floor. It was tilting at an alarming angle, causing his furniture to shift into a pile against the back wall. Deciding to sacrifice the collection of his belongings, Jago unlocked the front door and jumped in the car. As he started his car, Jago spotted Guy Blackthorn and Jake Treen racing up the hill towards him, so with angry intent, he drove at them, hitting Jake and narrowly missing Guy, who leapt to the side of the road to avoid him. Without stopping at the junction at the bottom of his road, he sped off up Poldhu Hill, shouting obscenities to the occupant of Wild Cliff Farm as he passed it - on his way to his new life.

*

Guy picked himself up as Jago's car sped away but found Jake could not stand on his leg.

'Oh, Christ! It's broken, I think. Go on ahead, Guy, go help Fee,' Jake urged as Agnes tended to him.

Inside the house, Jimmy had heard Jago's car drive off. He had recovered enough to pick himself up, and he began to scramble up the stairs. Suddenly, the house shifted again, and the staircase began to crumble, causing him to almost fall back down the stairs. He turned when Guy burst through the door, calling his daughter's name.

'Fee!' Oh, Jesus Christ!' Guy uttered as the house lurched again. 'Where is she? Please tell me Jago didn't have her in that car!' he said, following Jimmy up the crumbling stairs.

'No, she's in this house somewhere, but I don't know where yet.' Jimmy said as dust and debris pelted them from the crumbling ceiling.

'Fee. Where are you?' Guy yelled, overtaking Jimmy on the landing, but there was no sound. 'You search that room; I'll look in here.'

When Jimmy opened a bedroom door, he was confronted with a huge gaping hole and nothing else. He shouted, 'Christ, Fee, where are you?'

Guy found the second bedroom in complete disarray. The wardrobe had crashed to the floor, and broken lamps and ornaments were strewn everywhere. The house creaked and shifted, and then Guy heard the pitiful groan coming from under the wardrobe. 'Jimmy,' Guy yelled, 'Get here quick.'

The house was making the most alarming sounds, with timbers creaking and cracking. A huge split opened up down the back wall as Guy frantically tried to move the rubble so he could get to his daughter. When Jimmy appeared at the bedroom door, Guy shouted, 'I've found her. She's trapped under the wardrobe. Quick, help me lift it.'

It was a heavy, sturdy oak wardrobe, but with sheer, brute strength, they managed to push it back towards the wall, but it would not stay there.

'I'll hold it back, you see to her,' Jimmy said.

Fee moaned incoherently when Guy reached her. 'Oh, my darling girl.' He could see she was injured, and, for a moment, he dared not move her in case he would do her more harm.

'Guy. Get hold of her,' Jimmy yelled, his arms straining to hold back the wardrobe.

'She's hurt too bad.'

'Guy, for Christ's sake, she'll be dead if you don't move her now! The room next door has already gone over the cliff, and look!' The crack in the back wall opened up to a gaping hole, allowing the wind to whistle through the room. Suddenly, the whole wall fell away, revealing the cove.

'Guy, we need to get out,' Jimmy yelled as the bed and wardrobe began to slide towards where the wall had been. 'Guy, grab her, NOW!'

Guy grabbed Fee by the arms, and Jimmy let the wardrobe go. A moment later, the bedroom furniture slid away and disappeared over the cliff. Jimmy had to leap to solid ground as a great cavern opened up on the floor between himself and Guy, and although Guy was holding on to his daughter, Fee was hanging over the edge!

'I can't hold her,' Guy shouted, and Jimmy dived to the floor, grabbed her arms, and together they pulled her to more solid ground.

'We need to get out, Guy, or we're all going over,' Jimmy said, gathering Fee into his arms and pulling Guy towards the bedroom door and onto the landing. Timbers split above them, and the roof began to cave in, pelting them with years of rotting wood, dust, and thatch. With grit and grime crunching between their teeth, they both spat out the foul stone dust from their mouths.

'Quickly.' Jimmy beckoned Guy.

They made for the stairs, but as they descended, the house suddenly broke in half, and the stone stairs beneath their feet cracked open. They all crashed down to the ground floor, and a roof timber fell, hitting Guy square on the shoulder and head. When Jimmy heard Guy gasp in pain, he scrambled to his feet, picked Fee up from the rubble, and ran outside to place her on the grass.

Agnes, who had been tending to Jake, scrambled over to Fee and screamed, 'Where is Pa?' They all turned as the next part of the house slipped, causing a great cloud of dust.

'Pa!' Agnes shrieked as she left Fee to run to the door of the house, but Jimmy pulled her back.

'Stay back, for God's sake,' Jimmy ordered. 'I'm going back in for him.'

When Jimmy entered the building again, all that remained of the house was the floor at the bottom of the stairs and the front walls. Guy was on his feet, but staggering around, dazed, and disorientated on the edge of the precipice.

'Oh, Christ, Guy,' Jimmy shouted as he saw the ground beneath Guy fall away.

40

Having passed Prudence into the safe and healing hands of Ryan Penrose, Freddy was in the police station at Mullion, reporting the attack on Maia, when a small boy burst breathlessly into the office.

'P.C. Thomas, come quick! We've just driven through Poldhu on the wagon, and Jago Penhallow's house has fallen down the cliff. Ma reckons she saw people lying on the grass near where the house used to stand. She reckons you need to call an ambulance.'

'Right, lad, I'm on it.' P.C. Thomas grabbed his helmet. 'I must go, but rest assured, I'll log the report for Maia,' he said to Freddy as he dialled through to Helston for backup and an ambulance.

*

When the ground gave way beneath Guy, Jimmy grasped the front door jamb with one hand and reached out to grab Guy's shirt with the other. Guy was dangling over the edge, mud and shale pelting him, the shock rendering him speechless. The veins in Jimmy's arms bulged with the strain, and a slick of sweat coated his body as the hand holding Guy trembled with the tension. When Jimmy felt Guy's shirt begin to rip, he yelled, '*Agnes. Help!*'

Agnes was beside Jimmy in an instant. 'Oh, no, Pa!' she shrieked.

'Agnes. Help me pull him up. I'm not sure how long I can hold him.'

Shuffling forward on her belly, Agnes reached far enough down to grasp Guy's waistband. 'I have him,' she said.

'*Heave then*,' he ordered, and with almighty effort, they pulled Guy to safety.

They dragged Guy out onto the damp grass. Then clutching each other in horror, Jimmy and Agnes stood looking at the edge of the cliff – there was nothing left of

Penn als Cottage except the front door frame and one side of the front wall.

*

Ellie Blackthorne was carrying a tray of crockery into the back kitchen of the tearoom when she heard the almighty rumble and felt the ground shake beneath her. An earth tremor perhaps - they did get them very occasionally.

Expecting to see Fee washing up, she frowned when she found the kitchen empty and none of the washing up done! Where on earth was she? Fee had told her ages ago that she was going to the privy - she must have gone home for something!

'Ma! Ma!' Ellie nearly jumped out of her skin when Agnes burst through the back kitchen door.

'Goodness, Agnes!' Ellie placed her hand on her chest. 'You nearly gave me a heart attack. What is it?'

'It's Pa, Fee, and Jake – they're up the road – hurt.'

'Hurt!' Ellie felt suddenly faint.

'Yes, we need an ambulance quick!'

Meg Williams, who had been having tea with her husband, Tobias, outside, had seen the house fall down the cliff and had rushed through to the back of the kitchen to tell Ellie.

'Good grief, Ellie,' Meg said in alarm. 'The Penhallow's house has just tumbled down the cliff!' She stopped dead when she realised she had heard the word ambulance. 'Who needs an ambulance?'

'Pa, Fee, and Jake need one!' Agnes cried. 'Fee was inside Jago's house when it started to fall over the cliff!'

'What!' Ellie felt shockwaves searing through her. 'What on earth was she doing in his house?'

'Jago abducted her. Fortunately, I heard her scream, and so did Jimmy Trevorrow. He went in to rescue her while I went for Pa and Jake.'

'Oh, good God!' Ellie felt the ground sway under her, but Agnes caught her. 'Ma, you must come.'

'Ellie, you must go up to them.' Meg tapped her cheek to stop her from fainting. 'I'll get Tobias to go home and call for an ambulance while I see to the tearoom with Betsy for you.'

Coming to her senses, Ellie cried, 'Bless you, Meg.'

By the time Ellie and Agnes arrived at the scene, Jake had dragged himself to where the others were sitting.

'Jago left Fee in the house,' Agnes explained, 'and when he drove away, he hit Jake and broke his leg.'

'Good God!' Ellie cried and then almost fainted again when she reached Guy, Jimmy, and Fee; all three of them were covered from head to foot in blood and grey dust.

'Fee! My poor love.' Ellie gathered her daughter's limp, filthy body into her arms and rocked backward and forward. 'Is she alive?' Ellie searched the others for an answer.

'Yes, she had been knocked out and crushed under a wardrobe when we found her,' Jimmy answered, coughing the dust from his lungs.

'Oh, sweet Jesus! My poor girl.' Ellie wept.

Everyone looked up at Tobias running up the hill towards them with P.C. Thomas in tow.

'Is an ambulance coming?' Ellie cried out in panic to them.

'Yes. It's on its way. The police were already aware of the situation,' Tobias said breathlessly.

They all turned as Guy moaned in pain, clutching his shoulder. Agnes fell to her knees and cradled his head on his lap. 'It's all right, Pa. Help is coming.'

Guy's eyes opened, blinking the grey dust from his lashes. 'Fee? Did we get Fee out?'

'She's right here, Guy,' Ellie said. 'And she's alive.'

'And Jimmy saved your life, Pa,' Agnes said proudly. 'He pulled you to safety just as the house went over.'

'Not without your help, I didn't,' Jimmy replied, brushing away the accolade.

'He was an absolute hero, Ma!'

'I'll second that,' Guy agreed as great fat tears trickled down his dusty face.

*

Maia and Kitty had just finished tea and were washing up when they heard the almighty rumble in the distance.

'Thunder?' Kitty asked.

'I'm not sure.' Maia frowned, wiping her damp hands down her apron.

Out in the yard, all they could see was a great plume of dust filling the cove below.

'Is it a fire?' Kitty asked, standing alongside her.

'No, the house that stood on the hill has just gone over the cliff by the look of it.'

'Goodness me!' Kitty cried. 'I remember that house. Freddy showed it to me the first time he took me out all those years ago; he said his pa could not believe it had withstood all the storms, and that was then! I do hope the occupants were not inside.'

'Well, I sincerely hope he *was* inside.'

'Oh?' Kitty turned and looked at Maia in astonishment.

'That was Jago Penhallow's house – the man who just tried to rape me!'

Kitty's mouth made a large O.

'It would be sweet revenge if he was in there.' Maia smiled.

'Amen to that,' Kitty agreed.

As they turned to go back to the kitchen, Maia felt a curl of unease when she heard a car pull into the yard behind them. Grasping Kitty's arm in panic, thinking Jago had returned, she was just about to run indoors and lock the door until she saw it was Lord Dunstan's car, and relief swept over her.

'Gosh, what's happening down there?' Peter Dunstan asked when he got out of the car and looked towards the cove.

'Penn als Cottage has just slipped down the cliff.' Maia answered.

'Is that not Jago's house?'

'Yes, my lord.' Maia glanced at the cove. 'Karma, perhaps,' she muttered out of earshot.

'Goodness, Maia, what has happened to you,' he asked when he saw the state of her face.'

'Jago attack me,' she said grimly.

'Good God,' he said truly shocked. 'I'll have him arrested for that!'

'It's already been reported to the police. Thankfully, Freddy Hubbard saved me from worse. Please come in.' She gestured Peter into her kitchen.

Peter Dunstan stepped over the threshold and noticed Kitty sitting at the table. 'I do beg your pardon, Maia; I did not realise you had a visitor.'

'No matter, my lord. This is Mrs Kitty Walsh, Josh's grandmother!'

Kitty stood wide-eyed at the man before her. Suddenly, she was a young girl at the manor again and quickly lowered her eyes and stood to bob a curtsy.

'Oh! I see,' Peter said. There was an awkward silence before Peter cleared his throat. 'Forgive me, Mrs Walsh. I suspect I am the last person you wish to see.'

Kitty looked up and shook her head. 'On the contrary, my lord. I understand you are helping my grandson, and for that, I am so grateful. I must admit though, you do look like my son,' she grimaced. 'For a moment, I thought it was he who was coming through the door. It gave me quite a turn.'

'Ah, yes....my illegitimate half-brother?' Peter said cautiously.

'I suppose he is, my lord,' Kitty answered. 'But I beseech you to never claim kinship to him. I do not wish him to know of the blood connection!'

Peter tipped his head.

'I never told him about your father. If he ever found out, your family would never be rid of him. Trust me, he is a deeply unpleasant person. I know he is my son, but he is a spiteful, cruel, and manipulative individual who would make your life intolerable, as he has done with his son, Josh.'

'I see.' Peter seemed to breathe a sigh of relief. 'I know this does not go even half way to right the wrong my father did, but please accept my heartfelt apologies for the dreadful treatment you endured when you lived in our household. If I can do anything to make amends to you, I will.'

'You're very kind.' *Not at all like your father.* Kitty smiled, making the fine lines around her eyes more prominent. 'All I ask is that you help our poor Josh.'

'I shall do everything in my power. Now, Josh is the reason for my visit. My lawyer has learned that his trial will be the day after tomorrow.'

'Goodness that is quick!' Maia reached out to steady herself on the chair.

'Swift justice, it seems. I shall drive up tomorrow morning and meet Mr Sheldon, my lawyer, in Portsmouth. I wondered if you would like to accompany me, Maia?'

'I would, thank you. My lord, Kitty, is also going back to Portsmouth tomorrow.'

'Then you are also welcome to accompany us, Mrs Walsh. I shall pick you both up from here at eight in the morning.'

'Thank you, my lord. I'll show you out.'

When Maia returned, Kitty was biting her lip nervously.

Maia frowned. 'Are you all right? That must have been very strange for you to come face to face with a Dunstan.'

'Indeed, it was, but what is bothering me now is that Freddy was to pick me up to take me to the train station tomorrow morning. How am I going to get a message to him? The poor man will think I've abandoned him again if I'm not here when he comes.'

'No matter.' Maia smiled. 'Write a note, and I will get someone to give it to him. I need to go across the fields to organise someone to look after my livestock while I'm away.'

They both stopped speaking when an ambulance and police car rushed by with bells ringing.

'There must be casualties in the cove by the look of it,' Maia said, uncharitably hoping and praying that Jago had gone over with his house.

*

When help arrived at the scene, Fee and Guy were placed in the ambulance, while Jake was offered a lift to the hospital in the back of the police car. As Agnes was about to get in with him, she clutched her tummy and doubled over in pain.

'Darling. What is it?' Ellie said, putting her arm around her.

Agnes turned to her ma. 'I think I must have strained myself when I helped to pull Pa up,' she gasped.

'Agnes. There is blood on the back of your skirt!' Jake said in alarm. 'The baby!'

Agnes shot a look of despair between her ma and Jake, then her eyes filled with tears.

'Oh, sweetheart,' Ellie said softly as she pulled her daughter to her breast to comfort her.

P.C. Thomas watched the scene unfold. 'In you get, love,' he said gently to Agnes. 'We'll get the hospital to check you over as well.'

*

With great trepidation, Maia clutched the note Kitty had given her for Freddy and ran across the fields towards David Trevorrow's farm. She was constantly looking behind her, fearful that Jago would jump out at her from somewhere. She hoped with all her heart that he had gone over with his house, but if not, she knew only too well how much Jago disliked being thwarted and she did not trust him not to return to try and hurt her again.

After passing Kitty's note onto Ben Pearson, the saddler, for him to take to Freddy Hubbard, she went to see David Trevorrow to arrange for him to look after her stock while she was away.

As it had with Ben, shock also registered on David's face when he saw the large graze down Maia's cheek. 'What on earth has happened to you, Maia?'

Just as she had told Ben, she had to retell her story. 'Jago paid me a visit,' she answered gravely. 'He tried to rape me. He said he had come to take what should have belonged to him!' Her voice cracked, and despite her resolve to be brave, her eyes filled with tears.

David frowned angrily. 'Oh, goodness, Maia, did he... I mean, are you all right?'

She nodded. 'A bit battered,' she said, touching her face, 'he kicked me, but I am otherwise unscathed. Fortunately, Freddy Hubbard from Bochym called at the farm just in time to beat him off me.'

'Christ, Maia.' David was fuming now. 'Have you reported him to the police?'

'Freddy did that for me.'

'Good, because if the police do not deal with him, I bloody will! He shook his head. 'It seems Jago is having quite an *eventful* day,' he said grimly. 'Did you see his house go over the cliff? We watched from up here!'

Maia nodded. 'I was hoping he went over with it, but knowing Jago, he'll have escaped. But now he has nowhere to go,' she shuddered. 'I'm fearful Jago will still be lurking somewhere around here.'

David put his hand on her sleeve. 'Do you want me to come and stay with you just in case?'

'No, thank you. I'll be fine. I'll keep my doors and windows locked. I have Josh's grandma staying with me now, and she is one feisty woman. She beat Jago over the head with a chair while Freddy pulled him away from me.'

'She sounds like a formidable woman.' He smiled. 'Well, the offer is there if you need me.'

They both turned as David's son, Jimmy, walked up the path to the dairy farm, covered from head to foot in muck and dust.

'What the hell happened to you?' David asked, startled. 'You went for a swim a couple of hours ago!'

After drinking a glass of milk David thrust at him to moisten his parched throat, Jimmy relayed the shocking events of what had happened at Poldhu Cove that day.

'My goodness!' Maia murmured fearfully. 'That man really is a maniac. Where the hell is he now?'

'Scarpered he did, but when I gave my statement to the police, they said a country-wide manhunt was in place. Jago is wanted for assault, kidnapping, and attempted manslaughter. They interviewed his car showroom assistant, who told them that he had overheard Jago on the phone to Southampton docks this morning. It looks like he's planning to leave the country, so they're watching for him at all the ports.'

Maia nodded. 'When Jago attacked me, I told him I would report him, but he just laughed and said no one would find him because he was going away. I hope they catch him and hang him.' She clenched her teeth. 'Will they... hang him... do you think... If and when they catch him?' she asked hopefully.

'If they can prove he intended Fee to go over with that house, yes, but if not, I'm not sure. More is the pity,' David said dryly.

'I see,' Maia breathed.

*

When Maia returned to Wild Cliff Farm, she felt more settled regarding Jago, but she had something much more pressing to contemplate – something that she would see to later.

Kitty was snoozing in the chair but stirred when Maia entered and opened her eyes.

'All sorted with your friend David?' She asked with a smile.

'Yes. And I have found out what happened down at Poldhu Cove. My friends, the Blackthorns, have been in the thick of it. Some of them are badly injured and have gone to the hospital,' she sighed. 'Apparently, Jago abducted the Blackthorn's youngest daughter, after he left here.'

'My goodness, that man is a monster!' Kitty proclaimed.

Maia nodded in agreement. 'From what I can gather, David's son, Jimmy, managed to help a couple of people out of the house before it went over.'

'Not that monster, I hope?' Kitty said in disgust.

'No. Apparently, Jago drove off and left them all to perish. The police are on his trail now.'

'Good! At least, for once, the police will arrest a real criminal instead of putting innocent young lads in prison, like our Josh!' she said, trying to stop her lip from trembling.

'Hear, hear!' Maia placed her hand on Kitty's. 'Now, Kitty, would you mind if I pop down to the cove after I've milked the goats? I want to see if the Blackthorns are all right.'

'Of course you must go. I'll be fine here.'

41

Maia walked down to the cove before supper, just as the sun was setting on a calm and sedate sea. The air had cleared of dust, and the gentle shush of surf on the golden beach made it hard to believe the occupants of the cove had experienced so much havoc that day. Maia watched as a steady stream of people came down the beach to pick over the broken furniture from the pile of rubble that had once been Penn als Cottage. Wooden beams were being carried up the beach by strong men, obviously to build another structure somewhere in the village.

Maia walked over to P.C. Thomas, who was overseeing the scavenging. 'Pickings for all, I see, constable?' she said.

The constable nodded. 'Well, we are in Cornwall! They can take the wood, but I am telling everyone that if they find any personal items belonging to Jago, they must hand them over.' The constable's voice turned softer. 'Maia. I am so glad I have seen you. Freddy Hubbard reported what had happened to you with Jago, and then this happened, so I haven't had a chance yet to come and see you.'

'Please don't worry. You have your hands full here at the moment.'

'Are you really all right, though?' His eyes and voice were sympathetic, noting her grazed face.

'Yes, I'm fine. Thanks to Freddy intervening when he did.'

'Amen to that!' The constable glanced up and smiled. 'Ah, good. It looks like Ellie Blackthorn is back from the hospital.'

'Excuse me then. I need to go and see her.' Maia walked over to meet Ellie, noting that her friend looked tired and weary, and despite her own many worries, Ellie's first reaction was shock upon seeing the angry graze on Maia's face.

'Maia. Goodness. What has happened to you?'

'An encounter with Jago's boot before he came to wreak havoc here,' she answered grimly as she touched her painful cheek.

'That's shocking!'

'Yes, but thankfully, he was thwarted from doing worse when help conveniently arrived in the shape of Freddy Hubbard. Anyway, how are things with you? I spoke to Jimmy Trevorrow earlier, and he explained that he helped with the rescue.'

'Helped!' Ellie looked astounded. 'He did more than help. If not for Jimmy, Fee and Guy would be dead and buried under this rubble!' Ellie glanced at the debris of the house and shuddered. 'Jimmy was an absolute hero today!'

'I understand they've gone to the hospital.' Maia placed a comforting hand on Ellie's sleeve. 'Do you have any news? I do hope they're not all badly injured.'

'They're all going to be all right, thank goodness. Fee and Guy have a concussion, and Guy has also broken his collarbone. Jake suffered a broken leg when Jago ran over him when he was fleeing the scene, and Agnes...' Ellie put her hand on her chest. 'Oh, but Maia, can you believe that some good news actually came out of this awful incident?'

Maia tipped her head questioningly.

'When Agnes helped Jimmy pull Guy to safety, she strained her tummy. When we noticed there was blood on the back of her skirt, the poor girl looked stricken. It was then that she and Jake told me she was eight weeks pregnant. They'd been keeping it a secret!'

'Oh dear.' Maia looked puzzled. 'But you said good news!'

'Yes. When Agnes got to the hospital, they found the blood had not come from a miscarriage but from accidentally sitting in a pool of blood when she was caring for Guy until the ambulance came. So....,' Ellie's eyes shone with happy tears. 'I'm going to be a granny! Guy and I are going to be grandparents!'

Maia gathered her friend into a hug. 'Ellie. That is wonderful news on such a day.'

'They're keeping Agnes in the hospital with the others, though, because she strained herself, but all seems well. Tobias had just brought me back from the hospital when I saw you on the beach.' Suddenly, Ellie's eyes grew dark with anger. 'I swear I will swing for Jago if he sets one foot near my family again! Do you know that the bastard abducted Fee, took her to his house, and then left her there unconscious, knowing full well that the house was going to go over the cliff?'

'If it weren't for Agnes and Jimmy hearing Fee scream when Jago abducted her and Jimmy going in after her, well, goodness knows what would have happened,' Ellie's voice began to waver.

'Well, thank goodness everyone got out,' Maia breathed.

'It's a bloody shame Jago didn't go over with the house?' Ellie fumed.

'Yes. More's the pity.'

'I hope they catch the bastard,' Ellie said, then shook her head. 'That man is turning me into a potty mouth! I don't think I have ever sworn as much as I have these last few hours.'

'Oh, my dear, Ellie, I think you have good cause to swear. Tell me, have you been able to speak to Fee?'

'Yes, briefly, she said Jago wanted revenge because she had exposed his plans for the mining project. She said he was intent on raping her when the house started to crumble around them.'

'He didn't…..' Maia asked gravely.

'No, thank goodness. She said she put up a good fight, but...' Ellie began to cry. 'It greaves me that my poor little girl has been subjected to something like that!'

'Come on, Ellie, I'll walk you back to your house and make you a nice cup of tea. You look like you could do with one.'

'I'm tempted to partake in something a little stronger,' Ellie said wryly. 'But I suppose tea will suffice.'

As they sat in Ellie's cosy kitchen with a cup of tea and a shot of brandy in it, Ellie sighed wearily. 'What a day!' Then she looked up at Maia, wide-eyed. 'Oh, my goodness, I'm so sorry, Maia. I completely forgot what with everything that has happened here, but Guy told me that they arrested Josh this morning on information Jago had given to the police. What's to be done about that?'

'I can categorically say that Josh has done nothing wrong, but thankfully, Lord Dunstan has instructed his lawyer to help. We're going to go to Portsmouth in the morning. Josh has his trial date set for the day after tomorrow. Jago has a lot to answer for this day.'

'Well, Peter Dunstan's lawyer is the best; he has helped us in the past. Let's hope he brings Josh back home to you.'

'I'll drink to that.'

*

Freddy Hubbard doffed his hat to Ben Pearson and took the note from him with interest.

'Freddy, Maia asked me to pass this on to you. She also tells me you were her saviour today!'

'Well,' he said, looking sheepishly at Ben. 'Thankfully, I was just in the right place at the right time.'

'Nevertheless, I commend you for your actions.'

'Thank you.' Freddy waited until Ben had left before he slit the note open. As he read, his heart sank. It said that Kitty had got a lift back to Portsmouth in the morning, so he didn't need to take her to the train station. Damn! That meant that he wouldn't have a chance to tell her what he had wanted to say to her. He glanced around his little cottage. He had been visualising Kitty being here with him. He would have to wait now, but he was worried and kept thinking, What if, God forbid, Josh was sent to prison in Portsmouth? Because if he was, then Kitty may not want to return to Cornwall. Freddy screwed the note up and threw it at the fire. He had waited over forty years for her and he did not want to wait any longer.

*

It had been a long drive to Portsmouth, and though goaded and questioned about his desertion, Josh refused to say anything on the subject. He had not eaten all day and had only been offered a sip of water for his reluctance to engage with his captors.

'Let the deserter starve; it might loosen his tongue,' one of them said when the other was just about to offer a morsel of sandwich to him.

So, Josh watched as they feasted on fruit and sandwiches while he went without.

When they arrived in Portsmouth, Josh was placed in a cold cell containing a hard bunk, one blanket, and a bucket. He had no food, only water, and as the prison fell silent for the night, the only noise came from his rumbling stomach and the scratch of a mouse as it scampered in and out through the bars of his cell window.

He looked up at the darkening sky and tried to imagine Maia's arms around him, comforting him. His was a hopeless case, and his sentence would be of some duration - he knew that! Would Maia still want a jailbird for a husband? Would she still be waiting for him?

*

The sun had set when Maia reached the top of Poldhu Hill and turned to look down at the gaping hole in the cliff face. The beach was empty now, and the police presence had gone. Everyone knew there was a neap tide tonight, meaning none of the rubble would be disturbed. Maia thought of poor Fee, how terrified she must have been, and how Guy and Jimmy had risked their lives because of what Jago had done. She also thought of Josh alone in a cell. Every muscle in her body tensed, thinking that Josh would be frightened of the outcome of his trial. My God, but she hated Jago for all the hurt he had caused.

Turning her face to the sky, she whispered into the night. 'Stay strong, Josh, my love. I'll be waiting with open arms to hold you when you come home.'

She glanced again at the pile of rubble that had been Jago's house. The trip to the beach had settled something in her mind. She smiled to herself. Well, Jago, two can play the revenge game.

*

Kitty woke at around three in the morning. It was dark, making her feel disorientated. Then she remembered - she was in Maia's spare bedroom - the room where Maia had told her she had nursed Josh through a bout of malaria. Kitty liked Maia; she would make the perfect wife for her beloved grandson. If only... oh, if only all went well with the trial. Kitty was not a churchgoer, but as always, even if you didn't believe, when all else seemed lost, people often prayed to a higher being, and, kneeling by her bed, which was what Kitty had done last night, she had prayed for Josh's conviction to be overturned.

Suddenly, Kitty's train of thought broke when she heard someone walking about in the attic. A ghost? Fortunately, that didn't spook her; she had encountered spirits when she'd worked at Bochym, but never one since. Slipping out of bed, she opened her bedroom door slightly.

*

Maia hung the Tilley lamp on a hook in the eaves and opened the lid of the heavy chest. Moving the lamp to see more clearly, she lifted the lump hammer from its depths and closed the lid. Placing the weighty object in her leather shoulder bag, she picked up the lamp and crept back downstairs. Trying to be as quiet as a mouse, Maia opened the latch on the back door and slipped outside, locking the door behind her. Clutching the bag to her side, she set off down the garden.

*

Kitty had watched Maia walk fully clothed past the opening of her bedroom door, seemingly clutching something to her side. With her keen sense of hearing, she had heard Maia leave the house, and then, from the landing window, Kitty watched Maia walk down the garden with a Tilley lamp. A few minutes later, Kitty saw Maia return from the garden and extinguished the light. She waited, but Maia did not enter the house again. After a while, Kitty returned to bed, but not to sleep. Twenty minutes later, the back door opened again, and she heard movement downstairs and the kitchen tap running - the sound of Maia washing her hands. Ten minutes later, the house fell silent again, but sleep still evaded Kitty. She couldn't help but wonder where Maia had been in the dead of night.

*

Maia was up bright and early to see to the livestock before breakfast. She smiled when Kitty came downstairs.

'Good morning, Kitty. Did you sleep well?'

'Yes, thank you. Until about three o'clock,' Kitty answered, watching Maia's reaction, but none came.

'Oh dear. Perhaps you can catch forty winks in the car if you feel tired.'

'Did *you* sleep well, Maia?'

Maia laughed. 'I won't sleep easy until Jago Penhallow is locked up and Josh is safely back with us.'

*

Once David Trevorrow had milked his cattle and turned them out into the field, he called on Ben Pearson at the saddlery to see if he and Jimmy wanted a walk to the cove to see the remains of Jago's house.

As they walked onto the beach, Jimmy was greeted with applause by the many who were sifting through the wreckage of Penn als Cottage. Jimmy, reluctant hero that he was, wanted to turn tail and go back home, but his proud father held fast to his arm and made him take all the praise bestowed on him.

The wreckage covered a good third of the width of the beach. P.C. Thomas, who was back on watch, told them, as he had told everyone, that they were free to take any broken wood, but if they found any personal belongings, they had to hand them in.

David kicked aimlessly through the edge of the debris until his foot hit something quite solid. He bent down and pulled a leather money bag from the pile of rubble with the initials H. W. P. engraved into the leather.

'Christ, this is heavy! Look, Ben. If I'm not mistaken, these are Henry Penhallow's initials?' He passed the pouch to him.

'Indeed, they are. I made this money pouch for Henry a few years ago.'

P.C. Thomas moved forward. 'What have you there then?'

David handed the constable the money pouch, who almost dropped it when he felt the weight of it!

'Ben said he made this for Henry Penhallow,' David offered.

'P.C. Thomas frowned. 'If I remember rightly, this pouch was cut and stolen from Henry's person the night he was set upon and murdered.'

'What the devil is it doing here then?' Ben asked. Everyone looked at each other, all with raised eyebrows.

'Perhaps it was buried in Jago's garden!' David answered knowingly.

When P.C. Thomas opened the pouch, they found inside a lump hammer and a penknife wrapped in a piece of darkly stained hessian sacking.

'Would that be blood?' David gasped.

P.C. Thomas nodded. 'It could well be,' he said as they inspected the lump hammer and penknife, engraved with Jago's initials!

'Christ, does that mean Jago murdered Henry? His own brother!' Ben said.

'Well.' P.C. Thomas scratched his head. 'I think I need to get this up to the station in Helston. It looks like Jago will be charged with murder now.'

*

For Maia and Kitty, it seemed like a long journey by car to Portsmouth, and Kitty did indeed sleep for the best part of the journey, waking just as they approached the town. Peter drove into the centre of Portsmouth and insisted on taking Kitty to her house. Once there, he got out and carried her bag as she unlocked the door.

'No, my lord! Please don't come in – it's terribly damp here,' Kitty fretted.

Peter brushed away her argument and followed her in. 'Good grief,' he said, his nose twitching at the smell of decay. 'How long have you lived here, Mrs Walsh?'

'A few months – since my husband died, we had a tied cottage before that, a lovely place on a big estate. I'm looking for somewhere else. My son, Jacob, found this house for me but seems to have abandoned me to it and the ever-growing mould.'

'Well, this will never do! Gather some belongings and come with me.'

'But....'

'No buts. You'll stay in a hotel until we find more suitable accommodation.'

Kitty's eyes watered at his kindness as Maia put her arm around her shoulders and led her back to the car.

When they arrived at the hotel, Mr Sheldon, Peter's lawyer, was waiting for them. As the ladies settled into their rooms, Peter asked his lawyer if he had seen Josh.

'I have, my lord, and taken a full statement from him.'

'What are his chances?'

'It depends. This Captain Wright seems to be a clever man. He has covered the cruelty inflicted on his fellow shipmates well, and he has even been honoured for his impeccable service. People are afraid of him. It's a case of Josh's word against his.'

Deflated, Peter answered, 'Don't say any of this to the ladies.'

'Of course not, my lord.'

'I wonder, will you dine with them this evening? I plan to dine at the Gentleman's Club; there is someone there I would like to speak with.'

'Nobody involved with this trial, I hope. You may compromise the outcome if you meddle,' Mr Sheldon warned.

'I won't compromise anything. I promise.'

42

After dining in the Gentlemen's Club, Peter sat in the member's room, an opulent room filled with the aroma of old leather, polish, and Cuban cigars. As he enjoyed his brandy, he glanced around the room at the men relaxing. Some were dozing, some reading newly ironed crisp newspapers, but Peter was looking specifically for one person. Judge Robert Kirkwood. He had served alongside him as an officer in the Great War, and they had remained firm friends since.

Peter smiled when he saw his old comrade sitting in the corner of the room. He did not go over; he just sipped his brandy, hoping that his friend would notice him, and thankfully he did.

When Peter saw him get up, collect his drink, and walk over to him, he stood to greet him.

'Peter!' Judge Kirkwood shook his hand. 'I have not seen you for a while. How is life in Cornwall? Good, I trust?'

'Very good, Robert. Thank you. How are you?'

'Cannot complain. May I?' He gestured to the seat in front of him.

'Be my guest.'

'So, what brings you to Portsmouth? Business?'

'No. Actually, a distant relative of mine is to be tried in the morning.'

'Good God! For what?'

'Alleged desertion from the Navy.'

'Is he by God? Court martial?'

'No. A judicial hearing case.'

'And...erm, you wish to be associated with this relative?'

'I believe he's a good man, and not just because he's a distant relative!' Peter smiled.

'How distant a relative?'

'He is the fruit of my odious father's loins.'

Judge Kirkwood's eyebrows lifted. 'Ah, I see. How very charitable of you.'

Peter brushed an invisible speck from his trousers. 'I do not like to see anyone wrongly charged. I hate injustice.'

Judge Kirkwood took a drag of his cigar, spitting a stray piece of tobacco from his lip. 'And you believe him to be innocent of all charges?'

'I do.'

Judge Kirkwood glanced around the room and then back at Peter. 'I know the case of which you are speaking. You do realise that I'm not presiding over that case, don't you?'

'I would not have spoken to you about it if you were,' Peter said, taking a sip of brandy.

Judge Kirkwood nodded in grateful acknowledgement. 'Judge George Thomas is seeing the case in the morning. He is a fair judge; he will do the right thing.'

'I do hope so.' Peter smiled and then changed the subject. 'Come and visit Bochym and take in some of our Cornish air. Bring your good lady wife too. Sarah would love to see you both.'

'I will. Thank you. Good health.' He raised his glass.

*

The next morning, after arriving early at court, Peter and the others were milling about in the foyer, waiting to be called. As Peter surveyed his surroundings, he saw Judge Robert Kirkwood speaking with another judge. Kirkwood's eyes momentarily glanced in Peter's direction, and then, as he moved on, he gave Peter a slight nod.

'I see Josh has made the local newspaper.' Mr Sheldon broke Peter's concentration. 'No doubt Captain Wright has called in a favour with the owner of this gutter press report.

They all glanced at the headline.

SLIPPERY DESERTER, GIDEON WALSH TO STAND TRIAL.

The story went on to say that Walsh had duped his fellow shipmates into thinking he had fallen overboard, when in fact he had stolen a vital piece of the ship's safety equipment, putting the crew at risk of drowning should their ship have gone down, by taking a lifejacket and jumping ship.

It was reported that Walsh had taken on a pseudonym and wormed his way into a young widow's affection, hoping to take her farm from her. His lies and deceit came to light when the widow's brother-in-law became suspicious and saw Walsh for the fraud that he was, bringing to a close a ten-week manhunt for him.

On reading the story, Maia and Kitty sat down and held onto each other, distraught after reading all the lies.

'How do you think this article will affect the trial, Sheldon?' Peter asked.

'In all honesty, I do not know, my lord. Josh's version of the story could be deemed unbelievable. What ship captain would throw a member of his crew overboard? It's unheard of! The character references you handed me may help. They all say much the same: that Josh is a good man. But....'

'Excuse me, sir.'

Both men turned to see a nervous-looking man standing beside them with the newspaper in hand.

'Yes?' They said in unison.

'Are you defending Walsh in this case?' He asked Mr Sheldon.

'I am.'

'Then I have some information you need to know. Can we go somewhere private?'

*

It was hot and stuffy in the courtroom. Shafts of light from the high windows filled the room with dust motes. Captain Wright had given his embellished account of what had happened. According to him, Josh had refused to honour the document he had allegedly signed, which was to partake in another five years of service working under the captain's command.

'Walsh completely refused to honour the document,' Captain Wright said incredulously. 'When I told him it was legally binding, Walsh stormed out, and the next thing we knew, he had gone AWOL. We later realised he had jumped ship, taking a valuable item of safety equipment to aid his disgraceful endeavour.'

Josh looked on in despair. How could Captain Wright stand here in a court of law and tell such a bare-faced lie, especially after having sworn an oath to the truth on the Bible?

When Josh was finally called into the dock to defend himself, his heart was pounding so much that he thought it would burst out of his shirt. If this judge believed Captain Wright's pack of lies, what hope was there for him? He began to tremble for his future. Not only was he facing a prison sentence, but if found guilty, he would have to serve another five years in the Navy! According to Captain Wright, Josh had signed the five-year contract of service!

Josh looked around the courtroom at the sea of faces. His father, damn his eyes, was sitting back, arms folded and legs crossed, apparently enjoying the trial. He knew for sure now where his father's evil traits came from. Josh cast his eyes over the crowd. He knew Lord Dunstan was here somewhere, incognito, and was so grateful to learn that the Earl had granted him the use of his lawyer free of charge. He had also spotted his beloved grandma sitting next to Maia! How on earth had that happened? When he first locked eyes on Maia in the courtroom, he noticed the graze down her face. He frowned and gestured at what had happened by touching his own face. Maia just smiled and shook her head to dismiss it, but it did not ease his concern for her. Now, after hearing Captain Wright's version of events, Josh looked at Maia and his grandma - the two people that he loved more than anything in the world, and they were both ashen-faced; he suspected that his pallor was likewise. Only his lawyer, Mr Sheldon, seemed pleased with himself.

Mr Dickens, the barrister working on behalf of Captain Wright, stood and straightened his gown, addressed the judge and courtroom, before turning to Josh.

'Mr Walsh. We have heard Captain Wright's account. He says that you refused to honour the document you signed in agreement to work another five years on the ship. Is this true?'

'I did refuse, yes. Because I didn't sign it!'

'He then said that you deserted your ship.'

'I did not!'

'He said you took with you a lifejacket - a vital piece of Navy safety equipment - putting others at risk should there have been an emergency. I put it to you that you jumped ship.'

'I did not jump ship. I was thrown overboard at Captain Wright's orders.'

'Were you in possession of a lifejacket when you were allegedly thrown overboard?'

'I was.'

A murmur travelled around the courtroom, before once again, Josh recalled the story of that night and that the lifejacket was obsolete stock and, therefore, no longer a vital item of safety equipment.

'A tall tale indeed.' Mr Dickens smirked.

'It's the honest truth.'

'So, you say that the lifejacket was pushed into your arms by one of the men tasked with throwing you overboard?'

'Yes, sir.'

'Can you name this man?'

'No, sir. I do not want to get him into trouble. He could be court-martialled for disobeying Captain Wright's orders and helping me.'

'How convenient.'

Suddenly, a voice rang out in the courtroom, and a man stood up.

'It was me! I pushed that lifejacket into Walsh's arms before following orders from Captain Wright to chuck him overboard!'

Josh looked startled as everyone stood and turned towards the voice. Unfortunately, Josh could not see the man who had spoken before he was pulled back down to his seat.

The courtroom erupted into loud murmurings.

'Silence in court!' The judge ordered.

Josh saw Mr Sheldon frowning, frantically waving the man in the crowd to stay seated before he stood and addressed the judge. 'Forgive the outburst, Your Honour. The gentleman who spoke is actually a witness for the accused.'

'Then he shall speak when called to the dock - and not before!' The judge said sternly.

'Yes, Your Honour.' Mr Sheldon sat down and lifted his eyes skyward as if praying his witness would stay silent.

Mr Dickins carried on his interrogation. 'So, you say you washed up in Zennor, West Cornwall?'

'I did.'

'Why did you not contact the Admiralty as soon as possible to report this crime? It has been over two months since you came ashore.'

'It was due to what Captain Wright said when he ordered my shipmates to throw me overboard.'

Mr Dickins smiled without humour and glanced around the courtroom. 'And what, pray, did he say?'

'When he told my shipmates that I was deserting the ship, he said to them, "If, and that is a big if, Walsh survives and is found, rest assured he'll be court-martialled and imprisoned for desertion."'

Another murmur circulated in the court.

'I don't deserve to be imprisoned for what that man did to me!' Josh added vehemently.

Mr Dickens raised an eyebrow. 'Well, I think we must let the jury decide your fate!' He turned to address the judge. 'I have no more questions, Your Honour,' he said, smirking, knowing that his learned colleague's rogue witness had done nothing to help Walsh with his outburst.

'Mr Sheldon, I trust you have a statement from the witness you wish to call to the dock?' the judge asked.

'I do, Your Honour, and I apologise for the lateness in presenting it to you. The witness has only just come forward.' He passed the statement to the judge, who took his time to read it. Presently, he said, 'You can call your witness now.'

The man who had spoken out of turn walked up to the dock to take the oath, and Josh sat open-mouthed when he recognised who was about to speak up for him.

'Name.'

'Harry Flintman.'

'Are you a serving member of one of the armed forces?'

'Not any more, Your Honour. I quit the Navy when we docked shortly after this event. I have spent sleepless nights since the day I was ordered to throw Walsh overboard to an almost certain death. I did not join the Navy to kill innocent people. I had served during the Great War and intended to continue my service for at least another five years, but I could not work under *that* man a moment longer.' He pointed at Captain Wright, who snorted derisively. 'Captain Wright was cruel beyond belief to Walsh – on Walsh's father's orders, I might add.'

'On his father's orders, you say?'

'Yes, Your Honour. I was on deck five years ago when Jacob Walsh came aboard to speak to Captain Wright about his son. I believe they were drinking partners while the captain was on shore leave. Mr Walsh ordered Captain Wright to flog his son regularly for being a coward and refusing to fight for his country in the Great War, when actually Gideon Walsh was not old enough to serve. I witnessed Mr Jacob Walsh sign the papers to enlist him. He also postdated a second document to keep young Walsh in the Navy for a second term of five years when the first five were over.'

'And did he flog the accused regularly?'

'Yes, Your Honour. For many minor misdemeanours.'

'Such as?'

'Missing a corner of the deck when he scrubbed it. Or losing his footing in rough seas, which is an occupational hazard on a ship. He even had him dragged from his sick bed once to flog him for laziness when Walsh had been suffering from malaria. Six other men, currently serving in the Royal Navy under Captain Wright, are sitting outside the courtroom now, fearful of coming in for the risk of Captain Wright seeing them. They have all willingly signed an affidavit to back up my claims of Captain Wright's cruelty during the last five years, as long as you grant them anonymity.'

'Mr Sheldon. Do you have this affidavit?' the judge asked.

'I do, Your Honour. All six men will be happy to see you in private should you need to.'

Captain Wright's face turned puce, and he stood up. 'Your Honour, I order that man,' he pointed at Harry Flintman, 'and the others, to be arrested for defamation of my character,' he demanded.

'And I order you, sir, to keep quiet!' The judge warned the captain. 'Mr Flintman, please proceed.'

Harry Flintman wrung his hands anxiously. 'I cannot tell you how glad I am that Walsh survived. I can sleep easier now. It has played on my conscience all this time.' He glanced at Josh, who was openly tearful – relieved that Harry had verified his story.

'Witness to stand down.' The judge ordered. 'May I see the contract documents allegedly signed by Mr Jacob Walsh?'

The judge looked between the documents, noted the signature - Gideon Walsh - written in a shaky hand, and then handed them down to the jury.

'May I see Gideon Walsh's signature? If you could write it now!' the judge asked.

With the handwriting his grandmother had taught him, Josh signed the name he hated with his usual flair of hand: Gideon Walsh.

This too was passed to the judge, who looked at it before handing it to the jury.

'Mr Sheldon, do you have any scribbled notes that Mr Walsh gave you as you were building this case that I can inspect?'

'Yes, Your Honour.' He passed several pages of beautifully written script to the judge, who, in turn, passed them onto the jury.

'Gentlemen of the jury, you have listened to all the evidence in this hearing. I ask you now to retire with me to a private room to meet the gentlemen whose names are on this affidavit, and then you can deliberate on your verdict. Please take the accused down to wait until called for.'

As Josh left the courtroom, he shot a hopeful glance at Maia.

Outside, in the courtroom foyer, Mr Sheldon, Maia and Kitty huddled together. Peter stood a short distance from them, although still in earshot. While sitting high up in the courtroom, Peter had regarded Jacob Walsh and his unpleasant demeanour with interest. He noted the striking resemblance to himself - after all, he was his half-brother - it was almost a mirror image, albeit Walsh's looks were coarse. It would not do for him to come face-to-face with that man – in case Jacob saw the connection himself. He could see Jacob Walsh now standing at the other side of the foyer, glowering at Kitty, his mother. It took all his reserve not to intervene when he saw Walsh stride over to her.

'What are you doing here, Mother? Get yourself back home,' Jacob snarled at Kitty.

'Don't you dare *Mother* me!' Kitty snapped. 'You are no son of mine; I disown you for what you have done to that poor lad in there.'

'Is that so?' He laughed in her face and bared down on her with his fist clenched. For a horrible moment, Kitty was back in the hell that was the Earl's bedchamber all those years ago, until Mr Sheldon intervened.

'Mr Walsh.' Mr Sheldon stepped between them. 'I insist you leave Mrs Walsh alone, or I shall call security and have you removed and arrested for threatening behaviour.'

Jacob Walsh glared at Mr Sheldon and then prodded Kitty in the chest. 'I'll see you at home,' he said before storming away.

Peter Dunstan waited until Walsh was out of sight and moved closer to Kitty; he could see genuine fear in her eyes.

'Mrs Walsh. Would you allow me to offer you a cottage on the Bochym Manor estate?'

'Oh, goodness, my lord,' Kitty said tearfully. 'That is so kind of you, but if Josh is found guilty and sent to HMP Kingston here, I shall have to stay close so I can visit him.'

Peter nodded. 'Hopefully, it will not come to that, but if it does, you are welcome to stay in the hotel until we have found you more suitable accommodation – well away from your son. But, if all goes well, the offer of a cottage stands.'

'You are so good, my lord. Thank you for the offer.'

They all looked up when a court official approached Mr Sheldon.

'The jury is returning. The courtroom is to reconvene.'

'Oh, dear! That was a little too quick,' Mr Sheldon murmured to Peter.

'Sheldon. If the jury goes against Josh and finds him guilty, and I claim him as kin, will that reduce his sentence?' Peter asked hopefully.

'Perhaps.' Mr Sheldon answered doubtfully. 'We shall have to see.'

43

At Wild Cliff Farm, David Trevorrow and one of his dairy maids were finishing their chores on behalf of Maia when Ryan Penrose walked across to the pigsty to speak to him.

'Is Maia about?' Ryan asked. 'I've knocked, but there is no answer.'

David lowered his pitchfork and swotted the flies away. 'She's gone to Portsmouth for Josh's trial, I'm afraid.'

'Oh!' Ryan looked crestfallen.

'What's amiss?'

'I have Maia's cat at home. It was brought to me a couple of days ago after Jago had kicked it and injured it quite badly.'

David felt a strong sense of foreboding. 'Did she die?' he asked.

'No. You know cats - they can put up with an awful lot of pain before they give up the ghost, but she is awfully poorly. I think I should put her out of her misery.'

'But I take it you don't want to do that without Maia's consent?'

'No. But I hate to see any animal suffer.'

'You must do what you must do, Ryan.'

Ryan looked to the ground and kicked at a piece of turf. 'When does Maia come home?'

'The trial was today. So, I should think tomorrow at the latest.'

Ryan nodded sadly. 'I will wait another day then.'

David leaned on his pitchfork. 'I should think you're going to be shorthanded in the Thatching business after what has happened with the Blackthorns.'

'I'll say. There is only me and Agnes left unscathed; having said that, she is still in the hospital for some reason!'

'It could have been so much worse,' David breathed. 'At least they will live to thatch another day.'

'Amen to that, and all thanks to your Jimmy.'

David laughed. 'He is such a reluctant hero.'

'Well, I can safely say he has the admiration of the whole village. You must be very proud of him.'

'I am.' David beamed.

*

Jago had booked into a hotel in Exeter the night he left Cornwall. It was almost dark when he got there, so he dined late, and if the thought of leaving the Blackthorn girl trapped under his wardrobe bothered him, it had not affected his sleep that night - he slept like the dead.

Jago was up with the lark to breakfast before continuing his journey to Southampton. He knew he had left a trail of trouble behind him, so the sooner he was on that ship, the better. As he approached Southampton at about eleven o'clock, he saw the signpost for Portsmouth and gave a wry smile. Josh Harding would be in some prison cell there by now. He may not have had his satisfaction with Maia, or indeed that little sneak, Fay Blackthorn, but because of his intervention, he was confident Harding would rot away in some awful prison for a few years. It was a shame that he would never hear the outcome of his trial. Jago had no idea how swift the justice would be, but whenever it was, he would be long gone – on the high Atlantic sea en route to a better life.

Jago drove into the centre of the town and grudgingly sold his beloved Alvis 12/50 at a nearby showroom, peeved that he did not get what it was worth. Still, with the money he received and the money he had cleared from his bank account, he had more than enough to buy a completely new set of clothes, pay for his First Class boat ticket, and live very comfortably for a good few weeks in New York until he could establish another car showroom there.

At the Cunard ticket office at the docks, Jago paid for and picked up his one-way ticket on the RMS Berengaria.

'Be aboard at two p.m. The ship sails at four,' the ticket officer told him.

Somewhere Out There

Jago found a men's outfitter, where he purchased a trunk of new clothes to be sent ahead of him to his ship. He took a late luncheon in a local inn, savouring his last meal on English ground - a rich beef and ale pie and a glass of beer. 'To the new world.' He raised his glass and toasted himself.

*

In Portsmouth, Josh was standing pale and anxious in the dock. He glanced at Maia, who blew him a kiss. Josh hoped that they would give him a chance to speak to Maia before they sent him down. He would reluctantly tell her not to wait for him as it may be almost seven years before they could be together again.

Josh watched nervously as the jury filed in. He saw his father grinning and heard him say, 'Look at the jury. They can't look at Gideon. They have clearly found the scoundrel guilty.'

Others had also heard him, and Josh glanced fearfully at his grandma, who was openly crying, while Maia comforted her.

When the judge came in, everyone stood. Only Josh remained standing as everyone sat down again. He could feel his body trembling, resigning himself to years of hell - first in prison and then sailing on the high seas again.

'Members of the jury, have you come to a decision?'

'We have, Your Honour.'

'Do you find the accused guilty or not guilty?'

*

At half past one, and with a spring in his step, Jago stepped off English soil and walked up the gangway of the magnificent vessel. He nodded to the steward, who took his ticket, and glanced around the deck of people waiting to wave to their families on the dock.

'Mr Jago Penhallow?'

'Correct,' he answered assertively.

The steward nodded to two officers standing in the background who stepped forward and hooked an arm under each of Jago's arms.

'Hey, hey! What is this?' Jago struggled under their hold.

'Jago Penhallow. We are arresting you on five counts. Two counts of attempted rape, two counts of attempted manslaughter, and the murder of Mr Henry Penhallow.'

'What? Now, wait a minute.'

'You do not have to say anything. But it may harm your defence if you do not mention when questioned something which you later rely on in court. Anything you do say may be given in evidence.'

Jago looked around at the interested bystanders who would have been his fellow passengers. They were all watching agog!

'This is preposterous,' Jago spluttered. 'These allegations are completely fabricated. Murder, you say - of Henry Penhallow! Henry was my brother, for Christ's sake!' Jago shouted as they escorted him back down the gangway.

*

In the courtroom in Portsmouth, Josh shut his ears to everything around him. For one sweet moment, he let his mind drift to better times - when he had lain in Maia's arms after making love. His sweet reverie broke when the court erupted. Josh's eyes snapped open, and he saw Captain Wright, his face florid with anger, stand up and shout, 'What the devil do you mean, not guilty? You bloody fools! Of course, he's guilty. I demand an appeal!'

Josh frowned and glanced around the courtroom as happy faces looked back at him.

The judge brought the courtroom to silence. 'One more word from you, Captain Wright, and I will also charge you with contempt of court.'

'Also!' Captain Wright blustered. 'What do you mean, also?'

'I must inform you and Mr Jacob Walsh that you must remain seated when this court is adjourned, as your names are with the prosecution office for perverting the course of justice. They will deal with you accordingly.'

Josh glanced at the faces of his father and Captain Wright - the two men who had made his life hell, and felt a bubble of delight seeing them both shocked into silence.

The judge then turned to Josh and then to Mr Sheldon. 'The accused is free to go.'

Josh gasped and dropped his face into his hands. A moment later, he was encompassed in Maia's loving arms, drinking in the sweet fragrance of jasmine infused in her beautiful, soft, fiery curls.

'You're free, my darling, free!' she cried.

*

Outside the courthouse, everyone stood in a circle, celebrating the outcome. Josh shook the hand of Harry Flintman, the man who had undoubtedly saved him from drowning and years of imprisonment.

'Thank you, my friend. I owe you a great debt of gratitude.'

Harry clamped his hand over Josh's. 'We can both sleep easily in our beds from now on. I wish you the best of luck in the future.'

'Thank you, Harry. Please, could you thank the others who were brave enough to come forward and speak up for me?'

'I will,' Harry said. 'Godspeed, my friend.'

Peter Dunstan checked his watch. 'Well then, it's half past two. Shall we all set off back home?'

'Kitty! Kitty!' a voice shouted from across the street. They all turned to see Freddy, red-faced and puffing like Billy O as he manoeuvred across the busy road.

'Hubbard!' Peter frowned. 'What the devil are you doing here?'

'Begging your pardon, my lord.' Freddy touched his hat, clearly shocked to find His Lordship with the group. 'I have come to ask Kitty a question. But first,' he looked at Josh, 'have you been acquitted?'

Josh beamed a smile and nodded.

'Splendid news. Because if not...,' he turned to Kitty. 'I would have come up here to live with you.'

'*Live* with me?' Kitty teased.

'Married, of course!' He said quickly. 'You promised you would over forty years ago.'

'Yes, I did, Freddy.' Kitty smiled, gently masking the hurt of the separation that followed the proposal.

'So, Kitty, will you keep your promise?' Freddy got down on one knee. 'Will you marry me now? Will you return to Cornwall to be my wife and live in the cottage as we once planned?' He shot an anxious glance at Peter. 'Would that be acceptable, my lord?'

Peter laughed and nodded. 'Perfectly acceptable, Hubbard.'

Freddy turned back to Kitty for her answer.

Kitty's eyes were watering with happy tears. 'Oh, Freddy. Yes, please. I want that more than anything. Now, do get up, or you'll get rheumatism in your knee!'

'I spend my life on my knees,' Freddy joked, 'but I must admit, I'm struggling to get up off this hard pavement.'

Josh and Peter hooked a hand under each of Freddy's arms and helped him up.

'Well, we do have a jolly little party on the drive home then!' Peter mused. 'Hubbard, you will join us!' It was a statement rather than a question.

'Oh, erm, if you don't mind, my lord. Yes, yes, I will.' He clasped Kitty's hand, determined never to let her go again.

'What about your belongings in the house, Mrs Walsh?' Peter asked.

'In truth, the furniture was there when I took it on. There are only a few books – everything that means anything to me I collected yesterday.'

'Onward to Cornwall then?' Peter said, and everyone happily agreed.

*

Just as the Bochym car set off from Portsmouth back to Cornwall, Tobias Williams was driving the *walking wounded* – Guy Blackthorn and Jake Treen - home from the hospital. Guy was nursing a broken collar bone and a bandaged head, which covered a nasty gash sporting ten stitches. Jake was on crutches; his left leg clad in plaster of Paris from foot to thigh. Agnes had returned home the previous afternoon with instructions to rest, which went completely against the grain for her, but Ellie was determined that she would do as she was told. Fee was to spend another night in the hospital as her concussion had been quite severe, and they had also found a small fracture to her elbow and a broken rib, which was making it hard for her to breathe easily. It could all have been so much worse. No one dared think of the outcome if the house had gone over with them in it.

*

Later that same evening, P.C. Thomas called on the Blackthorns to inform them that Jago had been arrested, imprisoned, and was awaiting trial in Exeter jail. Apart from being charged with what he had done to Maia and the Blackthorn family, Jago was on an additional, more serious charge - of murdering his brother Henry - a charge Jago refuted quite vehemently, P.C. Thomas told them.

Guy huffed. 'I wouldn't put it past Jago,' he said, grimacing in pain as he adjusted his sling.

*

When word got out in Mullion about Jago's arrest, there was a general consensus amongst the regular customers at The Old Inn later that evening that the murder was probably a crime of passion. Everyone knew he coveted Henry's wife, Maia. Jago had never hidden the fact that he was desperate to take her as his own and take control of the farm. Therefore, the collective opinion was that Jago was most definitely guilty as charged!

*

After a long and tiring drive from Southampton, during which Maia and Josh had invited Kitty to live with them at the farm until her wedding to Freddy, Peter Dunstan dropped Maia, Josh and Kitty back at Wild Cliff Farm just after midnight. Peter had asked everyone for their assurance that his involvement in Josh's case could be kept secret. Peter had been happy to help Josh, but he did not want to encourage any more of his father's illegitimate offspring to appear out of the woodwork - or have Jacob Walsh knocking on his door. They all agreed that Peter had gone above and beyond to heal the wounds of the past.

The first thing Maia did after opening the farmhouse door was glance around for Prudence, who would have usually greeted her with a purr and by winding her way through her legs to the point of almost tripping her up. Maia felt a pang of sadness amid all the euphoria at having Josh home, as she wondered if her beloved pet had survived and if Ryan had worked his magic on her.

'I'll move back to the shepherd's hut, Maia, you know, with Grandma being here,' Josh offered.

'Oh, no, you will not!' Kitty and Maia said in unison, laughing heartily at how vehemently they refuted his suggestion.

'We are married, remember,' Maia said, slipping her arms around Josh's waist.

'Not really. I mean, we shouldn't.'

'To all intents and purposes, we are married in the eyes of most people. It was good enough before all this trial happened, so it's good enough now. Besides, I do not want to spend another night without you,' Maia said, looking deep into his eyes.

'My darling, Maia, I don't want that either, if the truth be told.' Josh wrapped his arms around her and kissed her.

'Well then!' Kitty said. 'I feel a little like a gooseberry, so I will take myself off to bed and leave you two love birds to your reunion. I have a busy day tomorrow. Freddy and I are to see the vicar at Cury Church to arrange for the banns to be read!' She smiled and then looked more serious. 'You don't mind me marrying Freddy, do you, Josh?'

'Mind!' He laughed. 'Of course not, Grandma.'

'It's just that, well…. you and your grandpa were very close.'

Josh let go of Maia and wrapped his arms around Kitty. 'We were, but all I wish for now is for you to be as happy as I am with Maia.'

'Why don't you and Maia come to the church with us then? Have your banns read too?'

Maia grimaced. 'I'm not sure the vicar will look favourably on us.'

'No.' Josh laughed. 'Especially as we have so blatantly been living in sin,' he added.

'It is no sin to love, Josh,' Kitty said, reaching out to touch his arm.

'No, but I think we'll go and give notice at the registry office in Helston tomorrow and arrange to get married quietly.' He glanced at Maia, who nodded happily at this suggestion.

44

Josh and Maia returned from Helston the next day, happy that they had set a date for their wedding for ten o'clock on Monday, the 10th of September. They had chosen Monday so that Ellie Blackthorn could be Maia's witness. Maia had very few female friends; Henry would never allow her any, so it was only since his death that Maia had connected with Ellie Blackthorn, and they had remained firm friends since. Josh had decided to ask David Trevorrow to stand up for him. The wedding would be an intimate, albeit secret affair if possible, as most people in the village still thought Maia and Josh were already married, and they had no intention of letting them believe otherwise.

As they manoeuvred the horse and cart into the yard, Ryan Penrose was waiting for them with a bundle of fur in his arms.

Maia jumped down from the cart. 'Prudence!'

'Oh, Maia.' Ryan's eyes and his voice were sympathetic. 'I'm sorry, but she just will not rally for me. I have done my best, and I do not believe she sustained any broken bones, but she is still badly bruised and could even have internal damage - I don't know. Maybe you need to take her to someone more knowledgeable about animals.'

'Has she eaten anything?' Maia asked, stricken.

'Only a morsel. Perhaps it would be kinder to...' He looked away, unable to finish the sentence.

'I see.' Maia's voice fractured. When Ryan passed her cat to her, Maia glanced first at Josh with tear-filled eyes, but when she kissed the cat's soft head, Prudence responded with a soft purr.

Ryan looked astonished. 'Well, I'll be! That is the first time I have heard her purr. Maybe I'm wrong. Maybe she was just missing you.' He smiled. 'I'll leave her with you now. If you need me to... well,' he smiled thinly, 'call me if you need me for anything.'

'Thank you for all you have done for her, Ryan,' Maia said tearfully.

Ryan shrugged. 'I wish I could have done more.' As he turned to leave, he placed his hand on Josh's arm. 'I'm glad you had your conviction quashed, Josh. The whole village is behind you now they know the full story. Come and share a drink with us in The Old Inn sometime.'

Josh smiled. 'I will, thank you,' he answered, his voice cracking with emotion.

Maia's eyes glistened. 'You are definitely part of the community now, Josh,' she said as she carried her precious cargo into her kitchen. Placing Prudence down on her favourite cushion, Maia fished a piece of chicken out of the pot she had put in the range earlier that day to cook and cut it into tiny pieces. Prudence sniffed the warm morsel, licked her lips, and took the chicken from Maia's fingers, thanking her with another purr.

'I think all she needed was you,' Josh said, putting his arm around Maia's shoulder. 'I know how she feels. Your love mends all wounds.' He lifted her hair to kiss the nape of her neck. 'Everything is going to be all right now,' he whispered, and Maia sighed contentedly.

*

Two days later, Fee Blackthorn returned home from the hospital. She was under strict instructions to rest, but rest was the last thing she wanted to do. Besides, she was sharing the house with her disgruntled Pa, who also had to take things easy, and the situation did not sit easy with him either.

It was Sunday, and though she was unable to work in the tearoom for the next few weeks as she was nursing a rather painful rib and a fractured elbow, Fee was keen to be near the tearoom in case a certain *hero* visited, as he had done most Sundays recently. After studiously averting her eyes from the diminishing pile of what used to be Jago's house, Fee sat on the tearoom veranda, waiting in anticipation, but Jimmy Trevorrow never turned up. She was desperate to go up to the saddlery, where Jimmy worked, but her ma would not let her, reminding her of the hospital orders to rest. Also, with her pa and Jake out of action, no one was able to drive her there at this moment in time.

'Why don't you write to Jimmy if you want to say thank you?' Ellie suggested. 'I am sure he would appreciate that. Tell him he will never have to pay for another cream tea in his life,' she added with a smile.

'No, Ma. I need to speak to him in person,' she answered seriously. So, she waited another week, and still, he did not come to the tearoom to see her on Sunday. He didn't even come down to the beach for a swim! That was it, she decided. She would take the matter into her own hands. On the following Monday, she waited until her ma had gone to Helston on the wagon, and with Pa dozing in the chair, Fee slipped out of the house. Fee knew it would be a slow walk because she still suffered from a dull headache and dizziness, but with determination, she set off to Polhormon Saddlery.

*

Jimmy was helping Ben Pearson cut a large piece of leather to make a saddle.

Ben regarded his assistant; Jimmy had barely raised a smile since he had helped to rescue the Blackthorn girl.

'Go and see her,' Ben urged.

'I can't, Ben. Fee will think I am fishing for thanks for saving her.'

'I'm sure she would be happy to see you.'

'She never normally is!' he answered gloomily. 'Don't get me wrong; she is always nice and polite, but I always think I'm cramping her style.'

Ben laughed and shook his head, then they both looked up when a knock came to the door, and Fee popped her head around it.

'Fee!' Jimmy said. His heart was hammering in his chest.

'Hello,' she trilled. 'Sorry to disturb you, but I would dearly like a word with my saviour, please?' She smiled at Jimmy, who had been rendered speechless.

'I think she means you, Jimmy.' Ben laughed.

'Oh!' he said, feeling a prickle of nervous excitement.

'Well, go on then!' Ben shoved him towards the door.

Outside, in the bright August sunshine, puffs of dandelion seeds floated in the air like confetti. Standing at the edge of the meadow filled with fragrant, creamy-white meadowsweet flowers, Fee reached out her hands to his, which he gave her hesitantly.

'My hero!' she said with the brightest smile.

Jimmy frowned and looked to the floor.

'My hero!' she reiterated, squeezing his hands. When he lifted his eyes to meet hers, she kissed him passionately.

Jimmy felt a tingle from his lips to his toes, and, if he was honest, he felt it in places he had never felt that sort of tingle before! When their lips parted, he gasped, 'Gosh, Fee. I never thought that would happen, I.....'

'Will you walk out with me?' She asked, cutting him off mid-sentence.

He regarded her for a moment. 'You mean go for a walk on Sunday?'

'No. I mean, will you *walk out* with me?

He straightened his back. 'And be your sweetheart?' he asked tentatively, excitement beginning to swirl inside him again.

'Yes, Jimmy, and be my sweetheart,' she said firmly. 'You saved my life, and I want you to be very much in my life from now on.'

'Oh!' he said breathlessly. 'Can we just do that kiss again?'

'We can do that kiss forever more if you agree.'

'I heartily agree to be in your life for as long as you want me,' he laughed, wrapping his arms around her. Suddenly, the weeks that had dragged by in his lonely desperation for her melted away as Fee gave way to his soft, tender kisses.

*

Freddy and Kitty had set the date for their wedding at Cury Church for Friday, September 7th.

When Sissy Blair conveyed the news to Sarah during their morning meeting and stated that she would very much like to cater for her friends, Sarah, delighted to hear the news, told Sissy to give them a reception and cake fit for royalty. The Dunstans would foot the bill.

After her meeting with Mrs Blair, Sarah headed straight for the gardens to find Freddy. When she approached him, he was kneeling in the fragrant flower borders, whistling a happy tune – his persona was very different from the Mr Hubbard of late.

'I believe congratulations are in order, Mr Hubbard. You've set a date to marry your childhood sweetheart, I understand!'

Freddy scrambled to his feet and touched his cap. 'I have, yes. Thank you, my lady.'

'You have had me so worried recently, Mr Hubbard. I thought you were seriously ill or something - you were so unhappy.'

'I apologise, my lady. I didn't mean to cause you any concern. It's just that, I...well, I simply did not know what to say to you about the whole business – after all, the Earl was your father-in-law.'

Sarah hummed in her throat. 'A man I never met – thank the Lord. Thankfully, his evil traits died with him.'

'Oh, yes, my lady. Lord Dunstan and Lord William have none of his traits.'

'And Josh, Mrs Walsh's grandson, does not show any either, so I'm to understand from my husband?'

'No, my lady. Not a one. He may have Dunstan genes and looks like one of the family, but he certainly has my Kitty's lovely character, even if it is one generation removed.'

'I suppose you knew my father-in-law well!'

'Not well, no. He never ventured into the garden. I spent more time with Lady Lucinda, who was pleasant enough to work with, but she was more of an observer in the garden than any help – unlike you, my lady. There were rumours about the old Earl's wicked ways. He and Mr Lanfear were as thick as thieves. If I had known what they did to my Kitty, I would have...' He stopped to check himself. 'Begging your pardon, my lady, to speak so out of turn.'

'I fully understand your anger, Mr Hubbard – it is to be expected. Hopefully, now is the time to put past grievances aside and let peace and harmony settle on you both.'

'It's what I wish for, my lady.'

'Come, let us stroll around the garden for a while, for it still looks as splendid as it did for the garden party!'

After inspecting the parterre garden and speaking about the spring bulb planting, they walked down the avenue of lime trees towards the orchard.

'Mr Hubbard. I understand you are to marry at Cury Church,' Sarah said casually.

'Yes, my lady, on the 7th of September at two o'clock.'

'And Mrs Walsh, or Mrs Hubbard, as she will be then, is happy to live in the gardeners' cottage on the estate?'

'Indeed. Kitty is more than happy.'

'Splendid. Now, Lord Dunstan and I have spoken about your retirement when it happens, though we know it is not for a good while yet. But we want you to know that the gardeners' cottage will be at you and your wife's disposal for as long as you wish it to be after retirement.'

'Oh!' Freddy's voice wavered a little. 'Thank you both so very much.'

'It's our pleasure. Do you have plans for where to hold your reception yet?'

'We thought we would just have an open house at the cottage. Sissy, I mean Mrs Blair, wants to make the cake and a small buffet for us so that all my friends and colleagues here can pop in when they have a few minutes.'

'Well, I think we can do a little more than that. If Mrs Walsh agrees, we would like to offer you the use of the conservatory for your wedding breakfast.'

'Goodness!' Freddy was quite taken aback. 'That is so very kind of you and His Lordship. I shall ask Kitty, but I'm sure she will say yes and be overjoyed with your kind offer.'

'Well, Mr Hubbard, you're a special and valued member of staff. I don't know what I would do without you. You make the Bochym gardens bloom and smell so fragrant. It's the least we can do for you.'

'There will not be many guests.' He tried to assure her.

Sarah smiled and placed her hand on his sleeve. 'I'm sure all your colleagues here would wish to attend. Feel free to invite them all; they can take time off to attend. I have just spoken to Mrs Blair, and she is happy to cater for everyone.'

*

The day before Kitty and Freddy's wedding ceremony, Josh offered them the four-leaf clover in copal.

'I believe you gave this to Grandma!' Josh said to Freddy.

Freddy inspected it and nodded. 'Indeed, I did. It has been in our family for generations.'

Kitty placed the charm on her palm as Freddy looked on. 'I'm not sure if it ever brought us any luck,' she said gravely. 'When you gave me this Freddy on the day you proposed, I had not had it in my possession a day before our lives were turned upside down.'

Freddy put his hand on Kitty's arm to try and dispel that terrible memory.

Kitty looked up into Josh's blue eyes. 'I remember when you asked me if you could have this, Josh. I was in two minds about whether to give it to you.'

Josh nodded in agreement. 'Thinking about it, my life too changed for the worse after I started to carry it around. Although I felt it did give me some degree of luck sometimes, I think it also brings its share of bad luck.'

'I suggest we keep it somewhere safe, but agree that none of us carry it again,' Freddy suggested.

*

Friday, the 7th of September, was a day of brilliant sunshine and gentle breezes as Freddy and Kitty were married in front of a small congregation.

Kitty wore a beautiful Victorian cream lace dress selected from Maia's wardrobe of vintage clothes. It was in keeping with the 1880s – the era they should have originally married. She wore a wide-brimmed hat of cream feathers to complement the dress and held a posy of flowers picked, especially by Freddy, that morning.

Freddy was resplendent in a new suit and shiny new shoes – garments he had never had a need for before.

Leaving Vicky to finish preparing the buffet in the conservatory, Sissy stood as Kitty's attendant, and a very special guest, Mr John Bolitho, now 96 years old and confined to his wheelchair, was also there. Once John had heard that Kitty and Freddy were to be married at last, nothing, not even the long drive from Falmouth to Cury, would keep him away from seeing this happy day. So, accompanied by his elderly son, John was at Freddy's side to hand the wedding ring to him – just as he would have been all those years ago!

The reception was a glorious affair. Sissy had done them proud, and it had not cost them a penny. As they cut the cake, they kissed and sealed their love in front of all who knew them.

Later, as the guests dispersed, Freddy walked home, hand in hand with Kitty, to the gardeners' cottage. There they were met by Sissy, who had been the first to leave the reception in order to get the family's evening meal started but was now waiting to present them with salt and pepper.

'To give flavour to your new life together,' Sissy beamed.

Kitty laughed. 'The perfect present from a cook to a cook.'

'I shall leave you now to start your life together,' Sissy said, kissing them both on the cheek.

When they had waved Sissy off, Freddy scooped Kitty into his arms.

'Freddy! What are you doing?' Kitty giggled like a young girl.

'I'm doing what I wanted to do forty-one years ago. I'm carrying my bride, Kitty, over the threshold of our home.'

Once inside, Kitty found the cottage to be cosy and warm. Cushions had been plumped on the chairs by the fireside, and Sarah had filled the house with fragrant blooms from the garden. They wrapped their arms around each other, slightly nervous now about starting their lives together at last.

Freddy kissed her and gave her a raffish grin. 'Shall we go upstairs, Mrs Hubbard?'

'Yes, please,' Kitty answered with delight.

45

Josh and Maia's wedding was a quiet, intimate affair the following Monday at the Helston Registry Office. Maia, dressed in an Edwardian pale green silk gown and an embroidered jacket, wore a simple sprig of myrtle in her red hair. Josh, resplendent in a new suit of clothes and clean-shaven, stood proudly by Maia's side as she held out her left hand for him to replace the wedding band she had taken off just before the ceremony. To keep their assumed marital status secret, only eight people attended the wedding. Apart from the bride and groom, there were David and Alice Trevorrow, Ellie and Guy Blackthorn – still sporting a sling - and newlyweds Freddy and Kitty. Afterwards, to celebrate, they all took tea in Bumbles Tea Room in Coinage Hall Street, Helston. Josh and Maia did not need a splendid reception; they had enjoyed Kitty and Freddy's reception the previous Friday. All they needed was to feel safe and secure that their union was legal and that nothing could separate them now. After saying their goodbyes and thanks to their guests, Josh and Maia returned to their farm to be greeted with a purr when Prudence saw them. Maia bent down to stroke her beloved pet, now well on her way to recovery, having used up one of her nine lives!

With the farmhouse door firmly closed on the world, Josh and Maia smiled happily at each other.

'Hello, Mrs Walsh.'

Maia laughed. 'How are we going to explain to people that I'm not Mrs Harding anymore, but Mrs Walsh?'

Josh shrugged. 'I'll just say that Harding is my professional *artist* name, and that is what I'm known by, although Walsh is my given name.'

'So, you're going to take up painting professionally, are you?'

'You never know, Maia, anything can happen. The world is our oyster now. If this mining project goes ahead and we have to sell up, we can go and travel - do anything we wish.'

'I know what I want to do at this very moment,' she said with a twinkle in her eye.

'Your wish is my command.' Kissing her passionately, he scooped her into his arms and carried her up the stairs to bed.

They lay spent and happy in blissful contentment, with the early afternoon sun streaming through the window. Birds sang, goats bleated in their pen, and the hens clucked contentedly in the yard below, all redolent of a farm in late summer.

Josh shifted onto his elbow and gazed happily at Maia; her fiery red hair splayed across the white pillow.

'How lucky can a man be to find such a woman as you in his arms?' He murmured, kissing the pale skin at her throat.

Lifting her slender fingers to his face, she smiled gently. 'The luck is mine also. I never knew a love like this was possible.'

Curling his fingers around hers, he brought her hand to his lips and kissed the gold wedding band. 'There is always someone for everyone, somewhere out there. We found each other and will be forever together, from this day forward.'

Having been wrapped in each other's arms until the sun moved slowly to the western afternoon sky, the farm animals beckoned, and they reluctantly left their marital bed.

'I think a cup of tea is in order before we feed and milk the livestock?' Maia suggested as she put the kettle on to boil.

'Sounds perfect,' Josh answered, opening the West Briton newspaper that David had brought over that morning, and in which was the story of Jago's hanging.

Josh shuddered at the thought of such a thing, especially on a beautiful day like this, but since learning how Jago attacked Maia when Josh was awaiting trial and what he did to the Blackthorns, the man deserved his fate, so he felt compelled to read the report:

CORNISH BUSINESSMAN - JAGO PENHALLOW - HANGED FOR HIS HEINOUS CRIMES.

Following an extensive manhunt, the Cornish businessman Jago Penhallow was detained as he tried to board a ship bound for America. He was arrested and charged with four criminal offences, namely, grievous bodily harm and sexual violence towards two women. A hit-and-run incident causing actual bodily harm. Attempted manslaughter, following his abduction and abandonment of a young woman, leaving her unconscious in an unstable house, and in which, if not for a daring rescue by the girl's father and another man, she would have fallen to her death. Jago Penhallow was also charged with the most serious offence: the murder of his brother, Henry Penhallow, who had been robbed and killed the previous year.

This latter conviction came from incriminating evidence found in the rubble of Jago Penhallow's collapsed property following a cliff fall. The evidence, namely the deceased's money pouch bearing the initials H.J.P., a piece of blood-soaked sacking and two items of tools bearing Jago Penhallow's initials - one of which – a lump hammer was thought to be the murder weapon. Though Jago Penhallow pleaded guilty to the first three charges, he pleaded not guilty to the murder of his brother. The jury, however, found Penhallow guilty on all counts, and he was sentenced to hang on Friday 7th of September 1923. Penhallow pleaded his innocence to his brother's murder right up to the last breath he took.

Josh sat back in his chair, digesting the report. He cast his mind back to the day he had gone to Maia's attic to retrieve the spare mattress and found the lump hammer in a chest bearing Jago's initials. He had not meant to pry, but curiosity had urged him to open the lid of the old chest and look inside. He then thought back to when he had been digging in the wilderness in the far corner of Maia's land and had uncovered a hessian cloth containing a personalised money pouch and pen knife. Initially, he had thought Maia might have buried these personal items of Henry's to rid herself of anything that reminded her of him. But these were the items allegedly found in the rubble of Jago's house!

Josh suddenly felt a chill down his spine. He glanced at Maia, who was singing happily while she brewed the tea, and a strange feeling swept over Josh. Was Maia perhaps withholding a dark secret? He swallowed hard and locked his eyes on his new bride as Maia placed the teapot on the table.

She kissed him warmly on the cheek and smiled brilliantly at him. 'Tea for my gorgeous husband.'

Josh caught her hand by the wrist. 'Maia. I need to ask you something.' He saw Maia frown at his serious tone, and she tipped her head, waiting for his question. 'Did *you* kill Henry?'

Maia gasped, pulled her wrist from Josh's hold, and grasped the top of a chair. Her lips moved, but she didn't speak; she just stared back at Josh.

Prudence, sleeping peacefully on her cushion, suddenly woke, and the fur on her back stood on end, picking up on the tension in the room.

Staring at Maia, Josh noted that her face had blanched, and there was a sudden intensity in her eyes as she desperately tried to evade his question. He arched his eyebrows as his interest in her answer grew.

'Your silence speaks volumes.'

Maia began to shiver, though it was not cold.

'You see, Maia. Those items of Henry's, found in the rubble of Jago's house, were, at one time, buried in the far corner of your land! I know this because I accidentally dug them up. So, Maia. Did you kill Henry?'

'Yes,' she whispered tremulously before crumpling to the floor in a dead faint.

*

When Maia came around a few seconds later, Josh was cradling her head in his arms. When he passed her a glass of water, she looked searchingly into his eyes for love but only found a sombre, intense gaze looking back. Maia felt her heart fill with a sense of dread. Was the happiness she had found with this wonderful man about to crumble before her eyes?

After allowing her time to recover, Josh helped her onto a chair. He clasped his hands on the tabletop and looked seriously at her. 'Maia. You must tell me everything.'

Maia closed her eyes to the strong sense of foreboding.

'Maia, you must!'

She nodded slowly.

'That day.' She swallowed the lump that was forming in her throat. 'That day, we had been to Helston Market. I had sold all the eggs, and the preserves I had made, and I even got a fair price for the piglets. I made enough money to buy seeds for the vegetable plot and enough to live on for a few weeks.' She lowered her eyes. 'But Henry was angry with me that day. He said I had been making eyes at the buyers to get a better price and that he had seen a man touching me.'

Maia fell silent and began to wring her hands, not wishing to relive the memory of that day.

'Maia. Go on,' Josh urged.

Maia bit down on her lip and shuddered as she began to recount the events leading up to Henry's death.

'Henry had been in the Blue Anchor drinking most of the day. It was late in the afternoon when I saw a face from the past walking towards me; his name was Graham Elliot. Well, I say walked - he was on crutches, having lost a leg. I knew Graham well; he'd been at school with my brother and conscripted into the war with Alec, Henry, and another friend called Roger Eddy. I honestly thought that Graham had died in the same battle as Roger and Alec because he never came back after the war. I was delighted to see him, and we kissed warmly on the cheek like old friends do. I laughed and said, How wonderful to see him. But that I thought he had died.

"Alas," he answered. "For better or worse, I survived, albeit without a leg."

I explained that because he had never come back, we had all thought the worst.

"Ah, well." He grinned. "I met a pretty nurse in the London hospital who didn't find my missing leg uncomfortable to look at. We married and settled there." I felt so happy for him and so glad that he had survived, as so many had not, and then Graham's face turned sombre. "It was shocking what happened to your Alec," he said.

I answered that the war had indeed been shocking, and Graham suddenly wore a more serious look.

"Yes, but I mean what Henry Penhallow did to your Alec!" I was puzzled by this statement, and Graham could see that, so he added, "You are aware that Henry used Alec as a human shield on the battlefield? I hope Henry got his comeuppance."

All I could do was gasp in horror. I suddenly felt lightheaded, as though the world were spinning, so Graham reached out to steady me. "Oh, God, Maia. Did you not know? I thought Roger Eddy reported Henry to the commanding officer." I shook my head, and then Graham told me what he knew about the incident.

"Roger and I were taken to the clearing hospital together, and before I lost consciousness with the loss of blood, he told me he had seen Henry hiding behind Alec on the battlefield, using him as a shield to deflect the gunshots away from himself. There had been an altercation earlier in the day. Henry and Alec were arguing over you. We all heard the row. Henry had told Alec that he intended to marry you after the war, and we heard Alec retort, "Over my dead body you are." The next minute, we went over the top. I took a hit in the leg within seconds, but Roger told me he was running alongside Henry and Alec, and saw Henry grab Alec and move him into the firing line. That was the last Roger saw, because seconds later, a bullet hit him. After the battle, we, who were wounded, were taken off the battlefield and sent to the clearing hospital. That's when Roger told me what had happened - he said he would report Henry as soon as possible. I don't remember anything else after that."

Maia paused and looked up at Josh, who was listening intently but he said nothing, so she carried on.

'I felt cold with what he had told me, and couldn't stop my body from trembling. I told Graham that word came through to us that Roger Eddy had died from a catastrophic wound to his stomach – he died the same day as Alec. Graham looked as stricken as I felt.

"Is Penhallow still living in Poldhu?" he asked. All I could do was nod. He then added, "That is a pity. It is probably too late to do anything about it now. Unfortunately, I didn't see the incident, so I cannot report it or vouch that it's true. But Penhallow should have been shot for cowardice. I would give him a wide berth if I were you." Again, I nodded, and he put his hand on my arm. "I'm that sorry, Maia," he said. "I thought justice would have prevailed for your Alec. There was no finer fellow than he."

I was near to tears and could hardly speak without trembling. Then Graham had to leave; he was meeting his wife to catch a train home.

"Take care, lovely Maia. Your brother loved you very much," he said, and he was gone.'

Maia ceased her narrative for a moment while she collected herself. She glanced again at Josh, who looked stony-faced.

'Graham had not been gone more than a few seconds when Henry arrived back. I was packing the cart up to return home, and my mind was in a whirl having heard what Graham had told me. I now knew that Henry was more of a monster than I thought him to be. I didn't pick up on Henry's anger until he grabbed me by my hair, dragged me down an alleyway, and punched me in the face. I felt my lip split and blood trickle from my nose, and I could feel the skin around my eye start to swell almost immediately. Henry grabbed me by the chin and banged my head against the wall.

"That should stop anyone from taking you up on your enticements. I saw that man touching you," he said, and then bared his teeth and wiped the blood from my nose across my face with his thumb. I could hear his breathing heighten and knew he was excited - he liked to see me battered and bleeding.

"You want to act like a whore, so I'll treat you like one," he said, reaching down to lift my skirt.

I knew he intended to take me there and then, in broad daylight! Thankfully, someone walked down the alley and that stopped Henry's intent, thus saving me the indignity and embarrassment.

"We'll finish this later, at home," Henry warned, and banged my head against the wall again.

We set off home, but Henry got off the wagon at Cury Cross Lanes to go to the Wheelwright Inn, taking with him the money pouch. Though I was glad to be rid of him for a few hours, I knew he would drink most of the money away in the inn. I set off towards home, shattered at what had happened to Alec, and it was just as I was passing the steps to Cury Church when I came across Clem, the iceman, who had shed his load of ice blocks. I stopped to help, but his ice had smashed and scattered across the dusty road. We knew we needed to stack the blocks of ice tightly back on the trailer bed so that they didn't completely melt, but because Clem's wagon was on the tilt due to the lost wheel, it was an impossible task. We gave up in the end, and Clem admitted that by the time the wheelwright got to him, the ice would have melted anyway. I helped him kick the dirty ice into the hedgerows so that no one would slip on it and break their neck.'

Maia paused in her story and smiled.

'Clem was so kind to me. I remember he was deeply concerned about the state of my face. I dared not tell him Henry had done it, but I knew Clem suspected as much. Clem had seen me in a similar state many times. He put a block of ice on my wagon to take home and wrapped some crushed ice into a piece of hessian sacking for me to hold next to my eye to bring down the swelling. He then thanked me for my help and sent me on my way.

Here at home, I waited as the clock ticked the minutes away. I was terrified of what was to come when Henry got home. Henry often liked to beat me before taking me – it proved he was my master. I kept thinking about my poor brother and what Henry had done. I started to wonder that if we hadn't kicked all that ice into the hedgerows, Henry, being drunk enough, could have slipped on it and broken his neck. I started to fantasise that if Henry died, it would be justice for Alec, and I would no longer have to endure this terrible life. If I could just get back there and scatter the ice in his path...'

Maia paused and gathered herself.

'Once the idea popped into my head, I couldn't ignore it. I took with me the hessian sacking that Clem had given me. I thought I could use it to pick up one of the blocks of ice – to stop it from burning my fingers. I returned to the church steps where the ice wagon had shed its load, and I managed to retrieve, smash, and scatter one block of ice on the path. I'd just picked up another block of ice when I heard Henry coming along the road. I knew it was him from the familiar disgusting phlegmy snort he always did when he was drunk. It was too late to smash the next block of ice I held in my hands because Henry would have heard me, so I ran up the church steps with it and hid behind the wall.

As Henry approached the steps to Cury Church, he belched loudly and laughed, then suddenly slipped on the ice. His feet went from under him, and he hit his face on the road. He was howling in pain as he pushed himself up with the flat palms of his hands. Using the church step wall to help drag himself up, he rested one hand against the wall as he tried to steady himself and cupped the other hand under his bleeding nose. He spat the blood and began to curse loudly, then started muttering to himself about the ice scattered by his feet.

"What the devil is this? Snow, in bloody June!" he shouted.

I could feel the ice burning my hands through the hessian, and then it slipped from my grip. I caught it, but the movement made Henry look up at me.

"You!" he roared.

Then, the ice I was holding slipped from my grasp and hit him clean on the top of his head with a sickening crunch. He fell forward onto his face. The ice slithered into the road, leaving only the hessian covering his head. I could see the blood oozing from the gash in his head, soaking the hessian and pooling onto the ice I had scattered. I panicked then because I realised that I'd probably killed him! I frantically tried to get the money pouch off of him so it would look like he had been set upon and robbed, but the strap to his money pouch was across his body. I had a penknife in my skirt pocket; it had once belonged to Jago. He'd left it at the farm one day, and I put it in my pocket. I had a wild idea that I could use it to defend myself from Henry.' Maia laughed at herself. 'As if I could ever have fought him off with it.'

She shook her head to gather herself again.

'I cut the straps of the money pouch with the penknife, grabbed the piece of hessian to leave no evidence, kicked the block of ice into the hedgerow, and ran home. When I counted the money, I found only a fraction left of what we had earned. I knew I must get rid of the pouch, so I wrapped it up in the hessian sacking with the penknife and buried it in the far corner of my land, where I thought no one would find it.'

With her story finished, she glanced at Josh's serious face.

'Tell me about the lump hammer,' Josh asked. 'Why did you steal that from Jago? I distinctly remember him coming to look for it, but hearing you deny all knowledge of it, even though I knew you had it!'

Maia looked up at him questioningly.

'I took a sneaky peek in the chest in the attic – the day I brought my mattress down.'

'Oh!' Maia answered a little crossly.

'Were you always going to blame Henry's death on Jago? It says in the paper that a lump hammer was with the other items.'

She shook her head. 'No. I took his lump hammer because he was starting to get angry with me after I had taken you on at the farm. When I found his hammer on my chair, it took me back to what P.C. Thomas had said to me when they found Henry dead. He suggested that Henry had been hit and killed with something heavy - something like a lump hammer. I was always frightened of Jago. I knew he had similar traits to his brother, and I didn't like to think he had a lump hammer that he could use as a weapon against you or me. So, I hid it. As far as I was concerned, the hammer would have stayed in the loft, and the bag and penknife would have stayed buried forever. That was until he did what he did to you, and then when he tried to rape me. I knew I needed to rid ourselves of him once and for all, so the house going over the cliff presented me with the opportunity. I put the bag and contents in the rubble of Jago's house the night before we came up to Portsmouth for your trial.'

With the confession over, silence ensued. Maia lifted her eyes to the man she loved with every fibre of her body.

'What are you going to do?' She asked tremulously.

'Do?' Josh tipped his head.

Lowering her eyes, she said tearfully, 'Now that you know.'

Josh sighed and stood up. He folded the newspaper and walked around the table towards her. He gently reached for her hands and made her stand before him.

Maia trembled as frightened tears streamed down her face, waiting for his condemnation.

'Maia.'

She looked deep into his startlingly blue eyes but couldn't read his thoughts.

'You want to know what I'm going to do?'

'Yes,' she whispered.

He brought her hands to his lips and kissed them. 'I'm going to make sure that I never hurt you or give you a moment of unhappiness. Otherwise, I shall have to watch my back, especially when I know there's a block of ice in the larder!' he joked. 'I love you, my darling Maia, you brave, brave girl. That man deserved everything he got,' he said, folding her into his loving arms - a place where she knew she would be forever safe.

⋙ ⋘
End
⋙ ⋘

Footnote

Although 'Somewhere Out There' is a work of fiction, the threat of mining in Mullion was very true. I read this following post, taken from the Mullion Old Cornwall Society Facebook site, written by Katrina Griffiths - Recorder for Mullion Old Cornwall Society. It was this story which set my creative juices flowing, and led me to incorporate this within the novel: -

Mullion Was Nearly Changed Forever.

When we look at the quiet village of Mullion today, we see a picturesque village surrounded by green and fertile fields, a pretty harbour set against the dramatic dark cliffs, and the popular coves and beaches that has attracted thousands of visitors since the Victorian times. The landscape has changed little over the years. However, in 1923, the destiny of the village of Mullion was about to change and was soon to find itself in the centre of a major mining development.

Recently discovered at Kresen Kernow, the home to the Cornish archives, a bundle of eight documents consisting of setts and correspondence between the Tehidy Minerals Limited, Camborne, the company who had granted permission to the Mullion United Mines Cornwall Limited and the Somerset Oxide and Ochre Company Limited to work serpentine rock and metallic minerals around Mullion.

The company called The Somerset Oxide and Ochre Company Limited, was given full and free liberty to dig, work and search for decomposed serpentine rock or green or other coloured earth in under and throughout the fields or enclosures of land situate in the parish of Mullion. The sett gave the company the term of 21 years from 25 March 1923.

Can you imagine what that would have meant? The village

would have been surrounded by quarries and the impact that would have on the inhabitants. They would have been subjected to pollution, noise, traffic, smoke, dust, damage to caves, loss of land, a deterioration to the water quality, living with an eyesore of the damage to the landscape and the biodiversity of the environment. It is staggering to think on just how much of the village would have been changed, probably beyond recognition.

So, what happened, you might ask?

The answer to that can be found within the correspondence which reveals that The Somerset Oxide and Ochre Company Limited went bankrupt, and the dream of the mining project in Mullion was dead in the water.

You are welcome to see the original documents at any time by visiting Kresen Kernow in Redruth. The collection number is TEM/337 holding setts and correspondence.
Katrina Griffiths
Recorder for Mullion Old Cornwall Society.

∽ ∾

BOCHYM MANOR

Please note, Bochym Manor is a private family home, and the house and gardens are not open to the public. They do however have holiday cottages available. Take a look at Bochym Manor Events on Facebook and Instagram for more information.

❧

Please, if you can, share your love of this book by writing a short review on Amazon I would be so grateful.
Thank you. Ann x

❧

Printed in Great Britain
by Amazon